A CAULEY MACKINNON
Novel

FORTHCOMING BY KIT FRAZIER

Dead Copy
(A Cauley MacKinnon Novel)

Kit Frazier

SCOOP

A CAULEY MACKINNON
Novel

MIDNIGHT INK
WOODBURY, MINNESOTA

FIRST EDITION
First Printing, 2006

Book design by Donna Burch
Cover design by Ellen L. Dahl
Cover photo © 2006 by Leo Tushaus
Editing and layout by Rebecca Zins

Midnight Ink, an imprint of Llewellyn Publications

Cover model(s) used for illustrative purposes only
and may not endorse or represent the book's subject

Library of Congress Cataloging-in-Publication Data
Frazier, Kit, 1965–
    Scoop : a Cauley MacKinnon novel / Kit Frazier.—1st ed.
        p.   cm.
    ISBN-13: 978-0-7387-0915-4
    ISBN-10: 0-7387-0915-8
    1. Women journalists—Texas—Austin—Fiction. 2. Austin (Tex.)—Fiction.
I. Title.

PS3606.R428S23 2006
813'.6—dc22

                                                                2006044892

Midnight Ink
2143 Wooddale Drive, Dept. 0-7387-0915-8
Woodbury, MN 55125-2989

www.midnightinkbooks.com

Printed in the United States of America

ONE

I DUCKED UNDER THE crime scene tape the way I always do, like I know exactly what I'm doing, but this time I was a little more careful on account of the black-clad SWAT guys drawing down around the perimeter. Sometimes I think the only things standing between me and certain doom are instinct, pure dumb luck, and a kick-ass hairdresser.

"Little early, aren't you, Cauley?" Jim Cantu was lounging against his cruiser looking like a Hispanic Marlboro Man as he surveyed the rugged limestone hills and gnarled oaks at the back of the Barnes' ranch. "What we got here is your basic suicide threat," he continued, squinting into the hot Central Texas sun. "Don't obituaries get written *after* somebody's turned up a corpse?"

"This isn't for the *Sentinel*," I said, swatting dirt from the seat of my jeans. "Scooter called me this morning and said he wanted to talk."

"Doesn't matter. No media behind the line," he said, nodding toward the SWAT guys. "You're lucky you didn't get shot."

"Calling me *media* is pure charity on your part," I said. "And I almost never get shot."

Cantu grinned down at me as I settled in beside him. Every now and then, Cantu cuts me a break because once upon a time, he'd been a rookie beat cop when my dad was a detective, and he sometimes steps in where my dad left off.

Cantu and I stood, staring at the tumble of weathered planks that comprised the shed where Scott "Scooter" Barnes had holed up, presumably sucking on the business end of a shotgun.

This wasn't the earth-shattering incident it might seem elsewhere in the world. Here, you don't ask if you have any crazy people in the family; you ask which side they're on. In Texas, we believe our own myths, and the wet heat of summer presses heavily on already fanciful minds.

Crossing his arms, Cantu looked at the bruise that was blooming on my forehead. "All right, blondie, I give. What happened to your head?"

"Banged it on a big piece of wood," I said. Despite a raging hangover, I'd climbed a crosstie fence to get past the police line. I was hot and sweaty, and I had enough dirt under my nails to repot a geranium. Plus, now I had a bump on my head and a hole in my jeans, which showed a big patch of Wal-Mart underwear. These things almost never happen when you're wearing nice undies.

"Hurricane Cauley." Cantu shook his head. "You want off obits? Go chase a real story. I hear El Patron's on the move."

I had to stop myself from growling. Cantu knew I'd sell my great aunt Kat's china for a story that would get me off the obituary page, and while I'd been assigned to do some of the research on El Patron—the latest South American syndicate to set up shop in Central Texas—the News Boys on the City Desk got the byline on the story. For the most part, I spend my days rewriting death notices, and if I'm lucky, I occasionally get to do legwork for the real reporters.

But getting something on El Patron could fix that for me. Organized crime was nothing new in Texas, but El Patron crossed the city limits into Looneyville when they shoved a heavy-duty Firestone around some poor bastard's shoulders and burned him alive. Talk about a front-page scoop.

"Yeah, well, El Patron will have to wait," I said, and winced as one of the SWAT guys with an orange-stocked sniper rifle disappeared into a thicket of sage. "Did you have to call the Jump-Out Boys?" I said, staring at the rest of the SWAT team, which was scattered among bushes and perched in the gnarled forks of live oaks.

"Had to," Cantu said. "I got dinner duty tonight."

"You called SWAT because it's your turn to *cook?*" I said, thinking of Cantu's three kids, who could make a sane person call SWAT on a good day. "You know Scooter would never hurt anybody."

"And he won't hurt anybody. Captain's called a negotiator."

"We don't need a negotiator. Let me talk to him."

"You talked to him last time."

"Hey," I said. "That thing with the goats was not my fault."

Cantu snorted. "You busted in the back of that pet store and scared *los cabras* so bad they passed out cold."

"They were those weird *fainting* goats," I said, staring at the shed. I shook my head. "Exotic animals. I don't know why Scooter can't sell dogs and cats like a normal person."

"He's not a normal person. He's a serial suicide. This is the second time he's threatened to bite a bullet this month. It's standard procedure to call SWAT and I shoulda never let you talk me out of it the first time."

I started to say that *serial suicide* was an oxymoron and that Scooter had issues, what with his wife leaving him and all, when I sucked in a breath and stopped dead in my tracks. "Who is *that?*"

Near the fence line, a lone man loomed, speaking into a cell phone as he surveyed the scene. I'd practically grown up in the West Side substation, and I knew all the precinct cops and most of the usual suspects.

This guy was no usual suspect.

Tall and bronzed, with a wide-legged stance, he was a dead ringer for Captain America. I had to remind myself to close my mouth. Probably my hormones. The closest I've been to a steady relationship has been since I set my cell phone to vibrate.

"Tom Logan." Cantu scowled. "FBI."

"You don't like him?"

"Nothing personal. We just don't need a bunch of feds fucking up a local case."

"They're here on a suicide threat? Why would the feds care if Scooter Barnes is having a bad day?" I said, but the rumble of an engine rolled over my voice.

"*Miranda*," I swore.

Miranda Phillips stepped out of a white van, shook out her platinum hair, smoothed her slim skirt, and tapped her Ferragamo-heeled foot while her television crew set up outside the flapping yellow crime scene tape. She might have been annoyed. It was hard to tell because her face never moved. It was frozen in a permanent look of surprise on account of all those Botox injections.

Miranda has her own wildly successful syndicated column at the *Austin Journal*, the *Sentinel's* flashier, better-funded rival newspaper, and she's broadening her already triumphant résumé by breaking into television.

Miranda never did time on the obituary page.

Miranda is Barbie, if Barbie gave up her Malibu Beach house to pursue a career in journalism. She's tall and blond and has all the accessories, including a closet full of fuck-me pumps. I, on the other hand, look like Skipper, Barbie's little sister. Permanently disheveled and always trying to keep up.

As long as I've known Miranda, I've never seen her sweat. She uses pretentious words like "exquisite" and "extraordinary" at inappropriate times.

I know this because a couple of Christmases ago I walked in on her riding my former husband like a wild, wet pony. *Exquisite*, she'd panted. *Extraordinary*.

"How'd she find us so fast?"

"Probably she has that OnStar navigation thing," Cantu said. He looked down at the hole in my jeans. "You should get that."

"I don't need any help," I said. The old shed was hard to find if you didn't know where to look. It was perched on a wooded knoll behind Scooter's dad's house on a bend in the Pedernales River near Paradise Falls. My friends and I used to spend sultry summer afternoons skinny-dipping in the cold spring waters, a memory not even two years in northern California could extinguish.

"You are sneaking into a crime scene," Cantu pointed out. "You're not supposed to be here at all."

"Yeah, well, if it makes you feel any better, these were my favorite jeans."

Miranda had finished tossing her hair and did a double take when she caught sight of me and Cantu.

"Well, hello, Carrie," Miranda purred as she prowled toward us, but she looked right past me like one of those smart bombs in search of a target.

"Cauley," I said, like she didn't already know.

"Right," she said without looking at me. "Like the dog."

I narrowed my eyes.

"What do we have here?" she said, and I was about to think of something really clever to say, but it didn't matter because she was staring at Captain America, who was still stalking the fence line, talking on his cell phone.

I glanced over the horizon expectantly. The News Boys would be on the scene soon.

Luckily, I had anticipated this. You can only screw me four or five times before I start to notice a pattern. From somewhere down the tree-lined road, a red Toyota 4 × 4 rolled up and slid to a stop next to Miranda's van.

A rangy, pimply faced kid climbed out of the truck and yelled, "Somebody order a pizza?" His voice only cracked a little, and it was hardly noticeable, what with all the sniper rifles ratcheting his direction.

"Thirty minutes or less." I grinned at Cantu. "Just like the ad says."

The kid was reaching across the passenger seat to pull out a big white pizza box when a deep voice yelled, "Freeze!"

I watched as six SWAT guys had the pizza kid spread-eagled on the ground and Miranda was mobilizing her troop of television techs. Seeing as folks were busy, I made a break toward some business of my own.

"You could go to hell for this," Cantu called after me.

"They're trained professionals," I called back. "They almost never shoot anybody."

I COULD HEAR THE falls rushing in the near distance as I scrambled toward the backside of the shed. The natural spring plunges down a forty-foot cliff to rush nearly fifteen miles through the Hill Country, pooling in Paradise Cove—not what most people picture when they think of Texas.

Texas is hot, but it's not all barren and rocky like the movies, where John Wayne rides into the sunset over a desert dotted with saguaro cactus. The only pitchfork-shaped cacti here are imported from Arizona, and John Wayne was born in Iowa. Not that we let little things like facts get in our way.

I pounded on the back door. "Don't shoot, Scooter! It's me, Cauley."

A rustling sound came from inside, followed by a half-hearted sigh. Scooter's voice drifted through the back door. "You're too late. Go away."

"Can't do that, Scooter. They've got the place surrounded. You're going to have to come out."

I tried the door and heard a chain rattle from the inside. Scooter didn't say anything. It was getting hotter by the minute and the smell of cut grass was about to pitch me headlong into an allergy attack. Mindful of the SWAT team perched around the perimeter, I crept around the corner of the shed until I found a hole just big enough for a smallish body.

"Well, crap," I growled. With much bitching and moaning, I shimmied through the narrow hole, tearing my shirt on a splintered board. Apparently I wasn't as small as I thought.

"Ow!" I swore, and spit out a mouthful of red dirt while my eyes adjusted to the darkness. The shed was about fifteen by fifteen, and its most prominent feature was a warped box-bench against the far wall. A bare bulb hung from a frayed wire, and a few rusty tools and half a dozen sagging cardboard boxes were scattered along the side and back walls. I pulled my mini recorder out of my back pocket, more out of habit than anything else, and hit the *record* button.

"Go away," Scooter said. He was sitting on the box-bench in the corner near a pyramid of old paint cans, where he'd surrounded himself with a semicircle of assorted weaponry.

I heard a loud squawk and blinked in the dim light. The big blue parrot that always hung out near the cash register at Scooter's pet store was perched atop the paint cans.

"Hey, Scooter," I said amiably, still eyeing the bird as I smacked red dirt off the back of my jeans. "Rough day?"

I started to sit down next to Scooter when the bird shrieked and threw open his enormous blue wings.

I yelped and almost tripped backward over an old, rusty shovel.

"Why'd you bring the parrot?"

"Sam's a macaw," Scooter said dully. The man was no MENSA candidate, but he was practically a savant with animals. The bird ducked his great feathered head at Scooter, who reached out and scratched the bird's fluffy neck.

"Sam's good company," Scooter said absently. "Did you know miners used to take birds with 'em down into the mine shafts? They're sensitive to fumes."

"The birds alerted when there was a gas leak?"

"No. They dropped dead. It was a sign things were about to go south."

Wow. I hoped that wasn't an omen.

Sam made a garbled noise that almost sounded human. "I know, buddy," Scooter said, staring at him sadly.

I winced. When Scooter called me earlier that morning, I'd been taping *The Maltese Falcon* on Turner Classic Movies. I'd seen what could happen when people got obsessed with birds. But then, I have found that most of life's problems can be solved with wisdom gleaned from Bogart movies.

"You know," I said in my best Bogart, watching as Scooter picked at the rusty lid of avocado green interior-exterior, "if you want to off yourself with paint fumes, you're going to have to do better than a can of twenty-year-old latex."

"A lot you know," he muttered. "She left me."

"I know," I said and sighed. If we were going to talk about Scooter's wife, it was going to take a while. Searching in the dust-moted shafts of light, I found a big, musty box. I shoved it closer to Scooter, coughing at the cloud of dust I'd stirred up, hoping I hadn't stirred up anything worse than dust, like a nest of nasty brown recluse spiders or a pack of red stinging scorpions. Settling in on the box, I really looked at Scooter. I almost didn't recognize him.

Scott Barnes slumped on the box-bench, a shadow of the big, blond legend he'd been at Marshall High School. Once upon a time, he'd been a kick-ass running back, which was how he got his nickname. Scooter wasn't the brightest match in the box, but he could blaze through a defensive line like Sherman through Georgia, so much so that he got a full ride to the University of Texas.

He left school early for a coveted contract with the Dallas Cowboys and made front pages all over Texas when he married Selena Obregon, first runner-up in the Miss Texas pageant. Once upon a time, his life had seemed charmed.

"Have you talked to Selena?" I said, hating the question. I wasn't comfortable playing marriage counselor because I wasn't qualified, and if I was going to be brutally honest, I wasn't wild about Selena. Oh, sure, she was small and fragile, with hair the color of spun gold and big, morning-glory-blue eyes and the faintest trace of an Argentinean accent that made men lose twenty IQ points. Selena and I had gone to school together, and she beat me two years running in all-state drama with her heart-rending portrayal of Blanche DuBois. *I have always depended on the kindness of strangers . . .*

"*Zorrita*," Scooter said, and I couldn't help but smile. *Little Fox.* In the South, nicknames tell as much about the person who gives them as the person who wears them. "I can't find her."

No big surprise there. Just after the honeymoon, their little southern-fried fairy tale went sour when Scooter blew out one of his million-dollar knees line-dancing in a honky-tonk in Oklahoma, ending what would have been a stellar career. No gazillion-dollar contract. No shopping sprees at Tiffany's. Just a quasi-normal life changing cat boxes in a little pet store west of Austin.

Sighing, I thought about hitting the *off* button on my mini recorder, but I didn't want Scooter to know I had been taping our conversation in the first place. This was about an old friend. There would be no scoop today.

"Scooter," I said carefully. "When you called this morning— you said you wanted to talk to me about something?"

Scooter stared blankly at the front door. "Why'd they have to go and call SWAT? I never hurt anybody."

"You threatened to hurt *yourself*," I pointed out, accepting the change of subject. Whatever the reason he'd called me, he clearly wasn't ready to talk about it.

"You don't want to do this," I said, and Sam squawked, ruffling his feathers. "What about your pet store?"

Scooter shook his head. "I got a guy helps out, looks after the animals, cleans the kennels. Does some computer-type stuff at the shop."

"A Renaissance man."

"He needed a job when he got out of prison."

Scooter always did have a soft spot for strays. I wiped my damp forehead. It had to be a hundred and ten degrees inside the shed, and the smell of mold and motor oil was making my throat close. And I couldn't think of a single thing that would ease his mind. Surely there had to be life beyond Selena. I was running low on ideas.

"You know what I like?" I finally said. "The sound of the lake lapping the shoreline on a hot summer night."

I looked at Scooter and he seemed to be listening, so I went on. "I like the taste of a Fredericksburg peach late in the season, all sweet and so juicy it runs down your chin when you take a big bite . . . I like the smell of mountain laurel, right when it first blooms—"

"Smells like grapes," he said.

I nodded.

"You remember when we were kids and we played dodge ball?" he said.

I barely remembered. Scooter was three grades ahead of me and I hated dodge ball, but I nodded.

"You run and run, and they hit you with that ball," he said. "No matter what you do, you can't get away, and even if you win, you lose because they're still gunning for you with that god-damned ball."

I stared at him. Scooter had enough testosterone to fuel a Third World army. He kicked butt at every sport known to mankind. But I had a feeling we weren't talking about the playground anymore.

"Yes," I said. "But you could always yell *do over!* And you got to start some other game with a clean slate."

"Not always." He looked so unhappy I wasn't sure what to say.

I took a deep breath. "You know what I used to do when I was a kid? I used to make grass skirts out of newspaper, get a couple of cans of pineapples, and drag a box out on the roof. Then my sister and I would climb out the window and sit in the box and wish we were in Hawaii."

Scooter stared at me. "You were a weird kid."

"Maybe. But I thought if you wanted anything bad enough, you could have it. I thought I could get us to Hawaii with the sheer power of my brain."

Scooter snorted. "Did it work?"

"No," I said. "But I didn't break my neck goofing around on the roof, so now I can go to Hawaii if I want."

Silence stretched between us as he sat, picking at the paint can. "What happens if I walk out of here?" he said. "You know, with SWAT?"

"Well, the guns had orange stocks, which means they're loaded less-than-lethal."

"They're gonna shoot me with beanbags?"

"Probably they won't shoot you at all, but if they do, a beanbag won't kill you. Most likely."

"Still hurts."

This from a guy who used to make a living getting charged by linebackers the size of bull elephants. I'd bet half my student loans it wasn't physical pain Scooter was worried about.

"Probably hurts like a sonovabitch," I agreed. "But if we don't come out soon, they're going to start lobbing tear gas in here, and that can't be good for your bird."

"Am I gonna get arrested? They never called SWAT before."

I shrugged. "I think they're finished cutting you breaks. You'll probably have to go to a hospital for some sort of psych evaluation."

Scooter considered that. "What about Sam?"

The bird snapped his big beak at me and I flinched. I'd seen parrots bend spoons with their beaks, and Sam was much bigger than your garden-variety bird. "You said you had somebody to take care of the animals," I said. "Give me the number and I'll give him a call."

Scooter nodded, then reached into his shirt pocket. "Will you give this to Selena?" I looked down as he pressed a worn gold coin with something that looked like a two-headed bird into my palm. "It's for luck."

I looked at Scooter's sallow face and thought *Fat lot of luck it's brought you, buddy,* but I said, "You can give it to her yourself."

I tried to give the coin back to him, but he just sat there, staring at the thin shafts of sunlight streaming through the door and then around at the old shed.

His red-rimmed eyes seemed to sink deeper in his gaunt face and he let out a long sigh. "I wish I was in Hawaii."

"I know," I said. I leaned in and took his hand. "Me too."

14

"WE'RE COMING OUT!" I yelled. "We're unarmed!"

Scooter locked the rickety door behind us and we walked out of the darkness, blinking in the bright afternoon sunlight.

A deep voice yelled, "Hold it right there!"

Like a rolling black thunderstorm, the SWAT guys charged in and had Scooter facedown and frisked. A bit excessive for a suicide threat, I thought.

They cuffed him and stuffed him into the back seat of an idling blue and white, and as the cruiser pulled down the tree-lined drive, I could see Scooter through the back window, his head down, like things just couldn't get any worse.

A smooth, familiar voice startled me. "Well, if it isn't the Obituary Babe. Little early, aren't you, Cauley?"

I came up short when a microphone was shoved under my nose, and I turned and stared into the too-handsome face of Alex "Live-at-Five" Salazar.

"You know, when y'all call me that it wreaks havoc on my social life," I said. "And this isn't for the paper."

Ignoring me, he turned to his cameraman. "Cauley MacKinnon was taken hostage by a desperate man earlier this morning," Salazar said to the camera. "Down-on-his-luck Dallas Cowboy Scott 'Scooter' Barnes barricaded himself in a shed at the back of his parents' property . . ."

Great. The News Boys had officially arrived. As he spoke into the camera, Salazar discretely signaled the KTEX television crew into position. All four local affiliates were roaming the scene, and I could hear Miranda with the KFXX crew interviewing the pizza kid about police brutality.

SWAT always drew a crowd.

"Can you tell us his demands, Cauley?"

"Scooter Barnes did not take me hostage, and there were no demands," I said, shoving my hair out of my eyes and the microphone out of my face. "He just wanted to talk."

"You've spent nearly an hour negotiating with an armed man," Salazar went on, his big white teeth glinting in the sun. "How does it feel to be a hero?"

I squinted against the glare off his incisors. I was hot and sweaty, and the last thing I wanted was to wind up on television in ripped jeans, Wal-Mart underwear, and hair that looked like it'd barely survived a nuclear disaster. I popped the tape out of the mini recorder and shoved it and Scooter's coin into my back pocket.

"It wasn't an hour, I'm not a hero, and you can read all about it in the *Sentinel*," I said, which was a big fat lie. I'd never spill ink on a friend's personal tragedy, even if it meant getting off the obituary page, but Salazar didn't need to know that. I pushed past him to head for my old, stripped-down Jeep.

I didn't look back.

All's well that ends well, I figured. Miranda had her exclusive, I talked Scooter out of the shed and the shotgun, and Cantu had his dinner if he could get to the pizza before the SWAT guys.

I was about to congratulate myself when I looked toward the fence line and noticed something was missing.

Captain America was gone.

When I finally pointed my Jeep down Lakeside Boulevard toward home, it was late afternoon. I was dirty and sticky and my hair felt like twenty pounds of blond mattress stuffing. Despite the lingering effects of a monstrous hangover, I'd called Burt Buggess, Scooter's lawbreaking bird man, to go wrangle Sam and take care of the store until Scooter got out of stir.

The warm wind whipped around in the open Jeep, making me feel marginally better. Now all I needed was a shower and a nap and a half-pound of Prozac. I glanced into the rear-view mirror. *And* an emergency hair appointment.

Drumming my fingers on the steering wheel, I stared absently through the windshield, the winding road ahead of me shaded by a leafy arbor of oak trees.

"Why on earth is an FBI agent interested in Scooter Barnes, and why did the SWAT guys come down so hard on the pizza kid?" I said to no one. "I mean, it was a suicide standoff, not some Waco-type siege. It wasn't like the pizza kid was smuggling guns or bombs into the shed for Scooter."

Maybe I'd just find that FBI agent and pump him for information . . .

I almost didn't see the dog in the road. My heart jammed in my throat and I stomped on the break. The Jeep jerked and skipped toward the animal.

The dog had a strange white face and he looked a lot like a wolf. I yanked the wheel a hard right, tires squealing, horn honking as I spun onto the gravel shoulder. The dog stood, staring at me.

"Jeez!" I yelled. There were strict leash laws in my neighborhood. Dogs didn't just roam the streets like wild animals.

I turned in my seat. "Good grief, dog, who the heck left you in the middle of the road?" But I was yelling at nothing. The dog was gone. I sat for a moment, trying to catch my breath.

When I got my pulse under three hundred thirty, I put the Jeep in gear and headed up the steep hill toward Arroyo Trail and felt marginally better when my eclectic little neighborhood unfolded on the hilltop before me. I live in one of those 1940s lake-area neighborhoods that started out as a resort community and evolved into a funky little soccer-mom neighborhood. It's settled along the banks of Lake Austin, but it's still excitingly close to the downtown corridor of tie-dyed hair and body piercing.

Turning into my drive, I slowed to a stop and stared at my sprawling white porch, where a large man lounged on the porch swing.

"Captain America," I whispered and sucked in a breath.

Glancing at my reflection in the rear-view mirror, I swore every swear I could think of and made up a few more for good measure. My cheeks were smudged with red dirt and my hair was an unmitigated disaster. Not exactly a *Chic* magazine Glamour Girl moment.

"Cauley MacKinnon?" the man said as he rose from the swing. He was a lot taller and way better looking up close. I sat, glued to the driver's seat. Why on earth was the hot FBI guy camped out on my doorstep?

"Special Agent Tom Logan, Federal Bureau of Investigation."
He held up his badge. "Do you have a minute?"

I blinked at him. "How did you find me?"

"Hey." He grinned. "I'm FBI."

TWO

"Oh. Right," I said, climbing out of the Jeep. Cauley MacKinnon, mistress of witty repartee.

Tom Logan had a nice smile. He reminded me of Gregory Peck in *To Kill a Mockingbird*, good looking in a quiet way. Dark hair, dark eyes, a strong chin, and no wedding ring. Did I mention tall?

I smacked the dust off the back of my torn jeans and tried to smooth out my hair, wishing I had a ponytail holder.

Special Agent Tom Logan held out a hand and helped me up the steps. Strong grip, and a lefty, too. Looking up, I couldn't help getting a better look at those dark eyes.

He looked down at me. "You okay?"

"Hmm? I just . . . had a bad night," I stammered, reaching up to smooth my hair. "I mean, a bad day."

He grinned. "I see that. I noticed you made it through the police line."

I smiled as winsomely as I could, given that I looked like a ragamuffin. "That's not a federal offense, is it, Agent Logan?"

"That crime scene tape is there for a reason."

I sighed. "I know, but Scooter's a friend. He's done this before. He wasn't really going to commit suicide."

Logan nodded. "A repeat suicide attempt. Maybe your friend should have had professional help the first time he tried to bite a bullet."

I looked up at him and he seemed almost amused, which irritated the hell out of me. Not to mention that he was probably right.

Straightening my shoulders, I said, "Is there a reason for this visit, Agent Logan?"

"Just a couple questions," he said. "And you don't have to call me *agent.*"

His dark eyes flicked toward the door, and I could tell he was waiting for me to invite him in. I bit my lip.

I'd spent the previous evening drinking my body weight in bourbon and Diet Coke, bemoaning my current man problems. There were dishes in the sink, and, if I remembered correctly, I'd stripped in the living room and left my clothes where they'd dropped. Thank God the stained glass in the front door didn't allow Agent Logan a clear view into my living room.

"I have a few minutes, but I have a big evening planned," I said, sliding a glance at the sky, hoping God wouldn't strike me dead for lying.

Logan looked at me like he knew I was lying and pulled a plain black notebook and pen from a pocket inside his suit jacket. "You mind?" he said.

I narrowed my eyes, but shook my head. What harm could come from answering a few questions?

"Could you take me through your conversation with Mr. Barnes while you were breaching the police line?"

He looked up from his notebook. Humor glinted in his dark eyes, and I could see little crinkle lines at the corners. He probably got that humor-glint a lot.

I shrugged. "Nothing to take you through. Scooter called me early this morning and said he wanted to talk, but I was a little late getting out to the shed—"

"He said he wanted to talk to you?"

"Yeah," I said. "But that's the weird thing. When I got there, he didn't really say anything. We talked about when we were kids, a little about his wife, that sort of thing."

"His wife?"

I narrowed my eyes, wondering why an FBI agent was interested in Scooter's wife. "Honestly. He didn't say anything, only that she's leaving him," I said, and I rose to my tiptoes, trying to sneak a peek at what he was scribbling. "What does this have to do with anything?"

Logan smiled enigmatically. I don't know how he did it, but his body seemed to shield his notebook without him moving a muscle.

Dropping to normal height, I frowned. "Is the FBI involved with Scott Barnes, or is this personal?"

Logan flipped his pad closed and smiled. "I'll let you know. Any chance I can talk you into staying out of this?"

I stared at him.

"Yeah, that's what I thought," he said. He shook his head. "Thanks for your time."

I watched as he tucked his notebook back into his official, dark gray federal suit jacket.

Before I could stop myself, I tipped my chin and said, "I'm sure you've got better things to do than sit around worrying about me."

"Just doing my job," he said, and a vague sense of disappointment washed over me.

"See ya 'round," Logan said, and he shot me a little salute. Turning, he took the stairs two at a time, heading for his white bureau car, which was parked in front of my neighbor's house. Some reporter I'm going to be. I hadn't even noticed.

Halfway down the stone path, Logan turned toward me. "Take care of yourself. And keep your doors locked."

"Hey," I said, regaining the use of my gray matter. "I have a few questions for you."

But Logan had already slid into his car and started the engine. I stood on my porch, staring as his taillights skimmed down the street.

And as I turned to the door, I realized the only person who'd been pumped for information was me.

"Stay out of it, my butt," I swore, twisting the doorknob. It gave without the key.

Ack. I'd forgotten to lock my door. Again. Had Logan noticed and let himself in? I was pretty sure that was illegal. You at least needed a warrant, and the only crime I'd committed was monumental stupidity.

My phone was making a muffled shriek somewhere down the hall, and the noise cut through my frontal lobe like a buzz saw, being's how I was still queasy from the bourbon and Diet Coke the night before.

There were probably better ways to deal with man trouble, like doing ten miles on a treadmill with Aretha belting *R-E-S-P-E-C-T* on really great speakers. Maybe I'd try it sometime. But then I'd have to buy a better sound system and a treadmill, and there wasn't enough room in my little house.

Okay, it's not really *my* little house. I'm sort of buying it from my great aunt Katherine, who is a fabulously famous romance author with jet-black hair and exotic, dark eyes. She was once voted one of *Chic* magazine's Most Beautiful People of the Year. Aunt Kat is the most elegant, talented person I know. I don't look a thing like her.

My name is Cauley MacKinnon. I was born and raised in Austin, Texas, an oasis of rivers and trees and an endangered population of card-carrying liberals in the middle of the rest of God-fearing, gun-toting, right-wing Texas.

After five years in a disastrous marriage to Dr. Frank Peters, the lying, cheating sonovabitch my friends kindly refer to as Dr. Dick, I wound up with little more than a divorce decree and a very bad attitude. If there was ever a time to yell *do over,* that was it.

So, I did the only thing I could do. I burned all his underwear and worked brief intervals between getting hired and fired until I'd saved up enough cash to buy an old CJ-7 Jeep and head to California, where I got a truly crappy efficiency apartment and applied for a mountain of student loans. I worked the night shift at an emergency vet clinic and finally, finally finished the journalism degree I'd abandoned when I'd married Dr. Dick.

I came back home for a yearlong internship at the *Austin Journal,* where I learned the second rule of Cauley's Code of Conduct—*Never, Ever Date Your Boss.*

It's not so easy to land a job in print media, so after my debacle at the *Journal,* I was lucky to land the obituary slot at the *Austin Sentinel.* Being an obituary writer is what happens to interns who've been very good or reporters who've been very bad. Somehow I'd managed to be both.

Getting another newspaper gig in Austin was fortuitous, but it's a known fact that as an obituary writer, my core readership was made up of hypochondriacs, octogenarians, and people in search of downtown apartment space. No doubt about it: I'd hit rock bottom.

At the *Sentinel's* west Austin field office, I rewrite death notices and research other people's stories for a salary that almost balances out to minimum wage. But Aunt Kat began her fabulous career as a novelist by starting out as a society reporter, and hopefully, the apple doesn't fall far from the worm. Or something like that.

I followed the chirp of the phone through the bungalow, which is pretty much what you'd expect in a funky lake-area abode—wide windows and hardwood floors. The foyer flows into a large living room, flanked by a short hallway and library in front, kitchen facing the living room, and a longer hall leading to a small den and bedroom in the back. It's cute and cozy in a rambling sort of way, and crammed to the ceiling with Aunt Kat's eclectic jumble of antiques.

"Hold on, hold on," I grumbled at the ringing phone. I was having trouble finding the cordless handset until I remembered that I'd stuck it in the refrigerator so I wouldn't return calls from Mark the Shark, my former boss and present ex-boyfriend, after I got all warm and fuzzy on the effects of way too much alcohol.

I have a strict No Poaching policy, and Mark Ramsey is the reason I've amended the first question in my Potential Boyfriend Quiz from "Do you have a girlfriend?" to "Is there anyone out there who *thinks* she's your girlfriend?"

"Hello?" I finally said, pulling the phone out of the barren vegetable crisper. It was nice to know the refrigerator was good for something.

"Hey, *chica, que pasa?*" Marina Conchita Santiago's voice breezed through the receiver like a tropical wind chime. Despite her long, dark curls and liquid brown eyes, Mia is like a human firecracker, small but loud, and she knows how to make an entrance. She's a *Girls Gone Bad* video just waiting to happen, and even worse, she's got a way of dragging you into whatever Pandora's box she happens to be ripping open at the moment. We worked on the yearbook staff together in seventh grade, but I've loved her like a sister ever since we wound up in detention for boycotting Biology for the poor treatment of the class's lab rats.

Well. I boycotted. Mia burned her sports bra. But you've got to admire that kind of commitment.

One of the best things about Mia is that you can say anything and she'll either ignore you or find a way to make whatever you've said the best thing since the anthrax vaccine.

"What am I doing?" I repeated, glancing around the house. Dirty dishes from the previous night's cooking disaster lined the counter, and Muse, Aunt Kat's mean little calico, glowered at me from beneath a withering ficus. "Systematically destroying my houseplants."

"Oh, good, then I didn't disturb you. Sorry I didn't make it to shoot the photos on that hostage thingy this morning. Phil and I had a reading with that new pet psychic. It took me almost two months to get him in."

"Not a problem," I said. Mia and some of her more militant friends had liberated Phil the cat during a raid on an animal-testing facility near San Antonio. Therapy, psychic or otherwise, probably couldn't hurt the little beast.

"There were no hostages, and it wasn't really a photo op," I said. "Scooter decided not to shoot himself again, so your job is safe."

Even as I said the words, the image of Captain America bumped the back of my brain, and all the cells in my body leapt simultaneously. That couldn't be good.

"You know what?" Mia went on. "You should take Muse to Mrs. Littlefield for a reading. It turns out Phil was Cleopatra in a previous life. He has gender issues."

"The pet psychic said your cat was gay?"

27

"Yes, and it explains a lot. Hey, what are you doing tonight?" she said, reminding me that I had no life. I stared into my empty refrigerator. Half a jar of fat-free mayonnaise, a plastic container of biohazard, and two bottles of Corona Light beer. Nothing had materialized in the crisper since I'd taken out the phone.

"I don't know," I said, but really I did. It was a tossup between ordering Chinese or eating my last package of ramen noodles. I was reluctant to eat the noodles, because the package was the foundation for a network of cobwebs at the back of my pantry and it had developed its own ecosystem. It's good to have some order in life.

I pulled a Corona from the fridge and scavenged for a lime. Finding none, I popped the top off the beer.

Mia remained undaunted. "I just finished your horoscope and guess what?"

"Travel is in my future and I'll meet a dark-haired, mysterious man?"

"You got the second part right. Why don't you come out with me and Roger? Brynn's coming and she's bringing the new guy," Mia said, and I wanted to say *I'm not coming because Roger is a pompous ass and I'd rather poke my eye out with a sharp stick,* but I said, "I asked you not to do my horoscope. I've got some research I need to get started on."

Yeah, right. I was going to pop *Casablanca* into the DVD player and numb out in the black-and-white clarity of a world where people do the right thing instead of the easy thing and the good girl always gets the guy. Or, in Ingrid Bergman's case, two guys.

"Oh," Mia said, sounding like a disappointed cruise director. "You know, you'll never meet anybody if you don't get out there and circulate."

"Mia, the arteries in my brain aren't even circulating," I said. "I just need to take it easy for a while."

"Roger has this friend—" Mia began, and I said, "I sincerely doubt that."

"Oh, come on. This guy is really nice. He could be the man of your dreams."

"That's what you said about the last guy, and then I caught him trying on my underwear."

There was a moment of silence on the line and I knew I was being disapproved of, but Mia finally said, "Okay. Call me if you change your mind."

I was snapping the phone into the charge stand on the kitchen counter when I heard a bang at the front door, which sounded suspiciously like a baseball slamming against my stained glass window.

"The Bobs," I swore.

I love most of my neighbors, particularly Beckett and Jenks, the guys in the townhouse next door. But the Bobs, who live on the other side of my bungalow, are a different story. Bob, Mrs. Bob, and all the baby Bobs. Their dog craps on my sidewalk and their kids play shredder with my newspaper.

The Bobs have the Cool House on the block. All the kids in the neighborhood play ball there, and they all seem to aim right at my front door, which, according to the baby Bobs, is third base.

Funny, since my social life sucks and I haven't even seen third base since the Clinton administration.

Muse hopped down from the ficus and scowled at me.

"Okay, okay, I'll tell them to knock it off. Just don't pee in the plant again," I told the cat. I opened the door to check for damage. No visible cracks in the glass or leading. I leaned over the white porch rail and snagged the ball from Aunt Kat's bed of antique roses, which had gone wild and rangy in her absence. Heaving back, I lobbed the ball to the oldest of the baby Bobs.

"Wow," he said, taking in my sweaty hair, damp tee shirt, and torn jeans. "Scary."

He made a motor noise with his lips and hurled the ball at his sister. He missed by a mile and hit his dad's car. Narrowing my eyes, I skulked back into my house.

There was still nothing in the refrigerator, and I'd already eaten all the Pop-Tarts. The ramen noodles were still an option, but I didn't feel like cooking, and I know from experience that if you eat ramen noodles without cooking them first they expand in your stomach and give you a stomachache from hell.

Since I didn't have time to get sick, I pulled the China Pacific menu from a drawer and was trying to decide if my checkbook could sustain almond chicken when another *bang!* sounded at the door.

"*This is not third base!*" I yelled, swinging the door open to find Mark the Shark Ramsey standing on my front porch.

My heart dropped to my stomach.

"I guess not," he said. His gaze slid over me. "Hello, gorgeous."

THREE

SHIT, SHIT, SHIT. MARK always ignited a weird flash of emotions, and I was never sure whether I wanted to slug him or jump him. There are certain lines that, once you cross them, are very hard to uncross.

Leaning against the doorjamb, he looked the way he always did, his sandy hair artfully mussed, and he was dressed like he'd stepped right out of an Abercrombie and Fitch ad. He was smiling and holding a dozen roses.

I hate roses. Roses are for funerals and men who've been mean to their wives. The one time I'd told him I liked peonies, he'd told me I should read Freud.

Mark leaned in and tucked my hair behind my ear, and I wished the floor would open up and swallow me. Despite my best efforts, my skin went warm where he'd touched me.

I squared my shoulders. "Hello, Ramsey," I said. "How's your girlfriend?"

"There never was a girlfriend," he said, and I snorted.

Maneuvering past me, he made his way to the kitchen where he retrieved a vase from my otherwise empty pantry and manipulated the flowers into a perfect arrangement. He was good at manipulating, and I watched him as he moved. Mark Ramsey had the kind of easy grace that comes from growing up in piles and piles of old money and the carefully cultivated charm that only prep school can provide.

"What are you doing here?" I said, wishing I'd had time to take a shower and do something with my hair. No point in seeing an old boyfriend if you can't make him suffer.

"Loosen up, sugar. You are one of the most uptight people I know."

I stood there, staring at him. I'd read this book before and I didn't like the ending. Ramsey's ten years older than me, and the entire time we were together he'd made it his personal ambition to run my life and correct my grammar. If I was going to be fair, as the executive editor at the *Austin Journal*, it had been his job to correct my grammar, but fairness is often overrated.

Oh, and the girlfriend thing. I know this because she e-mailed me some really nice candid shots of them doing the mattress mambo on the purple chenille I gave him for his birthday. Getting naked with the boss is one of the worst mistakes you can make, and after I'd seen those porno-mails, I couldn't stand being in the same office.

My daddy used to say there's an ass for every saddle. I don't know if there's such a thing as Mr. Right, but I do know I'm sick of settling for Mr. Good Enough for Right Now.

Even before the porno-mails, I knew inviting Ramsey into my house was a mistake. He's like one of those vampires in really bad B movies—slick and disreputably handsome. You can't see them in mirrors, you can't turn your back on them, and once you invite them in, you can never get them out. The only difference between Ramsey and a vampire is that instead of sucking out my blood, he'd ripped out my heart.

He turned to me and smiled, and I looked twice at his teeth to make sure they weren't pointed.

"What the hell are you doing here?"

He grinned. "You have to ask?"

I thought about that. The phone had been in the refrigerator, so I knew I hadn't called him during a moment of alcohol-induced weakness.

"So," he said. "How is our hometown hero?"

My eyebrows shot somewhere near my hairline.

"Saw you on the five o'clock news," he said, and my stomach pitched.

"Oh. Great." How was I going to explain *that* to my mother? "Is this about the takedown this morning?" I was being evasive, but he already knew what happened, right down to the last detail. Ramsey had the best contacts money could buy.

"What kind of takedown did you have in mind?" he said, and his voice lowered an octave as he moved toward me. He hooked a finger into the loop of my jeans and pulled me to him.

"Mark," I said. To my horror, it came out a little breathy.

"What happened with Barnes this morning?" he said, his gaze on mine.

I cleared my throat. "I told Scooter I'd seen him shoot and his aim is worse than mine, and that could be *real* embarrassing in front of all those SWAT guys."

Mark tipped his head back and laughed, then he leaned forward and pressed a kiss to my forehead. "Cauley, you're killing me," he said. "I've missed you."

I felt the warmth of his lips and I thought about how easy it would be to just let go, to slip back into the routine that was once so familiar to me.

"Barnes say anything interesting?" Mark went on, his voice as soothing as a favorite old song.

"Hmm?" I said, but I was distracted, thinking about his lips. "What difference does it make?"

"Cauley, Scott Barnes is in big trouble."

"I've known Scooter since we were kids," I said. "I didn't go there to snag a story that'll get me off obits. There's not going to be a story."

"There is a story, Cauley, and it's a big one. *Line-Dancing Dallas Cowboy Threatens to Bite Bullet.*" He announced the words like he was reading a headline.

"*Former* Cowboy," I countered.

"Football players are big news in Texas, especially when they crash and burn. You'd have an exclusive if you played it right—a scoop that could make your career. But you're too close to this to be objective and you don't have the kind of backup you need at the *Sentinel*. Why don't you take a pass on this one?"

I stared at him. "You think I'm a mercenary?"

tempted to throw the vase anyway, but then I'd just have a mess to clean up. That's the bitch about living by yourself.

"I never called him," I grumbled to Muse, who sat on the counter, twitching the tip of her tail and glaring at me dubiously. I frowned, staring at the door, wondering why on earth two totally different men had warned me to keep my nose out of a friend's business.

I sighed and dropped the gun in my purse. Despite my better judgment, I leaned in and breathed the sweet scent of the roses. Suddenly, I felt incredibly empty.

I stared around the room where my aunt's antiques loomed solidly in the silence. I kicked off my shoes, grabbed the flowers and the last Corona Light from the fridge, and wandered down the short front hall, past the old Wurlitzer jukebox and into the library.

The small, cozy room was filled with the peppery smell of aging paper and the lingering scent of history. Hardbound books lined the walls from floor to ceiling. The dusty Remington Scout typewriter sat dormant near a ream of crisp white paper on an old desk. I moved the flowers to the desk and ran my fingers along the round, cool metal keys of the Jurassic typewriter. Aunt Kat had given it to me when she'd headed for the south of France to finish researching her latest endeavor, a page-turner she'd titled *Beauty and the Baron*. I sighed. Probably hoped I'd follow in her footsteps.

From the hallway outside the library, I looked around the quiet house filled with other people's things and felt utterly, completely alone. Muse leapt up on the colorful, rounded top of the Wurlitzer and stared at me.

I sighed. "You want music?" I said to the cat, and punched the familiar series of yellowing plastic buttons. What can I say? The cat's got a thing for Aretha Franklin.

Inside the glass dome, the forty-five record swung around and plopped onto the felt-covered base. The speakers hissed when the needle hit the record, and before I knew it, Aretha was wailing about feeling down and uninspired.

"Oh, cat," I said, "what am I going to do?"

Muse sat on top of the jukebox, her white chest puffed imperiously, reminding me an awful lot of Aunt Kat.

In the library, I picked up the brass compass my father had given me for my eighth birthday, and in that moment I felt his absence like a sharp stab to the heart. Setting the compass aside, I picked up my old Magic 8 Ball and shook it. The compass might be a more sensible choice when trying to find your way, but I've always chosen destiny over discipline.

Peering into the small plastic window at the bottom of the black ball, I narrowed my eyes and said, "Will I ever get my life together?"

The answer appeared in the inky blue liquid.

ASK AGAIN LATER.

"Great."

Sighing, I put the 8 Ball back, feeling restless and annoyed and dirtier than I had when I'd arrived home. What I needed was a shower.

As I made my way down the back hall to the bathroom, I passed the den. The room was dark except for a tiny light blinking like a cyber beacon.

Aha! I wasn't totally alone. I had e-mail.

I pulled up the Internet *welcome* screen and felt instantly better when the screen announced *I had mail!*

Then I saw my outgoing message.

"Oh, no," I groaned.

Here alone, my message read. *Not wearing panties.*

See you at six, read Mark Ramsey's reply.

I beat my head on the desk in three short thumps and came up with a little yellow Post-it Note stuck to my forehead.

I peeled it off and read, *Note to self: never drink and e-mail.*

FOUR

I'd balanced my checkbook and discovered I couldn't even afford a bowl of China Pacific's egg drop soup. How is it mathematically possible to have less than a zero balance? If I couldn't find a way to cut expenses, I was going to have to pick up some freelance articles just to break even.

Depressed beyond what I'd previously thought possible, I stripped, showered, and slipped on a fresh pair of jeans and a tee shirt and headed for my mom's, trying to figure out why a bank would charge twenty dollars for insufficient funds when they know you don't have it.

I turned my Jeep down Texas 71 and onto Hamilton Pool Road, through a leafy canopy of oak trees, past some of Austin's more historic ranches. As impressive as all those old landmark homes are, they aren't what told me I was close to home.

More than anything, I can tell when I get close to home because I start to regress. That and the smell of Fresh Scent Clorox looms heavily over a three-block area.

The old Victorian where I grew up was nestled on forty rolling acres of Hill Country. It had wide, shiny windows and lots of bushy, green ferns. As long as I could remember, the house had been polished and scrubbed within an inch of its life, as though at any moment our family would be ambushed by a pack of feral photographers from *Southern Homes and Gardens.*

I pulled past the wide wraparound porch, turned the key, and sat while the engine rattled to a halt. I should have stopped for gas, but there's always a fifty-fifty chance I can't get the Jeep started again. So I dropped my head to the steering wheel and waited, calling up courage and resolve before walking into the high drama that is the MacKinnon household.

Home was always home, but it was different since Daddy died, and not even the Colonel's steadfast presence could fill the void. Stephan Connor, who everybody called the Colonel, was family by proxy. He was also the best stepfather a girl could ever hope for. He made my mother happy, and while he didn't pretend to have all the answers, he always had good advice, which was more than half the reason I'd made the trek over to my mom's house in the middle of the week.

Between Scooter and Mark and life in general, I was feeling a little lost. And, truth be told, Mark had spooked me. I kept getting the creepy feeling that someone was watching me.

The hot Texas sun raged red on the horizon as it grudgingly yielded to twilight, and if Aunt Kat had seen it, she'd have breathed low, Celtic words about a bad storm rising.

I took a deep breath. Time to go in.

The screen door banged shut behind me and I went through the mudroom into the kitchen, where the aroma of fried chicken conjured memories of Sunday dinners, cousins tumbling in the living room, and the steady rumble of football on television.

Mama had just sliced a big tomato and was drying her hands on the dishtowel she'd tossed next to her martini.

"Is Clairee back from the Charity League?" I said. If there was fried chicken, it was a pretty good bet Clairee was nearby. Mama never made it past *canapés* during her misspent youth at Miss Mona's School for Fine Young Ladies, where all budding Austin debutantes are whipped into marriageable shape.

"Here somewhere," Mama said, her voice soft as a southern breeze.

Lilianna Cauley MacKinnon Connor always reminded me of Barbara Eden from the *I Dream of Jeannie* reruns. She'd aged with grace, and I couldn't remember ever seeing her without a full face of makeup and perfectly pouffed hair. When I was a little girl, I used to lay in bed and wish I had one of those warm, round Pepperidge Farm mothers. Mama had never been big, but she'd always been larger than life.

She turned from the counter and her hands flew to her perfectly rouged cheeks.

"Ah!" she said. She always did that, and it sounded like someone stepped on her foot. "Good lord, Cauley! What have you done to your hair?"

Mama made a beeline toward me and pressed her flawlessly manicured fingertips to my forehead. "What's wrong? You've got

a fever. I knew it. You've come down with the West Nile virus."
She yelled over her shoulder, "Clairee! Get me the VapoRub!"

My mother would put VapoRub on a brain tumor. And the
truth is, out of sheer will and determination, she would probably
get results.

"No, Mama, there's no virus." I snitched a slice of tomato. I
hadn't made it out of *canapés* at Miss Mona's either.

In the near distance, I could hear a newspaper rattling and the
Colonel swearing softly at CNN as it droned in the living room.
Thank God for cable television.

They'd obviously been watching national news and hadn't
seen local coverage of my misadventures with Scooter. I knew this
because if they had seen my altercation with SWAT on the local
news, they'd have been combing my neighborhood and speed-
dialing my cell phone.

Mama narrowed her eyes when she noticed the technicolor
bump on my forehead. "Good gawd, Cauley, what have you
done?"

"Hunting accident," I said, wincing as she brushed my hair
back for a better look.

"Does it hurt?" she said and pressed on the bruise.

"Ow!" I said. "It does now."

"Did I hear Cauley? It's not Sunday." Mama's friend Clairee
swept around the corner, the sound of jangling bracelets and the
scent of gardenias swirling around her. She lifted Mama's martini. "Good lord, Cauley, what's happened to your hair? And
you're pale. Have you come down with The Fever?"

"I don't have a fever," I said, ducking out of Clairee's red-tipped grasp. "Y'all watch too much CNN."

They stood, staring at me like the Sisters Grimm.

I brushed past them and into the living room to kiss the Colonel on his silver-tinged temple. "Hey, Colonel."

"It's not Sunday." The newspaper crinkled as he looked up from the obituary page in the *Sentinel*. The Colonel is not a hypochondriac or an octogenarian, but he is loyal to a fault. His sharp, blue eyes studied the bump on my head and he frowned. "You okay, Cauley Kat?"

"Jeez!" I said, but I smiled at the sound of my childhood name. I wanted to ask him what he knew about the FBI, to see if he had any speculations on why the feds would be interested in a local suicide attempt, but that would have to wait until we were out of earshot of Thelma and Louise.

I wandered back to the kitchen where Mama and Clairee were leaning against the counter, arms crossed.

"What?" I said. "I'm fine. Can't a girl come visit her own family in the middle of the week?"

They stared at me.

"Okay," I said. "It's work."

"You've pissed somebody off," Clairee announced as though she'd suspected it all along.

"I haven't been at the *Sentinel* long enough to piss anybody off."

Mama rolled her eyes and handed me a stack of plates. "Make yourself useful," she said and sighed one of her trademark sighs. *Great*, I thought. *Here it comes.*

"Writing those awful obituaries. Cauley, honey, it just seems so depressing."

"Well, Mama, I write about dead people. It is kind of depressing."

What I didn't say was that the truly depressing part of my newfound career was that because I'd screwed up at the *Journal,* I was stuck writing obituaries at the *Sentinel,* and I would stay stuck until pigs sprouted wings and flew over Congress Avenue or I got the scoop on a real story.

"You know, your Aunt Shirley mentioned an opening down at Balcones Temps. It's nice and safe and secretarial, and you don't have to deal with any of that nasty death business. That's how she met your Uncle Dave."

"Mama," I said, placing the plates on the cheery yellow tablecloth. "Uncle Dave is in prison."

"Don't say *prison,* Cauley, it's not nice."

The woman swore like a sailor everywhere but church, and she was telling me not to say "prison."

"Besides," Mama went on, "Your Uncle Dave's unfortunate incarceration was nothing but a teeny little bookkeeping discrepancy. He misplaced a comma. People don't get shot over commas."

"No, they go to jail over embezzling," I said, "and I hardly ever get shot at."

"You know, if you think about it, that prison thing isn't so bad," Clairee said around a sip of martini. "Now Shirley has a nice house and plenty of free time."

Clairee had a point, but I could feel a headache coming on.

"Dinner," Mama shouted, right in my ear. Like clockwork, the Colonel rounded the corner and we all sat.

The Colonel said grace and passed me the plate of fried chicken. Because my older sister, Suzanne the Perfect, wasn't there to fight over it, I chose the wishbone.

"So what's the trouble at work, honey?" Clairee said, handing me a bowl of fried okra. "Is it that man again? Mark is too old for you. Remember what happened with your husband."

"*Ex*-husband," I said.

The Colonel growled and I felt a stiff breeze blow past my shin as Mama kicked Clairee under the table. Dr. Dick was a sore subject in this household. He had hurt me. You hurt one MacKinnon, you hurt us all.

"What?" Clairee said, ignoring the fact that my mother had probably given her a hematoma just above her ankle. "I hear he's selling body parts over the Internet."

"He's a broker for an organ donation center," I said. "He makes sure people get the organs they need."

"For a price." Clairee forked a big chicken breast onto her plate.

I didn't know what to say, so I busied myself by pouring gravy onto my potatoes, careful not to let it seep over onto the okra.

"You know who called me today at the Charity League?" Clairee went on. "Diego DeLeon. Turns out he just got a divorce."

"Annulment," my mother said. "Catholics don't get divorced."

I sucked in a breath, preparing for the worst. Diego's several years older than me, and even in school he'd been a player. He was terminally hung up on *The Godfather* trilogy and there were rumors his uncle was a money man with the Texas Syndicate.

"Anyway, do you know why he called the League?" Clairee said.

I shrugged. "To donate a big briefcase full of unmarked tens and twenties?"

"He wanted your number." Clairee actually beamed.

I dropped my fork. "My number's unlisted."

"I know," Clairee said. "That's why he asked for it."

I felt like I'd swallowed the wishbone. "Clairee, my number's unlisted for a reason. Besides, I haven't seen Diego DeLeon in years," I said. "Why in the world would he just all of a sudden want my number?"

Clairee shrugged.

"And I suppose he just volunteered information on his lack of marital status?" I said.

"Of course not. I had to pry it out of him."

I rolled my eyes so hard I almost gave myself a concussion. "I don't have time for a man," I said.

"There is *always* time for a man, honey," she said, waggling her gravy-coated fork at me.

Mama looked at me expectantly. I was already as uncomfortable as I could get, so I took a deep breath and jumped right in.

"I've already got man trouble," I muttered, pushing the okra around my plate. They were going to see the local news sooner or later. "Scooter Barnes."

"What the hell's a scooterbarnes?" The Colonel said, and Clairee's perfectly plucked brow arched like a bat wing.

"It's not a *what*, it's a *who*," I said. "Remember him from school, Mama?"

"Scooter Barnes, who went off with the Cowboys?" Mama said. "Didn't his wife just leave him?"

"The *Dallas* Cowboys?" Clairee said and clutched a hand to her heart like she was in the middle of a fully involved triple coronary.

"He married Miss Texas," Mama said and cast me a rueful glance.

"First runner-up," I said, like Mama didn't know. Beauty pageants are blood sport in Texas.

"You know, if you'd kept up your piano lessons, you could have placed . . ." Mama said, and I sighed. Genetics have been kind to me, but those cosmetically enhanced Amazon pageant pros would have eaten me alive.

"One pageant does not a beauty queen make," I said, trying to sound wise.

"Well, you didn't have to do that ridiculous Indian dance for the talent competition. Right out of the blue. You looked like you were having a convulsion."

I thought about squinting my eyes and wheezing, "I coulda been a contendah," but reason prevailed. In Texas, there's a pageant for every imaginable event, and even as a little girl, I knew I'd never live down being crowned Miss Elgin Grain and Feed.

"Yes, well, I don't think Selena should have gotten as far as she did, not being a real American and all," Clairee said.

"She's naturalized," I said. "She was born in Argentina, but she's lived here in Austin since she was a baby."

"I'm just saying . . ." Clairee said.

Mama blew out an elegant snort and then sighed. "At least I never pushed you like Selena's mother, that awful Obregon woman," she said.

"Yeah," I said, smiling to myself. "Good thing."

Mama had always pushed, but not like Selena's mother. I remembered Selena's mom standing off-stage, cool and beautiful but with a permanent frown. She reminded me of Grace Kelly's evil clone, watching every move Selena made like an Iraqi Olympic coach. In retrospect, I wondered if Mama was envious of Selena's mother the way I was envious of Selena.

"Selena was such a sweet little thing," Mama said, but I could practically see the gears churning inside her pretty platinum head. "Are you going to call Scooter?"

"The man just tried to kill himself for the second time this month."

"Does insurance pay on suicide?" Clairee said. The Colonel choked on a big bite of chicken.

"What?" Clairee said. "These things are important when you're starting a new relationship."

"I'm not starting a new relationship, unless you call stopping Scooter from a date with a Derringer a relationship," I said. "But," I shook my head and put my fork down. "There's something weird going on."

"I understand his business has picked up after he started importing all those bizarre little animals from South Africa," Mama said.

"South America," I corrected.

"Whatever," Mama said. "You know, last time I saw him at the Chamber of Commerce luncheon he was wearing Armani."

Mama and Clairee cast me identical stares.

"You should call him," my mother said.

"And shave everything that needs shaving," Clairee said. "Because you just never know."

"What kind of weird thing is going on?" the Colonel said, stoically blowing right by the shaving comment like he always did.

"Nothing worth mentioning," I said, thinking of Captain America roaming the fence line. I'd wanted to run the whole thing by the Colonel—the over-enthusiastic SWAT team and the FBI involvement—which, aside from dinner, was the main reason I'd come over. But I didn't want a bunch of meddling from the Sisters Grimm. I shrugged. "Just a feeling."

"What you need is a gun," Clairee announced. "Come back to the condo with me and you can pick out one of mine."

"I have a gun," I said.

Everyone stopped eating and stared at me.

The Colonel dropped his fork. "What?"

"Do you have bullets?" Clairee said, dabbing her perfectly lined lips with her napkin. "Let me get my purse . . ."

I walked out of my mom's with a raging headache, a Tupperware full of fried chicken, and a big box of bullets. And to my utter horror, I'd agreed to accept a phone call from Diego DeLeon. I wasn't sure why he was sniffing around after nearly ten years, but it might be interesting to find out.

The Colonel walked me to the Jeep and stood, rubbing the back of his neck. "Ya know," he said, "I saw a nice big Impala at the police auction last week. Still had the spotlight on the driver's side door."

"I like my Jeep." I smiled and rose on my tiptoes to kiss his cheek.

"The Impala has a top and doors," he said, kicking a tire on my topless, doorless CJ-7.

I could tell he was trying to work his way around to a difficult subject, and it was never easy for him to talk without doing something constructive like mowing the lawn or fixing the toilet or gutting catfish in the kitchen sink.

The warm, wet air was heavy with the scent of fresh-cut grass and the chirring of night insects. In the gentle din, I tried to think of a way to ask him what he thought of an FBI agent skulking around a local suicide attempt that didn't make me sound like I was either paranoid or in trouble.

"You know anybody in the FBI?" I finally said.

The Colonel's sharp blue eyes narrowed. "Used to. But FBI mandatory retires at fifty-seven. Guys I know've been out for a while."

"Do you know anything about them—you know, the FBI?" I said. "I mean, do you know anything about their jurisdiction?"

The Colonel gazed down at me intently. "Well, for the feds to get involved there'd have to be some kind of federal offense. Something like interstate crime or terrorism. Or when a kid's disappeared, or if local law invited them in. Or organized crime."

A shiver of unease skittered up my spine. What in the world had Scooter gotten himself into?

The Colonel probably sensed I wanted to ask him something but wasn't sure what to say, because he leaned in to kiss one of those smacking little kisses on the top of my head. "You need any money?"

I always need money, but I shook my head.

"About that gun," he finally said. "Be careful, hon. Don't let anybody take it and use it on you."

It was late when I pulled into the deserted Texaco a block and a half from my house, and I was pondering what I'd learned at dinner in between getting grilled on my un-social life and berated for my lack of respectable employment.

I thought about what the Colonel had said about FBI jurisdiction and wondered what Scooter had done to get the attention of the feds.

So far, all I knew was that Scooter had called me at the crack of dawn wanting to talk, then promptly holed himself up in a shed in the back of his parents' ranch with a shotgun, babbling about Selena.

I'd been able to talk Scooter out of doing himself in, but I couldn't get him to tell me what was up with the sudden rash of suicide attempts. Was it just Selena? And if so, why was the FBI so interested?

Idling at the gas pump, I hesitated at pulling the key from the Jeep's ignition. I never knew if the engine was going to start again. It's my understanding, however, that leaving the car running while you pump gas can spark an inferno that could obliterate an entire block, and I figured I was at my catastrophe quota for the day.

It was dark and the station was closed, so I was going to have to do the pay-at-the-pump thing, but Dr. Dick and a stack of student loans had burned me out of an A-1 credit rating. I was down to one credit card and I was pretty sure I was close to my limit.

I climbed out the doorless entry and selected the cheapest fuel grade. In my peripheral vision, a shadow flickered in the pink neon light.

"Great," I grumbled, glancing around the empty parking lot, thinking of Ramsey's ominous warning earlier in the evening. "He finally has me completely paranoid."

I muttered a prayer to the Visa gods as I swiped my card through the slot, looking nervously over my shoulder. The pump chugged and churned, then took my card. I sighed in relief and pumped the gas.

Tearing the receipt from the slot, I climbed back into the Jeep and turned the key in the ignition. Nothing.

"Perfect," I said to no one. I jumped out of the Jeep, pulled a toolbox from the back cargo area, and popped the hood. I have one tool. A hammer. I've found that if you can't beat an auto part into working, you can at least beat it into submission.

Extracting the hammer from the box, I reared back and smacked the crap out of the starter. A good solid *clang* of metal on metal, and I leaned in the driver's side, still staring at the exposed motor. Holding my breath, I turned the key.

The starter ratcheted. The engine coughed, sputtered, and turned over. Smiling a little smugly, I slammed the hood and wiped my free hand on my jeans.

I climbed into the driver's seat and pulled up short when I came face to face with a big bald man with little beady eyes.

I couldn't stop staring at the misshapen nub the size of a baby's finger in the place where his left ear should've been.

"Oh!" I tried to scream, but it came out as a squeak and I could practically feel his caustic gaze rake the length of my body.

My heart banged against my rib cage so hard I thought I'd go into cardiac arrest. I wondered if the bald guy knew CPR. My gaze dropped to his fat, wet lips. I hoped not.

"Ew, ew, ew," I said, knowing it's not nice to make fun of the infirm, but I stopped talking when he pulled out a big knife with an odd bone handle. The blade glinted pink in the neon light. My breath caught in my throat.

In a weird, feathery voice, he said, "Shut up and drive, *Hure*."

"*Hure?* Who the hell is Hure?" I said. "Look, mister. You've got the wrong girl."

The man slugged me hard in the back of my head. I nearly wet my pants. And I would have, if my brain hadn't shut down all my involuntary functions.

I write obituaries for a living and I know a little about the way these things turn out. It's better to fight an attacker at the scene of the crime and risk getting killed than to leave with him, which almost guarantees getting killed and usually involves some pretty gruesome pre-mortem activities.

"Be a clever girl and fucking drive," he wheezed in some sort of muddled German accent.

I stared at his missing ear. Great. I was about to get car-jacked by Van Gogh.

Panic pulsed through my veins and my brain tumbled through two million thoughts. *The gun in my purse.* Was it loaded? Did it matter? What if I just showed him the gun and he got so scared *he* wet *his* pants?

I looked at him in the dim, neon light. His eyes seemed glazed and lifeless, and frankly, kind of stupid. Maybe I could distract him. It was worth a shot. Plus, I still had my hammer . . .

"Wait!" I yelled, pointing over his shoulder. "What the hell is that?"

"What the fuck you talk about," he said, but he twisted his fat neck in the direction I'd pointed. I heaved back and swung the hammer at his head.

"I don't see nothing . . . Ow!" The blow bounced off his big bald head. He didn't fall over unconscious like they do in the movies, but he was bleeding and he appeared to be momentarily stunned. His knife clattered to the bare floorboard. I grabbed my purse.

Frantically, I rummaged. Lipstick, wallet, mini recorder . . . *weapon!* I caught hold of the grip and juggled the gun, aiming it in the vicinity of his missing ear.

"Freeze!" I yelled, just like I'd seen the SWAT guys do with the pizza kid, with only one real difference. I don't think the SWAT guys' hands shook. Swallowing hard, I narrowed my eyes. "Don't make me go Annie Oakley on your ass!"

The bald guy stared at me, rubbing the bloody dent on his head. "You hit me!"

He might have said *You heet me*, but his i's sounded like e's, so it was hard to tell.

He rubbed the gash on his head. "You fucking hit me! What, are you crazy?"

I thought about that. I was sitting in an open Jeep in the middle of the night with a gun that may or may not be loaded, next to a big bald guy who at best intended to kill me, and at worst . . . I didn't want to think about it.

"I'm so crazy it'd make your head spin," I said in my best Bogart.

He shook his bleeding head.

"Give me that," he said, and he reached over the console and took my gun.

I couldn't believe it. I was about to get shot with my own gun.

"You took my gun," I said, and I heard my voice crack. "Give it back!"

He looked at me like I'd spoken Swahili, but at this point, I had nothing to lose. I didn't want the Colonel, not to mention Mark, to read in the morning paper that I'd been loitering in a dark, deserted parking lot where an earless bald guy took my gun and used it on me.

Van Gogh shoved the cold, hard barrel under my chin. "We have a party, you and me."

I reached for the bloody hammer, but he yanked it out of my hand and tossed it into the parking lot.

"Drive. Don't talk. And keep your fucking hands on the wheel where I see them."

FIVE

"Drive," he growled. Van Gogh was fat, but it was hard fat, the kind that fighters get as they age, and his neck was as big as my waist. He pressed the barrel of the gun beneath my chin, and despite the heat of the summer night, I broke out in a cold sweat. My teeth chattered and my hands were shaking, but I jammed the stick shift into first and pulled out of the parking lot, aware of gravel crunching as we inched over the shoulder and onto the deserted road.

"What did he say?" Van Gogh snarled, and I couldn't help staring at his mangled stump of an ear in my rear-view mirror.

"What?"

"Don't fuck with me, *Hure*," he said. "Mr. Barnes has taken something that does not belong to him."

He slammed the pistol against my temple.

I screamed. Pain burst through my brain. My body rocked to the left as the Jeep ran off the road. I could smell the man's rancid breath from where I was sitting, and if I'd had some Tic Tacs, I'd have offered him a handful.

"Pull over!" he yelled, which was moot, because I'd already lost control of the Jeep. We were careening into the parking area at Lakeside Park, high on the limestone cliff overlooking Lake Austin.

The sweet scent of the lake after a good rain loomed in the air. Romantic, if you weren't tearing around in a topless Jeep with an earless homicidal maniac.

Over the noise of the engine I heard water lapping against the shoreline below. My stomach pitched. I was going to be sick.

Van Gogh reached over and jammed the stick shift into park. The gears ground and the Jeep jerked to a stop, bouncing my forehead off the steering wheel.

"I lost my patience when you brain me with that hammer. You must tell me what happen in that shed."

My head pounded like thunder. My nose was running and hot tears streamed down my cheeks. "Honest to God," I said. "I don't know what you're talking about."

"Barnes! What happen with Barnes?" He reached over and grabbed a handful of my hair and yanked. "I am not kidding with you. You must tell me where he put it!"

"Put what?" I said, and he jerked my hair hard. Pain streaked from my scalp to my collarbone. "I swear," I squeaked. "I don't know!"

"You want to go hard?" he said. "We go hard."

He laughed a horrible, wheezy little laugh and wrapped my hair around his fist. My head jerked painfully downward as he grappled for his knife on the floorboard. "You know what it feel like to lose an ear?"

Here's the thing. I'm often critical of myself, but I kind of like my ears, and every other part of my body, right where they are.

Van Gogh had my head wedged beneath the dash and I could smell the sweat that pooled in the apex of his polyester pants. A surge of hot adrenaline rushed to the back of my brain.

"No!" I heard myself scream. I yanked up and hit the shift with the back of my head.

Gravel crunched beneath the tires as the Jeep began to roll. Van Gogh still had me by the hair, so I stomped on the gas. The Jeep lurched as I floored it.

I saw my life flash before my eyes. I wondered who would write my obituary. I hoped it wasn't Mark.

"Stop!" Van Gogh yelled. I couldn't see over the dash, but we were picking up speed. He jerked my hair hard and I screamed in pain and then, strangely, felt my stomach lurch, the way it does on the downward swing of a roller coaster.

We were airborne.

"Fu-u-u-uck!" Van Gogh roared. Right before we hit the water.

The Jeep slammed into the lake. The impact smashed me into the dash and my head hit so hard I thought I'd split my skull. Stars burst behind my eyes and the rebound sent me flying.

I felt my body arc high in the air like a ragdoll right before I belly-flopped hard into the lake. The water was cold, and as I went under, it closed around me like a liquid grave, the slimy hydrilla weeds snaking around my arms and legs.

My temple throbbed where Van Gogh had hit me, and I was dizzy and nauseated. I felt frozen, and I couldn't move my arms or legs. As I sank into the cold water, I thought, "Huh. So this is how I'm going to die."

I supposed it was better than getting carved up by the likes of Van Gogh. Sinking deep in the dark water, I thought about how easy it would be to close my eyes and let the lake take me.

Then I heard it. A deep, smoky voice whispering beyond the waves.

"Swim, Cauley."

I blinked and my eyes stung in the murky water.

"Swim."

It was my father's voice, just as it was the summer he'd taught me to swim.

"Swim, Cauley." His voice was young and strong and sure, just as I remembered it.

"Swim," he whispered. And I swam.

My head hurt, my lungs burned, and my eyes stung, but my body seemed to come back to my brain, and I bucked, fighting the duckweed. My jeans and tee shirt clung heavily in the water, threatening to draw me down, but I kicked as hard as I could. Fighting my way to the surface, I gasped in a big, warm, welcoming gulp of air. Sputtering and coughing, I struggled to catch my breath. Kicking my legs toward the surface, I stretched out on my back, filling my lungs with air. For a few heartbeats, I floated, breathing until my lungs got used to the idea. I felt the cold, wet pull of the water at my back and the warm, dark sky above. The stars were bright in the sapphire night, and the North Star seemed to flash, and in that fleeting moment, I thought, "I'm going to be all right."

In the near distance, I heard Van Gogh choking. "I can't swim!"

I blinked, suddenly sucked back to the present. "You should have thought about that before you tried to cut my ear off!" I yelled into the darkness.

I righted myself and began to tread water, trying to get my bearings. Under normal circumstances, swimming is the one form of exercise I actually enjoy. You can work out, get a tan, and if you go to the right places you can get poolside margaritas served by men who look like finalists for Chippendales. But here in the cold, weed-infested lake, I could hear Van Gogh and his big, puffy lips desperately gasping for air.

The man had just tried to slice off one of my favorite body parts, but did I really want him dead? It was Darwinian, really—nature's way of thinning the herd . . .

I didn't worry about it long, because a big, fat forearm buckled around my neck.

Van Gogh.

"Let go!" I gasped. "Get off me or we're both going to drown!" He squeezed harder, choking me, and I did the only thing I could think to do.

I bit him.

He made some guttural, unintelligible sound, and I sputtered as he dragged me under. I wasn't prepared, and I sucked water up my nose as we sank. We hit the muddy, weed-choked bottom, where I scrambled and found a foothold against a rock. I pushed off, hard.

Struggling up and wheezing under Van Gogh's grip, my face broke the surface and I gasped, coughing up water. My lungs stung and my nose hurt, but hey, I was tough. I'd lived through a truly bad marriage and two years of night school. I was not a quitter.

Turning my head as much as I could in his corpulent grip, I scanned the darkness for shoreline. We were about fifteen feet deep, I guessed. If I could get just a few yards inland, I could stand up and wade right out.

Then what? Van Gogh had me in a chokehold. If we both made it to shore, he would catch his breath and find new and inventive ways to inflict pain on my body. His arm was bleeding where I'd bitten him and he still hadn't let go. Apparently Van Gogh was no quitter either.

In the dark, I squinted toward the shadowy strip of land beneath the cliffs. There was no way I could climb the steep rock-face, but there was a shallow bit of shoreline that went on about a half mile upstream. It was clear that whatever I planned to do was going to involve a great deal of running. I wished I'd gone ahead and dropped the dough for that damned treadmill.

My gun, cell phone, and hammer were history, and my Tupperware of fried chicken was floating across the narrows somewhere near the Fat Farm on the other side of the lake. I could kiss that chicken goodbye.

Van Gogh still had a death grip on my neck, so I flipped over until I was floating half out of the water on top of his whale-like body. I paddled for all I was worth.

"Let go," I gasped, but he was choking and sputtering, squeezing my neck until I thought my collarbone would break.

He's going to kill me, I thought. *Here in the water, or when we reach shore, this man is going to kill me.*

He squeezed harder. I fought to swim with his fat arms around my neck, but his big body felt like I was dragging my Jeep instead of a person as I struggled, propelling us slowly toward the shore. I wasn't going to let this idiot drown me; from somewhere deep inside, I found a strength I didn't know I had. As I paddled, I periodically did a half-dive, submerging his big face until he gurgled for air. If I couldn't make him let go, I could at least keep him breathless.

When I got close enough to shore to make a break for it, I gave him one final shove, pushing with every ounce of strength. He was still sputtering from the last time we'd gone under, and this time, he stayed under. I wriggled out of his grip and swam wildly for the shallows.

I didn't look back. Choking in big breaths of air, I scrambled up the slick, wet bank, grabbing at twigs and rocks until I could dig my waterlogged Keds into the mud, slipping and sliding up the shoreline, where I ran.

MY LUNGS BURNED AND my body ached. My teeth were still chattering and I was muddy and soaked to the skin when I made it to the gas station, where I called Cantu collect from the pay phone.

He arrived at the Texaco, siren blaring, lights flashing, and I still couldn't shake the feeling someone was watching me. The adrenaline that had rushed hot was gone, and my blood felt like cold sludge oozing through my veins. The muscles in my arms and legs felt like I'd been stricken with polio. *I had to get back to the gym.*

"I'm really sorry about this," I said. "When Arlene answered I told her I could call somebody else."

Cantu snorted. "She said she'd knock me into next week if I passed off the call," he said. He was smiling, but the smile was tight, and I could see he was mad as hell.

"You're mad?" I said, watching as two uniforms roared onto the scene.

"Not at you," he said. Draping his jacket over my shoulders, Cantu listened as I told him what happened. He drove me back to the cliffs, where I stood, shivering, as we watched the tow truck from Shay's Auto Body pull my CJ-7 out of the lake. I always hated calling Shay Turner for help.

Shay is one of my neighbors, and he's always trying to give me appliances and vehicles with no traceable serial numbers. He reminds me of a big, dopey Lab puppy—entirely too friendly and always goes straight for the crotch.

"So this earless guy was asking you about what happened in the shed with Scott Barnes?" Cantu said.

"Yeah," I said. Shay's tow truck beeped loudly as it backed to the cliff's edge.

"Did you ask him why he wanted to know?"

"I was busy worrying about not getting my ears chopped off," I said. "I didn't have time to quiz him about motivation. But he said Scooter had something that didn't belong to him."

"And he had an accent?"

I nodded. "Almost like German," I said, and Cantu frowned.

"Did you see what he was driving? We found a hopped-up blue El Camino abandoned out behind the Texaco."

"I never saw him coming," I said. "I'm going to be a helluva reporter. I should have gone to cooking school."

Cantu snorted. "Warn me if you do."

The tow truck was still beeping and the lift-gears made a metallic, grinding sound as my Jeep topped the cliff, water gushing from the open doorways. The wheels made contact with dry land and the Jeep tipped, crashing a big wave of lake water all over me and Cantu.

"You know, if it was anybody else, this might seem unusual," Cantu said, wiping strands of duckweed out of his face. "How in the hell do you get yourself into these things?"

"If I knew that, I could avoid it," I said, wringing out the front of my shirt.

A long shadow passed over us. I turned to look and saw the white-faced dog I'd almost run over peering out of a clump of sage. It stood, staring at me.

"Did you see that?" I said.

"What?" Cantu said.

"A white-faced dog. Right there." I pointed toward the bushes, but the dog was gone.

Cantu looked at me like I had finally lost my mind. Maybe I had. I'd never been threatened before. Hell, I'd never even hit anybody before, and now I'd brained somebody with a hammer and left him in the lake. Yes, he was a thug, and yes, he had it coming, but I didn't like the way it made me feel.

"Look, Cauley. We got most of what we need. You can come by the station in the morning and swear out a statement," Cantu said.

I nodded, but my chest hurt, like someone was sitting on my sternum. I could feel a big crying jag coming on, and I really, really hate crying jags.

Cantu must have sensed it, because he said, "Come on," and he put his arm around me and gave a quick hug. "The boys will take care of your car. Let's get you home."

BACK AT HOME, CANTU checked the house and gave me the all clear. I double-locked my door, something I never do, stripped my wet clothes in a puddle on the living room floor and then stood in the shower until all the hot water and most of my tears were gone.

Wincing, I stoically sprayed Bactine on my cuts, praying I wouldn't come down with a bad case of some mutant water-borne microbe. I stumbled over to stare at myself in the mirror.

Bruises bloomed interesting shades of blue and green all over my face and body, and I thought if I stood there long enough, I could watch them develop. But as I stared at my reflection, I watched something else develop: the realization that I had been attacked.

I had actually inflicted bodily harm on another human being, and I wasn't entirely sure he'd made it out of the lake alive. I felt sick.

In my head, I knew it had been him or me, but my heart was saying "Something was taken away from me tonight and I will never get it back."

I pulled an old football jersey over my head and crawled between my cool white sheets. In the darkness, I felt Aunt Kat's old typewriter silently tugging at me in the dark. *Write*, it whispered.

"Not tonight," I said to the empty room. "I can't do this tonight."

I curled my arms around the unoccupied pillow next to me and felt more alone than I'd felt since I sat on those cold courthouse steps three years ago. I rarely missed being married. Dr. Dick was, after all, a dick. But sometimes I missed snuggling up to a warm body at night.

All I had to do was make a phone call and Mark would be at the door with warm milk and soothing words. He'd fold me into his arms and, for the time being, make the world go away. He was good at that.

I considered getting up and playing his old messages on my answering machine just to hear the sound of his voice. But that was the very same feeling that made me hide my cordless phone in the vegetable crisper.

I had made my own bed, so to speak, and now I was going to lie in it. By myself. I flopped onto my back and stared at the ceiling.

Van Gogh had vanished. By now, some of Austin's finest would be out searching for him. But Lake Austin is a long, winding bend in the Lower Colorado River. It's lined with large-tracted neighborhoods and miles of thick, rambling woodlands. It would take time to find Van Gogh—if he made it out of the lake alive.

Every time I closed my eyes, I could see him, big and bald and earless, glaring at me with that weird, beady stare. I could smell his rancid breath, feel his hands fisting my hair, clinging to my neck, dragging me deeper and deeper into the cold, weed-choked water . . .

A cold chill skittered up my spine. Climbing back out of bed, I put the phone on my nightstand in case Van Gogh made an unscheduled appearance, then I popped *The Thin Man* into my little TV/DVD combo near the foot of my bed. I plumped the pillow and snuggled in, but even Nick and Nora couldn't take my mind off the events of the day. Besides, I should probably be listening in case Van Gogh showed up on my doorstep.

And what if he did? I had no car, no gun, and nobody. I threw the pillow over my head. If I stopped to think about it, I was lucky. I was alive. And despite a profusion of bumps and bruises, I was relatively healthy. Everything seemed dark now, but I could work through my problems alone. Lots of women did. All I had to do was get through the night.

From down the hall, I heard a weird, creaky noise. My breath caught.

Tossing the pillow aside, I listened, straining against the thick silence.

Had I locked all the windows? I rarely lock anything. Cantu had gone back home to his family and Van Gogh was at large. Hell would freeze over before I called Mark.

I held my breath, but all I could hear were the sounds of the soft southern night. A silvery breeze whispered through the live oaks outside my bedroom window and echoed in the canyon below. In the near distance, the river gently lapped at the shoreline. The old house settled on a sigh. No ex-boyfriends. No ear-chopping, homicidal maniacs.

A board squeaked. I stifled a scream and grabbed the phone from the nightstand.

A bounce at the edge of the bed sent the breath clogging in my throat.

And then I heard it. A soft whirring noise, followed by the pressure of tiny paws pressing into the mattress.

"What are you doing?" I said to Muse as she made her way to the head of the bed. "You hate me." Fresh tears stung the backs of my eyes as the cat bumped her head against my chin. She curled her warm, fuzzy body into the crook of my neck.

"Oh, cat," I said, and then I let loose with an honest-to-god crying jag. "I never cry. Well. Almost never."

Muse wriggled, turned twice, then settled in, brushing my tear-streaked cheek with her long, curled whiskers, and then she softly purred me to sleep.

SIX

SOMETIMES IT DOESN'T PAY to get out of bed. My alarm clock shrieked at the crack of seven and I woke up swearing. After a night of wrestling with a homicidal maniac, I couldn't imagine going to work. I wondered if it was possible to write obituaries by telekinesis. Does *thinking* about writing count?

My whole body felt like I'd been beaten with a ball bat and I thought about calling in dead, but then I was back to who would write *my* obituary. Rolling over, I smacked the *snooze* button. I felt a tickle on my cheek and I smacked that too and then swore when I realized it was Muse.

"Shit!" I swore. She glared at me with the profound animosity mastered only by cats, and I reached out to scratch her little round chin. "I'm sorry, cat. I didn't know it was you."

She cast me a mutinous glare, then leapt out of bed, the tip of her tail twitching as she sashayed down the hall.

Great. Now I was a cat beater who may or may not have left somebody to die in Lake Austin. I wasn't sure which was worse.

The phone rang, and I thought about letting the machine pick up, but it could have been Publishers Clearing House calling to say they were circling the block with a big fake check for a million dollars. Hey. I'd barely survived an attack by an earless bald guy. My luck was bound to improve.

"Hey, *chica, que pasa?*" Mia's voice rang over the receiver.

"What's happening?" I flopped over on the bed and dragged the pillow over my head. "I'm dying a slow and painful death," I mumbled through the pillow.

"Oh, good, then I didn't disturb you. I got the CliffsNotes on what happened yesterday at the standoff thingy. Sorry I wasn't there," she said, her voice soaked with sympathy. "But see? I told you your horoscope said you would meet a dark, mysterious man."

"You don't know the half of it," I said, thinking of Van Gogh.

"What you need is a smudge ceremony—you know, where you burn little bundles of sage in the wonky parts of your house to clean up all the bad karma."

My eyes crossed involuntarily. "Mia, I'm not setting a brush fire in the middle of my aunt's living room."

"We'll get this taken care of," Mia said. *"Asi esta bien."*

Under the pillow, I shook my head. Mia's Colombian roots tangled wildly with her Texas upbringing. She'd always been wired differently than most but I was convinced it was that extended stay at aromatherapy camp that pushed her over the edge.

"Maybe later," I said, my voice muffled by the pillow. "My Jeep and I took a swan dive into Lake Austin last night. I need to figure out how I'm going to get to work."

"I could be over there in an hour," she said brightly. "I could bring you some tea."

I almost perked up. "Not green," I said, but she'd already hung up. *Be here in an hour,* my butt. Mia was never on time.

I rolled out of bed and checked my windows and doors for latent signs of Van Gogh, then called Cantu on his cell. He had no real news to report, except that they were going to release Scooter from the hospital that afternoon.

Almost as an afterthought, I said, "What's up with the FBI?"

"Tom Logan," he said with a growl.

"You boys and your pissing matches," I said, and decided to take a chance. "Hey. Why would the feds care about a local suicide threat?"

There was a long silence on the line, and I figured either Cantu couldn't tell me or he didn't know. Sighing, I thanked him anyway, told him to say *hey* to Arlene, and clicked off the phone. Stumbling into and out of the shower, I rinsed off and wrapped myself in a towel before wandering to the vanity, where I stared at myself in the mirror.

My bruises were so bright they were almost festive, and my hair was an unmitigated disaster. There wasn't much I could do about either, so I didn't. I'd wander next door to Beckett's later to see if he could perform one of his miracles on my hair.

I was headed back to my bedroom when the phone rang again, and I was surprised to hear Diego DeLeon on the other end of the line.

"Cauley?" he said in a smooth Latino accent. "Can you spare an evening for a friend?"

My eyes narrowed involuntarily. *Friend* was stretching the meaning of the word. "Any particular reason?"

Diego chuckled. "The policeman's daughter, suspicious as always. Can't we say just for old time's sake?"

I supposed I could, but I'm not a big believer in coincidence. "Fine," I said. "Where and when?"

"Tonight, then, *bonita*. It's all arranged. I'll be over to pick you up at seven."

I started to say that I'd had a rough couple of days and didn't feel up to an evening out, but I was talking to a dial tone.

Resigned, I snapped the phone back into the charge stand and laid a pair of shorts and a tee shirt with the *Sentinel* logo on my bed. Austin didn't invent business casual, but it certainly did its part to sink the concept to exciting new lows. The only people who wear suits in Austin are feds and morticians. And speaking of feds, I wondered how on earth I was going to find out why a federal agent was interested in Scooter Barnes. Scooter was my friend, and whatever he'd done to attract the attention of the feds had to be a mistake. Besides, there were rules about federal jurisdiction, and while the Patriot Act had broadened some of the bureau's power, they still had limits. I wondered what those limits were. Perhaps I'd just hunt down a certain FBI agent and find out.

I wrapped my towel more tightly around me, retrieved the phone book from the library, and flipped until I found the number to the FBI's Austin field office. According to the listing, the office was located near the Arboretum—the Mecca of Central Texas shopping. I picked up the phone and dialed.

When a bored female voice answered, I asked for Special Agent Tom Logan and was immediately channeled into his message system, where I listened to the sound of his voice. He really did have a nice voice.

I didn't leave a message. Law enforcement types typically mistrust media in any form and funnel even the most simple requests through Public Information Officers.

PIOs are journalists who've gone over to the dark side. Getting useful information out of a PIO is like teaching a pig to sing. It wastes your time and annoys the pig.

I punched "0" for operator.

"Federal Bureau of Investigation, Austin," she droned.

"Hi," I said. See? Cheery. Harmless. "My name is Cauley MacKinnon and I'm with the *Austin Sentinel*—"

It wasn't exactly a lie, but I rarely find it helpful to announce that my job with the *Sentinel* is confined to the Dead Beat.

"Media?" she said. "You have to talk with our Public Information Officer."

"Wow," I said into the phone. "You're very good. What was your name again?"

There was a long silence on the line. "Jennifer James."

"Jennifer," I said, just to keep her talking. "Thanks, Jennifer. I was just sitting here wondering who I should talk to. Who is your PIO, anyway?"

"Susan Grimes."

"And Special Agent Logan is white collar crime?"

"Agent Logan's in Organized Crime, but you're going to have to talk with Special Agent Grimes about that."

I would have smiled at my own cleverness if I hadn't been so stunned. Organized crime? What the hell had Scooter done that would draw the attention of the FBI's Organized Crime division? And was Logan's interest professional or personal? I wasn't sure which was worse.

The best approach, I figured, was the direct approach. I'd just go find Agent Logan and ask him. And if I couldn't weasel my way in to talk to Logan, I could swing by the Arboretum for a new pair of Manolos—once I got my insurance check cashed. And my Jeep back.

Still wrapped in my big bath towel, I opened a can of tuna for Muse and filled her champagne glass with fresh water. My aunt had started this little compulsion with her cat, and now the animal goes on a Ghandi-like hunger strike if she isn't wined and dined in her customary cut crystal.

I scavenged an old purse out of the back of my closet, a useless gesture since all my earthly purse-type possessions were languishing at the bottom of Lake Austin. If the cops dragged the lake for Van Gogh, I wondered if they'd mind looking for my purse. While I was momentarily delighted to discover a much-needed, forgotten twenty-dollar bill in there, I still had to cancel one credit card, thanks to Dr. Dick, and I was going to have to go down to the DMV and stand in line for three and a half years to get a new driver's license. Sighing, I fished a spare house key out of the junk drawer and wished like hell I had my Jeep.

And then what? Go to the office, sit in front of the computer, glassy-eyed, obsessing about the past twenty-four hours? I thought about Scooter's pale face in that shed and the ghastly face of Van Gogh, interrogating me about anything Scooter might have said, and for the first time, I considered the hideous thought that I might have actually had to write the obituary of a friend.

Shivering against a sudden chill, I wandered into the den and booted up my desktop and Googled Scott Barnes, hoping to find something—anything—that might be a clue that would explain what Scooter had gotten himself into.

Muse hopped up onto the desk and peered at the monitor as the search results appeared.

"Thirteen thousand hits?" I sighed. "Well, I'll do better when I hit the search engines at the office."

Muse didn't say anything. I scrolled through the top ten results. The first three hits were inane statistics from Scooter's brief brush with fame through NFL.com, followed by a two-page *Lone Star Observer* spread regarding Scooter's marriage to Selena. There was also an article on the grand opening of Scooter's pet store.

Just for grins, I entered "Earless German Guy" into the search engine.

There had to be a link between Scooter and Van Gogh, or some perceived link. Otherwise, why would Van Gogh care what Scooter said in the shed, and more importantly, why would Van Gogh think Scooter had something that didn't belong to him? And then there was the ear thing. While I've had more than my fair share of men mad at me, none of them had ever threatened to chop off one of my ears. And the FBI involvement thing really bothered me too.

The search on earless German guys came up with a couple of role-playing computer games and a link that turned out to be a truly disgusting S&M site.

After a brief moment of trying to figure out why anyone would want to see stuff like that, I printed the articles on Scooter, grabbed a manila file folder from the drawer and moved to the living room so I could spread the articles out on the living room floor and see if I couldn't stumble over a clue.

Tucking the towel more tightly around me, I popped a copy of *Casablanca* into the DVD player. I always think better with Bogey growling in the background.

Settling onto the Turkish rug, I skimmed a short clip and photo of the pet store grand opening. In the picture, Scooter stood behind a big red ribbon, flanked by his father and mother—Coach and Golly Barnes. I looked closer at the photo. Where was Selena? Surely a person's wife would be present at such an event.

Sighing, I laid the printout near the file folder where Muse sat, twitching her tail.

Rifling through the rest of the printouts, I wished like hell my mini recorder wasn't rusting at the bottom of the lake. Maybe Scooter really had said something important and I'd missed it.

I picked up the clip of Scooter's wedding, which featured a full-page wedding photo of the happy couple racing through a hail of rice in front of St. Stephen's Cathedral. It also featured an inset of Selena as first runner-up in the Miss Texas pageant.

She looked very much like she had in high school, only more so. Fine blond hair and delicate cheekbones. Her big morning-glory eyes practically melted the camera lens.

Not knowing what else to do, I got a legal pad from the desk in the library and made a flow chart of the timeline with players and possible connections. Scooter, Selena, and a mysterious FBI agent. And an ear-chopping homicidal maniac.

When I got back to the *Sentinel* office, I'd run a proper background check with public records and possible police connections. Of course, I'd have to do it during my lunch break . . .

I stared down at the printouts and my notes strewn about the Turkish rug. The business article about the pet store grand opening was bugging me. It was pretty ironic that a big, testosterone-pumped running back would open a pet store, although anybody who knew Scooter knew he was a gentle giant around animals. He seemed so happy in the photo.

What in his life could be so awful that Scooter would go on a bullet binge? Sure, he had been a ball player and he'd blown his knee. He'd lost out on a million-dollar contract, and I supposed that was enough to make anybody suicidal. But as far as I knew he seemed to be doing okay. A year ago, he and Selena changed the name of the store to the Blue Parrot and started importing all kinds of funny little animals.

So why the sudden rash of suicide attempts? Was Scooter's sudden death wish a result of Selena leaving him? Since I was pretty sure the FBI is not routinely called in for marital disputes, it was clear that I was going to have to dig deeper.

"Suicide," I said, thinking aloud. I got up and pulled a big book of medical research from the library, flipping pages as I drifted back into the living room, with Muse doing her best to trip me by doing figure eights around my calves. I was running my finger across the header *suicide* when something banged at the door. Muse shot down the hall and disappeared.

"Mia?" I said, tucking the towel tighter around me. "You're early."

I swung open the door and came face to face with what might have been the dark, mysterious man that Mia had predicted in her stars.

I couldn't move. He was a little taller than me, not quite six feet, I guessed, and looked like he was on his way to a shoot for GQ. I swallowed hard. This guy had the kind of green eyes that could trigger a public orgasm.

He smiled. "Cauley MacKinnon?"

I slammed the door.

"John Fiennes, United States Customs Service," he said through the stained glass. "I have a few questions. Is this a bad time?"

Customs? Peeking through a transparent piece in the stained glass panel, I noticed that not only was he drop-dead gorgeous, he was wearing a suit and holding a badge.

Well, crap. I'd been months without a man and now they were popping out of the woodwork. I took another peek. He wasn't Pierce Brosnan, but I supposed he was as close as a tough guy was going to get.

"Just a minute!" I yelled through the door.

He wanted to know if this was a bad time. Ha. Lately, every time was a bad time, but a customs agent with questions? I had a few questions of my own.

I scooped last night's damp clothes from the living room floor and raced to the bedroom, yanked on the shirt and shorts I'd laid out, and hurried back, slipping and sliding on scraps of research. The house was a wreck, but there wasn't a lot I could do about it, and with all the trouble I was having getting information out of Agent Logan, I wasn't going to let *this* fed get away.

Breathless from months of inertia, I swung open the door. Fiennes stared at me, not quite hiding a grin. I felt a jolt of electricity and took a step backward. Men like him should have warning labels stamped on their foreheads.

"I can come back later," he said, eyeing the mess in my living room. He had the barest hint of a European accent, and if dark velvet had a sound, it would have been this guy's voice.

"Um, no, it's okay, I thought you were someone else. Come in."

His gaze flicked toward the television, where Rick and Ilsa were romping through Paris as Nazi cannons boomed in the background.

"*Casablanca?*" he said, and grinned.

"Um, it helps me think," I said, fumbling for the clicker.

Fiennes raised a brow but didn't comment. He followed me into the house, carefully stepping over scattered printouts.

"Ignore the mess," I said. "I'm in the middle of a project."

He glanced at the papers with interest, and then looked at me, studying the road map of bruises on my face. He hadn't stepped any closer, but I could feel his presence like a physical thing.

He wasn't as tall as Logan, but he had a nice face, the kind that was handsome without being pretty, and he had tiny lines around his eyes, probably more from enthusiasm than age.

"I don't mean to be politically incorrect," I said, "but a U.S. Customs agent with a European accent?"

"Clever girl." Fiennes smiled. "My father was in the United States Air Force. I speak five languages, an advantage in my line of business."

"Oh," I said, feeling a bit like a xenophobe.

"I understand you had a rough night," he said, his voice warm and low. He moved my hair out of my face for a better look at my bruises and frowned. "Have you seen a doctor?"

Heat rushed to my face and I touched my bruised cheek. "A couple of medics looked me over at the scene. How'd you know about last night?"

"Actually, that's why I'm here."

"Hmm," I said, not knowing what else to say. "May I get you a glass of tea?"

"Do you have coffee?"

"I don't drink coffee, so it's nothing fancy."

"Fancy doesn't suit me," he said, and I almost thought he was flirting with me.

I set about brewing a pot of the year-old store brand I keep in the freezer, a grim reminder of my days with Mark Ramsey.

"What kind of a name is Cauley?" he said as coffee plopped noisily into the old pot.

"Actually, it's my mother's maiden name," I said, flattered at his interest.

When I handed him the cup, he took it in his hands, and something about those hands sent a warm chill straight through me. They were large, his fingers long, their movements precise, like those of a physician. Or a musician. Or a sharpshooter.

The kind of hands that could drive a girl crazy.

Jeez, I thought. *I'd been lusting after everything in pants. I'd better get a boyfriend. Fast.*

"Do you have any idea who abducted you?" he said.

"What?" I said, tearing my gaze away from his hands. "Abducted?" I hadn't thought of it like that. "Um. No." I said, and at least I didn't stutter.

"And you don't know why you were abducted?" Fiennes took a big slug of my hideous coffee. To his credit, he didn't flinch.

I fidgeted. Spilling your guts is sticky business for someone trying to make ranks as a reporter—protecting your sources and all—and at some point, I hoped to get off the Dead Beat.

I watched as John Fiennes took another drink of coffee and my eyes narrowed. Why would a customs agent be interested in Van Gogh? Which brought me back around to Van Gogh's interest in Scooter.

"Is this just about the German guy, or are you after Scott Barnes, too?"

"German," Fiennes muttered, looking like he'd heard a private joke. He extracted a leather-bound notepad that didn't look anything like Agent Logan's. "What would make you think there is a connection between the two?"

"Well, let's see . . . Scooter's sudden rash of suicide attempts, a customs agent at my front door, and an FBI agent lurking around a SWAT suicide standoff. And then there's the little matter of how I got attacked by Van Gogh, who was grilling me about what Scooter said while we were in the shed, something Scooter was hiding."

Fiennes's jaw muscles tightened. "FBI?"

"Yes," I said, looking at his dark suit and crisply pressed dark shirt. His clothes were tailored and he smelled of some sort of expensive cologne I didn't recognize. "What, are you some sort of customs agency spy?"

He smiled. "What would make you think so?"

"I don't know. I thought customs agents were those geeks at the airport who ask if you have anything to declare. You look sort of like James Bond."

Fiennes chuckled at that. "We're on the frontline of homeland defense," he said, and I could feel the warmth flooding into my cheeks.

"Do you know this 'Van Gogh'?" he said, steering the conversation back to its source.

"Oh. The earless guy. That's not his name. That's just what I call him."

Fiennes smiled. "What did you tell your, uh, Mr. Van Gogh?"

"I told him I didn't know what he was talking about, and then we drove into the lake."

"And your friend—this 'Scooter.' This would be Mr. Barnes?"

I nodded.

"And he told you nothing?"

I shook my head. "See? That's what I can't figure out. The only thing we talked about was his wife. That and his glory days back in high school."

"His wife?" Fiennes was scribbling in his notebook, and while I caught a peek, it was some sort of shorthand I couldn't read.

"Well, yeah," I said, "but he didn't say anything. Just that she was leaving him."

Fiennes nodded, his eyes narrowed. "He said nothing odd or unusual?"

"This whole thing is odd and unusual."

Fiennes looked at me for a long moment, and then his gaze drifted around my house.

"You live here alone," he said. It wasn't a question. "Do you have a gun?"

"I had a gun. It sort of got taken away from me."

He blew out a breath with the patience reserved for the very young or the very stupid. "You need a security system. And you must think about bringing your dog inside."

"Dog?" I said, but Fiennes was already moving toward the door.

"If you remember anything more, you must call me on my cell phone," he said. "And if you get in over your head, tag it *Urgent*. These men are not playing, Miss MacKinnon."

"Cauley," I said. Our gazes locked and his eyes were so green I went speechless.

He handed me his card, his gaze still on mine. "In case of emergency."

Did flashes of pure lust count as an emergency?

He looked down at me intently. "And you must be more careful when opening your door."

"I thought you were somebody else."

"There are dangerous men about, Miss MacKinnon. Be careful," he said. "And lock your door."

And then he opened the door and was gone.

I stood, staring at the closed door. Dangerous men indeed.

I hadn't gotten any more information from John Fiennes than I had from Tom Logan. But when Tom Logan showed up at my door, he'd said it was business. Whatever John Fiennes was up to, he didn't mention anything about being just business. Things were looking up.

"U.S. Customs. Curiouser and curiouser," I said to myself, and looked down when I felt Muse winding her furry little body around my bare calves. I tucked the hot customs guy's card into my old purse.

"Did you see the butt on that guy?" I said to the cat, but she ignored me, so I headed toward my blow dryer to get ready for the day.

I was dried and dressed and rearranging the printouts when the front door rattled.

"Hey! *Todo bien?*" Mia yelled through the door. "Your door's locked!"

"Hold on a minute." I tossed the book on suicide to the floor, which sent a stack of notes flying like oversized confetti.

I grabbed the old purse and a spare pair of Ray-Bans and swung the door open, looking around for signs of hot customs guys and big, swampy-looking earless thugs. "Yeah," I said. "I'm locking my doors now."

"Ts, ts," Mia tutted, popping her gum and peering at me over the rims of her little round sunglasses. Standing on the porch, she looked like ninety-eight pounds of pure dynamite packed in a swingy orange skirt and strappy matching sandals. She was holding a paper cup I knew wasn't from Starbucks.

"Smell this," she said, rising on her tiptoes to shove a sprig of lavender under my nose.

I winced. In my family, when someone asks you to smell something, it's usually spoiled milk or bad meat.

I locked the door behind me with the spare key and was headed down the porch steps when the white-faced dog flashed in my peripheral vision.

I stopped. "Did you see that?"

"See what?"

"A white-faced dog," I said. That dog had to belong to somebody. My neighborhood has a lot of wildlife, partially because it has strict ordinances on stray dogs. If the dog was still hanging around when I got home, maybe I'd print out some lost and found flyers.

"You know," Mia said. "In some cultures, seeing a phantom dog is a harbinger of death."

"That's very comforting."

"But usually those harbinger-dogs are black."

She handed me the little cup of tea and I took a drink. "Green," I growled, and Mia ignored me.

"Speaking of seeing things, have you seen the front page of the *Journal* today?" she said.

"No. Why?"

She shrugged. Opening the door to her yellow Beetle, she tucked the sprig of lavender into the dandy little bud vase attached to the dash. "No reason."

MIA HIT THE GAS and my head jerked back, which I always think is funny in a Beetle. The air conditioner was broken, so we cranked down the windows and I was windblown and hot when she dropped me off at the police substation. Windblown and hot never bothers me in my Jeep, but riding around with no air conditioning in Mia's little Beetle reminded me of being trapped in an Easy-Bake Oven.

Luckily, the police substation is only about fifteen minutes from my house. Mia let me out in the parking lot, and I thanked her before she peeled out and tore down the road.

There isn't a whole lot of crime in west Austin, and the substation shows it. It's shiny and clean, with tract lighting and gleaming floors. The downtown cops call it Club West. Fort Apache, the cop shop in east Austin, is where most of the real action goes down.

I signed in and Cantu walked me back to his office, where I made a statement and did the paperwork on my run-in with Van Gogh. The cops who usually flirt and make wildly inappropriate suggestions were grim and attentive as I browsed through pages of mug shots that all seemed to blur together.

It didn't matter. I wouldn't find Van Gogh in those books. Not with that weird, pseudo-German accent. Austin is such a melting pot that if you stay here long enough, the drawl invades your speech patterns.

Cantu gave me a report to file with my insurance company for my Jeep, and after filling out a pile of perfunctory paperwork, I called a cab.

I ASKED THE CABDRIVER to wait when we stopped at the FBI field office near the Arboretum to see if I could weasel a couple of questions out of Special Agent Logan. Logan wasn't there, but the receptionist eyed my bruised face with thinly veiled suspicion. I declined her offer to leave Logan a message. I would look for him later, and I figured he'd be easier to find if he didn't know I was looking for him.

The cabdriver hooked a left on Loop 360 and headed for my office, and as we passed the Arboretum, I gazed longingly at Saks, thinking about rows of kicky summer sandals in need of a good home.

In nearly thirty minutes, we slid into the parking lot at the *Sentinel's* west Austin satellite office. I paid the driver and over-tipped him for waiting—which is one of the reasons I'm always broke. I was aware of every sore muscle in my body when I pushed open the glass door and stalked into the *Sentinel's* lobby at noon.

"Wow," Paul Shiner said. Shiner is a big, blond sports reporter in line for a shot at the City Desk, which put us in direct competition. If I'd had anything to compete with.

He'd been heading out of the lobby with a big stack of sports scores. "Hey!" he said.

"Not now, Shiner."

Shiner U-turned and fell into step beside me, and we breezed by the security desk where Harold, the heavyset guard, was keeping watch over a box of donuts. We did the badge flash thing and Harold nodded us in with a big powdered-sugar grin.

"What happened to you?" Shiner said, crowding in front of me, staring at my bruised face.

"Hunting accident," I said, and pushed past his big shoulders to march down the main hall toward the Bull Pen. The Bull Pen is a maze of cubicles divided in the middle by a long aisle, all monitored from the Cage, the glass-enclosed office where the *Sentinel* satellite's managing editor sits in a swivel chair eating red meat, smoking designer cigars—which he swears he's quitting—and ripping our stories to smithereens with his little red pen.

The satellite office is located between a bank and a meat market, giving it the unique smell of old money and fresh meat. The walls are pus yellow, the carpet is burgundy, and none of the equipment works the way it's supposed to. My boss, Mike Tanner, says the satellite is where the main office sends you when you're on your way up or on your way out. I didn't care to speculate on my place in that scenario.

The best thing about the remote office is that it's laid back. We get all kinds of community drop-ins who report the best, most insane story ideas. My favorite is the Laser Lady. She comes in once a week swearing that aliens abducted her and used lasers to redistribute the fat in her body—a neat trick if you can get them to do it.

I strode past Remie at the front desk, who was chattering warp-speed on the phone, yelling something to one of her juvenile delinquents about not flushing the cat down the toilet.

I made my way down the aisle, which opens up to the Bull Pen, where all of the *Sentinel's* second-string reporters and copy editors were busy clattering away at keyboards.

I'd nearly reached my desk when I stopped dead in my tracks.

Selena Obregon gleamed blondly out of the ladies' room at the back of the office. She moved through the aisle of cubicles with aristocratic grace, even more beautiful than I remembered. A thin man with gold-rimmed glasses fell into step behind her.

As she moved, the heads of every male, not to mention a few females, turned from their monitors to admire the beauty-pageant sway of her behind. Her expensive pink handbag matched her expensive pink shoes, and as she walked, she dabbed a starched linen handkerchief to her flawless cheek. I was suddenly aware of every bruise on my face.

Selena stopped in front of me and leveled her big, blue gaze on me.

"Selena," the accountant-guy said. He gently touched her arm, but Selena shook her head, still staring at me.

She had her own gravitational pull and you'd have to be dead not to notice. Selena stared at me for a long, uncomfortable moment, and then she strode past, the accountant scrambling to catch up.

The pneumatic door sighed as it closed behind her. Selena had the same effect on a lot of people.

"What was that all about?" I mouthed to Remie, who was watching the whole thing from the front desk.

Shrugging, Remie hung up the phone, reattached her big silver dollar-sized earring, and said, "Tanner's lookin' for you," in that sing-songy voice that means *Girl, are you in trouble.*

"What now?" I grumbled. My whole body hurt from the previous night and I had a lot of research to do. I didn't feel like being on the business end of one of Tanner's legendary temper fits.

"Cauley MacKinnon!"

Too late.

"I am going to take a gun and shoot you!" he yelled from the back of the office, and Merrily March, the *Sentinel's* most irritating advertising rep, popped her rigid blond head out of the warren of cubicles, probably hoping for bloodshed.

"You wanna shoot me, you better get in line," I yelled back.

Throwing my broken purse under my desk, I shoved aside a stack of death notices before booting up my computer. I logged on and pulled up the FBI website, looking for boundaries, jurisdiction, and job description.

In my peripheral vision, I could see Tanner storming down the aisle toward me. He looked almost as menacing as Hugh Grant on a bad hair day.

"Hurry, hurry," I muttered to the hard drive.

Ever since Logan's secretary let slip that Logan was assigned to Organized Crime, I'd been more concerned about what kind of trouble Scooter was in. I leaned closer to the monitor. According to the documents that popped up on my screen, FBI agents were often cross-trained and didn't always work within their assigned field. I hit a link labeled *primary function* and pulled up a brief description of jurisdiction:

> The FBI's investigative functions fall into the categories of applicant matters; civil rights; counterterrorism; foreign counter-intelligence; organized crime/drugs; violent crimes and major offenders; and financial crime.

Hmm. That didn't sound like Scooter.

Tanner was spouting steam from his ears by the time he got to my desk. I hit *print,* then exited the site and crossed my arms, arranging an innocent look on my face.

"What in the hell is this?" Tanner said. Death notices fluttered from my desk as he smacked the morning copy of the *Journal* on top of my bulging in-box.

"What?" I said, but I picked up the copy of the *Sentinel's* main competitor. On the front page was a picture of me, scary hair and all, squinting in the sunlight as I led Scooter Barnes from the shed.

I swallowed. *Former Dallas Cowboy Threatens to Bite Bullet,* the headline read. The byline read *Miranda Phillips.*

"*Ramsey,*" I swore.

I could hear Mark Ramsey's words echo in the back of my brain, *You may not write this story, but somebody's going to . . .*

"Why am I reading about a *Sentinel* reporter on the front page of our rival-fucking newspaper?" Tanner roared. "Reporters *write* the news, Cauley. They don't fucking *make* it!"

I snorted. "Are you calling me a reporter?" I said, but I stared at my awful picture.

"Wow. Look at your hair," Mia said, poking her head around the corner. "You should call Beckett for an appointment."

I turned to look at her. "You knew about this?"

She shrugged. "I asked if you saw the *Journal*."

"Wow," echoed Shiner, who'd sidled into my cubicle next to Mia. I turned and stared at his perfect boy-band hair and scowled.

"What?" he said. "Oh, come on. It's not that bad."

Tanner stalked past us to the Cage, which is conveniently located right across from my desk, where he can hear every inappropriate word that pops out of my mouth.

"Wait a minute," I yelled after him.

I jumped up, all but knocking over my chair as I scrambled after him. In the Cage, I tossed the *Journal* on his keyboard, shoved aside a big jar of red licorice whips, and hopped up to sit on his paper-strewn desk.

Tanner is a former ESPN anchor and he prides himself on being a premature curmudgeon. He's pushing forty, but his stubborn hold on newspaper nostalgia is one of the reasons I genuinely like and respect the big jerk.

Tanner stared at my knees, then yanked a press release from under my behind and grumbled, "Do you even know how to use a chair?"

I ignored him. "What was Selena Barnes doing here?"

Tanner was aggressively chewing a licorice whip and didn't answer. The office smelled like a cigar, and I glanced up at the mangled smoke detector. "I thought you were going to quit."

"I'm not the one on trial here," he said, pointing the rubbery whip at my picture in the *Journal*.

Scanning the front page, I was glad to see the *Journal's* crack reporters hadn't gotten wind of my altercation with Van Gogh.

"You've got no business on a crime scene." Tanner shoved his free hand through his network-news-anchor hair and I swear I heard it crinkle.

"Scooter called and said he wanted to talk to me," I said. "I didn't know it was going to turn into a crime scene."

"You've got a whole stack of death notices and releases to rewrite in your in-box and a four o'clock deadline." Tanner rubbed the back of his neck. "Second chances don't come so easy in this business."

Okay, that stung. Tanner had put his neck on the line to get me this job after I'd blown it at the *Journal*.

"I know, and I appreciate it," I mumbled. "I've got ninety-eight minutes to get my in-box out, and I will."

Tanner leaned back in his chair. "What the hell happened last night? Shiner said he heard a call go out near midnight."

Shiner and his damn scanner. The man needed a hobby.

Sighing, I told Tanner about Scooter and the feds, Van Gogh, and my trip to the cop shop to file a report earlier in the morning.

Tanner's left eye twitched as I told him about the carjacking and winding up in the lake.

I leaned forward. "Doesn't it bother you that two branches of the federal government are skulking around an apparent suicide attempt? And why would a man threaten to chop off my ear to find out what Scooter said in that shed?" I shook my head. "He also said something about Scooter having something that didn't belong to him. Something he was hiding."

"You believe him?"

"Seemed pretty serious when he pulled that knife on me."

Tanner's nostrils flared like he could smell a scoop, but his gaze lingered over my bruises. "D'you go to the hospital?"

"The paramedics checked me out."

He shook his head and sighed. "Who knows about this?"

"Cantu buried the report. He'll keep it out of print and off air as long as he can. So far, I'm the only witness, and the cops don't want to tip their hand, I think."

"And the feds?"

"Customs and FBI. They never talk to media anyway."

Tanner nodded, but he was quiet for a long time.

"You should have called me," he finally said. He got up and looked out his wide window where upscale suburban tract houses were steadily eating away at the rolling green hillsides. "You were hired to write obituaries, Cauley, and you're still on new-hire probation." He turned to look at me. "We all start at the bottom and work our way up. That's how the news business works. You'll get your break, but right now, you need to toe the line. You got to be patient or you're going to blow your career before you even get started."

"It's not like I did this on purpose."

Tanner moved to the door and opened it. "Give your file on Barnes to Shiner on your way out."

I sat, perched on his desk, and didn't move. "Shiner is a sports reporter."

"He's on his way to City Desk," Tanner said, giving me a poignant look.

I gritted my teeth. He and Shiner had sports in common, and there was no way I could breach that kind of male bonding.

"I can do this, Tanner," I said, trying to steady my voice. "And besides, I can't give it to him. I left my notes at home."

Tanner ran his hand over his face and slammed the door shut. When he got his blood pressure below boiling, he said, "I shouldn't have to find out what you're doing in somebody else's newspaper."

"You're right," I said. "I'm sorry." And I was. "I'll do a better job of keeping you informed."

"Doesn't matter. You're off Barnes."

"Is this because Selena stopped by this morning? And what's with the geek slobbering around after her?"

"Her attorney." Tanner looked away from me. "I'm going to ask you a question, and I'm only going to ask you once." He turned to look at me. "You got anything funny going on with Scott Barnes?"

"What?" I hopped down off the desk, memos and reports fluttering around me. "You would never ask Shiner something like that."

"This isn't a gender thing and you know it."

I closed my eyes. "Is this because of Mark Ramsey?" I said. Some mistakes never really go away.

"I've always been honest with you, Cauley. Your past doesn't bother me. But the news business—it's a small community. Word's got a way of getting out and your little fling with your ex-boss at the *Journal* put a big dent in your reputation."

"I know," I said quietly, but I looked at him dead-on. "Tanner, the only relationship I have with Scott Barnes is friendship."

Tanner studied me for a long time and then nodded. "Okay."

"That's it? I can have Barnes?"

"Cauley," he said wearily. "You say you didn't sleep with Barnes, I believe you. But Selena Barnes is in a delicate place right now. You'll get other opportunities for ink."

"Tanner, Selena's leaving her husband. That's why he keeps threatening suicide."

"Selena said they're trying to work things out. She came by this morning to ask me to keep you away from her husband. Says you're making things worse." Tanner leaned down, scooping up the papers I'd knocked to the floor. "Editorial meeting tomorrow at ten. Don't miss it."

I was being dismissed.

"I wouldn't dare," I said. Squaring my shoulders, I headed for the door with as much dignity as I could muster. "I'll have the obits before four."

"Leave Barnes alone," he yelled after me.

"Leave Barnes alone, my ass," I grumbled, and I stalked back to my computer.

"I HEAR YOU HAD a big evening," Shiner said as he passed me on his way into the Cage.

"I handled it."

"Yeah, I heard." He snorted, handing me a stack of press releases I was supposed to sort. His blue eyes moved only slightly as he studied my bruises and scrapes. "Need some help?"

"No," I said, and I knew he wasn't talking about the jumbled stack of reports. "But I appreciate it."

He shook his head. "Call me if you need me," he said, and sauntered into Tanner's office.

"Thanks, buddy," I called after him.

Tanner slammed his door shut and yanked down the blinds so he and Shiner could discuss *my* story.

Almost resigned, I settled in to look at the death notices the funeral homes had e-mailed. Obituary writers write obituaries, but for the most part, we copyedit death notices sent in by funeral homes. Occasionally, we do the legwork for hotshots on the City Desk, which can be pretty interesting.

But there was no research today. There were, however, fourteen death notices, which meant there would be fourteen little paragraphs that summed up fourteen lives. Fourteen families whose lives had changed permanently overnight. I supposed if you did this long enough, you'd get some sort of sick sense of humor about it, or at least a tougher skin.

Like most medium-market newspapers, the *Sentinel* only runs one actual obituary each week. If more than one high-profile or interesting person dies in a week, it usually gets bumped up to City Desk.

The rest of the death page is reserved for death notices, which are provided by the funeral homes, and memorials, which are paid announcements placed through classified advertising.

I glanced up at my degree, which my mom had double-matted and framed in gold filigree. "I am one step up from the classified department," I muttered.

Sighing, I printed out the e-mails the funeral homes had sent. I would rewrite each of the death notices so they'd appear in tomorrow's paper in neat, clean Associated Press style. I would choose one of the dearly departed this week and write a concise, twelve-inch obituary that would encapsulate their life and herald them on into the hereafter.

I stared at my computer screen. "This is not how I thought my life would be."

"Ahem," Merrily March cleared her throat. She rounded the partition and was clutching her clipboard close to her chest. "Aren't you supposed to be working on your obits?"

I narrowed my eyes. Merrily was a self-appointed office monitor and took scrupulous notes on everything from office supplies to employee efficiency. The new partitions that carved the satellite office into cubicles were one of Merrily's brilliant ideas.

"Did you need something, Merrily, or is this just a courtesy call?"

She pursed her lips. "You owe me twenty dollars," she said.

"What?"

"For Melissa's baby shower."

"Who's Melissa?" I said, but Merrily had already minced back to her cubicle.

I sighed out loud, glancing at the big clock above Tanner's office. Eighty-two minutes to deadline. Which meant sixty-two minutes to sneak in some research on Scooter and twenty minutes to rewrite the death notices.

Plenty of time.

I logged on to Lexis-Nexis, a legal-slash-news database for media, and ran a search for *S. Barnes,* Scott or Selena, it didn't matter, but I keyed in Austin to narrow the results. Fifty-six articles on Scooter and eight on Selena popped up on the screen.

"You know, Merrily should have been a hall monitor," Remie said. I looked up from my computer to find Remie filing her nails as she perched on the corner of my desk.

"I guess." I sighed. "What do you expect from a woman whose name is an adverb?"

Mia rounded the corner of my cubicle, set mismatched china cups on my desk and began pouring green tea.

I looked back at my computer screen. "Anything bother y'all about Selena?"

"Want a list?" Remie said.

"You're just jealous because she won Miss Texas," Mia said.

"First runner-up," Remie snipped. "You're just defending her because she's Hispanic."

"Argentine," Mia said. "*Hispanic* is just a word y'all Anglos made up so you don't have to learn geography."

Half-listening to them argue, I stared at the screen. "Maybe. But she accused me of having an affair with Scooter."

Mia laughed out loud.

"Okay," I said. "I'm going to pretend that did not hurt my feelings."

"Oh, come on, Miss Digging for Compliments. It's just that Scooter's a one-woman man," Mia said.

Remie snorted. "No such thing." She turned to me. "You comin' out tonight?"

"She can't," Mia chimed in. "Cauley's got a date."

"With a man?" Remie said.

"No, with a goat," I said, and glared at Mia.

"You do need to start dating, *querida*. We'll be over at six to help you get ready."

"Yeah," Remie said, inspecting the bruises on my face. "You're going to need all the help you can get."

Mia nodded. "We're only telling you this because we love you."

I looked back at the death notices on my desk.

"God protect me from those who love me," I muttered and turned back to my computer to get some work done.

SEVEN

I'D MANAGED TO REWRITE most of the death notices, but I just couldn't concentrate with the front page of the *Journal* taunting me from the top of my in-box.

Staring at my full-color photo, I picked up the phone, punched speed dial, and waited for Mark Ramsey's secretary to pick up. By the time she patched me through, I was so mad I was grinding the enamel off my back teeth.

"Ramsey," he said absently.

"You *jerk!*"

"In general or is this something specific?" he said, and I could practically feel him smiling over the line.

"The front page, Ramsey! The freaking front page!"

"Liked that, did you?"

I stifled the urge to scream. "You could have told me."

"I would have if you hadn't thrown me out."

"That's not the point and you know it."

"You want to be the Obituary Babe forever?"

"I'm going to do this the right way this time," I said, hoping I didn't sound as bitter as I felt.

"Listen, hot shot. We got a couple solutions here. You could come back to the *Journal* and be a real reporter . . ."

"I would rather drip honey in my navel and roll in a mound of fire ants."

"Better uses for honey, babe," he said.

I growled.

"Or we could work this thing together. Share information. Call it a *détente*."

"Share information, my butt," I said. Mark already knew more than he was letting on or we wouldn't be having this conversation. "I'm not in the mood for a truce."

"Not even a French one?" he said, and I could tell he was still smiling. "What are you doing for dinner tonight?"

I twisted the phone cord around my finger. "I have plans."

There was a long silence on the line, and I started to feel guilty. The truth is, sometimes I miss Mark. He gave me my first break in journalism. But he'd also taught me the disappointing difference between the way you think things will work out and the way they eventually do.

I sighed. Maybe going out with a new guy would help get me over him, since I apparently couldn't be trusted with bourbon and e-mail.

"I see," he said, and I was afraid he really could. "Well, then, take care, Cauley. And try to stay out of trouble."

He disconnected, and I could feel the weight of the silence on the line. I thought about calling him back.

Opting to err on the side of discretion for a change, I hung up and checked my messages. I had about thirteen thousand calls from my mother and one from the Colonel, with my mother shrieking in the background. Apparently the *Journal's* front page had made its way through the fog of CNN. Thank God they hadn't caught wind of my episode with Van Gogh. Some things, I decided, you just shouldn't tell your family.

I'd return their calls later.

Resigned, I turned back to my computer and finished up the last notice, rewrote a press release, and e-mailed the whole she-bang to Tanner with ten minutes to spare.

I got up and peeked through the blinds and watched Tanner print out my stuff. That ought to keep him busy for at least the next twenty minutes. Twenty minutes I could spend snooping.

I headed back to my desk to search public records for Scott Barnes. I didn't know what I was looking for, but when you cast a wide net you can just keep sifting until you find something that makes sense, or until you find something that doesn't fit. I pulled up public licenses and notices, including marriage, divorce, property tax, deeds, and bankruptcy.

It felt like I was going through my friend's dirty laundry. You think you know someone until you start poking around in the nooks and crannies of their life. I winced, hoping no one would ever get the urge to poke around in mine.

I clicked link after link, turning circles in cyberspace until I landed on a link mentioning an arrest at a high school football game. Scooter was a gentle giant, and for the life of me, I couldn't remember Scooter getting arrested.

I sent everything to the printer at the back of the office, where I surreptitiously whisked the printouts back to my desk, tucked them in a big white envelope, and stuffed the whole thing in my purse. I'd sort them out when I got home.

I picked up the phone and called Cantu.

"Hey," I said when he answered. "You know anything about an arrest on Scooter?"

"Hello to you too, Cauley. How's the family?"

"I'm sorry," I said. "What are you up to?"

"Running the plates on the abandoned El Camino we found out behind the Texaco," he said. "Belongs to a guy named Burt Buggess."

"Buggess?" I said, tapping my pen against my lips. Scooter's pet shop guy? Apparently I wasn't the first person Van Gogh had interrogated. I hoped Mr. Buggess had met a better fate than I had. Clearing my throat, I said, "Let me guess. Our Mr. Buggess lives in close proximity to Scooter's pet store."

"Stay out of this, Cauley," Cantu warned, and I snorted.

"You were going to say something about Scooter's arrest record?"

There was a long silence, and he said, "Is it important?"

"I don't know."

"And not for the paper?"

I pulled the handset away from my ear and stared at it. "I can't believe you said that."

Cantu sighed over the line. "You give me what you got and I'll see what I can do," he said.

I told him, then smiled happily and disconnected, then yellow-paged the number for Brackenridge Hospital and asked the receptionist for Scott Barnes.

After some shuffling and clicking, she came back with a bored, nasally voice. "I'm sorry, ma'am. Mr. Barnes is in a no-call area."

"The psych ward?"

"I can't give out that information," she said.

"Can you tell me when he'll be released?"

"I'm afraid I can't tell you that, either."

"Is there anything you can tell me?"

"I get off at five."

"Thanks," I said. "You've been a huge help."

I hung up the phone and stared around the warren of cubicles. I'd done as much damage as I could for one day. I turned the events of yesterday over in my mind, from Scooter, the SWAT team, the bald earless guy, the abandoned El Camino . . .

"El Camino," I muttered. Cantu seemed to think it was important, so I ran a search. The car was listed as a Chevy, but it looked like it was half car, half truck.

I Googled Burt Buggess and double-checked his number against the one Scooter'd given me in the shed.

"Bingo," I whispered. "Same Burt Buggess."

I ran MapQuest, which indicated that Mr. Buggess lived in Paradise Cove, a little community on Lake Travis that resembled paradise by nobody's standards. It was, however, temptingly close to the Blue Parrot, Scooter's pet shop, just as Cantu had said. I printed out the map and the information on the El Camino site, just in case.

"Wow, are you getting an El Camino?" Remie said dreamily. She'd been heading back to the front office from the breakroom and stopped to peek at my monitor. "I once lost something very important in the back seat of an El Camino."

I doubted that Remie'd ever lost anything once, but I pointed to the web page.

"I just want to know what it looks like," I said.

Mia, who'd been following Remie, wrinkled her nose. "And you need to know this because . . . ?"

"It could be another piece to a puzzle I'm working on," I said. I hit *print* and casually sauntered down the aisle to swipe the web info off the printer. Snagging a fresh manila folder from the supply room, I made a new file and marked it *Buggess*.

Back at my desk, Remie cocked her hip. "You're going to get in big trouble."

"Me?" I said, tucking the newly constructed file under my arm. "I'm not sure I've ever been *out* of trouble."

Grabbing my purse, I dialed up Shay at his auto shop, who reported he'd taken my motor apart to drain the lake water, and not only was it going to cost a small fortune to dry it out and put it back together, it wouldn't be ready for at least another day. Thanking him, I disconnected and sighed.

I was going to have to bum a ride to Paradise.

"Mia," I said. "Did *you* ever lose anything in an El Camino?"

HOT WIND BLISTERED US through the Beetle's open windows as Mia and I zoomed down the rolling hillsides of Ranch Road 620, past the bait shops and liquor stores on Hudson Bend and into Paradise Cove.

Paradise was wedged between two affluent neighborhoods, a proud throwback to a time when libertarians ruled Central Texas and Texas Rangers wrote official reports on cigarette wrappers. In its heyday, the little Lake Travis community was a place for families to rent cabins for quiet country weekends outside of the hustle and bustle of 1940s Austin. As the sprawling city limits of Austin crept closer, the cove gave way to decaying mobile homes and world-weary lake houses patched together with tar paper and plywood.

We turned down Doss Road, where single-wide trailers perched precariously on cinder blocks, surrounded by tall, twisted trees and patches of fenced-in dirt. A rangy-looking guy with piercings on every part of his body I could see—and probably parts I couldn't—wandered into the road.

"What's the matter?" Mia said.

"Just trying to remember the last time I had a tetanus shot." I looked down at the map printout. "This is it, I think," I said, biting my lower lip as I tried to match the address in Shiner's file to anything other than the solitary stone fence circling a row of shiny, chrome-covered motorcycles.

"I think we're here, but this doesn't seem right," I said, looking at the map.

"I guess we just pull in the drive," Mia said, nosing the Beetle up to the fence. A pack of dogs in assorted shapes and sizes scrambled out of the gate, the smallest of which was barking so hard his hind legs lifted with the effort.

"Is that a dog or a rat?" I said. Mia uncapped her Nikon and fired off a shot.

The barking came to an abrupt halt as an ominous shadow slid over the passenger-side door.

"Uh-oh," Mia whispered.

Uh-oh was right. A fleeting image of Van Gogh rushed through my mind and I cringed. Peering over my Ray-Bans through the open car window, I saw the dark form of a man who eclipsed the hot afternoon sun.

"You need somethin'?"

He wasn't Van Gogh, but his voice boomed over me. My heart pounded in my throat. *Get a grip, Cauley,* I thought. *You're overreacting.*

I swallowed hard. "Burt Buggess?"

His dark eyes narrowed and he looked as though he was considering the pros and cons of ripping us limb from limb.

"I'm the one who called you yesterday. You know—about Scott Barnes? I asked you to pick up Sam and look after the shop for a couple of days?"

After a few moments, in which I swear I could hear his synapses firing, a smile split his shaggy black beard. "You're Scooter's friend," he said, nodding. "Come on back, then."

The man's arms were scrawled with prison tattoos, and he had one of those permanent teardrops inked below his left eye, signifying a gang kill. I swallowed hard. "Uh, Mr. Buggess, I just have a few questions. We could take care of it out here."

"My friends call me Bug," he said over his shoulder, and he disappeared into a thick patch of gnarled mesquite trees.

Mia shrugged. "He seems nice," she said, slipping her camera strap around her neck. "And he likes dogs."

"So did Hitler."

Mia peered at me over her little round sunglasses. "You're the one who wanted to come out here, and you gotta get this done before your big date."

The dogs resumed leaping and yipping, jumping so high they were level with the passenger door.

"Hey!" I yelped. The rat-dog vaulted through the window and landed in my lap.

"Oh, look!" Mia said. "She likes you."

"I see that." I stared at the wriggling rodent in my lap. I wondered if this was some kind of omen about my so-called date. The little dog licked me right in the mouth. Apparently so.

"Yuck!" I said, spitting and hacking, probably more than necessary. I got the sinking feeling this was going to be the high point of my day.

Scooping up the hairless beast, I bundled it across the seat to Mia. "It's drooling."

"Oh, come on, she's sweet," Mia said, making smoochie noises as she accepted the dog.

"So's my great aunt Irene, but that doesn't mean I want to kiss her on the mouth."

"Your aunt drools?"

"Only when she's awake."

I climbed out of the Beetle and waded through a sea of wagging tails and twitching noses. Mia trotted along behind, clutching the rat-dog.

We followed the path through the thicket until a perfectly manicured lawn unfolded around a tidy stone cabin. Flower beds rioted with plants I recognized as rosemary and mint and a dozen other herbs I couldn't identify without a field guide.

"Come on in," the man called from somewhere inside. The door was open. "I'll get you some tea."

"We don't need any tea, Mr. Bug," I said, but I did as I was told. The Bug rounded the corner with two cups of tea, which were dwarfed in his ham-sized hands.

The floors were hardwood, the walls whitewashed, and crocheted doilies dotted the surfaces of polished antique end tables. It looked and smelled like a grandma house, except for the wall-to-wall cages and aquariums stocked with strange little animals. And there, on top of an old 1940s radio, perched Sam.

"Hey, buddy!" I said, moving to scratch his neck. Mia set the rat-dog on the floor and snapped a photograph of the cages.

"Have some tea," the Bug said. "I grow the leaves myself."

I sniffed at it and took a sip, hoping the contents were legal. I winced. It was so acidic it stung the roof of my mouth, but it didn't seem to burn the enamel off my teeth. Things were looking up.

"Mr. Bug, you work with Scott Barnes?" I said, and the man let loose a laugh so deep it made his considerable girth shake.

"Ah, Scooter. Good man in a bad situation, and I know a fair bit about bad situations."

I raised my eyebrows and waited. The effective use of silence was one of the many things Mark Ramsey had taught me.

"Yeah," the Bug said, running his hand over his shaggy beard. "I went over to the shed for Sam and then on to the Blue Parrot right after you called me. Went in, fed the critters, cleaned cages, took care of a few things here and there, and I went out to the parking lot and damned if my car was gone."

"An El Camino?"

"Yeah," he said, nodding his head so hard I feared it would snap right off his big neck. "It was the darndest thing . . ."

His voice trailed off when a small, fluffy white dog with a tiny, bandaged foot thumped around the corner.

"'Scuse me," the Bug said, his big, bearded face breaking into a wide grin. "You needin' your bandages changed, there, Muffin?"

I smiled involuntarily at the tiny dog. "What a sweet little puppy," I said, trying not to succumb to whatever instinct it is that makes you talk baby talk when you see something that cute. I reached out to pat the ball of fluff as it limped pitifully past my leg.

"Ouch!" I yelped. "It bit me!"

"Oh, she don't mean nothin' by it," said the Bug.

"I think she did," I said. "She's not letting go."

Flash! Mia snapped a picture.

"Here, now, Muffin. There's a good girl," the Bug said. He pried the dog off my hand, taking a fair-sized chunk of my thumb with it.

"Let me have a look at that," he said, restraining the snarling fuzzball under one big, tattooed arm as he looked at the puncture holes between my thumb and index finger. "Got somethin' that'll fix that right up."

"No, really, I'm fine . . ." The Bug's tea tasted like battery acid. I didn't even want to know what he thought would fix a dog bite.

But he'd already retrieved a jar of something that smelled like old socks and was spreading it on my bleeding bite wound.

"There now." He grinned and turned his ministrations to the dog. Mia trotted over to study his handiwork.

"Some people say I got a way with animals," he said.

Nearby, a sugar glider with a nasty gash to the head lounged in a bed of cedar shavings next to an aquarium of tiny, colorful frogs. The frogs were making small chirping noises like tiny tropical birds. The whole place looked like the Betty Ford center for animals. Soft hearts and weird animals. I could see why the Bug and Scooter were friends.

I cleared my throat. "Mr. Bug," I began, hoping to get down to business. I pulled my little red spiral notebook, a pen, and the file I'd started out of my purse. "May I ask you a few questions?"

"Bug," he said, rebandaging the dog's tiny white paw. "You cut your hand so don't touch those frogs."

"Not a problem," I said, looking into the aquarium of tiny frogs, which were such bright hues of electric blue and candy-apple red that they didn't look real. I hadn't cut my hand, I'd been attacked by a fuzzball, but I didn't see the need to belabor the point.

"Poison dart frogs," the Bug said, and his tone reminded me of Scooter when he was in the middle of one of his lectures on obscure animal facts. "From Argentina. Indians used to boil the skins and dip their arrows in the poison. Paralyzes the prey."

I moved away from the aquarium. "Is it legal to own these things?"

"No law against it in Texas." He shrugged. "They're safe long as you don't have a cut."

"Or a dart," I said.

"This is so cool," Mia said and snapped a picture of the neon frogs. "I saw some cages around the side of the house. Do you mind if I go snap a few shots?"

The big guy shrugged. "Please yourself."

"Exotic animals," I said, watching as Mia wandered out the back door. "And you're taking care of these animals for Scott?"

"Some of 'em. I do his rehab," he said. "I don't know what company he's got importing those animals, but some of those little fellas get here in real bad shape. I take 'em to the vet, get 'em fixed, and if I need to, find 'em good homes."

I nodded, but wondered what kind of home would be good for poisonous frogs.

"What kind of bad shape are the animals in?" I said, hoping it wasn't something truly awful.

"Hungry," the Bug said. "Skinny. And real dirty. You know. Covered in their own filth."

I winced. "Do you mind if I ask what veterinarian you take them to?"

The Bug hesitated, and I knew I'd gone too far. *Great, Cauley. Now he's going to clam up.*

The Bug eyed me for a moment, and to my surprise, he said, "Doc Smit, out east in Bastrop. Only a few vets in town take exotic animals."

I nodded, trying not to breathe a sigh of relief when he didn't go quiet on me. I wanted to be able to talk to him again if I needed to, and, truth be told, I kind of liked the big guy.

"I use that El Camino to tote them around," the Bug said. "You know. To new homes, out to Doc Smit. That sort of thing."

I stared at the notebook on my lap. Scooter and his exotic animals were connected to the Bug, who'd had an El Camino that had been stolen in Scooter's parking lot yesterday. Cantu said he'd seen an abandoned El Camino at the Texaco where I'd been jumped by Van Gogh. Yesterday. Cantu told me this morning the El Camino had been traced back to the Bug. Standing near the cage of colorful frogs, I smelled a rat.

"Mr. Bug," I said, watching from the corner of my eye as Mia wandered back in, snapping pictures as she moved. "I think I may know how to get your car."

"Well, now. That's cause for celebration." He grinned and startled me when he scooped us both into a big group hug, and I could feel Mia stifling a giggle.

When he let go, I said, "Just one more thing, Mr. Buggess." I looked up at the gang-kill tear tattoo, which loomed high on his bushily bearded cheek.

"Mr. Buggess. Have you ever . . . killed anyone?"

Tucking the fluffy little dog into the crook of his arm, the Bug touched the tattoo on his cheek.

"Not on purpose," he said. "And nobody that didn't need it."

EIGHT

"You really think he killed somebody?" Mia said when we were back in the Beetle.

"I don't think he was lying," I said, shifting my knees so they didn't hit the dash. I could not wait to get my Jeep back.

"What I don't understand is that the Bug said Scooter's animals were in bad shape," I said as we snaked our way out of Paradise Cove and down 620, where Mia pulled into the perfectly landscaped parking lot at the Blue Parrot. "That doesn't sound like Scooter."

We climbed out of the car and peered through the window. The pet shop was closed, but it was neat and orderly, like a Disneyfied jungle crammed with tropical plants and colorful animals. Lizards and snakes lazed about in spacious, clean aquariums. A capuchin monkey chided us through a large brass cage.

"Well, it looks like our new friend Bug is taking good care of the place," I said.

Mia nodded. "When is Scooter getting out of stir?"

"Cantu said they're putting him on Prozac and turning him loose on the condition he gets some help," I said, trying the front door. "I wonder if the back door is open."

Mia narrowed her eyes. "You're not trying to get out of your date tonight . . . ?"

"Me?" I said. "Never."

Navigating the boxwood bushes that lined the outer walls of the limestone-bricked building, I made my way around to the back and tried the door. Locked. I jiggled a few windows and was considering climbing over the bushes and accidentally breaking one with a rock when Mia's cell phone chirped.

"It's for you," she said.

Rats. I took the phone and winced when I heard Tanner's voice roaring through the receiver.

"MacKinnon! You were supposed to get Shiner those notes on Barnes. There are only two newspapers in this town and you've already screwed one. Do I make myself clear?"

"Crystal," I said, staring at the glossy pane of the Blue Parrot's unbroken window.

Mia cocked her head. "What did he want?"

"My head on a platter," I said.

"Aren't we going to check on Scooter?"

"Later." I handed Mia her phone on the way back to the Beetle.

AT HOME, I PULLED the public records and the Lexis-Nexis printouts on Scooter and Selena and the Bug out of my purse and tucked them into the big book about suicide. I stuck the book next to my computer, where I could get to it later.

Going over my notes, I sat down at my desk and pecked out an outline on what I knew, what I supposed, and what was still anyone's guess on whatever kind of mess it was that Scooter had stumbled into. Muse sat on the desk, watching the words as they appeared onscreen. I got to the part about Doc Smit and stopped.

While it was true when the Bug said there weren't many vets in Austin who took in exotic animals, I knew there were at least two in west Austin, about sixty miles closer to the Bug's Paradise Cove home than a vet in Bastrop.

"Anything about this bother you, Muse?"

She stared at me with her round, yellow eyes.

"Yeah, me too," I said, reaching for the small Bastrop phone book.

I flipped through pages, looking for a Doctor Smit, and found squat.

Shelving the phone book, I dialed information.

"Dr. Henry Smit on Highway 29?" the operator repeated, then plugged me through to the automated voice that gave me the number and connected me.

A woman answered the phone. "Hello?"

I was expecting a veterinary clinic and her informal greeting threw me, but I recovered quickly and said, "May I speak with Doctor Smit?"

There was a long silence. "What do you want?"

The Bug said some of Scooter's animals were in bad shape, and I wanted to ask the Bastrop vet what kind of bad shape, and a couple of general questions about Scooter and the Bug, but I got the feeling a direct question like that would earn me a dial tone.

Racking my brain, I thought of Mia's cat, Phil, who Mia and some of her more militant animal-rights friends had rescued from an animal testing lab. Though he was healthy now, the cat was alarmingly skinny and so neurotic he compulsively sucked his own tail 'til it was bald.

"Um, I have a cat who's got some problems," I said, hoping to make an appointment.

"We're not accepting new clients," she said and hung up. I stared at the buzzing receiver in my hand.

"Well, Muse. Isn't that curious?"

She yawned and blinked at me. "Right," I said. "Let's call your vet and see if she knows anything about the mysterious Dr. Henry Smit."

I dialed Dr. Emily Madison's office, told the tech who I was, and she put me right through.

"Hey, Dr. Em," I said when she answered.

"Cauley?" she said. "What's the matter. Did Muse pee in the ficus again?"

I smiled. "No more than usual, but this isn't about Muse. I'm working on something about animal rehab and wondered if you knew anything about a Doctor Henry Smit in Bastrop."

"You mean Dr. Mengele?" she practically growled.

"Excuse me?"

"He's a butcher."

A butcher? I shook my head and wasn't sure what to ask next, but it didn't matter because Dr. Em was on a roll. "He does a lot of controversial procedures most Austin vets won't touch."

"Like what?" I said, my mind reeling.

"Well, like cutting a dog's vocal chords to prevent barking."

"Jeez!" I swore, and felt my whole body recoil. "Any reason somebody with abused animals would take them to this particular vet?"

She snorted. "Sure. Because Smit's notorious for not reporting animal abuse and neglect, even when it's bad enough for criminal charges. The Veterinary Practitioner's Board has been after his license for years, but it's hard to yank a license if it interferes with the practitioner's livelihood." She paused. "Cauley, what's going on?"

I blew out a breath. I'd known Scooter since we were kids, and I couldn't imagine him using a veterinarian with shady credentials. "I don't know yet. If I have any more questions, can I call you?"

She said I could, we said our goodbyes, and I sat staring at my computer screen, which glowed the outline on the Bug. I wasn't sure where this notorious Bastrop veterinarian fit into the outline, so I'd leave that out. For now.

I dropped back down in front of my computer and worked on the outline, sketching out the connection between Scooter and Buggess, Buggess and Van Gogh, and Buggess and the Bastrop vet, Dr. Smit.

"Who says I can't investigate?" I said to the cat, and logged online and e-mailed my notes to Tanner, tagging it with a subject header that read: *How's this for an obituary writer?*

Then I dialed Cantu. "You by the fax?"

"What have you got?"

"Maybe nothing. I'm sending you an e-mail and faxing a couple of notes now. You know anything about a Dr. Smit, some kind of veterinarian out in Bastrop?"

"No. Should I?"

"I don't know," I said. "He came up in a conversation today and I wondered if you'd ever run into him. I'm faxing you the notes I took. You get Scooter's old arrest record?"

"Yeah, I pulled them."

"That arrest . . . was it because of Selena?"

Cantu sighed. "I figured you'd ask that. I talked to the arresting officer, and yes, it was something about Selena."

"I owe you," I said. Thanking him profusely, I disconnected. I e-mailed my notes on Buggess and the conversation I'd had with Dr. Em about Dr. Smit to Cantu and tried not to get excited when he faxed me Scooter's arrest record. I smiled. *Quid pro quo.*

Settling back down at the computer, I browsed the report Cantu had faxed. At seventeen, Scooter'd been in a fight over a girl after a football game. That figured. The only thing that could incite good-natured Scooter to criminal activity was Selena.

Muse hopped down from the desk and circled my legs as I tucked the arrest record in with the other files and glanced over at Aunt Kat's old Regulator clock.

"Good grief, cat, do you know how late it is? I'm supposed to have a date!"

By the time I hit the shower, I was running abysmally late. I was rushing around the house in a towel when a knock sounded at the door.

"Well, crap," I muttered. The knocking quickly turned into a pounding. I wasn't dressed and my house was a wreck.

The dishwasher was full so I shoved the dirty dishes from the sink into the oven. In the bedroom, I kicked a pile of clothes under the bed. I hate having my house a mess, but I'm pretty single-minded, and when my head gets into something, everything else pretty much goes to hell.

The banging got louder and I yelled, "I'm coming, Mia!"

My wet hair was wrapped in a white towel, my wet body swathed in a big Turkish robe Aunt Kat had sent me from her research trip for *The Turk and the Temptress*. "You're on time," I said, swinging open the door.

"Of course I'm on time, what are you talking about," Mia said, Brynn following her in.

"Hello, Cauley," Brynn said. She strolled in like she always does—like all eyes are on her, which they usually are. Brynn Rosen is a preternaturally beautiful advertising executive with bronze hair and bronze eyes and a vocabulary like a whorehouse madam. Brynn, Mia, and I had been suitemates at the University of Texas before I dropped out to put Dr. Dick through medical school. The day I broke the news, I thought Brynn was going to accidentally back over Dr. Dick several times in the student parking lot with her zippy little Miata. Sometimes I wish she had.

"Remie said to tell you she would have been here, but one of her kids got meningitis," Mia said.

"Great," I said. Ought to make for an interesting week at work. "Why aren't you out with Roger?"

"Put him on hold," Mia said.

"I brought essentials," Brynn announced, dumping two shopping bags onto the counter next to Muse. Brynn arranged a plate of tortilla chips around a bowl of salsa and set to work on some exceptional Mexican martinis. I accepted a glass and headed back to my bedroom to dry my hair.

Brynn and Mia followed as Muse hopped down, circling their legs, bitching her little cat blues all the way down the hall and into the bedroom.

"I hear Rob Ryder's on the market again," Brynn said, draping herself over the chair near the vanity.

"You don't want Ryder," I said. "He's a News Boy. The man would bundle up all his ex-girlfriends and sell them to the Taliban if he thought it would get him a good story." I paused. "What happened to your new guy?"

"Archived," she said. "And it's not like I want Ryder forever. I'll put him back when I'm done."

Mia brandished a big embroidered bag and a stack of *Chic* magazines. "This is going to be so much fun. What's your new guy like?"

"He's not my 'new guy.' He called me out of the blue." I shrugged. "I haven't seen him since high school. For all I know he could be an axe murderer. There were rumors his family was—"

"Rumors! Ts, ts. You're such a pessimist," Mia said, thumbing through a magazine.

I'm a pessimist? Easy for her to say. She hadn't been run into a river by an earless homicidal maniac.

"Here. I brought this for you," Mia said, and handed me a dog-eared page in the latest edition of *Chic*.

"It says here if you want to have a successful relationship, you gotta know what you're looking for," Mia said. "You know. Like a list of requirements."

I snorted. "We're taking relationship advice from a magazine devoted to attracting a man, trapping said man, and lulling him into a stupor in the sack?"

"Now, Cauley. Mia's got a point," Brynn said. "So far your only requirement seems to be *must be a mammal.*"

"Hey," I said. "They've all walked upright."

Brynn shook her head. "Listen, honey, you have got to get yourself some standards. In my case, that means fat stock portfolio and stuffed jock."

Mia looked mortified. "Don't listen to Brynn. What you need is someone who's sweet and sensitive. You know, like Roger."

Brynn and I exchanged cynical glances. The only sensitive bone Corporate Raider Roger had in his body was below his belt.

"Look, y'all," I said. "I'm not like you. I've never expected fireworks. I just want someone I can spoil a little, someone who'll spoil me back. Someone who'll take out the trash, change the light bulbs, and kill the bugs."

Someone dependable, smart, and funny. Someone warm and safe to snuggle up to at night . . .

"Oh, for fuck's sake," Brynn said. "You get someone with a good balance sheet and you can buy the rest."

Sighing, I pulled a blue cotton sheath from my closet and tossed it onto the bed.

"You're not going to wear *that*, are you?" Brynn said, looking like someone had wafted a three-day-old catfish carcass under her nose.

"I happen to think I look pretty good in that dress," I said.

"Pretty good and drop-dead gorgeous are at least an hour of makeup and a pair of Prada apart," Brynn said, and pushed me into the chair in front of the vanity. "And we have got to do something about this hair."

"Let me," Mia said, flipping open a magazine. She took my brush and began back-combing my hair.

"Not so big," I said.

"There's no such thing as too big," Mia said. She teased and pouffed and spritzed and sprayed until I could feel a hole opening in the ozone above me.

Mia stood back to admire her work, then hopped up on the counter in front of me brandishing eye shadow and boob glitter.

My heart sank. "I don't wear makeup."

"Don't be ridiculous," Brynn said. "There's no such thing as natural beauty."

"True beauty comes from the inside," Mia said wisely.

"Oh, hell. That's just something the parents of ugly babies say." Brynn pulled a handful of Miracle Bras from a shopping bag.

"Here," Brynn said, tossing uber-padded bras at us. "I got the Miracle Bra campaign and I need field testing. Go forth. Improve your attributes."

"You got any other campaigns going on?" Mia wanted to know, arranging the bra cup on her head like a jaunty little cap before dabbing a brush into a pot of eye shadow that was two shades too dark for me.

"Yes, as a matter of fact," Brynn said. "Rave Ribbed Condoms."

Great. Brynn would be picking our brains for a month on the commendable qualities of contoured condoms. Not that there was anything in my life worthy of a report.

Ducking the trajectory of Mia's makeup brush, I lost the robe and packed myself into the monster bra Brynn had tossed me.

"Not like that," Brynn said. She pulled something at the back of the bra and before I knew it, my attributes were glittered and padded and strapped so high I could eat hors d'oeuvres off them.

My friends had taken turns with the makeup, leaving me with more foundation than face, and the ton and a half of mascara they'd applied to my lashes made the bruises around my eyes look even darker. I was about to say something pithy when I heard the front door fly open.

"Let's get ready to rumble!" Shiner's voice boomed down the hall. He appeared around the corner bearing a big white deli package.

I smiled. "Shiner to the rescue—and he brought reinforcements."

"Holy shit!" Beckett Gage, one of the neighbors I actually like, walked in behind Shiner, brandishing a big shopping bag.

Beckett is lethally beautiful, with dark hair and summer blue eyes, and he stood just outside my bedroom door, Muse draped around his neck.

"Good gawd, Cauley," Beckett said. "What have you done?"

"Help!" I said to Beckett, trying to appear both attractive and pitiful—no easy feat when your breasts are glittered and strapped up to your chin.

Muse hopped to the vanity as Beckett lifted a lock of my lacquered hair and sighed. "All right. Everybody out." He turned back toward me, reached into the shopping bag, and I heard the crinkle of dry cleaner's plastic. He swished a clingy slip of scarlet beneath my nose.

"Fuck-me red," he said, grinning a drop-dead grin.

I smiled. "How did you know?"

Beckett shook his head. "You haven't been over to model new clothes in six months."

Running the clingy fabric through my fingers, I asked, "Antoine won't mind me wearing his clothes?"

"Gowns he shares. Don't touch his shoes."

In my peripheral vision I saw Muse nearly climbing Shiner's leg. "Shiner, what is that?" I said, staring at the white package in his hand.

"Ham. For sandwiches. I knew Brynn was bringing yard clippings, so I brought some stuff we can actually eat."

Beckett rolled his eyes and took the pins out of my hair. "Now," he said. "Let's get that dress off you."

Shiner had a choking fit and excused himself to the kitchen, Mia trotting along behind him. Brynn went on a mission for more martinis, and within moments, I smelled burning rubber drifting in from the kitchen.

"Don't turn on the oven!" I yelled.

"Too late," Shiner yelled back. I heard dishes clattering onto the kitchen floor. "Ouch!" he yelled. "Don't worry. We got it under control."

LESS THAN THIRTY MINUTES later, my house was spotless, my friends were snacking on spinach quesadillas and ham sandwiches, drinking some tasty Mexican martinis and watching *The Maltese Falcon*, where a bunch of bottom-dwelling socialites were trying desperately to get their sticky fingers on a statue they thought was worth dying for. Or at least killing for.

Beckett had managed to get the glitter out of my cleavage, and the bruises on my face were barely visible beneath his artfully applied makeup. He'd tamed and trimmed my hair into a shiny chignon and I'd shimmied into the slut-red dress. We were arguing about whether or not I was going to wear pantyhose when he whirled me toward the mirror. I stared at my reflection.

I was pretty sure I wouldn't send Kate Hudson into a jealous rage, but not bad. We moved our makeover into the living room, where Humphrey Bogart was squaring off on Mary Astor in perfect shades of noir.

"I can't believe Bogey's going to turn the love of his life over to the police," Mia said, refilling her martini glass. "He doesn't even know if she's going to get hanged or what."

I shrugged. "She killed his partner. Who knows what else she'd do?"

"Well, I think he's stupid for falling for her in the first place," Brynn drawled. "I mean, look at her. She's not even that pretty."

"Yeah, but she looks like she'd be a pretty wild ride," Shiner said around a mouthful of ham sandwich. Mia hit him with a couch pillow.

"Oh, come on. You've never fallen for someone who was so bad for you they could have ended life as you know it?" I said.

"I know I'd commit a felony for Bogart," said Beckett, and I smiled.

"The point is, it doesn't matter how good the sex is," I said, listening as Bogey told Astor he hoped they didn't hang her by her pretty little neck. "Turning her in is the right thing to do."

Brynn stared at me. "Beckett, what did you use on her hair? It soaked into her brain."

"More martini, please," I said.

Shiner grinned. "Worried about your date?"

"*That* we can settle right now." Mia picked up my Magic 8 Ball and shook it. "Will Cauley have a good time tonight?"

She turned the ball over. "*ASK AGAIN LATER.*"

I rolled my eyes.

Beckett was dabbing my lipstick with a tissue when a thump sounded at the door. We all went quiet.

A voice outside the door said, "Yo. Is there anybody in there?"

"Great." I scowled. "A Pink Floyd aficionado. I'm about to get beamed back to the eighties."

"Hey," Shiner said. "Adam Sandler made a whole career out of it."

"Oh, stop it," Brynn said, hustling me toward the door.

Beckett almost teared up. "Our little Cauley has a date."

IF THERE'S ANYTHING I hate more than an ass, it's a pretentious ass, and Diego was definitely a pretentious ass. But curiosity had me wondering what would make a man take a sudden interest after years of no contact.

I winced as we pulled up to the Shoreline Grill, the restaurant where everybody who's anybody goes to pose, and is therefore a known haunt for that blood-sucking pseudo-reporter, Miranda Phillips.

As Diego steered me down the stairs onto the elegant outdoor patio, I wished I hadn't agreed to go in his car. It's good to have an escape route.

"Cauley, Cauley, Cauley," Diego said after we were seated at an excellent table. He was darkly handsome, his teeth unnaturally white.

The evening air was warm and wet with the threat of rain. The scent of fresh flowers mingled with the smell of good food, and I could hear Town Lake lapping the shoreline below. Despite the elegant atmosphere, I had the creepy feeling that someone was watching me.

Diego pulled out my chair, brushing against me at every given opportunity. Elegantly dressed society-types tittered around us, and I wondered what Tom Logan was doing tonight.

Sighing, I resigned myself to an irksome dinner at one of the best restaurants in Austin, determined to find out why I'd been summoned.

The Shoreline is at the foot of the Four Seasons Hotel, a stop for celebs like Kevin Costner and Clint Eastwood when they're shooting films in Central Texas. It's nestled along the rolling green shores of Town Lake, and in the summer, you can sit on the patio at sunset and watch the largest North American population of Mexican freetailed bats swoop out from beneath Congress Bridge.

From the way Diego was looking at me, the bats would be the high point of the evening.

Lilting strains of an opera spilled from the small special-events orchestra, and I looked at my program.

"You like the music? I arranged for it especially for you," Diego said with an oily smile. "It's a Czech opera. *The Cunning Little Vixen.*"

He looked at me like that was supposed to mean something. "It's about a little fox caught by a forester and turned into a beautiful young woman," he went on, "but the fox is clever. She escapes, returning to her beloved forest."

"Where she falls in love with another fox?"

Diego smiled. "And then she dies."

Diego snapped his fingers and the sommelier hustled out. If the wine steward was annoyed at the finger-snapping, he hid it well. The steward nodded, then scurried off, and in moments returned brandishing what was probably a very expensive bottle of white wine. Diego made a big production out of sniffing the cork.

"There is nothing like a good Sauvignon Blanc," he said, swirling the wine in his glass. He pursed his lips for a small sip. "Confident but not arrogant. Did you know that Sauvignon Blanc means the *savage white?*"

I didn't say anything because he was talking at me, not to me, and I was getting more irritated by the minute.

"Do you know anything about wine, Cauley?"

"Only when to put a cork in it."

He took out his cell phone and pushed the "off" button. "Now," he said. "You have my full attention."

Oh, goody. My patience was wearing thin.

I sat back and looked at him. If Diego was an axe murderer, he hid it well. He wore a silvery, slick-fabric suit and a salmon-colored shirt and tie, his dark hair crunchy with product. Just to confirm my suspicions, I sneaked a peek down his crossed legs. Yep. Salmon-colored socks.

Despite his flamboyant wardrobe, Diego was more sophisticated than I remembered, but time hadn't taken the predatory edge off him. He ordered for both of us without asking me what I wanted, then reached across the table and took my hand.

I knew this was more than a casual date, but I wasn't sure what. My eyes flicked around the twinkle-lighted patio, and I felt a bone-deep stab of envy when I caught sight of Miranda Phillips in a drop-dead black dress, fully engaged in an intimate conversation with a very handsome assistant district attorney who looked like he'd barely passed puberty.

"Are you all right?" Diego said.

"Yeah," I said, spreading my napkin in my lap and trying not to think evil thoughts about Miranda. "I thought I saw a snake."

Oh, well. I've never been a slave to the angels of my better nature.

The server came soundlessly with our spinach salads and semolina-crusted oysters.

"I understand you've gotten yourself in a bit of trouble," he said, forking an oyster and lifting it to my lips. "I may be able to help."

I sniffed the oyster and opted for the salad. "What are you talking about?"

He looked at me intently. "Scott Barnes."

I ate a forkful of baby spinach and raised a brow.

"I saw you in the newspaper. With Scott Barnes."

Great. The bad hair day that wouldn't die.

"I understand you are suffering a bit of fallout because of your conversation in the shed." He leaned forward. "I can offer you protection, but I must know what Mr. Barnes told you."

I stared at Diego, wondering when he had started talking like a mobster in a B movie. "Protection?"

"Of course," he said. His brows dipped sharply over his nose. "You are friends with Scott Barnes, and right now it seems you are his only friend. If you tell me what he said about El Patron, perhaps we could work a deal."

I nearly choked on my salad. "El Patron? The gang?"

Diego sat back in his chair. "El Patron is not a gang—more like a network. They finance a number of activities my family would like to know more about. And frankly . . ." Diego stopped and poured more wine. "We believe that Mr. Barnes has something that belongs to El Patron. We'd like to know what it is."

I shook my head, trying to get rid of the buzzing.

"You know people connected with El Patron?"

Ignoring the question, he said, "I like you, Cauley, I always have, and it would be mutually beneficial for both of our . . . businesses if you were to tell me what Scott Barnes said to you in that shed."

"What businesses?" I said, and my voice sounded high.

"You work for a newspaper." Diego waved his free hand in a bored manner. "I work with my family. Importing, exporting," he said. "Entrepreneurial financing."

I swallowed hard. "And financial compliance?"

"Only when absolutely necessary."

Well-dressed couples waltzed around the patio, keeping time with the music. The swollen sun hung low in the purple sky and patrons at the bar moved closer to the rail overlooking the water for a better look at the bats, which would soon make their exodus from beneath the Congress Bridge.

For the first time, I realized two dark-haired men who looked like they could be Diego's second cousins lounged bonelessly at the table behind us. Telltale bulges showed near their waistbands.

The voice of Tom Logan's secretary echoed in my brain. *Agent Logan's in Organized Crime.*

A surge of panic pooled in my stomach. *Oh, Scooter, what have you done?* And, more importantly, where was Tom Logan when you needed him?

I stared at Diego.

"You're Texas Syndicate," I said. "I'm on a date with the mafia?"

He smiled. "Not the whole mafia. Just me."

NINE

Diego smiled a shark's smile and I could practically hear the theme music from *Jaws* thrumming from the river below.

"Texas Syndicate," he said. "Let's just say we have mutual financial interests with our, uh, *colleagues* in El Patron."

Unease crept up my spine and I shook my head. "Then why the big pretense of a date?"

"Who says we can't mix business with pleasure?" he said. "I thought we could have a little drink. A little dance. I've taken a room here, if that would be more comfortable."

My heart thumped hard. Behind me, tiny wings began to thwack rhythmically from beneath the bridge. The sound quickened and grew to a fury and within moments, more than a million pairs of leathery wings pulsed on the evening air. The bats screeched, spiraling up from beneath the bridge, their small, brown velvet bodies snaking over the setting sun.

"Did your friend say anything odd or unusual?" Diego said. "Perhaps something about . . . *vixen?*"

I had a very bad feeling I was about to be in big trouble.

"Like the opera?" I was getting confused.

"No, not like the opera." Diego stared at me intently. "Did your friend mention Selena?"

"Of course he mentioned Selena, she's the one who started this whole thing. She left him. That's why he's been threatening to bite a bullet. But honestly, Scooter didn't say anything about El Patron or a vixen or anything else important."

"Perhaps he did and you weren't aware. Perhaps we would be more comfortable in my suite," Diego said, casting an uneasy glance at the bats. Probably afraid he'd turn into one.

"What?" I said, but Diego stood, his fingers gripping my upper arm. A sudden vision of my encounter with Van Gogh made my throat go dry. I would not go through that again. Eyes wide, I searched for something, anything, and found a butter knife on the table.

Diego jerked me toward him, rubbing a raging hard-on against my hip.

I felt sick. My heart hammered as I gripped the cool metal of the knife, and from somewhere in the near distance, a voice boomed through the twilight.

"Cauley! There you are."

I'd know that accent anywhere. The dark figure of John Fiennes parted the crowd, the cinnamon sky swirling with life behind him.

A vein popped on Diego's forehead, visible beneath his dark, perfectly groomed hair. "Who the hell is this?"

Grinning, Fiennes gave me a little wink. "My friends call me Bond."

"Back off, *cabron*." Diego tightened his grip on my arm. "This doesn't concern you."

"I think it does." Fiennes badged him and took my hand—the one that held the knife.

Diego's colleagues at the table behind us rose, their hands sliding inside their suit coats.

Fiennes and Diego stared at each other for what seemed a small eternity.

And from the din, a familiar female voice purred, "Well, hello, Cauley. And look what you brought."

"*Miranda,*" I swore as she prowled toward us.

"Is this a private party or can anyone join?" she said to Fiennes. Her black dress was cut to her navel, and she brushed her breasts against Fiennes' arm as she spoke.

Fiennes looked at her for a long moment, then at me. "I'm afraid this party is by invitation only," he said, and pulled me from Diego's clutches.

I smiled. The assistant DA rose to join her, and Miranda stood in the middle of the patio gaping like a catfish out of water.

I could have kissed Customs Agent Fiennes on the lips right then and there.

At that moment, a bulldog-shaped guy in a bad suit swaggered into the fray. He had a hotel security badge clipped to his belt. "Is there a problem here?"

"No," Diego said, glaring at me. He waved a hand at the men behind us. "No problem."

"Of course not," Fiennes said, and he brushed a soft kiss to my cheek.

Diego's hard gaze never left John's. "This isn't over, *chilito*," he said to Fiennes.

"It never is," Fiennes said. And then he pulled me close and led me out onto the dance floor. My heart was still pounding, but my knees were weak with relief.

As my pulse slowed to near normal, I noticed Fiennes was a very smooth dancer. I should have felt elated, but all I could feel was the hard gaze of Diego as he skulked to a dark corner, where he sat watching us from the shadows.

"THANK YOU FOR THAT," I said, my heart still skittering.

"For what?"

"That thing with Diego," I said and gave a nervous little laugh. "But mostly for Miranda. She beats me at everything."

He looked down at me, his gaze glinting green in the warm moonlight. "Not everything," he said, and a zip of electricity pulsed along my skin. "You should keep better company, Ms. MacKinnon."

I couldn't help but grin. "Thank you, Mr. Bond. How did you know I was here?"

"I didn't. I have a room here," he said, and I thought, *A federal employee with a room at the Four Seasons? That doesn't make sense.* He took the butter knife from my white-knuckled grip and set it on a nearby table, much to the chagrin of the elderly couple who were sitting there.

"What were you going to do?" he said. "Butter his toast?"

I relaxed a little and my breathing began to even, but I didn't respond.

"You're leading," he said.

"I'm sorry."

"I doubt that."

I smiled. "You know, Diego called you some pretty awful things."

"Small minds resort to small words," he said.

"Yes, but that's not what he was saying was small," I said.

"Envy is an ugly thing," Fiennes said.

I was quiet for a moment, trying to put all the events together as we glided across the dance floor. "You speak Spanish?"

"I have many useful skills," Fiennes said and dipped me low. My heart gave a hard thump against my chest.

"Let's give your friend a few minutes to cool down," he said, "then I'll take you home."

Righting me, Fiennes pulled me closer and I felt a great big gun-shaped bulge beneath his blazer. While I don't carry a gun and never have, I've been around enough of them to know that it was an unusually large piece of weaponry.

I raised my brows. "Happy to see me?"

"A Desert Eagle," he said and swung me into an exceptionally low dip. "Never leave home without it."

"And you just happen to have a room here?" I said.

Fiennes smiled. "What's the matter, Cauley—you don't believe in coincidence?"

THE TRUTH WAS I did not believe in coincidence. I was going to have to look for the connection. Why had Fiennes swooped in, just in the nick of time? My guess was that he was either following me or he was following Diego. Or he could have been following us both.

If Fiennes was following me, I wondered if Tom Logan was following me too, but it didn't seem likely. Tom Logan didn't seem like the kind of man who would keep still if a woman was about to get dragged up to a hotel room against her will.

With a word to the concierge, Fiennes had his car brought around and he held the door of his black convertible BMW for me. I wondered if lusting after his car made me shallow.

"A civil servant with a new BMW and a room at the Four Seasons?" I said when he got in and pulled out of the elegantly landscaped circle drive.

"The car is a rental."

"And the suite?"

"I have resources," he said. "And please, call me John."

I shot him a sidelong glance and wondered if he was doing some kind of sting in the hotel. That would explain the big budget and high profile. "Speaking of customs agents, can I ask you a question?"

"Fire away," he said easily.

"I met with a man today who has a tie to the animals at Scott Barnes's pet shop. He said some of Scooter's animals arrive in the United States in very bad shape. Is that why customs is involved?"

"There are a number of reasons we are involved," he said.

I was about to ask him about Smit, the disreputable veterinarian, but the look on his face said I was pushing my luck. I had a feeling this thing was far from over, and if I alienated him now, I'd lose a potential source of information forever.

"Anyway," I said. "Thanks for taking me home."

"My pleasure. My day hasn't been so hot, either."

"Tell me about a bad day in customs," I said, leaning back, enjoying the soft leather seat, the warm, wet night, and the soothing sound of his voice.

"I spent most of the day at a neo-Nazi rally."

I turned my head against the headrest. "As a participant or an observer?"

"You're quite the wit, Ms. MacKinnon."

"Anything you can talk about?"

"Not at the moment. Who was your friend back there?" he said, changing the subject.

"He wasn't a friend. It was supposed to be an evening out."

"A date."

"I wouldn't call it a date. More like a favor for my mom and a bout of my own sheer, morbid curiosity."

"A *blind* date."

"I don't do blind dates," I said. "He had a proposition."

John crooked a smile. "In that dress I'd be disappointed if he didn't."

I felt the blood rush to my cheeks. "Diego DeLeon wanted the same thing everyone else seems to want these days," I said.

"World peace?"

"Information about what Scooter said in the shed. Diego said he'd trade information for protection."

"Yours or his?" he said.

Smiling, I looked over at John's profile in the darkness. The violet glow of the city played along his elegant face as we headed west, down the winding cliffs of Ranch Road 2222, toward home. He looked so handsome in his dark shirt and jacket, and for some reason, I got a small pang and wondered what Logan was doing tonight. His job, as usual, I thought and sighed.

The balmy wind whirled around me, and with Agent Fiennes beside me, I felt warm and safe. Above, the stars were so bright that I contented myself to settle in and enjoy the ride.

John looked over at me and his smile was brilliant. "And what did you tell Mr. DeLeon?"

"Hmm? Oh. Name, rank, and serial number."

He laughed as we pulled into my drive. He got out and opened the passenger door. The evening was warm, and night insects chirred in the dark. On the porch, he turned to me and I could practically feel the heat radiating off him.

"I'm pleased I ran into you tonight," he said, and my heart did a little jazz riff against my rib cage. I was surprised he even remembered me after one meeting, and I said so.

"Cauley, if I lived to be a hundred years old and never saw you again, I would never forget you."

"Oh," I said and winced. One of these days, I was going to have to learn to flirt.

Chuckling, he pressed a kiss to my cheek, very close to my lips. "You're something else, you know that?" he said, and he looked down at me with those very green eyes.

"I have a proposition of my own," he said, and he slipped a finger beneath the lock of hair that had escaped my chignon and kept falling into my eyes. "I will get the information I need sooner or later, but there is an easier way. We could go see Barnes tomorrow. Together. You are friends with our Mr. Barnes. He would talk more freely if you accompany me."

I stared up at him. "You'd really share information with me?"

He smiled and ran his thumb over my lower lip.

"I really would," he said.

I took a deep breath, trying not to shiver at his touch. "Let me think about it," I said.

We stood there, bathed in moonlight, the cicadas serenading us in the warm, velvet night. I looked up at him and got a hot chill, and I knew he was waiting for me to ask him in. I'd have to think about that, too.

In the meantime, I rose to my tiptoes and kissed him on the cheek, then turned and unlocked my door.

"Cauley?" he said, and I stopped, just inside the door.

"Yes?"

"You look good in red."

I closed my eyes, wrapping myself in the pleasure of his words. He sauntered down the steps and I waited, listening, as the BMW's motor turned and revved, then faded into the night.

I FLOATED PAST THE open door and into the foyer on a cloud of pure happiness, lust, and something else I wasn't ready to define. I was perilously close to breaking into song when I flipped on the lights and jarred to a stop.

My little house was a wreck.

Not a clothes-on-the-floor, dishes-in-the-stove wreck. It was a certifiable disaster. Chairs overturned, lamps broken, empty file folders ripped and scattered like big, manila-colored confetti all over the living room.

Somebody had tossed my house.

I had the insane impulse to call out, to search my rooms, to touch each one of my things, to inventory them, but as a cop's daughter, I stifled that urge. Switching the light back off, I blinked as my eyes adjusted to the darkness.

In the dark entryway, I felt chaos all around me. I wanted to see the damage, but on some level I knew that was the most stupid thing I could do.

My stomach did a queasy slide and I glanced out the living room window into the moonlit darkness. John was gone. Someone had been in my house. I wasn't sure if Van Gogh was still alive, but I'd just left an up-and-coming mobster with a half-mast hard-on.

And he'd mentioned El Patron. Had I poked a stick in a hornets' nest?

In the darkness of my house, I was very aware that I was alone. I had no car and no cell phone. Only silence.

Oh, dear God. Where was Muse?

I knew I should back out and run next door to Beckett's, but I couldn't bear a *Godfather*-type message with Muse's fuzzy little tennis-ball-shaped head rolling around in my bed.

From somewhere in the dark house, I heard a muffled *gack-king* sound.

As quietly as I could, I felt my way toward the library, where the small choking noise grew louder. My heart pounded in my ears as I eased around small patches of starlight shining in through windows. I needed to stay out of the light in case someone was still in my house.

Gack! The noise was coming from the library sofa.

"Muse?" I whispered.

Gac-c-ck! The sound wasn't coming *from* the sofa. It was coming from *inside* the sofa.

"Shit, cat," I swore as quietly as I could, and I fumbled along the desktop for the letter opener.

"How the hell did you get in there?" I put my shoulder to the sofa and leaned it on its back legs, probing the fabric that lined the bottom until I found a writhing, hissing bulge.

"Hold on, kitty," I said and plunged the letter opener against the opposite end of the sofa.

Muse shrieked as the fabric tore. I reached for her and she spun and thrashed like the Tasmanian Devil. A small box tumbled out of the sofa after her. Muse hissed.

"Stop it," I hissed back. "I'm trying to help you!"

Grabbing the little maniac by the scruff, I tucked her under my arm, scooped up the box, and ran like hell next door toward my friend Beckett, toward a telephone, toward some semblance of safety.

TEN

"AN EAR? SOMEBODY LEFT a whacked ear in your living room?"

"Library," I said, snuggling into a Downy-soft blanket. I sipped a cup of Mexican hot chocolate, letting the warmth of the Kahlua slide down my throat while Beckett and Jenks soothed Muse into a purring stupor. Beckett and Jenks were both impossibly handsome and in their late twenties, and in a committed relationship for the past ten years.

We all sat in Beckett's living room, staring at the box with the severed ear, which lay in a profusion of Saran Wrap, rubber gloves, and Clorox Clean Wipes on the rough-hewn coffee table. We'd called the police and were sitting, staring at the severed ear, waiting for the welcome call of the sirens.

"Why on earth would they stuff poor Muse in the sofa?" Jenks said, staring at the box.

"Probably to make sure she found the ear," Beckett said.

I shuddered. "I think they're trying to scare me."

"Oh, honey. When someone leaves you a little box it ought to have something sparkly," Jenks said.

"It was a message," I said, still fighting nausea but feeling a little better as the Kahlua kicked in.

"You need a Xanax?" Jenks said. He took my glass and headed to the kitchen to freshen my drink.

"I need a new life," I said.

A knock sounded at the door.

Jenks grabbed a frying pan and assumed a kickboxer stance. It might not scare the burglar to death, but he might fall down laughing.

"Who is it?" Beckett called through the door.

"Special Agent Tom Logan, Federal Bureau of Investigation."

"I'll get it!" I yelled, tripping over the blanket as I scrambled toward the door. I swung it open and found Captain America standing on the front porch.

"Ms. MacKinnon?"

I stood blinking at his large frame silhouetted in the porch light. *I hadn't called the FBI.*

The sharp light cast Tom Logan's angular face in shadow, and I wondered if John Wayne had just swaggered in off a movie set. Behind me, I heard Beckett and Jenks go into a simultaneous sigh.

Logan grinned. "I hear you've been looking for me."

"Yes, I . . . how did you find me here?" I stuttered, looking back at my neighbors.

"Hey," he said. "I'm FBI."

"Right," I said. "I always forget that."

Logan slipped the severed ear and its box into an evidence bag, logging it as discreetly as he could.

Through small patches of moonlight, he led me across Beckett's manicured lawn and back to my house, where a team of crime scene techs were shooting photos and examining surfaces for stray hairs and latent fingerprints.

"You'll have to make a list of what's missing," Logan said.

"Missing?" I felt sick again.

With Muse still squirming in my arms, I rushed into the library and found my father's compass, untouched. I clutched it tightly to my chest. Muse calmed, and I exhaled.

Suddenly cold, I watched the controlled chaos of a crime scene investigation. I didn't know any of the cops roaming around my house, and I watched these strangers wandering through my living room, touching and examining what was left of my belongings.

I settled the compass into an old cigar box and set Muse on the rug. She hit the ground running, no doubt looking for some place to hide. I knew how she felt.

If I were a screamer, this would have been the perfect opportunity. Every stick of furniture in my living room had been smashed or overturned, books and files torn and tossed about the library and living room. My television was still intact, but my DVDs and videotapes were broken and scattered along the Turkish rug. I was going to have to call Aunt Kat and tell her about her Queen Anne chair.

Logan sniffed the air. "Smells like burning rubber," he said, and I winced.

"That was from before."

"Cooking accident?"

"Something like that," I said, staring into my kitchen where big, jagged pieces of my blue Spanish glasses and Aunt Kat's china lay shattered on the hardwood floor. A few hours ago, my friends and I had been here, laughing, accidentally torching my Tupperware in the oven, watching movies and scarfing down quesadillas and ham sandwiches.

"You've been through the house?" I asked Logan, trying to keep my voice even.

"Yeah," he said. "Whoever did this knew what they were after. The rest is for show. What was on your computer?"

I stared at him. "My computer?"

Without another word, I raced into my den, dodging broken furniture along the way. Standing in the doorway of my little home office, my heart slammed into my throat.

My hard drive was gone. The surface of my desk glittered with shattered glass from my monitor. The paper files in my desk had been ransacked. All of my computer disks were missing. The medical book where I'd tucked Scooter's file was gone.

Screw it. I went ahead and screamed. *My computer!*

Logan appeared beside me. "Was it insured?"

"That's not the point," I said, feeling like I'd lost everything. "I kept everything I ever wrote on that hard drive. Even my disks are gone!"

I dropped back against the wall with a hard thump and slid down until I landed on my butt. I was so upset I couldn't even cry.

"Was any of it worth stealing?"

"No," I said truthfully. My ransacked house had to be tied to Scooter somehow, but the joke was on the thief. My predilection for procrastination left the burglar with a half-finished outline on my suppositions about Scooter and a half-finished freelance article about liposuction.

I looked around at the carnage and said, "They weren't just searching, were they? This was personal."

Logan rubbed the back of his neck. "Looks like."

Looking up into Logan's dark eyes, I swallowed hard. "Do I even want to go into my bedroom?"

"Probably not," he said, but I pushed myself to my feet. Pressing past him, I swung open my bedroom door.

The breath caught in my throat. My dresser drawers were dumped on the floor, except for my lingerie drawer, which was overturned on the bed. Shredded remnants of my most personal garments were strewn about my bed, colorful slashes of fabric against my crisp, white sheets.

Someone had taken a knife to my panties.

Hands shaking, I picked up a soft scrap of ruined silk and I couldn't control the full-body shudder. All the crotches had been ripped out.

A fresh wave of nausea sent me running for the bathroom.

I didn't throw up, but it felt like I was going to. I heard running water at the vanity. Logan appeared in the doorway and pressed a cool, wet washcloth into my hand.

"You okay?"

"No." I wiped my face with the cool cloth and blew out a breath.

He nodded. "You know what's going on here?"

I shook my head. "I thought I had an idea but now I'm not so sure."

AN HOUR LATER, THE police were gone. Logan brewed us two cups of tea and helped me right the furniture that wasn't broken. I was going to have to call Aunt Kat and tell her half the furniture she'd entrusted to me had been reduced to a big pile of splinters.

Logan and I piled the broken furniture in the library near the ripped-up sofa. I'd figure out what to do with all the pieces later.

In the living room, Logan hooked the cables back into my television while I stacked a few undamaged DVDs and old videos back into the cabinet. Aunt Kat's sofa was overturned, and one of the claw-and-ball feet was missing.

"I cannot believe I got robbed," I said.

"Technically you were burgled," Logan said.

I turned to look at him. Odd, how someone could be handsome and rock solid and funny, all at the same time.

"Yeah, I know," I said, trying to make my voice sound light. "Robbery they'd have to confront me with a threat or place me in fear of imminent bodily injury or death, blah, blah, blah. Criminology 101."

"And I'm guessing it didn't hurt that your dad was on the job."

I shrugged. From the living room, I looked at the jagged remains of my blue Spanish glasses on my kitchen floor. "But breaking into my house *feels* like I've been threatened."

"I know," Logan said, sounding genuinely sympathetic. He took the video of *Key Largo* I was holding.

I cringed. "That's a copy."

Logan raised a brow.

"You know," I said. "The warning at the beginning of movies: *FBI Warning: Federal law provides civil and criminal penalties for the unauthorized reproduction, distribution, or exhibition of copyrighted motion pictures, video tapes, or video disks . . .*"

"You going to sell it?"

"I can't sell it, it's broken."

He smiled. "You have way too much time on your hands, kid." He nodded at my broken disks. "Noir, huh? These belong to your dad?"

I looked up at him, reassessing.

"Yeah," I said, watching Logan peruse my movies. "But I like everything old—furniture, books . . ."

"Typewriter," he said, nodding toward the library. "You planning on writing a book?"

He reached beneath the entertainment center and retrieved the sofa's missing claw foot.

"Someday," I said, genuinely surprised. "I've been thinking about writing a book about my dad. He was a real hot shot—a detective with APD. But," I sighed, "Aunt Kat is the real writer in the family."

"*The Pride and the Passion,*" Logan said, and I laughed out loud.

"You read romance?"

"I do my homework," he said.

I was about to say *I'm your homework?* when he said, "Speaking of old, what's with the Wurlitzer?" He was looking at the colorful old jukebox near the entrance to the library. Muse perched on the multicolored plastic arch of the jukebox, scowling around at the mess.

I smiled. "The cat's got a thing for Aretha."

I turned the movie over in my hands. "What about you? What do you do when you're not out chasing bad guys? Wait, let me guess. Westerns. You've got that John Wayne swagger."

He didn't say anything, but he seemed amused.

Sighing, I looked around at the broken antiques. "I guess I like old things because life seemed a lot simpler back then."

"Back when women weren't allowed to vote and there were separate drinking fountains marked *colored*?"

"Ouch."

"Life is always simpler when it's black and white, kid," he said in a pretty good Bogart impression. "In the movies, life sticks to the plot and has a point."

He screwed the clawfoot back on the sofa and flipped it upright, and I wished everything could be fixed so easily.

"Yeah, well, it's nice to believe in fairy tales," I said. "The good girl gets the guy, and then, boom. Fireworks."

"*To Catch a Thief,*" Logan said, and I smiled that he got the Cary Grant, Grace Kelly-fireworks reference.

"Ah." He grinned back at me. "A cynic underneath it all. You don't believe in fate?"

"I don't believe in fireworks."

"Too bad," he said, and I turned to look at him, feeling an odd little jolt.

Tom Logan was a pretty cool guy, for a fed. My gaze flicked down to his naked ring finger and I started to ask him why he wasn't married, but the moment had passed. It didn't matter. I was nothing but homework to Logan.

As we straightened out the worst of the mess, I told Logan about Van Gogh, about Diego, and about rehashing my last conversation with Scott Barnes, since that was what seemed to trigger the rest of it.

He listened, nodding, periodically stopping to jot notes in his notebook.

"Your friend DeLeon said Barnes has something that doesn't belong to him," Logan said. "You don't know what it is?"

"Diego DeLeon is not my friend, but yes, that's what he said."

"And he mentioned El Patron without you prompting?"

"I didn't know there was anything to prompt."

Logan nodded. "Any ideas on who belongs on the other end of that ear?"

My stomach lurched and I felt lightheaded again. "I don't know, but I think they're trying to scare me." I sighed. "It's working."

Turning to the newly righted end table, I picked up the cup of tea Logan had made and took a sip. It was warm and bitter and felt like heaven as it slid down my throat. "Do you know what it is that Scooter Barnes is supposed to have?"

Logan smiled enigmatically. "I'm more interested in your thoughts, since our band of thugs broke into your house and didn't take anything valuable."

I shrugged. "I think they did take something valuable, but I don't know how much good it'll do them."

Logan raised a brow.

"I'd started a file on Scooter. It's gone."

"You have a backup?"

"No." I muttered. "The bitch of it is, I was getting my clips organized and had some sketchy notes on a couple of connections. I think I was getting somewhere."

Logan raised a brow again.

"Well, Scooter started threatening suicide when Selena left him. I've been through their financials, and they aren't in any trouble that I can tell, and every time I turn around, I run into something about Selena. So whatever he's gotten himself into, it seems to revolve around Selena," I said. "Or that's what I thought until Diego started pumping me about El Patron and stolen merchandise."

"Stolen? You said that DeLeon said your friend Barnes had something that didn't belong to him."

I started to say *same difference* and stopped when I realized that it wasn't the same at all.

"You know what? Now that I think about it, Van Gogh asked about something Scooter had hidden," I said. "Diego said Scooter has something that belongs to El Patron. You think Scooter's involved with El Patron?" I bit my lip. "Or maybe Selena's involved with them and that's why Scooter called me? For help?"

Logan's expression didn't change, but he asked, "Why would you think so?"

"Well," I said. "Selena is the catalyst for Scooter's suicide attempts, which seem to be the beginning of this thing, and El Patron is the odd piece that doesn't seem to fit with anything else. And why would Diego DeLeon, who I haven't seen in years, go to all the trouble to make a date with me out of the blue and then get rough with me when I didn't know anything about some mysterious stolen—"

Logan looked at me.

"—I mean, mysterious *missing* property, which seems to have piqued the interest of El Patron?"

Logan was quiet for a long moment. "How did you end things with DeLeon?"

I snorted. "Not nice. A friend happened to have a suite at the Four Seasons and he helped me get out of it."

I wanted to tell him about Fiennes, but it felt weird, talking about Fiennes with Logan. Even though there was nothing between Logan and me and he was just doing his job, it felt funny bringing the subject of another man into the conversation. Of course, he would know all about Fiennes anyway, because they were both federal agents working the same case.

I noticed Logan's jaw muscles tighten. His gaze was hard, but he nodded, scanning my semi-trashed house. "You got a place to stay tonight?"

"I have friends," I said.

Logan looked at me like there was more to say. But he handed me a fresh business card, seeing as how the one he'd given me was at the bottom of the lake.

"You see any sign of your friendly neighborhood thugs or you get yourself into any more trouble, you dial 911, then call me on my cell," he said. He looked around my little house. "You have a gun?"

Thoughts of John Fiennes' unusually large gun bubbled to the top of my short-term memory. "You know anything about a Desert Eagle?"

Logan raised both brows. "You have a Desert Eagle?"

"No. It's for something I'm working on."

Logan eyed me. "An Eagle can drop a charging rhino."

I frowned. "And they're not standard issue for government agents?"

"Not our government agents," he said, stepping toward me. "Cauley . . . do you have a gun?"

"I had one. It sort of got taken away from me."

"Someone took a Desert Eagle from you?"

"No, a .38."

Logan looked confused, like he'd walked in on the middle of a conversation. "And this gun," he said. "You didn't get another one?"

"No."

"Good," he said. "Some people have no business carrying concealed."

"Hey. I could learn to use a gun if I wanted and I'd be very good at it. *Armed prophets conquer.*"

Logan stared at me for a long moment, then said, "You doing anything for lunch tomorrow?"

"You just said I was a maniac."

"No, I said some people are better off not carrying weapons they're not qualified to handle."

I thought about that. "What kind of lunch?"

"Your choice. You're tired tonight and you've had a rough day. I want to go over what you had in those files—see if we can reconstruct some of the information."

"Oh," I said, feeling vaguely disappointed. I thought he meant *lunch* lunch. Somehow I always managed to forget that this was just a job to him.

"This is a tough case." Logan picked up the Magic 8 Ball, which the thugs had tossed into the foyer. "Any chance I can talk you into staying out of this?"

It was my turn to smile enigmatically.

He grinned wryly and turned the ball in his big palms.

"*MY SOURCES SAY NO*," he read aloud. He shook his head. "That's what I thought. You need a ride somewhere?"

He tossed me the 8 Ball and I caught it neatly, first try. "No." I said. I didn't tell him I wasn't about to let a bunch of slimy bastards run me out of my own damn house.

I SET THE 8 Ball next to the typewriter in the library before walking Logan out to a big, battered gray car.

"A Mercury," I said. It was missing a side mirror and part of the front bumper. "What happened to the Crown Vic?"

"It went down in the line of duty," he said.

160

"High-speed chase?"

"Renegade stop sign," Logan said. "You going to be okay?"

I heard a noise near my house and noticed the white-faced dog lying under my porch swing, partially obscured by the big potted fern.

"Hmm?" I said, distracted by the dog. "Oh. I'm always okay."

He looked at me like he didn't believe a word I was saying. "You'll call me if you need me?"

"You don't have to be so nice," I said. "I know the drill. Just doing your job."

Logan looked like he wanted to say something and didn't. He nodded, folded himself into his car, started the engine, and drove away, muffler rattling noisily as he went.

I turned back to the house. The dog lifted his head and looked at me.

"Well, the prodigal phantom returns," I said.

The dog didn't say anything.

"I've had a really long day," I said to the dog as I climbed the porch steps. "So if you're going to bite me, please, just get it over with."

I knelt, extending my hand. The dog bellied forward from beneath the porch swing and drew himself into a sitting position. He sat stoically, chest out, head back, and I almost laughed because he reminded me a little bit of Logan. The dog leaned his head forward and sniffed. His fluffy tail thumped twice on the porch.

The dog's face was white, his back gray. Probably some sort of Siberian husky mix, but jeez, he looked like a wolf.

"It's a miracle you haven't been picked up by the pound," I said, scratching his chin. His eyes were clear, his coat clean and glossy, and he had a collar. This dog obviously belonged to someone, and if he spent the night on my porch he would probably earn himself a one-way ticket to the puppy pokey. "You got a name, big guy?"

He looked at me intently, like he was waiting for me to say something he understood.

"Strong silent type, huh?" I said, and reached for his collar. Expensive, worn brown leather with a rabies tag. No name or address.

"You want to come in for a drink?" I said, and chuckled aloud at the way it sounded, but the dog was up and by my side as I opened the door. "If I'd known I'd have company I'd have cleaned the place up."

Logan had helped me straighten up most of the mess. The dog picked his way around the rest, sniffing the coffee table and Turkish rug with interest. He turned around twice on the rug and made a strange warbling sound at me that reminded me of the way my dad's German shorthair pointers used to alert on duck hunts.

"What's the matter, boy? Are you hungry?" I said. At the word *hungry*, the dog left whatever was bothering him about the carpet and padded after me into the kitchen. He stopped in front of the refrigerator. Well, at least his hunting instincts were intact.

I made the dog one of Shiner's ham sandwiches and poured him a bowl of water, which he lapped noisily as I checked on Muse. The Queen of Cantankerous had vacated the Wurlitzer, annoyed that I hadn't cranked it up and probably utterly incensed about the dog. In a snit, she'd burrowed into one of my cashmere sweaters on the top shelf in my bedroom closet.

I peeked into the closet. "You okay in there?"

The cat scowled at me, and I quietly pulled the door nearly closed, leaving it open a small crack. I'd introduce her to the dog later.

I turned and looked at my panty-strewn bed and shivered. I had a big day tomorrow.

I'd make some "found dog" flyers to distribute around the neighborhood and finish some paperwork at the police substation. And somewhere along the way, I ought to stop by my office to remind Tanner I was still alive and willing to do my job. I would go check on Scooter, and at some point I was going to have to go panty shopping. I picked up a shredded scrap of silk and felt violently ill.

I may not be Nancy Drew, but I was fairly certain the severed ear was a clue. Because of it, I could surmise that Van Gogh had tossed my house.

I had to get some sleep, but I couldn't stand the thought of crawling into sheets that Van Gogh had probably touched. And God knew what else. *Yuck*.

Slipping off my undies, I swished them around in the sink with some hot water and liquid soap and hung them over the shower rod to dry. Ignoring Muse's protests, I dragged a blanket out of the closet, skimmed into a big tee shirt and went back to the living room, where I found an unbroken DVD to pop into the player.

The Big Sleep filled the screen, and I settled in on the sofa next to the dog.

"Now, see, dog, that's Philip Marlowe. He's handsome, smart, and funny, and he doesn't take crap from anyone," I said, pointing at the flickering black-and-white image. "He has his own code of ethics and he does the right thing, not the easy thing."

The dog seemed to be listening. He looked at the television, then back at me. Letting out a long sigh, he laid his head in my lap and went to sleep.

"Yeah," I said on a yawn, as I stroked his velvety ears. "Me too."

ELEVEN

I DREAMED OF PHILIP Marlowe that night and woke up sprawled on the couch in a very unflattering position. Static sputtered from the television. I had a crick in my neck and the distinct smell of dog breath in my face.

"Good morning, Mr. Marlowe," I said, my voice thick with sleep. "I see my luck is changing. A male spent the night in my house and he's still here."

The dog broke into a big doggie grin and hopped off the couch, his nails clicking along the hardwood floor as he danced his way to the front door.

"Can you give me a minute?"

The dog woofed, and I figured the last thing I needed after a drawer full of shredded underwear was dog doo in the foyer.

"All right, all right," I said. "Hold on."

I put on a pot of tea, slipped on a pair of shorts, and looked around for something to tie the dog with, settling on the strap from my purse. I decided not to brush my hair or teeth because

I'd have to look in the mirror, which might persuade me to do some damage control, which would mean the dog would have to wait.

The dog was shifting from paw to paw in the foyer, and I noticed a key had been shoved under the door. *My car key!*

I swung open the door to find my Jeep in the driveway, complete with an invoice tucked under the windshield wiper marked *no charge.* Not even for parts. God bless Shay and his felonious little heart.

The dog and I took a short stroll past the Bobs, where I encouraged him to pee on their rosemary bush, and we headed back to the house, where I fed him another of Shiner's ham sandwiches.

I showered, slipped into my last pair of undamaged undies, still damp from being washed in the sink, then yanked on a pair of jean shorts and a clean tee shirt. I blasted my hair with the blow dryer, then fed Muse, who was still on sabbatical in the closet. Chores done, I headed next door to Beckett's to borrow his computer to make some "found" flyers for the dog.

"You are a huge pain in the rear," I told the dog as we went for a longer stroll, tacking flyers along telephone poles and message boards through three blocks. More exercise than I'd had in months. Of course, when my friends and I work out, we spend about twenty minutes on the machines, then hit the Mexican martini happy hour at Flores'.

Posting the last of the flyers at the Methodist church, we headed home, where I sat at my kitchen counter and made a To

Do list. I wrote down *walk dog* and *create and distribute found dog flyers* so I'd have something on the list to check off.

Go by police station, get a new cell phone & mini recorder, make an appearance at the office, check on Scooter . . .

I wriggled, trying to ignore the damp panties creeping into my nether regions. *Quick stop at Victoria's Secret . . .*

I shut the door to the bedroom so Muse wouldn't run into the dog unannounced. I folded the To Do list, stuck it in my tee shirt pocket, and headed for the door.

As I stepped out onto the porch, the dog streaked past me and leapt into the topless Jeep. He sat smugly in the passenger seat, staring at me.

"Look, buddy. You are *not* going with me. It's going to be very hot today and you are way too furry."

The dog stared at me.

"Come on," I said, and reached for his collar. He growled. Great. The second time I'd been threatened in my own Jeep in a matter of days.

"Fine," I said. "I'll call a veterinarian and trace the number on your rabies tag when I get to the office. Then we'll see who's boss."

AT THE POLICE SUBSTATION, the guys all had nice things to say about the dog, but they all made sure to make fun of the purse strap I was using for a leash. I signed paperwork and requested copies of the incident report for my insurance company.

On the way out, I stopped by Cantu's office. He was out on a call, so I left him a note.

I climbed back into my Jeep, grateful to have it back, and pulled into a strip center on North 620. I went into Pet Guys for a bag of expensive dog food and a cheap leash. Tanner had given me an advance on my check, but I suspected he hadn't meant for me to spend it on stuff for a dog that wasn't even mine.

Because Marlowe scowled at everyone in a two-foot radius, I decided to forgo Victoria's Secret for the time being and popped into the discount store next to Pet Guys for new undies. Since they weren't a bastion of fine lingerie, I settled for a set of economy-size days-of-the-week granny panties before hitting the electronics store, glad, for once, that there was no one in my life to see the sorry state of my undergarments.

In the electronics store, the dog and I stood in line until half of hell froze over to get a new cell phone and another mini recorder. I was surprised to find that if you act like you know what you're doing, people don't question the dog. They might have thought he was a service dog if he hadn't made a low, rumbling noise at everybody who got too close.

With my new cell phone programmed by the pimply faced kid at the counter, I was ready to rock and made a command decision to postpone telling anyone remotely related to me that I was once again mobile and wireless.

BACK IN MY JEEP, I pulled out my To Do list and jumped when my new cell phone rang. I answered and was oddly pleased that it was Logan calling to check on me and, I suspect, to find out if any more catastrophes related to Scott Barnes had fallen on my front door step.

"I just got this phone. How did you get the number?" I said.

"I'm very good at finding people."

Seizing the opportunity, I asked him if he had any more news, and being Logan, he didn't tell me a thing.

"You still up for lunch?" he said.

"Um, I'm running some errands, and I sort of have a dog with me."

There was a long silence, and when Logan finally spoke, I could hear a smile in his voice. "Guero's has a patio."

"See you at noon," I said.

I CALLED HOME TO get my messages and cringed at Cantu's recorded voice. It didn't sound good. I dialed him on my new cell.

"You find your buddy, the earless guy?" he said, sounding grouchier than usual.

"Have you had any hysterical calls on your cell?" I said.

Cantu ignored my sarcasm. "We just got another Necklace. Found him on the eastern edge of Travis County, near Bastrop. He's missing an ear but he's still got some of his face. Want to come give him a look?"

My stomach folded in on itself. "A burning tire shoved down around his shoulders? Not drowned?" I said, and I got an unpleasant image of an earless Van Gogh crawling out of Lake Austin, draped in duckweed like a swamp monster.

"Not drowned," Cantu said, further supporting my fears that it really was Van Gogh who had broken into my house.

"You think the Necklace was El Patron?" I said, remembering my conversation with Diego DeLeon and his mysterious inquiries into the organization.

"We got no proof," he said. "But it's a pretty good bet. I'd like you to come down and make sure it's not your earless thug. You can look at pictures if you want. Avoid a trip to the M.E.'s office."

"Yeah," I said as I turned my Jeep back toward the police station. "See you in ten."

THE CRIME SCENE PHOTOS made my insides twist into a big, queasy knot. The face in the photo was scorched beyond recognition and his charred glasses were burned into what was left of his nose. I didn't know who this burned-up, earless guy was, but the body was too small to be Van Gogh's. I wasn't feeling up to lunch or anything else as I left the station. Cantu told me to keep in touch, and by the time I headed for Guero's, I was running abysmally late.

Flustered and nauseated and trying to wipe the image of those photographs from my long-term memory, I cruised down Congress, past the eclectic little shops and antique stores, thinking about the body the police had found in Bastrop, until I was waylaid by one of the Pixy Stix guys at the light at Riverside and Congress.

"Spare a dollar?" he said, leaning into my topless, doorless Jeep, offering me a giant Pixy Stix—those big, festively colored plastic straws filled with flavored sugar that tastes like unreconstituted Kool-Aid. The man's Army fatigues were tattered, his eyes tired, and his cheeks were hollow beneath his beard. "Whatever you can spare'll help."

"Right," I muttered, and gave him a five I really couldn't spare while politely declining the gigantic Pixy Stix.

I pulled the Jeep into the side street at Guero's about ten minutes late.

"Rats," I swore. Dressed in his usual suit and tie, Logan was seated outside at a table on the patio, reading a newspaper.

"Sorry I'm late," I said, fighting with Marlowe as he strained at his new leash.

Logan stood, pulled out my chair, and looked at me like he wasn't surprised that I was late, which irritated me even more. I'm usually on time. Okay, I'm rarely on time, but I'm working on it.

Choking against the leash, Marlowe pulled toward Logan, tail wagging, tongue lolling. Logan smiled down at the dog.

The host came out with menus and I ordered a margarita on the rocks with salt. Logan didn't say anything while the guy was there, but he looked at me intently.

"Rough day?" he said.

I nodded. "Cantu asked me to ID a body this morning."

"You know who it was?"

I shook my head. "No, but it was pretty gruesome. Another Necklace—the poor guy had a car tire shoved down around his shoulders and then they torched him. Found him out east between Austin and Bastrop."

"Lot of that going around," Logan said, shaking his head.

A server brought the margarita, and I sucked half of it down in one swallow.

"I don't know how people can do those kinds of things to each other," I said, licking the salt from my lower lip.

"People will do a lot of things, given proper motivation," Logan said, studying my face. "Explains why you're late. You want to do this some other time?"

"No," I said, the margarita warming my insides. "I need to get to the bottom of this. And I'm late because I got waylaid by a Pixy Stix guy."

Logan looked at me blankly.

"You know, those homeless guys down at the shelter on Manchaca? They bus them out to sell Pixy Stix at stoplights."

"I must have missed them," Logan said, shaking his head like I'd lost my mind.

Marlowe bumped Logan's hand with his nose, and Logan automatically scratched the dog's chin.

"He seems to like you," I said.

"No accounting for taste," Logan said, and I smiled when he scratched behind the dog's ear as he mulled over the lunch selection. Sighing, Marlowe curled up under the table at Logan's feet, quiet for a change. Traitor.

I watched Logan as his gaze swept the area periodically, and I wondered if he ever let his guard down.

The margarita was warming my cheeks and I glanced down at my menu. "I love the fajitas here, but I always feel terrible about ordering them because I can't eat the whole thing."

"Because children are starving in South America?"

"Your mom gave you the same speech?"

"No, I just know how you are."

I frowned. "How am I?"

"You're the only girl I know who falls over fences, quotes Machiavelli, and bats her eyelashes to get behind police lines."

I was very nearly offended. "I do not bat my eyelashes," I said. "Are you saying I use the fact that I'm a woman to get what I want?"

"I think you play to your strengths, which is exactly what you should do. You're a beautiful woman, Cauley. A bit eccentric, but there's nothing wrong with that."

I was trying not to get my feelings hurt when the waitress sauntered out of the patio door in typical South Austin style, flame-red hair piled high, skirt so tight it looked like two tomcats fighting in a denim sack. She set large glasses of water in front of us, and if she saw the dog at Logan's feet, she didn't say anything. "Y'all know what you want?"

Logan looked at me.

"I'll have an iced tea and a chalupa, please," I said, but my order was interrupted as two blue and whites whizzed down Congress, lights blazing, sirens blaring.

Marlowe's ears pricked and Logan's head barely moved as he and the dog watched the cop cars race by.

"Oh, hon." The waitress laughed. "You think that's bad, you shoulda been over to my house last weekend. My neighbor's brother was doin' this buy and he had a suitcase full of weed. Well, his scumbag brother-in-law was stayin' with him, and don't you know, the suitcase come up missin'. You know what my dumb-ass neighbor did? Called the cops to report the suitcase stolen."

I shook my head, hiding a smile. Logan practically had "fed" tattooed on his forehead, and this poor woman was prattling on about things you wouldn't even tell your own mother, let alone a federal agent. To his credit, Logan sat listening to the waitress, a trace of amusement in his eyes. The woman's chatter trailed off as she finally caught his gaze.

"What?" she said, cocking her helmet-haired head at Logan. "You're not a cop, are ya?"

Logan looked at her. "Not exactly."

She fidgeted. "Drug enforcement?"

"FBI."

The waitress stared first at him, then at me. "You're shittin' me."

"I would not shit you, ma'am." Logan didn't smile, but I could tell he wanted to.

"Y'all got a badge and everything?"

"And everything."

"Y'all carryin' a gun?"

"Always."

The waitress shifted her hip. "Can I see it?" I don't know how she did it, but the question sounded suggestive.

"I'll have the fajitas," he said, in a tone that said the conversation was over.

The waitress looked at me and I shrugged.

When she was out of earshot, I said, "You won't let her see your gun?"

"You let 'em see it, they want to touch it."

"All men think that," I said, and Logan actually laughed out loud. He had a really great laugh. He should do it more often.

I slipped my glass of water beneath the table and set it next to Marlowe, who lapped noisily.

The waitress didn't say a word when she brought our salads. Sprinkling cayenne on mine, I asked Logan, "Does that bother you?"

"What?"

"Being treated like that? You know, like you're not a real person."

He grinned. "Sometimes it's amusing."

I watched him drip ranch dressing on his salad. "Seems kind of lonely."

"We were going to talk about those Barnes files," Logan said, and I nodded, accepting the change of subject.

"Yeah," I said. "We were."

Logan, as always, was on the job.

"We've been over this before," I said.

"Doesn't hurt to go over it again," Logan said, and he transferred some of his fajita onto my plate.

I smiled. "Want some chalupa?" I said.

"Sure," he said. "I wouldn't want you feeling bad about starving South Americans."

"Even if I'm eccentric?"

"I didn't say eccentric was a bad thing."

I tried not to smile even wider, and over shared plates of some truly excellent *Tejana comida,* I started with everything I could remember about what Scooter said while we were in the shed. We both jotted notes as I told Logan everything I could remember about the photos, news clippings, and research I'd done on Scooter, from his family history to his football career to the pet store's resurrection as an upscale exotic pet boutique.

I scribbled notes to myself in my little red notebook as I tried to mentally reconstruct my file on Scooter.

"A flow chart?" Logan said, looking amused.

"More like a timeline with the players and their connections." I showed him my chart.

He smiled. "Anyone ever tell you you've got the handwriting of a serial killer?"

"All part of my plan. Anyone steals my research, they'll have to kidnap me to decipher it."

"Don't say that," he said, a bit gruffly. "What else you got?"

I told him about the Bug and the mysterious veterinarian in Bastrop. And although it wasn't part of my original research, I tried to remember most of the journalists' names who'd written articles about Scooter during his glory days, as well as those about Selena, and I jotted down approximate dates of clippings as best I could recall. Rob Ryder, one of the downtown News Boys, had written most of the sports articles before he'd made it to the City Desk. I was probably going to have to go down to the *Sentinel's* main office at some point and talk to him.

During a break in conversation, I looked at Logan across the table. It was amazing how much easier reconstructing my notes was when Logan and I went over it together. He listened, nodding as he ate, stopping periodically to take a few notes and frequently to slip bites of beef to the dog. I copped a look at his notebook. He didn't make a flow chart.

"I'm trying to figure out where to put this thing about Diego wanting to know what Scooter said about El Patron," I said. "The thing is, Scooter didn't say anything about El Patron, and I haven't seen any kind of a link at all. And I swear, Logan, Scooter wouldn't be mixed up in some gang."

"What makes you think he's involved in a gang?"

"Well, you're in FBI's Organized Crime division, right?"

Logan looked at me for a long time. Leaning back in his chair, he finally said, "This thing's all over the board, Cauley, and El Patron isn't a gang. They've got international ties and they like to think of themselves as businessmen. And don't underestimate your friend Barnes. Your friend is suicidal."

"So you're looking at Scooter?"

"Let's just say he's a person of interest."

"He wouldn't do anything with El Patron, he's got no reason. The Blue Parrot's doing great. I snooped around in public records and financials. The only thing that worries me about the pet store is that they seem to be importing animals that aren't well taken care of, and I know in my heart Scooter would never mistreat animals."

"Where'd he get the cash to import?" Logan said, and I blinked.

"He and Selena have money—not obscene amounts, but they seem to be doing okay. He spent a season with the Cowboys, and he's managed his money pretty well. And the only kind of trouble he's ever been in is for fighting over Selena. Scooter told me the suicide attempts are because Selena's leaving him. He said so that day in the shed."

"You talk to her?"

"Who?"

"The wife."

I felt my face color. "No," I admitted. "Until very recently, I thought I was just helping a friend out of a bad time. I didn't take this thing very seriously."

Logan nodded. "You know her?'

"You could say that. We were rivals in high school."

"Let me guess. Debate?"

"I was in debate, but Selena beat me at drama." I fidgeted, not wanting to tell him the rest of the rivalry.

Logan waited.

"We were in a pageant together," I muttered.

He grinned, and to my eternal horror, I felt my face go hot pink. "Like a beauty pageant?"

"It was a long time ago," I said, defensively. "Mama and my older sister, Suzanne, both finaled in the Miss Texas Pageant. Mama was going for a MacKinnon three-peat."

"What about Selena's mother?"

"She was the worst stage-mother I have ever seen," I said around a swallow of margarita. "The woman was beautiful and perfect, but I never saw her smile. Not even when Selena came up with a crown, which was most of the time. They went off on the pageant circuit and we lost touch. I never much liked Selena, but I always felt kind of sorry for her."

Logan sat very still, watching me.

Self-consciously, I swallowed a bite of fajita. "What I don't understand is what's with all the federal attention. Do you think Scooter's smuggling something? Drugs or weapons?" I stared down at my notes. "And maybe that's where the animals fit in."

"You think they've figured out a way to use the animals to smuggle something?"

I looked up from my notebook. "But they wouldn't still be at it if they knew you were on to them."

Logan shrugged. "Maybe they've done what they meant to do."

"But wouldn't we have heard about it before now?"

"When we do our job well, you never even know we were there," he said, and I got a cold chill.

Logan cocked his head. "Did your pals Diego and Barnes hang out together?"

"Diego's not my pal, and no, I don't think so. Why?"

"Just seems odd that in a city like Austin with a metro population of more than a million, everybody and their dog knows a small-time pet store owner."

"Scooter played for the Dallas Cowboys almost a season, and he married a beauty queen. Agree or not, that holds a lot of weight in this part of the country."

"Yeah," Logan said. "But you can't find that many people who know who the mayor is."

I thought about that as I sat, staring at the free association of events outlined in my notebook. "You make anything out of this?"

"I don't know yet. Right now we're looking at a lot of different pieces."

"But you'll tell me if any of this information helps?"

Logan looked at me for a long time. "How about I'll tell you whatever I can."

I wanted to be skeptical, but the thing was, I believed him. He wouldn't tell me everything, but he'd tell me what he could.

"How did you leave things with Diego?"

I sighed. "Not good."

Logan's eyes went dark and he nodded. "He won't bother you again," he said, and a cold chill settled over my insides.

Logan picked up the check, then rose and walked me to the Jeep, Marlowe trotting along at his side. Logan stood at the open door as I climbed in.

With his forearm resting against the roll bar, he looked down at me. "What was your talent?"

"What?"

"In the pageant."

I felt my face go beet red. I hesitated. "I was supposed to sing and play piano," I said. "But at the last minute, I did this, um, *enthusiastic* Mayan dance my friend Mia's grandma taught me. You should have seen my mother in the audience. She about had a cow."

"An enthusiastic dance, huh?" Logan grinned, stepping away from the Jeep. "You'll have to show me some time."

I was still gaping when he got in his old gray bureau car and pulled out of the parking lot behind us, heading north on Congress, back to our respective offices.

"Was he flirting with me?" I said to Marlowe. The dog looked skeptical. I eyed Logan in my rear-view mirror.

At the light at Riverside, Mr. Pixy Stix hobbled up, just like he hadn't hit me up an hour before. Sighing, I scrounged in my purse for a dollar.

My cell phone chirped.

"Cauley MacKinnon," I said, still searching for money.

"What the hell are you doing?" the voice said, and I looked back through my mirror to see Tom Logan on his cell phone, staring at me through his windshield.

I disconnected.

"Here," I said, and gave the guy my last buck. He smiled his hollow smile and started to hand me the three-foot, powder-filled Pixy Stix. The light turned green.

"Give it to the big guy in the ugly gray car behind me," I said. Grinning to myself, I stomped on the gas.

WITH THE FIRST HALF of the day wiped out, I parked in the loading zone at the *Sentinel* and swung past security, straight for my desk, Marlowe padding along beside me.

I checked my messages. Three from my mother, one from Mark, and one from Cantu.

I tossed my purse under my desk and speed-dialed Cantu's cell.

"Any more on the Necklace?"

"Been working it all last night and most of today," he said. "I meant to tell you—sorry I didn't make it out to your house last night."

"You can't come running every time I get in trouble," I said. "You link that burned body last night to El Patron?"

"Actually, yeah. We're waiting on forensics, but word is it's El Patron's attorney."

"Mafia have attorneys?" I said.

"Who needs attorneys more than crooks?"

"I briefly met Selena Barnes' attorney," I said, remembering the crime scene photo Cantu had asked me to look at and thinking about the bespectacled, blond man who'd followed Selena through the *Sentinel* office like a whipped puppy. "And he had glasses."

"Used to have glasses," Cantu said. "Lotta good now."

"I don't know," I said. "The burned guy seemed bigger built than Selena's attorney, but I've only seen him once."

"Forensics aren't back yet."

"But you'll check it out, right? And keep me posted?"

"Sure," he said. "I live to keep you informed."

"I know you don't, so thanks," I said. "I'll pay you back."

"Just stay out of trouble," he said, and disconnected.

I was hanging up the phone when I heard Tanner roar from inside the Cage.

"Is that a dog?"

"Looks like it," I said. I happen to know Tanner loves dogs, and it'd be a cold day in hell before he made me get rid of a husky in this heat.

"Get him under the desk," Tanner grumbled. "And I need to talk to you about the Buggess outline."

Rolling my eyes, I headed for Tanner's office, where I hopped up to sit on his desk.

Marlowe trotted in behind me and sat at Tanner's feet. The dog thumped his tail, and I could tell the gesture melted Tanner's Grinchy little heart.

"What's with the dog?" he said.

"He's been haunting the neighborhood. I put flyers out this morning and I'll place an ad with classifieds today. I didn't mean to bring him, but he sort of jumped in the Jeep and wouldn't get out."

Tanner made a rusty noise that almost sounded like a laugh. He cleared his throat. "About Buggess."

I shook my head. "What about Buggess?"

"I read the outline you e-mailed me, and it's pretty good," Tanner said, surprising me. "Not bad at all."

He turned and shut the door, rubbing the back of his neck. "What I don't like is what you're not saying."

I fidgeted, and I knew Tanner caught it.

"Are you working Barnes?"

I blew out a long breath.

"Goddamn it, Cauley." He wasn't old enough for the vein I saw pulsing in his forehead. "What have you got?"

I crossed my arms. "Are you going to make me turn it over to Shiner?"

"Let me hear what you've got and I'll let you know."

Sighing, I told him about the vandalism-slash-burglary and the missing Barnes file at my house last night, skillfully omitting the part about the mutilated underwear. I told him about the severed ear, the customs agent, and the FBI.

"And then there's the El Patron connection. Why would Diego DeLeon call me up out of the blue to quiz me about some nonexistent thing about Scott Barnes? He also asked me point-blank about some kind of vixen, and he was blabbing on and on about El Patron."

I leaned forward. "And here's the big thing. Agent Logan was surprised that DeLeon knew about the El Patron connection, but he didn't seem surprised by the connection itself."

Tanner shook his head, looking at my e-mailed outline. "And you think, what? Barnes is smuggling drugs in with the animals for El Patron?"

"I don't know, but I'm pretty sure the feds think he's smuggling something. Why else would two different federal agents give a rat's rear end that a washed-up jock keeps threatening suicide? And why are some of the animals neglected and in need of medical attention? Something is wrong, Tanner. I know Scooter, and he'd rather throw himself in front of a burning bus than hurt an animal. And he wouldn't knowingly break the law."

"People will do anything, given proper motivation," Tanner said.

I winced, thinking about Scooter's arrest record for fighting over Selena. At least once in his life, Scooter had broken the law, and he'd done it for Selena. Not a great precedent.

I shook my head. "It's all connected. Logan as much as admitted it. He said they were all pieces of the puzzle."

Tanner turned, looking out the window, fiddling with a licorice whip. "You spoke to two agents? In person?"

"Customs and fed, but it was off the record."

"Nothing's off the record," Tanner grunted, but I knew from the look on his face that Shiner hadn't been able to get squat on the story, let alone corroborate with two federal agents. Of course, Shiner hadn't been threatened at gunpoint, burgled, or menaced with a severed ear. Nice to know there's a bright side to everything.

"It is off the record. I won't use anything they've told me in confidence."

Tanner didn't say anything, so I decided to press my luck. "The customs guy said he'd let me tag along when he goes to interview Barnes. He thinks Scooter will talk more freely—I mean, he's called me wanting to talk about whatever's bothering him before."

"You want out of obits," Tanner said, and he didn't say it kindly.

"I want to know what's going on," I said, standing my ground. I knew he was thinking about the journalism hierarchy and the importance of paying your dues. And probably the trouble I'd gotten into at the *Journal*.

Tanner moved to the glass door of his office, looking out on the second-string reporters pecking away in the Bull Pen. Rolling the licorice stump along his lower lip, he reached down to scratch the dog on the chin.

"So," I said. "I've got the go-ahead on Barnes?"

Tanner turned and looked at me. "You name the dog?"

"Marlowe."

Tanner nodded. "Take him with you. And keep me posted, goddamn it."

I would have turned a cartwheel if I remembered how, and I almost kissed Tanner right on the lips, but there was that gummy licorice stump, and also, I'd already gotten myself a bad reputation for kissing my bosses. So I took the dog and high-tailed it out of Tanner's office before he could change his mind.

TWELVE

THE SKY WAS MGM Technicolor blue, the sun was high and the wind was hot when Marlowe and I hopped into the open Jeep to go see Scooter. I'd checked the weather forecast. Despite the heat, it wasn't an Ozone Action day and there wasn't a gulf hurricane in sight. It wasn't supposed to rain for another day or two, so I skipped the antihistamine and headed for the open road. A perfect Central Texas summer day.

I'd fished Fiennes' card from my purse and called him on my new cell phone, then left a voice mail when I got his message system.

Technically, I'd agreed that Fiennes and I would go talk to Scooter together, but Tanner had finally given me the green light and I wasn't about to wait around for a bureaucrat, no matter how hot, to decide to answer his cell.

I could always fill all the necessary feds in on the details later, I rationalized. In the meantime, maybe I could get Scooter to tell me what kind of trouble warranted the interest of at least two branches of the United States government. I was having a hard time thinking the El Patron connection was legit, but I would ask about that, too.

Besides, if I got to Scooter before the feds, he and I could sit down and work out a plan to get him out of whatever it was he'd gotten himself into *before* we got the feds involved.

"The man takes care of bunnies for a living, how bad could the trouble be?" I said to Marlowe.

Marlowe sat in the passenger seat, eyes front. No undignified hanging out the door, no tongue lolling in the slipstream. The wind whipped his fur to a frenzy, and the dog looked as happy as any mammal had the right to be. The feeling was contagious.

I cranked the radio up to *decimate* and sang along when Toni Price wailed *Low Down and Up,* and I smiled when Marlowe howled along. It could have been a critique on my vocal stylings, but I prefer to think we were sharing a moment. At any rate, we soared down Ranch Road 620 South on our way to the Blue Parrot.

"You're going to love this place," I told Marlowe as we pulled into Scooter's parking lot. "They have mice and parrots and rabbits and these funny little goats that faint."

No sooner had I said the words than a streak of unease spidered up my spine. The parking lot in front of the Blue Parrot was empty. No double-parked Beemers of the young and privileged, no nicely dressed techies hauling bags of designer dog chow to their idling SUVs.

"Well," I said to Marlowe as I cut the motor and the Jeep rattled to a halt. "Miranda and her team at the *Journal* seem to have put our old friend out of business."

I tried the door. Locked, but no *closed* sign in the window. Through the plate glass, I could see the lights were out. Scooter's macaw wasn't sitting on the perch next to the cash register.

"Where are all the animals?" I said to Marlowe. He didn't answer.

"Well, then. It's our civic duty to check it out."

The building was surrounded by a row of dense boxwood bushes, so there was no clear access to the windows. I squeezed behind the bushes and inched my way along the limestone ledge of the foundation to peer into a pane. Nothing.

Inside, the pet shop was dark and unnaturally quiet, but I noticed something else. Doors to the large cages were open, and there were no animals in sight. I wondered if the Bug had been by and taken the animals back to his place . . .

Bang!

Sharp white fangs in a wide pink mouth hit the window.

I heard a scream. It might have been me.

Arms flailing, I fell backward into the bush. Marlowe stood over me, his dark, almond-shaped eyes looking at me like I'd lost my mind. Flat on my back and stuck in the bush, I looked up to the window. A capuchin monkey was perched on the inside sill, screaming simian swears at me through the pane.

"Jeez!" I swore back, trying to get hold of something that wasn't sharp so I could pull myself to my feet. I was tangled in the bramble, so I rolled over, branches poking and scratching, until I could crawl out from underneath the bush.

Spitting out a mouthful of leaves, I stared back at the monkey. "What are you doing loose?"

I went to the back door and banged hard. "Scooter? Are you in there?"

When I hit the door, the room erupted in shrieks and screams. The sounds of animals under duress.

"Shit, Marlowe, how did they get loose? It sounds like they're going *Lord of the Flies* in there." Marlowe shifted from paw to paw, growling low in his throat.

"Scooter?" I yelled through the door.

Nothing.

With a growing sense of dread, I fished my new cell phone out of my purse and dialed the number to the Blue Parrot. No answer.

"Scooter!" I yelled at the door. Heaving back, I hit it with my shoulder. The door didn't bust down like it does in the movies, but I would probably have another neat little bruise to add to my collection.

Inside, the animals were going crazy. Outside, Marlowe was in a full-fledged snarl, scrabbling hard at the steel door.

I should call the police and let them handle it, but what would I say? Animals were rioting at the exotic pet store? Probably they'd just tell me to call the Humane Society.

I slipped Marlowe's leash over the knob at the back door and searched the ground for something big enough to break the window. I knew it was a bad idea, but I have a long history of being impervious to good sense.

"Shit, shit, shit." I flipped open my cell and dialed 911.

"Austin 911, what is your emergency?" droned the voice on the line.

"There's a woman breaking into the pet store on Ranch Road 620."

I disconnected.

I climbed over the bush, reared back, and hit the window with the rock. The window cracked but didn't break.

I bet Bogey would have broken it on the first try. I hit the window two more times and made a good-sized jagged hole. Levering myself between the ledge and the bush, I kicked the rest of the glass and made a hole big enough to get through.

"Scooter?" I yelled. "Bug? Anybody?"

Boosting off the ledge, I vaulted through the window, getting a handful of glass splinters from the shattered pane. Landing, my foot struck something wiggly.

"Blast it!" I swore, teetering briefly before I slipped and fell face-first on the linoleum. The giant lizard on the other end of the wiggling tail swung around, hissing and spitting.

I did what any sane person would do. I screamed. Outside, Marlowe went wild.

As my eyes adjusted to the dim light, the lizard scuttled away and I pushed up on my hands, mindful of the glass splinters and feeling like I'd been thrown into a reality show depraved enough for the Fox network.

The sound of skittering claws beneath a toppled store fixture sent my skin crawling. Colorful birds perched freely along bookshelves and store displays, and a white cockatoo flipped his orange crest at me from atop the silent ceiling fan. I didn't see Sam, Scooter's blue macaw.

The monkey continued his chiding, and I froze. All the cages were broken, overturned, and empty.

The musky smell of free-ranging animals was overwhelming, but I smelled something else, too. Thick and oppressive, almost sweet. In college I'd worked at an emergency vet clinic, and once I'd cared for a schnauzer that'd temporarily won a fight with a pit bull. Temporarily, because the schnauzer got a galloping case of gangrene from the bite wound in his neck. The dog literally rotted to death. Rotting flesh is a smell you never forget.

Like the calm before a storm, the animals went quiet, and then—

Crash!

The remaining glass in the pane shattered as Marlowe leapt through the broken window, torn leash flying like a thin, tattered flag.

"Marlowe, no!" I shouted. The dog landed in front of me, teeth bared at the monkey.

Faced with a snarling, sixty-pound dog, the monkey scampered behind a case of monkey chow. It could have been a blood bath, but Marlowe screeched to a halt, turned, and came back. Like a sentry, he circled me twice and then sat, staring at me expectantly.

"Who are you?" I said to the dog. If Mia's cat was Cleopatra in a previous life, it was entirely possible that Marlowe was John Wayne.

Marlowe rose, sniffing the floor like a bloodhound.

I blew out a breath, flinching at the glass splinters prickling my palms.

"Good grief," I said. "Will you look at this place?"

Marlowe didn't appear to be bothered with the animals. His mind was clearly on something else. He disappeared down an aisle of broken aquariums.

In the near distance, Marlowe yelped three strange little barks from deep inside the pet store. Scooter's office.

The little hairs on the back of my neck lifted.

"What is it, boy?" I said, but my voice quavered.

Maneuvering around upended cages, I moved toward Marlowe, toward Scooter's office. With each step, my feet felt heavier, my heart rose in my chest, and the odor of rotting schnauzer grew thicker.

"Marlowe? What is it?"

When I pushed the door wide, I saw what it was. Marlowe was standing alert, ears pricked, legs braced, almost in a pointer stance.

Scooter was seated in his ergonomically correct computer chair, his handsome, blond head slumped forward.

My breath caught in my throat.

Dried blood covered his mouse pad and crusted where it had pooled on the floor, most likely from the deep gash that spanned the width of his wrist. Beside the keyboard was an empty bottle of bourbon and a sharp-looking hunting knife, blade extended. It was coated with crusted blood.

"Scooter?" I said, but my voice rang hollow. "Scott!"

I moved toward him and a blur of blue feathers burst in front of me. Sam spread his enormous wings at me, shrieking like a banshee. Marlowe growled, the fur along his back bristling.

"Hey, buddy," I said to the bird, carefully sidestepping the sharp talons and big beak. "I'm just going to see if he's all right."

I edged closer, trying not to gag at the smell. Scooter's once-stunning blue eyes were milky and lifeless.

"Oh, Scooter." Grimacing, I reached for him, feeling for a pulse at his throat. He had both ears, but his skin felt unnaturally cold when I touched him. His stiff body toppled to the side.

Sam screamed and the computer beeped, the hard drive whirred, and the Word program blinked into focus. *"By the time you read this, I'll be gone . . ."*

I couldn't move.

Dim, dust-moted light from the windows cast long shadows over Scooter's ashen face. The computer's screen saver scrolled in continuum, as though waiting for its owner to finish whatever he'd been working on. Just another day at the office. Except for the dead body.

I don't know when I heard the sirens, and I didn't hear Logan enter the pet store, but I felt his hand, large and warm, on my shoulder. My knees buckled and he caught me, his arms strong around me. He smelled clean, like soap and leather, and I could feel the hard line of his shoulder holster tucked beneath his right arm. With his left hand, he patted my back, hesitantly at first, and then he pressed his cheek to the top of my head.

"You okay?" he asked.

"I'm going to be sick."

"Come on." He ushered me toward the back door.

"No," I whispered hoarsely. "Bathroom."

He got a pained look on his face, and said, "Can't. We've got to treat this like a crime scene."

I realized then that crime scene techs were combing the place, and my stomach lurched. Logan led me outside and gallantly turned away as I heaved and wretched and wished I'd never been born in a world where things like this were allowed to happen.

THIRTEEN

"THANK YOU FOR BRINGING me home," I said. I couldn't stop shaking, even as I stepped into the familiarity of my little house. Logan had packed me and the dog into his bureau car and driven us back to the bungalow.

"I'm sorry," I said. "Every time I see you I seem to be throwing up."

"Yeah, I've got a way with women. And if I remember correctly, you didn't actually throw up last time."

I almost laughed at that, and to my horror, burst into tears instead. "I'm sorry," I said. "I don't know what's wrong with me."

"You're in shock." Logan pulled a monogrammed handkerchief from inside his jacket.

I blew my nose. "Last year I aced two Criminology courses and held my own through three semesters of Forensic Science. I've been on ride-alongs with the APD, and the boys at the substation love showing me the Blood Book."

"Blood Book?"

"Forensic shots of burned bodies, decapitated bodies, severed penises." I shook my head.

Logan nodded. "Not the same, is it?"

"No," I said. "My dad was a detective with the APD, but he always kept that kind of thing at the office."

In my living room, Muse perched on the back of the sofa, bitching vociferously. Since Marlowe's appearance in the house, Muse had gone underground, probably plotting her revenge. Marlowe's ears perked, and before I could say a word, the dog dove for the cat. I suddenly realized that this was their first official meeting. I was not in the mood.

Muse lifted straight into the air as though she'd been yanked by stunt wires. She came down on the dog's head, and the heat was on.

There was a tumble of fur as the dog rolled, the cat orbiting about him, claws and teeth bared. When both animals righted themselves on all fours, Muse's sharp teeth sank into Marlowe's upper lip. The dog growled with a bit of a lisp.

"Stop." Logan's voice thundered through the living room.

The cat and dog froze as though they'd been handed an edict from God. The cat let go of the dog's lip. After a long moment of glaring at each other, Muse flipped her tail and stalked back to the bedroom. Marlowe circled Logan twice, then lay at his feet.

I stared at Logan. One of these days, I was going to ask him how he did that.

Logan sniffed the air. "Did somebody break into your house again?"

"My aunt's cat probably peed in the ficus. She does that when she doesn't get her way."

"You're batting a thousand, kid. Why don't you go wash up. You want some tea?"

I nodded. My bones felt like rubber and I couldn't remember ever feeling so tired. Nothing seemed to make sense anymore.

Making my way to the bathroom, I felt strangely safe, glad that Logan was in the living room. He had stopped Muse and Marlowe from the canine equivalent of World War III, and he'd taken total control at the Blue Parrot. He'd briefed the police and settled things with Cantu, who said he'd bring my Jeep by later.

Logan was a natural leader, I realized, dealing with Scott's body, organizing forensic search patterns, delegating tasks and ordering reports before quietly driving a hysterical, trouble-prone obituary writer back to her house.

Scott's body.

I nearly threw up again. Instead, I climbed into the shower and stood under the hot water until it went cold. Dressed in a big, soft tee shirt and a pair of faded shorts, I felt clean, but even then, the world seemed muted, out of focus.

In the living room, Logan handed me a cup of tea and I curled up on the sofa, my hair still damp, my feet bare. Logan dragged the overstuffed chair next to the sofa and sat, Marlowe at his heels.

"You want to talk?"

"No," I said. "But I suppose that's exactly what I should do. There have to be pieces missing. Something I've overlooked. None of this makes sense."

"The pieces may not make sense independently, but they do make sense. These things are like a puzzle."

"Fit them together for the big picture," I said, nodding numbly. "I faxed Cantu some of the notes you went over with me."

Logan nodded. "You up to starting at the beginning?"

I shook my head but said, "Yes."

The thought of going over everything again made my stomach feel even oilier, but I blew out a long breath and began, starting with Scooter in the shed, recalling our conversation, which was mostly about Selena, as best I could. About Van Gogh, the Bug, and the animals in bad shape, and his mysterious veterinarian. Then there was Diego's deliberate date, his questions about a vixen and references to El Patron, the break-in and stolen files I'd put together on Scooter, the severed ear in my couch, and the latest torched, ear-chopped, unidentified corpse, presumably the work of El Patron. And somehow it was all connected.

"I've got to be forgetting something," I said. "You know how something bumps at the edge of your brain but you can't quite see it clearly?"

Logan nodded. "It'll come to you."

I shook my head, trying to dislodge the memory of Scooter dead in the middle of his pet store. "Logan, the Blue Parrot was wrecked. You think somebody was looking for something?"

Logan's dark eyes narrowed. "Like what?"

"I don't know. It was just a thought." I rubbed my eyes. "Hey, how did you know about the Blue Parrot? Do you have a scanner?"

"Yes, I have a scanner," he said, and I didn't notice until later he'd skipped the first half of the question.

"The broken window?" he said.

"I did that."

"And the 911 call?"

"I did that, too."

He smiled and shook his head. "What were you doing skulking around, breaking windows?"

"My editor finally gave me the green light on a real story. I was going to talk to Scooter before Tanner changed his mind. I knew Scooter was out of the hospital and I wanted to get to the bottom of whatever's going on."

"And you went alone?"

"I called Fiennes but he wasn't there, so I left him a message and went myself to see if Scooter and I couldn't work out a plan before we got the authorities involved. Again."

"Fiennes?"

"You know. John Fiennes. The customs agent."

If I had just met Logan, I wouldn't have noticed the subtle change in his expression.

"You didn't mention a customs agent last time we spoke."

I shrugged. "I told him everything I told you, and I figured y'all were working together."

Logan pinched the bridge of his nose.

"Hey," I said. "You don't think this is about drugs, do you?"

"What would make you think so?"

"Well, the customs agent being involved and the animals being imported from South America. They could be using the animals as mules to smuggle illegal substances."

Logan looked at me levelly. "We've had dogs all over Barnes' store, truck, and house. If there were drugs or weapons, the dogs would've alerted."

I nodded, narrowing my eyes. "So how come you didn't know about the customs agent?"

Logan leaned back in the chair. "I'll tell you a little story. Off the record. A couple of years ago I was undercover at a Klan rally. While I was surveilling the bad guys, I happened to notice another assistant district attorney—also UC. Then I really looked around, and spotted a couple of local cops in on the gig, too."

"*Another* assistant district attorney?"

"Before I joined the bureau."

I blinked at him. "You're an attorney?"

"I know," he said. "All this and brains, too."

"But you didn't know someone at your own office was under cover at the same rally? What if things had gone south? Y'all could have been shooting at each other."

"There's always that."

I shook my head. "I wouldn't take your job for the world," I said.

"Right now, your job doesn't seem so hot either, kid," he said.

I was quiet for a long time.

Logan sat back, scratching the dog's chin. "Nice dog," he said. "You always take him with you?"

"You mean because of the restaurant? No." I sighed. "He's not really my dog. He's just hanging around here until I find his owner. In the meantime, I'm calling him Marlowe."

"Marlowe, huh?" Logan smiled like he'd heard a private joke. He rose and picked up his suit jacket. "Can I talk you into staying somewhere else tonight?"

"Probably not."

He nodded. "You going to be okay?"

"Someday."

I walked him to the door and felt an odd urge to ask him to stay. I wasn't about to embarrass myself. No matter how nice he was, he'd already made it clear this was just another job for him.

"Logan?" I finally said, and felt my voice stick in my throat. "About what happened back there. Scooter—I mean, Scott. Do you think it was suicide?"

Logan stopped. He studied my face. "That's for the M.E. to decide. Take care of yourself, kid, and do me a favor—" He opened the door. "Don't let anyone in or out." He looked pointedly down at the dog. "And don't talk to anybody without good ID."

From the front window, I watched him start up his old gray bureau car. He pulled out of the driveway.

Watching him leave, my stomach roiled on a fresh wave of nausea. Until now, I thought I'd convinced Scooter that life was worth living, when what I'd really done was prevent him from getting the kind of help he needed. Too late for help now.

Rubbing my forehead, I tried to erase the image of my friend slumped over his computer, blood caked at his wrists and crusting around his feet. I tried not to think about the authorities notifying his parents. His wife.

I leaned my head against the cool glass of my living room window and said a silent prayer for all of them. Scooter's wife, his parents, the police . . . and I watched the red glimmer of Logan's taillights skim into the night.

And I said a little prayer for him, too.

FOURTEEN

Former Dallas Cowboy running back Scott "Scooter" Barnes was found dead yesterday afternoon in an apparent suicide . . .

Suicide. My fingers stilled over the cool metal keys of the old typewriter. But I cleared my throat and pressed on.

. . . according to police officers on the scene. Barnes was 32.

Barnes was found with cuts to both wrists, slumped over his computer in the exotic pet store where he, along with his wife, former beauty queen Selena Obregon, had made a successful second career after his brief time in professional football.

"The pet store was in a state of disarray," acknowledged one crime scene investigator, who declined further comment, pending autopsy results.

By the time I finished the obituary, my head was pounding and my stomach was tied in knots. I knew Logan wouldn't mind being quoted if I kept his name out of it, but I felt sick when I ripped the paper out of Aunt Kat's typewriter and faxed it to Tanner, ensuring the *Sentinel* would get the story live on the web and scoop those troglodytes at the *Journal.*

Tomorrow I would make some calls, see if I could get the police to make a statement for the follow-up. Then I'd talk to Scott's parents. Maybe a former teammate or two. And then I'd have to call Selena.

The full effects of gravity pulled at me as I trudged off to bed. I didn't sleep and I'm not sure how I got up, showered, and dressed, except I didn't know what else to do. I ripped open my new pack of days-of-the-week granny panties and selected a pair that was Pepto Bismol pink to match my queasy mood. As I slid into the panties, I realized they were the wrong day, but who cared, because there was no man in my life to count the days of the week, anyway.

I still felt disoriented, like I was walking on the bottom of the ocean, when Cantu showed up early with my Jeep, a trough of iced tea, and, thank God, donuts. Marlowe sniffed Cantu with interest, but spared him the usual growling routine.

Sitting at the dining room table, Cantu helped me fill out paperwork, something we'd been doing a lot of lately.

"Have y'all located Selena?" I said.

"Didn't have to," Cantu said. "She held a press conference early this morning. You should have seen her. She looked like a princess or something."

"Let me guess. Her mother arranged the press conference and Miranda did the interview."

Cantu shot me an ironic grin.

"Hey," I said on a long shot. "How does this all fit in with El Patron?"

"Who says it does?" Cantu said. He unhooked his radio from his utility belt and called for a cruiser. "Why don't you take a couple days off?"

Avoidance. Practically a confession.

"Would *you* take a couple days off if you were in my position?" I said, giving the dog a bite of donut under the table.

"We're not talking about me," Cantu said, but he shook his head. I'd won this round. The cruiser must have been waiting nearby, because Cantu's radio squawked, and he rose from the table. "You gonna be okay?"

"I gotta get to work," I said, thinking about Miranda and her exclusive press conference with Selena.

"Thanks, buddy. Tell Arlene I said *hey*," I said, and ushered him out the door.

MARLOWE AND I SHOWED up at the office a half hour late, images of Scooter's empty eyes still haunting me. My stomach was tied in a perpetual knot, but I had to get out of the house and do something. Anything.

I flashed my badge at security and rushed through the lobby. Tanner stuck his head out of his office. "What are you doing here?"

"I still work here, right?"

Tanner stepped aside, meaning he wanted me in his office. Now.

I sighed, threw my purse under my desk, and trudged into the Cage. Marlowe skipped the invitation and padded down the hall toward the graphics department, hot on the trail of peanut butter cookies, Diet Coke, and Skittles.

"You look like hell."

"Thank you," I said. "I feel like hell." I didn't sit.

"Okay. Let's hear it," he said, dropping into his chair, his arms crossed behind his head. The obituary I'd faxed over that night was laying on his keyboard, and I noticed Tanner'd given me the front page of the Metro section. It was only a twelve-inch column, but it was above the fold.

"I just went to check on him," I said, amazed at how steady my voice sounded as I told Tanner about the pet shop in shambles, about Scooter's death, about how I was pretty sure it was going to be ruled suicide. I told Tanner about the animals running wild in the pet store and Selena's press conference earlier this morning.

Tanner rubbed his forehead as he listened.

"Why don't you go on home," he said. "Shiner can do the follow-up."

I gaped at him. "Now you're taking *obituaries* away from me?" I said. "Tanner, I am going to that funeral, I'm going to write the follow-up."

"Cauley. You're not responsible for Barnes' death."

His words struck like tinfoil against a loose filling, and I took a deep breath.

"Maybe I'm not responsible," I said. "But Scott Barnes called me for help, and the only real way I could have helped him was to make sure he got to a shrink. Scooter had real problems and I interfered. I never should have crossed that police line."

Tanner looked at me and didn't say anything.

"If I'd stayed out of it—"

"The guy had two prior suicide attempts. He left a note. Despite whatever you might think, the fate of the free world does not rest in your hands."

I swallowed hard, steeling myself for what I had to say. "Tanner," I said. "I don't think Scott Barnes committed suicide. I read up on the pathology. Men, especially former pro football players, do not slit their wrists. Besides, according to everything I've read, if you really want to kill yourself, you slash the length of your arm from wrist to elbow. Scooter's wounds spanned the width of his wrists."

"Leave it, Cauley. He was your friend. We got somebody else to cover the funeral."

"Yes, Scooter was my friend, but I was there at the beginning of this thing and I want to see it through. I need to do this, Tanner."

He rose, going for a licorice whip, and leaned against the glass door, watching reporters and copyeditors rush around the Bull Pen. It was quiet in the Cage, which magnified the clattering keyboards and chattering phone conversations on the other side of the door. Finally, he turned to me and said, "You may be sorry about crossing that police line, but you'd do it again."

Sighing, I nodded.

"All right," Tanner said. "Go to the funeral. And take Shiner with you."

I WASN'T ABOUT TO take Shiner or anyone else with me. I'd caused at least part of this mess, and I was going to see it through. I slouched out of Tanner's office and across the aisle to my desk, where Mia and Remie were waiting for me. The phone was ringing. Mia picked up the receiver and handed it to me.

"Front page above the fold," a familiar female voice purred over the line.

"*Miranda*," I swore.

"I guess you've found a nice little silver lining for yourself on your friend's suicide."

I slammed the phone down, gritting my teeth.

"Wow. You look terrible. What's going on?" Mia said. As much as I loved them, I didn't know if I could take any more at the moment.

"That was Miranda."

"So we gathered," Mia said, shooting Remie a concerned look.

"Something is very, very wrong," I said, almost to myself. "Why would Scooter's estranged wife hold a press conference the day after her husband supposedly killed himself?"

"Anything we can do to help?" Mia said.

"Look into the past," I said.

Remie jabbed Mia with her elbow. "Get your crystal ball."

"Don't be ridiculous," Mia snorted. "Crystal balls are for the future, not the past."

"Yeah, but there is a way to look into the past," I said, booting up my computer. "Background research. What I really need to do is sit my butt down and start over from the beginning."

Mia grinned. "Our butts are at your service."

REMIE, BLESS HER ALL the way up to her great big, ozone-destroying hair, took Shiner and went down to the KFXX station to get a copy of Selena's press conference video, and Mia called Jamal, the *Sentinal's* ace photographer, to come over after-hours and go through photo archives. Even if the photos they dug up didn't help with the investigation, we'd need them for the Metro story on Scooter, his football career, and his final days as the owner of an upscale exotic pet store.

Mark had been right. A star-crossed Dallas Cowboy with such a colorful past was a big story, and I would do it right. I owed Scooter that much.

Above the chattering keyboards, Scooter's voice echoed, soft and sad, as it had that day in the shed . . . *I wish I was in Hawaii.*

I created a new file on my computer desktop and labeled it *Hawaii.* My fingers stilled over the keys. I hoped Scooter was finally in a place where he felt safe and happy.

Opening the new file, I settled in and put my nose to the digital grindstone, hoping like hell I could do the man justice.

I picked up the phone and hit speed dial for Cantu so I could ask for another copy of Scooter's arrest record, which I'd forgotten to mention when he'd dropped off my Jeep that morning. "Also, can you fax me back the notes I faxed you on Barnes?"

"Anybody ever tell you you're a big pain in the ass?"

"You're the first today," I said, "but it's still early."

"What in hell did you do with the records I gave you?"

I bit my lip. "They got stolen when I got robbed."

"Burgled," he grumbled. "A robbery is—"

210

"Yeah, yeah, I know. Also, can I get a copy of the crime scene report from the Blue Parrot?"

"Sure. You want me to change your oil and rotate your tires while I'm at it?"

"No, thanks. Shay already took care of all that."

"You gonna give me what you got?" Cantu said.

"I'll give you whatever I can," I said.

He grunted and I said, "Thanks, buddy. I owe you."

"Yeah, ten transfusions, a kidney, and two weeks of babysitting."

"You'll have your kidney by tomorrow," I said. "And tell Arlene I said *hey*."

Turning back to my computer, I stared at a ten-year-old article in the online archives as it flickered on the monitor. There was Scooter, head lowered, football tucked in the crook of his arm as he mowed through San Francisco's defensive line. He was young and blond and unstoppable. Or so we thought.

I scrolled through document after document and stopped when I came to Scooter's archived wedding announcement. His handsome face shone, the prototypical golden boy as he stood with his arm around Selena. I stared at the monitor. As striking as Scooter was, it was Selena who absorbed the spotlight. In the photo, she looked sweet and fragile and very beautiful.

I looked at the notes I'd reconstructed with Logan. None of the pieces fit tidily, but there was one that didn't fit at all.

I typed in "El Patron" and got a page full of links about the group's ties to South America, most of which I'd already seen when I'd been assigned to research the group for Ryder the News Boy.

I sat, staring at the monitor. Why did Diego DeLeon think Scooter was involved with El Patron? And, not to sound politically incorrect, but why was El Patron, a group known to support anti-Hispanic sentiments, based in South America, where most people are Hispanic?

I sat, tapping my lips. Scooter died with both ears attached and he had not been treated to a Necklace. And if Scooter really was so depressed over Selena leaving him, why did he do two practice runs at suicide?

And why did El Patron use a burning tire as an M.O.? I keyed in "Necklace+Tire" and came up with side links leading to other gruesome forms of torture, and interestingly enough, some truly ghastly porn sites.

I clicked the two most legitimate-looking sites and got links to a group of Argentinean separatists.

"Separatists in Argentina? Well, now," I said. "Isn't that interesting?"

Frowning, I typed in a cross-reference for "Aryan" and a link halfway down the page marked *Vixen* caught my eye. Hitting the link, I scrolled through the site's pages. It seemed to be some kind of neo-Nazi recruiting port.

"Aryans, huh?" I printed the page and, on a hunch, pulled up the CIA World Fact Book and the Cromwell Intelligence site and cross-referenced "Vixen" with "El Patron."

"Holy shit," I whispered, when a list of connected names and descriptions appeared on the monitor. Some of the cross-connected people were currently cooling their jets in Huntsville Prison for illegally transporting "artifacts" from South America.

I sent the documents to the printer and nearly jumped out of my seat when a voice right behind me yelled, "Got it!"

"Good grief, Remie, make a noise or something."

"Sorry," Shiner said, jogging behind Remie at a reserved pace. "We got the tape and just wait 'til you see it."

We trooped through the aisle of cubicles, back to the conference room, and popped the tape into the machine, queuing until an image of Miranda appeared. She was doing some kind of "mi-mi-mi" musical scales before her interview and I tried not to scowl. The outtakes?

"You got raw tape?" I said. "How'd you pull that off?"

"That funny little guy in editing has a crush on Shiner," Remie said.

"Can we just watch the tape?" Shiner grumbled, and we all settled in. The video whirred in the machine and Selena appeared on the television screen, beautiful and blond, quietly sipping a glass of water, listening carefully as Miranda told her about camera angles and cue lights. Selena's mother lurked near the door. *Just like the old pageant days.*

Noticeably absent was Selena's clings-like-Saran-Wrap attorney. A makeup artist puffed and pouffed Selena's corn silk hair, an off-camera voice called, "And three, two . . ."

On cue, Selena's mother stepped out of the camera shot.

The transformation was nothing less than miraculous. When Selena turned to the lens, her beautiful face went carefully grief-stricken. Her posture was ramrod straight, her attire Donna

Karan. A single tear clung to her lower lashes. Hell, she almost had *me* crying.

"Shiner, you are the best," I said. Shiner's gaze flicked toward Mia and I swear I saw him blush.

Mia hopped up to sit on the conference table, a good portion of her bare legs in close proximity to Shiner. He sat, eyes straight, but I thought his head was going to explode.

The television flickered as the tape rolled. "Look at her. She's doing a young, blond Jackie Kennedy," I whispered. "She could win a Golden Globe."

Shiner fast-forwarded through the first part of the interview and hit *play*.

"All I wanted was to get Scott some help," Selena said in a hushed voice, with the barest trace of her Latina accent. "But there was so much interference. People meddling where they didn't belong . . ."

I sat on the table in front of the monitor. "Is it just me or does it sound like she's blaming me for Scooter's death?"

"Do you think it really was a suicide?" Remie said.

"No," I said, watching the monitor, "and I'm not sure Selena does, either."

"Cauley. Can I see you a minute?" Tanner stood in the doorway of the conference room, his hands in his front pockets. I didn't like the look on his face.

"Uh, yeah, sure," I said.

I followed Tanner down the hall. "What's going on?"

In his office, he shut the door behind us. I didn't sit.

"The M.E. called. They're ruling Barnes a suicide."

I blinked. "That was quick."

"Hey, you got a former Dallas Cowboy committing suicide, things get done."

"Tanner, it's not a suicide."

"Scott Barnes holed up in a shed two times trying to get up enough nerve to kill himself."

"With a shotgun. With SWAT drawing down around the perimeter, for Pete's sake. Testosterone junkies like Scooter go out with a bang and you know it. They don't trash their place of business, then slit their wrists."

"That's enough, Cauley."

I crossed my arms. "Did you see the M.E.'s documents?"

"They faxed them over a few minutes ago."

"I'd like to see them."

"Cauley," Tanner said. "It's over."

"Tanner, I just saw Selena Barnes giving the performance of her life. If you could just come look at it . . ."

"Doesn't matter. We got what we needed."

"Since when did you ever take the easy way out? You're the one who's always telling us to dig deeper. Check all the facts."

Tanner let out a deep sigh. "Show me what you got."

"I think it's got something to do with Selena," I said, leading him back to the conference room. When we rounded the corner, my friends scattered like rats.

I rewound the tape and hit *play*. Selena sat, her blue eyes shining with tears. Luminous. Perfect, if they didn't seem a little out of focus.

Tanner watched, and I saw his throat tighten when Selena teared up.

"See?" I said, skipping back to the outtakes where Selena seemed calm, cool, and reserved.

"People grieve in different ways," he said. "Look at her. The woman is obviously distraught."

I wanted to throttle him. "Women like Selena get away with this kind of thing because they're petite and beautiful. They depend on the kindness of strangers."

"Are you being objective or are you letting the past cloud your judgment?"

I bit my lip. "Maybe a little, but I know in my heart Scooter didn't commit suicide. If the APD would just look at this tape, if the M.E. would just—"

"Cauley, this isn't like the movies, where the entire Travis County Medical Examiner's office grinds to a halt for one death, especially for a guy with a record of multiple suicide attempts. He got some special treatment because he was a ballplayer, but they looked at the evidence, the facts, and the history and made a decision. Unless you can show me something—some shred of evidence that says otherwise—we're done."

"Done, my ass," I growled, stalking back to my computer. Dropping into my chair, I could still hear Selena's soft Argentinean voice ringing in my ears.

"There was so much interference. People meddling where they didn't belong . . ."

"Didn't belong," I muttered to myself. The CIA site was still flickering on my monitor. On a hunch, I typed in "Argentina." Maybe I'd look up little Miss Selena's family.

"What have we here?" I said, watching as numerous links to Aryan groups and El Patron popped up on the screen.

I clicked on several links and found an old *Sentinel* article dated 1997 about the Nazi flight from Germany, primarily to Argentina, but also to Chile and Brazil. The author of the article was Rob Ryder, the News Boy incarnate at the *Sentinel's* main office downtown. Scrolling down, there was a photo of a scattering of gold coins, each imprinted with an eagle, the tips of the wings pointing skyward. The caption read "Rare Gold Anschluss Eagle Coin Stash Found in Bastrop County."

Something about the coins seemed familiar—they looked an awful lot like the coin Scooter had given me to give to Selena. *For luck,* I thought wryly.

The coin was the thing I'd been trying to remember when Logan and I had gone to lunch.

Not that it mattered. That coin was at the bottom of the lake with everything else in my purse.

I hit *print* and snatched the article, as well as the hard copy of the search I'd done, from the printer, got a fresh manila folder from the supply closet, and went back to my desk, where I stuffed all of it into my purse.

I picked up the phone and called Cantu.

"Have you seen the M.E.'s report on Scooter?"

"Yeah, tough break, *mijita.*"

"Maybe not," I said. "How much do you know about El Patron?"

Cantu didn't say anything.

"Do you know anything about an Argentinean named Vix or Vixen?"

"Cauley," Cantu said. "The M.E. report didn't come out the way you wanted. I understand you feel bad about your friend, but he called you to the scene and you went. No one can blame you for what happened."

I felt like yelling at him, but for once discretion overcame drama and I said, "Did you find out for sure if that last Necklace was Selena's attorney?"

After a shuffling of papers, Cantu said, "Let's see. They ID'd him. A Dr. Henry Smit—he's some sort of exotic animal veterinarian out of Bastrop."

FIFTEEN

I'D NEVER SEEN DR. Smit, but apparently he wore glasses just like
Selena's attorney.

I sighed. I guess if I was honest with myself, I knew the M.E.
would call Scooter's death a suicide, but I'd been so sure that Van
Gogh and his legion of doom had something to do with Scooter's
death.

I supposed it was possible that Scooter committed suicide, but
the thought that he may have really killed himself made me phys-
ically ill.

"Suicide," I said aloud. The events of the past days started to
catch up with me and all I wanted to do was go home and pull
the covers up over my head. Feeling miserable, I called Marlowe
from the graphics department, and on the way home we went
through the drive-through liquor store and got two bottles of
Llano Estacado red wine.

At home, I ordered a pizza and a pint of Ben & Jerry's chocolate ice cream and stuffed *North by Northwest* into the player.

Misery is almost bearable when taken with Cary Grant, chocolate ice cream, and a mountain of mozzarella.

After the food was delivered, I stripped down to my tee shirt and my pink days-of-the-week granny panties. One day soon I was going to have to break down and go shopping for some presentable undies. But what difference did it make? There wasn't anybody around to see my undies anyway.

Wrapping myself in one of Aunt Kat's soft old quilts, I flopped onto the sofa next to Marlowe to watch the movie. I was just wondering how Eva Marie Saint got her hair to do that when my phone rang.

"Hey," Tom Logan said. "What are you doing?"

"Bingeing on Ben & Jerry's and wondering who did Eva Marie Saint's hair."

"You heard about Barnes, then."

"Yeah, I heard. That's why I'm wallowing."

"Have you heard from your customs agent?"

"No, and my nose is officially out of it."

"Sorry, kid. Tough break."

"Logan," I said, figuring I had nothing to lose. "Do you make this for a suicide?"

He didn't say anything for a long time. "Well," he said. "Let's put it this way: I'm still on the case. Are you going to the funeral?"

"Scooter was my friend."

Logan was quiet. "Don't wander off," he finally said. "Still got the dog?"

I looked at Marlowe, who was sitting next to me on the sofa, crunching on pizza crusts. "Still got the dog."

"Been outside lately?"

"No. Why? Is there a bald, earless guy sharpening his Bowie knife on my front porch?"

"No. Just a hell of a sunset."

I stared at the phone.

"See ya 'round, kid," he said and disconnected.

"Ya know," I told Marlowe, "I kind of like that guy."

Marlowe put his chin on my knee and sighed.

My ears were warm and my lips were numb from two glasses of wine, and I was lulled by the sound of Cary Grant's voice when a thump sounded at my door.

"Well, crap. What now?"

A low growl sounded deep in Marlowe's throat. Wrapped in the quilt, I grabbed the phone and got up, my trigger finger on speed dial for 911.

I peered through a clear spot in the stained glass. "Who is it?"

"John Fiennes."

I blew out a breath. I'd half hoped it was Logan. Sighing, I smoothed my hair and cursed myself for not jumping into the shower before cranking up the movie.

Cracking the door, I peeked out. Fiennes stood on the porch, the pale moon shining softly on his dark hair. Against my better judgment, I opened the door.

"Can I help you?"

"May I come in?"

The look on his face was strained. Curiosity got the best of me, and I pulled the quilt more tightly around me and let him in.

Marlowe bristled, and I laid my hand on his head. "Easy, boy," I said.

"Hello, dog," he said, and held out his hand for Marlowe's inspection. Nice.

The dog stood down, but made a big production of sniffing Fiennes in a very private manner. Fiennes redirected the dog's nose and scratched him on his neck.

Marlowe padded back to the sofa, turned three times and lay down, his little doggie eyebrows lifting as we spoke, as though he was following the conversation.

"I understand you had quite a time at the pet store. I know Mr. Barnes was a friend of yours and I am sorry for your loss."

"Yeah," I said miserably, dropping onto the sofa next to Marlowe. "Thanks."

Fiennes looked around the house. "I understand you've had trouble here as well?"

"I was burgled, if that's what you're talking about."

Fiennes pulled a chair closer to the sofa and sat, leaning forward, his elbows on his knees as he spoke.

"You should have waited for me," he said. His accent was smooth in the middle, rough around the edges. Not like Cary Grant, but very sexy just the same.

"I called you and got your voice mail," I said. "My boss finally gave me the go-ahead and I wanted to get to Scooter before he changed his mind." A sudden image of Scooter slumped over his computer made my stomach turn. "Can we talk about this some other time?"

"Yes," he said. "But I must ask you about the break-in at your home. Are you going to be all right?"

The wine was making me dizzy and my thoughts whiplashed from guilt over Scooter to the fact that I'd been yanked off a real story, and back to John Fiennes. I sat, listening to the poetry of his speech patterns.

"Where are you from?"

He didn't sit back, but I felt him draw away. "All over the world, really."

"You said that, but what kind of accent?"

"I was born at Ramstein."

"The U.S. air base in Germany?" I said. "Your parents were military?"

"My father was Air Force. My mother was a German national."

"Was?" I said.

"They are both gone."

I studied John's face, which had gone hard.

"I grew up with my aunt," he went on. "We moved around a lot."

"I'm sorry," I said. It seemed we had something in common. We'd both lost our fathers, and in that moment, I felt my heart shift.

He blew out a breath. "And so my accent is just an echo from a long time ago, and nothing to talk about on a moonlit night in the company of a beautiful woman."

"Well," I said warmly. "I like your accent. You sound like Jean Claude Van Damme."

"But better looking."

I smiled. "And way more humble."

Fiennes grinned. "I must know what was taken from your home."

"They trashed the place, took a file, my hard drive, and all my disks, then they busted up my computer." I shook my head, which was starting to throb from the wine. "Oh, yeah. They also stuffed my cat in the sofa and left me a severed ear."

"They took a file of papers and your hard drive?"

I nodded. "The file I was putting together on Scott Barnes."

Fiennes narrowed his eyes. "Do you remember what was in that file?"

"That's the bitch of it. There wasn't anything in that file worth taking."

"Perhaps there was something and you didn't recognize it."

"People keep saying that."

Fiennes looked at me intently. "How do you feel about searching your friend's belongings?"

I blinked, not sure I heard him correctly. "My boss pulled me off research, and I think he was right. I shouldn't have gotten personally involved. If I hadn't interfered, Scooter might still be alive."

"Perhaps," Fiennes said. "Perhaps not. Will you go to the funeral?"

I nodded, feeling miserable and tired.

Fiennes rose and I walked him to the door, with Marlowe trotting along with interest. "Glad to see you brought your dog inside."

"He's not my dog."

Fiennes smiled. "Of course he's not." He looked down at me. "You must consider dressing before answering the door."

I adjusted the quilt. "I knew it was you."

"And don't forget to lock up."

I opened the door and John stepped onto the porch and stopped, eyes sparking green in the moonlight. "Cauley?"

"Yeah?"

"Nice undies."

SIXTEEN

Tanner'd given me a couple of days off to get my act together, and then it was back to the obituaries. But the truth is, when I'm not writing—even if it's a batch of obituaries—I'm not quite sure what to do with myself.

I tried to read the rest of a Parker novel, watch old movies, and catch up on paying bills, which is hard to do when your bank account balances out to zero. I even did battle with the dust bunnies in the laundry room, but they battled right back, so I quit. I should have called the insurance company to find out when I would be able to replace the things that were broken or stolen, but it seemed like too much effort. Even deviant thoughts of chocolate lost their thrill. All I wanted to do was sleep.

I did, however, break down and call Aunt Kat at her place in Paris to give her an inventory on what had been broken, though I skipped the details of how it'd happened.

"Oh, sweetheart, are you okay?" she said, her voice choppy, like she was in the middle of a massage.

"Yes, I'm fine," I lied. If I'd told her the truth, she'd be on the first plane headed home.

"Things can be replaced, Cauley Kat," she said. "You, however, are priceless."

"I think some people would disagree with you, Aunt Kat."

"Nonsense," she said. "You take that insurance money and buy whatever you like. I've told you that the bungalow is yours now. Make it your own. I'll be home soon, and I'll bring you some things from the Riviera. Do you need a new bikini, hon? They're practically made of dental floss here."

"No," I said. "No floss. But thanks."

Over the line, I heard a man's voice calling for her. "Hey," I said. "You're busy. I'll see you when you get back."

"All right," she said doubtfully. "Just remember: if you can't be a good example . . ."

"Be a terrible warning," I finished for her, and I really did smile this time.

I disconnected and went back to the couch for some serious wallowing. With the exception of the call to Aunt Kat, I ignored the phone and all my friends, getting out of bed only to feed the cat and walk the dog, who were pretty good sports about my malaise.

I woke up early on the day of the funeral feeling like I was moving through a terrible dream, and I rummaged through my closet for a black dress that didn't scream "looking to get laid." I slid into a dress, slipped my Ray-Bans over my puffy eyes, and headed downtown.

I was surprised that the service was at St. Augustine's, on Brazos, where everybody who's anybody gets married and buried. I was surprised because Scooter's death had been ruled a suicide—a big no-no in the Catholic church—and because I would have thought Scooter would've wanted his send-off at Lake Travis Methodist, where he'd been an usher for the past five years. But Selena had gone to church at St. Augustine's, and funerals are for the living, not the dead.

I slid into the adjacent parking lot of the gothic cathedral, craning my neck for a better look at the elaborate spire.

Drawing a deep breath, I tucked my purse under my arm, crossed Brazos, and ducked into the church. I pulled off my sunglasses and stood in the enormous foyer, blinking as my eyes adjusted to the darkness. Despite the cavernous hall, the scent of funeral flowers loomed like a noxious fog. Stepping around me, the bereaved filed by the little water stand, dipping their fingers and crossing themselves, and I wondered if I was supposed to do the same.

The red-carpeted aisle seemed to roll on forever. The open casket at the end gleamed under a kaleidoscope of red and gold light from the stained glass windows. In that casket was what was left of Scott Barnes. My breath hitched in my throat.

I'd just talked to him a couple of days ago. Scooter had called me that day for help. Some help I turned out to be. I should have made sure he got the kind of psychological help he needed. If I had, maybe he wouldn't be lying in a box.

Above his casket a giant Jesus loomed, nailed to a big Plexiglas cross. I couldn't bring myself to make the long journey up the aisle to see Scooter, so I slipped into a pew near the back and found myself pressed into the solid, wide shoulders of the Bug. He was solemn and bleary eyed and dressed in a very expensive suit. Probably had his own wake the night before.

As I squeezed in, the big man shifted, his expensive suit jacket making silk shushing noises as he moved.

An enormous pipe organ boomed into the silence, thundering a dirge I didn't know. On cue, prepubescent boys dressed in white robes marched somberly down the aisle, carrying an assortment of candles, golden cups, and a gilded cross.

I watched, feeling a sense of awe, of something bigger than me. Still, I felt out of place in the regimented structure of the unfamiliar service, not knowing when to stand or kneel or sit, not understanding the songs that flowed in fluid, lilting Latin.

Down front, I saw the slight form of Selena tucked next to her attorney—the one that I'd thought had been torched in a tire. Selena's tiny form shook with grief. Despite her small stature, her presence seemed to fill the auditorium.

The music rose and even though I couldn't understand the words the boys were singing, my heart swelled with the song. Next to me, the Bug's shoulders shook. I handed him a Kleenex.

"I don't get it," he said. "Scooter woulda never done nothin' like this."

"You don't think he committed suicide?"

"Nope. He woulda never left Selena this way. He loved that girl like nobody's business."

The music changed and the hair on my neck prickled. My gaze drifted around the cathedral, and I wasn't sure what I was looking for until I found it.

Seated at the pew nearest the door was Tom Logan. He was dressed in a suit, as usual, and looking like the consummate fed that he was.

My heart gave a hard thump, and I wasn't sure if I should feel better or worse. Why was he still involved with the Barnes case if Scooter was gone? On the off chance Scooter had done something wrong, wouldn't the case be closed?

If Logan was here, would other law enforcement types be scattered among the mourners? I scanned the crowd, listening hard in the litany for the sound of Fiennes' voice, looking for anything familiar in the sea of unfamiliarity.

What I did understand of the service was beautiful, and after some time, the altar boys marched solemnly back down the aisle. Slowly, throngs of the bereaved filed out after them. This, I assumed, was the end of the service.

Taking a deep breath, I slipped out of the pew and crept down the aisle toward the front of the church, a thick sense of dread building with every step. Coach and Mrs. Barnes sat quietly in front in the pew opposite of Selena, their eyes steady on the body of their only child.

I stopped, closed my eyes, and prayed for the right words.

None came.

Swallowing hard and swearing I wouldn't cry, I sank to my knees in front of them. "I am so sorry for your loss."

"I know you are, darlin'," Coach said. "You did the best you could."

I wanted to say *Fat lot of good that did anybody,* but now was not the time for self-pity. These people were Scooter's parents, and they were hurting.

At a loss, I said, "If there's anything I can do, please, let me know."

They nodded, and a tear slipped down Golly's cheek. Taking a deep breath, I looked toward the casket. Time to say goodbye.

I thought of Scooter's words as we'd talked just a few days ago in his father's shed. I hadn't taken him seriously. I could still hear his voice. *I wish I was in Hawaii.*

"Oh, Scooter," I whispered. "I'm so sorry. I wanted to help."

People always say the dead look like they're sleeping. I haven't been to many funerals and I haven't seen many dead people, but Scott Barnes did not look like he was sleeping.

He didn't look like Scott at all. His face was pale and waxen, his cheeks and lips pink with rouge. Whatever was left of Scott was not in this still, cool body, and despite all reason, I could feel his presence as though he was looking over my shoulder.

In the stillness of the cathedral, a mellifluous voice hissed behind me.

"La asesina!"

I jumped and nearly fell over into the casket.

"Murderer!"

Selena's mother stood, staring at me, her elegant face twisted beneath her black veil. "You killed him!"

Time jarred to a stop and my heart jammed in my throat.

"He has lost his soul," she said, her voice leveling as she pointed straight at my heart. "You caused this as surely as if you'd held that knife yourself."

I felt like a deer caught in headlights. I couldn't move. Couldn't speak.

Behind her, Selena made a small sound and began to sob. The woman went on. "Scott could have had help, but you interfered and now he's committed a mortal sin."

I couldn't say a thing, because it was true. Selena's mother had given voice to every thought I'd played through my mind in the past few days.

I turned to Selena. Her blue eyes were misty and blank, quiet tears running down her cheeks.

"I'm sorry," I whispered. I didn't know what else to say.

My head reeled and I felt dizzy. As I turned to leave, the red, carpeted aisle seemed twice as long, and I felt every eye on me as I made my way to the door. Behind me, I could hear Selena sobbing softly over the body of her husband.

At the back of the cathedral, Logan was leaning against the door, where he fell into step behind me. He opened the cathedral door and followed me out into another perfect Central Texas summer day. The sun outside was bright and I blinked against it.

On the front steps, Logan looked down at me. "You okay, kid?"

I looked up at him. Hot tears slipped down my cheeks. "No. And I don't think I ever will be again."

SEVENTEEN

"CAULEY? I KNOW YOU'RE in there. I saw your trash can at the curb for pickup." Mama's voice trilled through my answering machine like fingernails scraping a chalkboard.

Safely back in my bungalow, I flopped face-down on my bed with a bad case of Holly Golightly's Mean Reds. I tried whining out loud for a while, but all I managed to do was get on my own nerves.

"We haven't heard from you in over a week! If you don't pick up that phone I'm sending the Colonel over." Her voice muffled. "Stephan! *Stephan!* . . . you've got to go check on Cauley . . ."

I pulled myself out of bed and shuffled through wads of crumpled-up Puffs Plus to plop down on the sofa. Looking around at the mess made me feel even worse.

I supposed the wrath of Mama was my own fault. I'd missed church and Sunday dinner twice in a row. But I'd been very busy wallowing.

Murderer.

I'd barricaded myself in the house and spent the week in my bathrobe, eating Spaghetti-Os out of a can and watching the Shopping Channel. I ordered the Super Elite Butt Cruncher exercise machine, a real bargain because it came with a set of complimentary leatherette swimwear. I finally got my insurance check to replace the broken furniture, and the Butt Cruncher would make a dandy coat rack, since I still had sense enough to know I'd never actually use the thing.

From my bunker of blankets on the sofa, I watched friends and family do slow drive-bys every few hours. My answering machine blinked mercilessly with unanswered calls. And I just couldn't make myself care. Outside, hurricane season was in full swing. The sky was that weird color of yellow that meant a tornado or a hell of a summer storm. I was about to make a resolution to start drinking before ten when Marlowe sat up, ears pricked.

I wondered what his problem was. Then I heard a knock at the door.

"Cauley?" Mia's voice sounded like cheerful, tinkling bells on my front porch. I was not in the mood for cheerful tinkling.

"I know you're in there. Brynn was watching the Shopping Channel and heard you order that stupid Butt Cruncher."

Marlowe growled. I knew how he felt. "Go away."

A rustling sound came from the magnolia tree that shades the porch, followed by a loud *thump!*

"Ow," Mia swore, and I knew she was going for my hidden key. Within moments, Mia, Shiner, and Brynn were barging through my front door like a pack of friendly bulldozers.

Marlowe bristled, and I reached down and stroked his head.

"Hey!" Mia said brightly. "You brought your dog inside?"

"He's not my dog."

"Oh," Mia said, like I'd explained everything. "Where's Muse?"

"She doesn't like the dog," I said, and Mia nodded.

"Maybe we should do proper introductions," she said. "You know. Help them get to know each other."

I groaned.

"Hey, sistah," Shiner said and gave me the kind of bear hug that only Shiner can give. "How you doin'?"

Marlowe eyed him suspiciously.

Brynn handed me a big, beautifully wrapped box on her way to the kitchen.

"Y'all didn't have to do that," I said, opening the gift box. Two dozen blue Spanish glasses gleamed inside a cloud of tissue paper. "Oh," I said on a breath, and I felt my heart warm. Great. I was going to burst into tears. Again.

"We needed something to drink out of," Brynn said, brandishing a martini shaker. "And all your stuff is broken."

I shook my head. "I appreciate it, but I don't feel like—"

"Look," Brynn said. "What that woman said at the funeral was awful, but you can't spend the rest of your life holed up in this little house."

"I don't want to spend the rest of my life here," I said. *Just the next ten years.*

Mia flicked opened her bag with a loud *pop.*

"Are those star charts?" I said. "I don't want you doing my horoscope." I wasn't sure I could take any more gloom and doom.

"Oh, come on. You ask that stupid 8 Ball questions all the time."

"I've had that 8 Ball since I was a kid," I said defensively. I didn't necessarily believe in any of that stuff, but I wasn't sure enough to disbelieve it either.

"You know what your problem is, *chica?* Your feng doesn't shui."

"Impossible," I said. "A friend helped me move all the broken furniture out to the garage. There's no feng *left* to shui."

"A friend?" Brynn said.

"Oh, Cauley! You met somebody?" Mia perked up.

"Not really." I sighed. "He's an FBI agent. He's just doing his job."

Shiner gave me a look. "It's not an FBI agent's job to rearrange your furniture. It's his job to rough people up and arrest 'em."

"Tom Logan does not rough people up," I said. I dropped onto the sofa. "At least I don't think he does."

Mia nodded. "Probably only people who really need it."

I rolled my eyes as Mia wedged an enormous compass out of her feng shui kit. I got out of her way as she took several readings.

"I knew it. This is all wrong." Mia lit a match and set fire to a small bowl of dried twigs and flowers that smelled like feet.

"I don't think you're supposed to light potpourri," I said, but Mia had moved on. A woman on a mission.

Brynn handed me a Mexican martini, shaking her head at Mia, who appeared to be upending my couch.

"What you need is a man who's available," Brynn said, extracting her Palm from her purse.

"Look, I already have a man. Sort of."

Everyone stopped where they were. "*You* have a *man?*" Brynn said.

They all stood, staring at me. I sighed.

"His name is John Fiennes and he's a customs agent," I said, and blushed at the collective whooping. "And no, there's nothing going on."

"*Yet,*" Mia corrected. "Just wait 'til we get you feng shui-ed properly. You'll have men dropping like flies. Shiner, will you give me a hand?"

While Shiner moved what was left of the furniture into what Mia thought was a more peaceful flow, Brynn tugged the sleeve of my robe, pulling me into the bedroom.

"You are never going to get out of this funk if you don't get dressed," she said, and started tossing clothes out of my drawers. "And for God's sake. Put on some makeup."

Pulling open my lingerie drawer, she gasped and picked up a pair of my provisional, super-sized, days-of-the-week underwear. "Good gawd, Cauley. No wonder you're sulking. Come on. We're going shopping."

AFTER SPENDING WHAT I thought was a disproportionate amount of my homeowner's claim at Victoria's Secret, I felt marginally better. I also splurged on a new Coach bag and a small throw rug to replace the one that used to be in front of the juke box, and on the way home we stopped at Computer Re-Store, where Shiner helped me pick out a secondhand iBook laptop. The rest of the money I would give to Aunt Kat. Despite what she'd said, most of the stuff destroyed in the break-in was hers.

My friends finally left and I stripped, slipped back into my bathrobe, and washed the department store makeover off my face.

Slouching into the living room, I grabbed the remote. Outside the wide living-room window, storm clouds roiled on the horizon, and I still didn't care. Marlowe and I sat on the rearranged sofa.

"Do you think our feng is shui-ing now?" I said. The dog didn't answer. "Sometimes," I told the dog, "it's best to wallow alone."

Muse sat, wide-eyed, on top of the television. She hadn't started anything with the dog since Logan had broken up their fight.

I popped *Key Largo*—the quintessential storm movie—into the player and resettled on the sofa, ready to get back to some serious wallowing, when I heard Mia on the front porch.

"What now?" I said, swinging open the door to find Logan on the front step. I hadn't seen him since the funeral, so I suppose I should have been surprised.

Logan shook his head. "Don't you ever look to see who it is?"

"I thought you were somebody else," I said, moving aside so he could come in. Marlowe danced around his legs, sniffing all kinds of interesting places, like he hadn't seen Logan in a year, let alone two weeks.

"Tough luck, kid," he said and grinned as he took in my disheveled state. I wrapped the robe tighter around me.

Grimacing, he sniffed the air. "Somebody break in again?"

"No," I said. "My friends were trying to cleanse my house of evil spirits."

"Did it work?"

"Depends on how you look at it. What do you want?" I said and cringed at my snippy tone.

Logan shook his head. "You lead an interesting life, Cauley MacKinnon."

"I'm ready for *un*interesting. I was thinking of finding a nice, boring accountant, getting married, and moving to the middle of a Kansas cornfield."

Logan snorted. "Yeah. That'll happen."

"You don't think I could marry an accountant?"

"I don't think you'd be happy with a boring life."

Without asking, he settled on the sofa. I joined him and we stared at the television, where Lauren Bacall was busy slapping the living daylights out of Edward G. Robinson. The gangster looked like he was going to kill her when Bogey stepped in.

I sighed. "Do you think Bogey really loved Bacall the way everybody makes out he did?"

"I don't see why not."

I watched the screen as it flickered in black-and-white clarity. "It's a big fat fairy tale. Nobody really believes in that stuff."

Logan shrugged. "Sometimes they do."

I turned and looked at him. "I'm sure you didn't come by to watch old movies and talk philosophy."

"I told you. I heard you were having a rough time."

"Have you been spying on me?"

"Should I be?"

I narrowed my eyes.

"Yeah, you caught me," he said. "FBI agents have nothing better to do with their time than monitor civilians."

I was half thinking about smacking him when he smiled. I had to admit, he had a really great smile.

"Hey," he said. "You haven't been calling my office and harassing my secretary for information. I thought I'd come by and see if you were okay."

"And see if any big earless guys left confession notes on my doorstep?" I said.

"It was a thought."

"Nothing to worry about," I said. "I'm back to writing obituaries and off Barnes for good."

"Yeah, right."

"I mean it, Logan. You were at the funeral—you heard her. Selena's mother called me a murderer in front of God and half of Austin. She said it was my fault Scooter killed himself. It would take an act of God to get me involved again."

Logan nodded. "I don't think I'd blame myself for someone else's actions."

"Obviously you don't know me very well."

"You hear from your customs agent?"

I stared at him. He almost sounded defensive when he said that. Maybe there was hope after all.

"No," I said, trying not to smile. "Right now I'm just slothing around, feeling sorry for myself."

"Anything I can do?"

"Prove Scooter didn't kill himself."

"Easier said than done." Logan rose. "Give it some time, kid."

Thunder rolled on the horizon and lightning flashed bright through the wide living room window.

Logan looked down at me. "An act of God, huh?"

"A *specific* act of God." I pulled my robe tightly around me and walked Logan to the door, Marlowe trotting alongside. I felt miserable and cold and I was about to be alone. Again.

Looking out the door, Logan turned to me.

"Storm's getting close," he said.

I shrugged but tipped my face skyward, and I could smell the threat of rain.

Logan stepped onto the porch and turned back to me. "You need anything, you call. I'll be there."

I nodded. The problem was, I wasn't sure what I needed—but I was pretty sure I was the only one who could give it to me.

IT RAINED HARD ALL night, a genuine Texas thunderstorm, and it rocked the house to the foundation. I slept in fits and starts, and when I wasn't dreaming of exercise equipment I would never use and swimwear I would never fit into, I could hear Selena's mother's voice hissing behind me.

Murderer.

Muse slept on my head, Marlowe on my feet, and as I dozed, I wondered if the animals were the only things anchoring me to the earth. The telephone trilled, puncturing my turbulent dreams.

Lightning snapped outside my bedroom window like a brilliant whip, and I rolled over to get the receiver, knocking both the dog and cat off the bed.

"Cauley?" A woman's voice quavered over the line. Even in my dream-induced stupor, there was something familiar about that voice.

"Yes?" I sat up, blinking and wiping my face to get Muse's orange and white fur off my face.

"It's Golly Barnes. You said if you could do anything to help . . . ?"

A phone call this early in the morning from Scooter's mom? I was wide awake. "What kind of help did you have in mind?"

"We—the Coach and I—we need to talk to you."

Thunder boomed outside my bedroom window and the hair lifted on the back of my neck.

I supposed I'd found my act of God.

EIGHTEEN

GREAT. SCOOTER'S PARENTS WANTED to talk to me. The thing is, they couldn't say anything worse to me than I was already saying to myself.

I climbed out of bed, showered, blasted my hair dry and pulled it into a ponytail holder, then fed the cat and put water down for the dog.

"You're going to have to stay here," I told Marlowe, who stared at me with a pained look in his dark almond eyes.

With a growing sense of dread, I stuffed my little notebook and mini recorder into my new purse and headed for the Jeep.

I stopped just outside the front door, looking up at the thick gray sky. The rain had let up, but it had poured buckets all night, and, as usual in these cases, I'd left the top of my Jeep off. The seats were going to be soaking wet. I headed back into the house for a towel to wipe the driver's seat when Marlowe flew by in a blur of gray and white fur. He leapt into the wet passenger seat and looked at me expectantly.

"You are obnoxious," I told the dog. "It is truly no wonder that your owner hasn't come to claim you."

The dog stuck out the tip of his tongue and ignored me.

"What do you suppose Mrs. Barnes wants from me?" I said to Marlowe as I unfolded the Jeep's canvas top and struggled to snap the gigantic snaps into place.

Murderer. Selena's mother's voice echoed in the damp air.

Whatever Scooter's parents wanted, I was going to do my best to give it to them—even if what they wanted was somebody to blame.

My hands were sweaty and my throat was tight when I nosed the Jeep down Creek Road toward Paradise Falls. I felt like I'd been sucked into a time warp. The towering live oaks were the same. So were the rolling hills. The only real change was that Scooter wasn't there.

I pulled past the old white farmhouse and into the separate garage out back, just as Golly Barnes had asked.

In the past month, I'd been threatened with a knife and run into the river. I'd lost a childhood friend and been called a murderer. I supposed there were a litany of reasons why I shouldn't be sitting in the garage of the parents of a man I may or may not have helped commit suicide.

At the back of the property, the shed where I'd last seen Scooter loomed like an old wooden grave marker.

"Stay," I said to Marlowe, and I swear the dog smirked at me. It didn't matter. The canvas top was snapped onto the Jeep's frame. This time he'd have to do what I said.

I climbed out of the Jeep, my chest going tighter with each step I took toward the back of the old farmhouse. I knocked on the screen door. "Mrs. Barnes?"

Golly Barnes appeared in the doorway. She was wearing a pale blue Mexican dress, looking exactly like what she was, an aging West Texas cheerleader with a kind face and bright eyes.

"You're alone?" she said, her gaze darting along the rolling hills behind her house.

"Mrs. Barnes, are you okay?" I said, with the sinking feeling that she wasn't okay at all.

I heard a popping noise like big, industrial-sized snaps unsnapping, and in a streak of white fur, Marlowe leapt to my side.

Mrs. Barnes let out a small yelp, and I grabbed the dog by the collar. "Blast it, Marlowe! I'm really sorry, Mrs. Barnes—"

Footfalls from deep in the house rang on terra-cotta tile, and I heard the Coach's voice rumbling down the hall like the voice of God, if God had been born in Lubbock.

"Is that little Cauley?"

"Hey, Coach," I said, offering my hand when the big man rounded the corner, and he looked so much like an older version of Scooter that my breath caught. Coach stepped inside the handshake and hugged me hard. Something in my chest tightened.

"I'm really sorry about Scott," I said, fighting back tears as Coach released me. They both seemed to have aged ten years since the funeral.

"I know you are, hon," he said.

Marlowe and I followed Coach and Golly through the mudroom into the kitchen. I sat at the red Formica and chrome table, where a bulging photo album lay next to the longhorn salt-and-pepper shakers. Marlowe settled in at my feet.

Mrs. Barnes slid me a glass of iced tea with a slice of lemon, then wiped her hands on a red-checked dishtowel and sat. "At the funeral, you said if we needed anything we should call?"

I nodded.

Her lips pressed into a thin pink line and she looked at me dead-on. "We want you to find out who killed Scooter."

My heart gave a thump and I wondered what to say. I had known these people since I was a kid, ate cookies at their kitchen table, skinny-dipped in their creek. Now they were asking for my help. As a peer.

Their only child was dead and the M.E. had ruled his death a suicide. My boss' needle was pegging the patience-meter and he'd practically forbidden this line of research.

But now the Barneses sat across from me at their kitchen table, watching me expectantly.

I blew out a long breath and pulled the little Sony and notebook out of my purse. "All right." I flipped the recorder on. "What makes you think Scott was murdered?"

"Scott wouldn't have killed himself," Coach said.

Mrs. Barnes flipped open the tattered photo album and pointed to photos of Scott and Selena on their wedding day. I looked closely. Captured on crystal clear Kodachrome, Scooter was beaming as he carefully offered Selena the first bite of expensively frosted white wedding cake—no obnoxious rubbing it in her face.

I looked at Coach and Golly and didn't know what to say. Since Scooter started having problems, I'd done some research on suicide. According to the books I'd read, relatives and friends often get mired in guilt or denial.

Mrs. Barnes looked at me sharply. "He had too much to live for."

"You mean the Blue Parrot?" I took a long drink of iced tea. It was good, like Nana MacKinnon used to make.

"That little pet shop was really taking off," Coach said. "But, no. There was more."

Mrs. Barnes leaned toward me. "Selena is expecting."

I nearly dropped my iced tea.

"You mean like a baby? How do you know?"

Scooter's parents stared at me like I'd lost my last shred of decency.

"I'm sorry," I said. "I know that sounded harsh and I apologize. But you asked for my help, and I have to know what leads to follow. Did Selena see a doctor?"

"You think she's not being truthful?" Mrs. Barnes said, her eyebrows raised so high they disappeared into the fringe of her platinum bangs.

"It's just to establish a time line and a paper trail," I said carefully. "And I'll probably need to go talk to Selena."

Coach nodded. "In case we wind up in court."

"Like Matlock," Mrs. Barnes said, brightening a little.

"Yeah," I said. "Just like that. Have you told the police about this?"

I was scribbling like crazy.

"We figured Selena told them," Coach said. "They interviewed her for at least an hour and then she did that press conference."

"And then those men stopped by yesterday," Mrs. Barnes said.

I stopped scribbling. "What men?"

"Strange thing. We don't get many people out here at the ranch just stopping by, and these two fellas stopped by, 'bout forty minutes apart."

I looked up from my notebook and the Coach went on. "The first fella was some kind of foreigner, German I think. He said he was with the State Treasurer's office and he was asking about stolen property."

"German guy?" I scribbled, keenly aware that my recorder was still whirring. "What did you tell him?"

"The truth: we don't know. But soon as he left, I got on the horn and called the State Treasurer's office. They said they don't have any German fellas and they aren't working on anything that has to do with Scott."

"Good for you," I said. "This, um, German guy—was he strange in any way?"

Mrs. Barnes pressed her lips together. "He was a big man. Very pushy. And he had on a sock hat pulled way down on his head over his ears and he didn't take it off when he sat down to the table. Imagine—a sock hat in this heat," Mrs. Barnes said, tutting as she spoke.

My stomach knotted. I'd bet this month's 401K deduction that the Barnes family had just had a visit with Van Gogh.

"Did the man threaten you in any way?"

"Hell, no," Coach said. "I don't get many people offering to run me 'round the barn."

I smiled, looking at Coach's arms, which were as big around as my head. "No, I imagine you don't. Did you tell the police about this?"

"Should we have?" Mrs. Barnes said, worry deepening the gentle lines in her face.

"I think you should talk to a detective, just in case," I said. "You mentioned a second guy?"

"A customs agent," Mrs. Barnes said, and she blushed like a schoolgirl.

There was only one customs agent I knew who could make a grown woman blush. Never mind that I only knew one customs agent. Maybe they were all hot enough to start a brush fire.

"He had a bit of an accent, too," she said.

I turned to Coach. "Did you call the customs office and ask about him?"

"No," Coach said, running a large hand over his balding head. "He showed us a badge and left a card. He seemed like a stand-up guy."

"Has anybody else been by?" I asked. "Say, like an FBI agent or a man named Diego DeLeon?"

"No," Mrs. Barnes said, looking more worried by the moment.

I stared down at my notes. There was a piece missing. "Did Scooter ever mention being in trouble? Ever mention any groups or organizations?"

They both stared at me blankly.

"Nothing like, say, El Patron?"

"Oh, hell, no," Coach said. "I woulda remembered that."

"And he never mentioned storing or hiding something?"

They looked at each other blankly, then back at me. "Like what?" Coach said.

I shrugged. "He never mentioned having something that didn't belong to him?"

They stared at me.

"There's an FBI agent in town who might want to talk to you about this," I said. "He's a good guy and very good at his job. Do you mind if I give him your number?"

Tears filled Mrs. Barnes' eyes and her face went tight. "Why can't we just talk to you? This has all been so . . . awful." I heard her heart shift in her voice.

"I know," I said. "I'm sorry. But this agent, Tom Logan, he's a professional and he's a really nice guy. He'll probably ask you things I didn't think to ask, and he has resources I don't. He'll help, I promise."

Mrs. Barnes fidgeted with the hem of her dress. "Do you know him?"

"Yes," I said. "And I know his kind. He reminds me a lot of my dad, and you know I don't say that lightly."

Mrs. Barnes nodded and swallowed hard. Coach reached across the photo album and took his wife's hand.

I looked down at the album. "Would you mind if I took the photo album? I promise I'll bring it back."

Coach nodded. "We'll do whatever it takes."

"I'm going to call a friend at APD and he'll probably be by to talk to you as well," I said, closing the photo album. I flipped open my notebook and stared at my own shorthand. Something in my notes, or something missing from them, nagged at me.

"Is there anything that's been bothering you? Anything that doesn't seem to fit?"

Mrs. Barnes glanced up into her husband's eyes. "One thing has been bothering me."

I waited.

"The Blue Parrot. It's been closed. It was in Scott's will that his friend Burt Buggess would run the store with Selena as a silent partner."

I looked up from my notes. "The store's still closed? Is the crime scene tape still up?"

"No. It seems to be cleared, or whatever you call it." Mrs. Barnes shook her head. "Scooter loved that store. He would want it open, you know, for Selena. And the baby."

"Do you have a copy of the will?" I said, and Mrs. Barnes got up and went to the living room. She came back with a fresh sheaf of papers.

The will was on new paper and it was dated two months ago. My hands stilled at the significance. "Is this a copy?"

"Yes," Mrs. Barnes said. "The original is with our attorney. You can take that one, dear."

Nodding, I folded the copy of the will and tucked it into my purse. "Have y'all spoken with Selena?"

Mrs. Barnes shifted uncomfortably.

"No," Coach said. "Her family never much liked the idea of her marrying a Texas boy. They were big shots from Argentina, you know. Thought they were some kind of royalty or something. When Scooter busted his knee and left pro ball, her family lost all use for us."

Mrs. Barnes nodded. "We offered to help with the Blue Parrot, but they don't want our help."

"Who is 'they'?" I said, just to clarify.

"Selena and her mother," Mrs. Barnes said, her mouth twisted around the word "mother" like she'd bitten into a bad apple.

"Have you seen Mr. Buggess?" I said.

"Not hide nor hair," Coach said. "We tried callin' Bug at his house but it sounds like the phone's been disconnected or off the hook or some such thing."

"I've met Mr. Buggess," I said, tucking the photo album under my arm. "I'll swing by and check on him. About that customs agent. Do you still have the card he gave you?"

Mrs. Barnes blushed again and pulled the card from the pocket in her dress. I looked down at the card and tried not to smile.

"John Fiennes," I said, like I didn't already know.

"You want the card?" Mrs. Barnes said.

"That's okay," I said, giving it back. "I have one of my own."

I RE-SNAPPED THE TOP onto the Jeep. Marlowe and I hopped in, and we hit the road with a renewed sense of energy. Every time I dug into this thing, I hit either Selena or El Patron. Heading east on Texas 71, I called Cantu to tell him what I'd learned.

"You think it was your pal the earless guy that went to visit them?" Cantu said.

"You know why anybody else would wear a ski cap over his ears in hundred-degree weather?"

Cantu grunted. "I'll file it and be out to see the Barneses this afternoon. I'm sending a uniform to do drive-bys on the house."

"Thanks."

"Hey, speaking of earless—the wife of the veterinarian burn victim called. She wanted to know about when she could pick up his missing ear. Said she wanted to bury him whole."

My stomach did a slow, sickening turn. "You mean the one that was stuffed in my sofa?"

"Yeah, well, it's in forensics—the geeks are working on matching that up right now. Told the wife it was evidence," Cantu said. "Sometimes I hate this job."

"I know," I said. "That's why you're good at it."

After a long pause, Cantu said, "Cauley?"

"Yeah?"

"Be careful."

"Don't worry. I like my ears and I don't want a repeat performance of my evening in the lake. Tell Arlene I said *hey*."

I disconnected, thinking about my next step. Maybe I'd swing by the *Sentinel's* main office downtown later in the afternoon to talk to Rob Ryder. He'd done a lot of interviews with Scooter over the years, and he'd had a half a dozen bylines on El Patron. Despite the fact that the investigation on El Patron hadn't gone past the low-level guys, Ryder might have some useful insight.

Before I did anything else, I called Tanner to tell him I was taking another week off.

"You okay?" Tanner said.

"Yeah, I just need some time to get my head straight."

"And you're not nosing around on Barnes?"

"Me?" I said. "I'm an obituary writer."

"Leave it, Cauley. APD still hasn't found your bald, earless guy."

Oh, they're closer to finding Van Gogh than you think, I mused.

I made a noise in the back of my throat. "Tanner, I can't hear you. Must be a bad connection."

I disconnected and called Logan and got his voice mail. I told his machine about what I'd learned and left the elder Barnes' address and telephone number so he wouldn't have to look it up or twist arms or use thumbscrews or whatever FBI agents did when they wanted telephone numbers.

Then I took a deep breath to calm the butterflies and dialed Fiennes. I would be cool and breezy. Just another business call.

When Fiennes picked up the phone I said, "Hey, stranger, it's me, Cauley. What are you doing?" See? Calm and casual.

"Breathlessly waiting for you to call."

I almost dropped the phone. When I didn't respond, he said, "Actually, I'm at a reading."

I stared at the phone. "Like a poetry reading?"

"Non-fiction. Ian Sayer."

"A literate customs agent," I said, racking my brain for literary references on Ian Sayer and wondering why I was constantly surprised by the men in my life.

"We've got some new developments," I said.

There was a long pause. "I thought you were off Barnes."

"Yeah, I thought so, too," I said, watching through the windshield as storm clouds gathered on the horizon. "There was an act of God."

"What?"

"Never mind."

"Can you meet me at the Blue Parrot at nine tonight?"

I glanced at the clock glued to the dash. Nine would be cutting it close, but it would give me a good excuse to cut my interview with Ryder short. "Sure," I said. "I'll call if I'm going to be late."

"Nine, then," he said. "And Cauley?"

"Yeah?"

"Wear black."

I stared at the phone. "For profession or pleasure?"

"Who says we can't have both?"

NINETEEN

I WAS IN A time crunch, and as usual, I was running late. Rush hour these days starts at four and doesn't trickle off until seven. If I was going to meet John at nine, I was going to have to haul ass.

I dropped Marlowe at home, and after a brief altercation over who was boss and a big distraction involving a ham sandwich, I zoomed downtown. I nearly swore when I hit Loop One just before afternoon crush and sat in traffic for nearly an hour. Lots of people visit Austin; no one seems to leave.

I pulled onto Congress Avenue and slid into the parking garage at the *Sentinel's* main office, squared my shoulders, and marched through the revolving doors of the sprawling, Lloyd-Wright-looking *Sentinel* building. I badged the security guard, signed in, and headed for Editorial on the fifth floor, armed with the yellow pad with dates and headlines that Logan and I had pieced together. The Barneses had asked me to find the truth about what happened to their son, and I was prepared to resort to drastic measures.

"Well, if it isn't the Obituary Babe."

I didn't have to find my drastic measure. It found me.

Rob Ryder came sauntering down the hall, carefully rumpled in that annoying polo the way that only a real News Boy can master. His blue shirt matched his eyes, his shirtsleeves were rolled up, and his trendy tie was carefully askew. Ryder's one of those rare breeds of male who can talk most women out of their panties and purse and make them feel like he'd done them a favor.

He stood in the spacious, carpeted hall, looking at me. He had a file tucked under one arm and he was eating an apple.

"Hello, Ryder," I said. "Still seeing Miranda?"

He laughed like I was being ridiculous. "What brings you to the corporate jungle?"

I smiled winsomely, stopping just short of batting my eyelashes. Two could play the charm game. "Just tying up some loose ends. Hey—you still have your notes on El Patron?"

Ryder's eyes sparked as he tried to figure out how to play me. "El Patron?" he drawled like he was thinking it over. "You were on that one for a while, too, weren't you?"

"Strictly research. I hit a dead end and got reassigned."

"I think I still have some notes and interviews," he said, his eyes narrowed. "Want to see?"

Did I.

"Yeah," I said, trying to sound bored. "What I really need are solid dates. I've got a list of approximates. The other stuff I can look up in the Morgue."

"Resource Recovery?" he said. He stopped walking, giving me his full attention. "Why aren't you using your own office?"

"Long story."

He nodded, and I could practically hear his brain churning as he tried to work an angle. "I was about to knock off for the day, but I could stay for you. Need some help?"

I narrowed my eyes.

"Now, Cauley," he said, sliding an arm around my shoulders so that his file folder brushed my waist. "We work for the same paper. We're on the same team."

Journalists guard information the way a pit bull guards a pork chop—especially when they're on the same team. I didn't want Ryder horning in on me. But I needed to pump him for information, a sort of informal interview.

Drastic measures.

"Yeah," I said. "Help would be great."

UNTANGLING MYSELF FROM HIS grip, I followed Ryder through the cavernous hallway back to his office, where his Texas Press Association awards gleamed neatly on the wall behind his European-style desk. An air purifier hummed quietly in the corner and a state-of-the-art police scanner buzzed quietly from the sleek bookshelf.

Suddenly, my inner Lauren Bacall surfaced, and I could see myself leaning back in this glass and chrome office, wearing a short black skirt that could make a bishop kick out a stained glass window, my feet kicked up in a perfect pair of red Manolos, a pearl-handled pistol perched next to my Remie Scout typewriter. Where's Raymond Chandler when you need him?

The view from his office was exquisite. Downtown Austin, complete with glittering glass cityscape and the sparkling blue ribbon of Town Lake. I supposed this is what your office is supposed to look like when you grow up.

Ryder moved behind his desk, ruining a perfectly good daydream. He caught my gaze and took a loud, obnoxious bite of the apple he'd been carrying, which I assumed was supposed to be sexy.

"Want a bite?" he said, holding the apple out to me, so close to my nose I could smell ripe fruit and expensive aftershave.

I wanted to say *I wouldn't eat after you if I was armed with a Kevlar vest and a can of Raid,* but I said, "No, thanks. I already ate."

"Suit yourself," he said, and tossed the rest of the apple through a miniature chrome basketball hoop over a shiny chrome wastebasket.

Ryder booted up a very expensive computer and I stood behind him, peering over his shoulder at the screen as he logged on and ran a Lexis-Nexis search for El Patron. I wanted to tap my foot and yell, "Oh, for the love of God, will you just hurry?" but letting him in on the urgency would cue him to just how important this project was. The search didn't take long, but Ryder's screen saver flashed as the hard drive whirred, and a photo of Ryder and a well-built blond frolicking on a sunny beach flashed into view. I rolled my eyes.

I supposed there were worse things in life than spending an afternoon with Rob Ryder. I would rate it somewhere between roasting in hell and rubbing my knuckles on a cheese grater.

But Mark Ramsey had taught me to start an investigation with people who'd walked the scene before you got there. And the people who walked the scene first were cops and news hounds. I stared steadily at Ryder. I hadn't handled anything right since I'd set foot in that shed, and I was determined to get it right, even if it meant rubbing noses with the devil.

"El Patron came to Texas through Argentina, and what's interesting is that they're more of an old-style family business. They buy up vulnerable businesses—you know, bars, restaurants, and car washes—wring 'em for everything they're worth, and then torch 'em for insurance, but occasionally they keep 'em around to clean the money," Ryder said. "I think they also do some small-time corporate takeover stuff and use the legitimate businesses to cover some of their more shady dealings."

"Like smuggling?"

"Peripherally they've been busted twice for smuggling—small-time stuff through a dirty shipping company name of Herrera Shipping. Some guns and dope that landed in northeast Austin via Buenos Aires. The feds pulled Herrera apart at the seams. But the long arm of the law never went above El Patron's low-level guys. When El Patron ran into trouble with Herrera, they shut that down and took over a little mom-and-pop shipping company, CenTex Distribution, and I guess it's legit. It's still up and running."

"Shipping." I thought about Scooter's exotic pet shop. "Did the old shipping service ever get busted for smuggling animals?"

"Animals? Not that I ever found. I tried to change the angle of the story during the last pitch meeting." He gazed out the wide windows overlooking downtown Austin. "There's something there, I can smell it."

"You got yanked off the assignment?"

Ryder scowled. "It was a mutual agreement." Turning back to his desk, he pulled up an Excel program filled with interview dates, times, and information. They were all color-coded and in alphabetical order. I stood, staring at the screen.

"Do you do this with all your interviews?" I said. I couldn't have been more awestruck if the man had just told me he was double jointed.

"Of course. How do you organize your data?"

There was no way to say "In a great big pile on my living room floor" and still look professional, so I said, "I'm in the process of developing my own system."

Ryder grinned. "You gonna tell me what this is all about?"

I had to tell him something. He was, after all, helping me. I knew if I told him the whole truth, the rat bastard would try to scoop me. But I had a couple of things going for me, and it would take Ryder a long time to trump an FBI agent, a customs guy, and the entire Barnes family. Not to mention an up-close and personal relationship with an earless maniac who wanted me dead. You just can't cultivate better sources than mine.

I blew out a long breath. "I don't think Scott Barnes committed suicide," I said, and watched as Ryder's face remained carefully composed. He blinked rapidly, but otherwise showed no outward sign that he wanted to turn cartwheels in the middle of his office.

"And you think he's tied to El Patron?"

"I don't have proof," I said.

Ryder adjusted his tie, never breaking eye contact. "What makes you think there's a connection?"

"Nothing concrete. But every time I dig around in the Barnes thing, I keep running into El Patron. I don't think it's a coincidence that Barnes called me the morning he holed up in the shed. He was my friend. He knew I'd done some of the legwork for your articles on El Patron."

"And you don't think Barnes committed suicide?"

"I've got some German guy chasing me around, threatening to chop off my ears if I don't tell him what Scooter said in the shed—which was the last time anybody saw him alive in public."

Ryder tried to contain his excitement and almost succeeded. "Oh yeah? What did Barnes tell you?"

"That's the bitch of it. He didn't tell me anything."

"Why didn't I hear about the German guy on the scanner or see it in the beat report?"

"Cantu came to get me off the clock so the initial incident didn't make the scanner, and you probably didn't know what to look for in the beat report."

Ryder looked at me the way my mom looks at the expiration date on questionable lunchmeat, but he pulled up another Excel document, did a couple of merges, and created a new document. He hit *print* and pulled the three documents from his laser printer.

"You want to access the Morgue from my computer?"

My fingers itched at the thought of skimming across that ergonomically correct keyboard. But every document that crosses a screen is accessible in the hard drive, even if you delete it. And the *Sentinel* had a battalion of computer geeks who had wet dreams over that kind of thing. It would be just like Ryder to cyber-siphon my research.

"Um," I stalled. "I need outside resources."

He frowned. "Outside Lexis-Nexis?"

"I want pictures," I said. "I'm heading to the main library."

"Hold up," Ryder said, grabbing his expensive leather messenger bag. "I'll go with you."

I GOT A SINKING feeling as Ryder followed me down Congress to Seventh and onto Guadalupe, but it was still a free country and I couldn't stop him from tagging along. I could, however, fake, deceive, and downright lie if it came down to him horning in on my research. Besides, he'd worked this thread longer than I had. Maybe I could learn something.

Armed with the dates of pertinent articles, Ryder followed me up to the second floor of the main library, where the city archived magazines, newspapers, and other bits of obscure information on outdated microfiche. I stopped at the top of the stairs and breathed deeply of historic headlines and the peppery smell of vintage paper. I just love libraries. I wanted to linger, but I was on a tight schedule.

Settling in next to the big metal file cabinets, I browsed through the notes I'd taken when Logan and I had reconstructed my original stolen Barnes file. I'd also brainstormed names of reporters and approximate dates for a timeline, which I added to the dates Ryder and I'd found in his Excel documents.

I pulled microfiche according to date, skimming the teasers under the projector. Anything related to Scooter's marriage, social obligations, and charity functions would be in the society pages, football and the knee injury in sports, pet shop in business. Anything on El Patron would most likely be state/metro, since there hadn't been any big federal breakthroughs on the growing crime syndicate.

Ryder had a file drawer out, doing his own search. Staring at me with a practiced lascivious stare, he said, "Hey, Cauley. How come you and I never . . . you know?"

"Because I have taste," I said, zipping through files.

"You ever thought about how beautiful our kids would be?"

"Every waking moment," I said. The machine rattled and I squinted at the flying typefaces on the microfiche, scrutinizing until my eyes hurt. I glanced up at the clock. I was supposed to meet Fiennes in two hours.

"I'll get the articles I wrote; I know where they are," Ryder said. He moved to a nearby aisle as I flipped madly though metro sections in papers dated close to the dates I'd written down.

I found an article on El Patron that Ryder hadn't written, pulled some change out of my pocket and made a copy, then thumbed through the rest of the fiche I'd retrieved. If I could make copies and spread it out on my living room floor, I could look for connections.

"Hey, Cauley, you got any change?" Ryder said, and as I dug into my jeans for a coin something hit me like a runaway delivery truck.

The coin.

"Ryder," I said. "Didn't you write an article about some rare coins found in Bastrop? Auschwitz Eagle or something."

Ryder stopped rifling through files. "*Anschluss* Eagle," he said. "Why?"

"Just curious. What's so hot about this coin?" I said, trying to look innocent, which is harder than it sounds.

"There were only nine-hundred-ninety-nine minted," he said, "but what makes them valuable is that they were cast by an Austrian jeweler in Anschluss the day the Nazis marched into Vienna."

I got a sick feeling in my stomach. "You're saying those coins are Nazi gold?"

Ryder shrugged. "In a manner of speaking. They found a small jar of the coins buried out behind a vet clinic in Bastrop."

"You're kidding. How on earth did they find it?"

Ryder grinned. "The guy's wife saw him buckle-rubbing with some big girl in a honky-tonk and dimed him out."

"Don't mess with Texas women," I said, but I was thinking about the coin Scooter had given me, which was now languishing on the bottom of Lake Austin, and wished I'd gotten a better look at it. Could that coin have been one of those weird eagle coins? It had to be, and the connection between the Bastrop veterinarian couldn't be a coincidence. And if Scooter had something to do with stashing those coins, it explained why everybody and his brother wanted to chop my ears off to find out what Scooter told me in the shed.

"Can I have a copy of that?" I said. Trying not to look excited, I went back to my microfiche, watching Ryder in my peripheral vision.

Just when I didn't think I could look at another article on hydrilla weeds invading Lake Austin, I found what I'd come for. It was an article in an old copy of the *Journal*, depicting the grand reopening of the Blue Parrot.

"Local Pet Store Goes Wild with Exotic Animals," the headline read. I peered into the monitor. *There was something about that photograph . . .*

Selena and her mother stood center stage in the photo, behind a big, red grand opening ribbon. They looked very slim and very blond, like a pair of European aristocrats you see in those old movie reels on Turner Classics. Standing next to each other, Selena seemed like a scanned copy of her mother: the same, but smaller and less defined, a little blurry around the edges.

Mother and daughter held the ceremonial scissors, smiling perfect publicity smiles. Selena's attorney stood between them, looking like a bespectacled, love-struck ferret. Selena's father stood a little off-center, dark and handsome and almost out of camera range, looking like an obsolete conquistador.

Scooter was standing in the back, near the door, with Sam perched on his forearm.

Interesting. I remembered the article of the grand opening with the Chamber of Commerce, back when the shop sold regular old dog food and held Humane Society pet adoption days under a tent in the parking lot. And I remembered thinking it was odd that Selena's mother wasn't in that picture. Neither was Selena.

Quietly, I made a copy of the microfiche article, folded it, and slipped the copy into my pocket before filing the fiche back in place. I nearly jumped out of my skin when Ryder rounded the corner.

"Mother lode," he said, waving a stack of sports and lifestyle copies at me.

"I need to get going," I said.

Ryder eyed me for a long moment. "You're not going to tell me what this is really about?"

"I already told you. I don't think Scooter's death was a suicide." I scooped up the last of my fiche and the articles I'd copied on Scooter's signing contract, his marriage to Selena, and his knee injury.

"Because some German guy threatened you?"

"Yep."

"And somebody said something about some obscure coin?"

I smiled.

Ryder stopped rustling through his copies and looked at me hard. "What did Barnes really tell you in that shed?"

"Just what I told you," I said, finishing up my copies. "He didn't say anything. Look, thanks for your help, but I really gotta run."

Ryder nodded. "Would you tell me if he had said something?"

I grinned. "Probably not. But thanks for your help."

Ryder laughed and shook his head, rifling through my stack of discarded fiche. "Now that I know what I'm looking for, I'll scoop *you*, you know."

"I know you'll try," I said, and headed for the stairs to keep a date with a certain customs agent who happened to look like James Bond.

TWENTY

Outside, the warring weather fronts had called a truce, so it wasn't raining, but the skies were a thick, iron gray and the streets were slick with drizzle. Driving in the rain in Austin is a full-contact sport. I ducked and dodged and slid through traffic, and it took me more than an hour to get home.

I fed the dog and cat and went back to my bedroom, where I yanked on a black tank top. The black jeans were a problem. I hadn't worn them since winter, and I had to shimmy into them, plopping back on my bed and sucking in a breath to get them zipped. Time to get back to the gym.

I slipped on a black pair of Prada riding boots, the only black shoe-type apparel I owned with less than three-inch heels. Besides, they were really great boots. I shoved my hair into a ponytail, ran some lipstick over my lips—no sense seeing the hot customs guy with chapped lips—popped a fresh tape in the mini recorder and I was ready to go.

In the kitchen, Muse lounged on the counter, twitching the tip of her tail as I filled her champagne glass with water. Marlowe trotted around the corner with his leash.

"Oh, no, buddy, can you hold it? I'm already running late."

The dog trotted to the door, shifting from paw to paw.

"Ahhhhh! All right, but please hurry!"

I took the dog-slobbered, broken leash from his mouth and snapped it to his collar, then rushed him over to the Bobs', where he promptly peed on the rosemary bush. I coaxed the dog back into the house, bribed him with the rest of Shiner's ham, jumped in the Jeep and hauled ass. I really hate being late. Amazing how often I am.

I squealed into the parking lot at the Blue Parrot about a quarter after nine. The lot was deserted, the windows in the pet shop were dark. A *closed* sign hung in the front door, just as Scooter's parents had said.

I looked around and caught sight of Fiennes. He was dressed in black chinos, a long-sleeved black polo shirt, and black leather jacket, leaning against his BMW in the restaurant parking lot next door. My heart stuttered.

I couldn't see it, but I knew he had the big, rhino-killing Desert Eagle tucked in his waistband. I'd never seen a spy, but I bet they looked a lot like Fiennes.

He motioned, and I nosed the Jeep into the next lot. I shoved my purse beneath the seat and climbed out, my black jeans catching on the door latch. I unhooked myself from the door latch and nearly fell over. *Way to go, Grace.* Somehow I always managed to look like an idiot when I was within ten feet of this guy.

The evening air was wet and it felt like breathing warm water. Luckily, I still had the canvas top on the Jeep in deference to the threat of rain.

"Emma Peel, as I live and breathe," he said, his gaze running from the tips of my boots to the scoop of my tank top.

"What?" I said, flushing as I tugged up on the top, which was cut lower than I remembered.

"*The Avengers.* I thought all Americans watched too much television." He reached into the back seat of the BMW and extracted a black leather bag.

"You're American, too," I said, still tugging. "Besides. *The Avengers* were British."

"My mistake. Do you own a watch, Cauley?"

I looked down at my bare wrist. "I have a watch. Somewhere."

"Watches only work when you wear them."

"Sorry about the late thing. Extenuating circumstances." I didn't feel compelled to say, *The dog who lives with me had to pee.*

"I'm prepared to finish this, whatever it takes, Cauley," he said. "Are you?"

My heart skipped a beat. Whatever it took? Was this going to get dangerous? Despite the damp heat of the evening, I shivered and nodded.

Fiennes grinned in the darkness. "Come on, then."

"Is this legal?" I said as we skulked toward the back of the pet store, staying close to the building and getting pricked and poked by the boxwood bushes.

"Didn't you break in here once before?"

"Yeah," I said. "I had a bad feeling about it then, and I have a bad feeling about it now."

As we rounded the corner, I stopped, staring at the window I'd broken two weeks ago. Someone had boarded it up with heavy plywood and tacked it with enough nails to restock a small hardware store. I'd been in such a hurry to meet Fiennes that it hadn't occurred to me I was going back to the place where I'd found my friend dead.

An image of Scooter slumped over his computer hit me hard. Suddenly, my feet felt heavy and I couldn't move. Fiennes turned to look at me.

"Hey." He slipped an arm around my waist. "Are you all right?"

I nodded. I think it was a nod.

"This was a mistake," Fiennes said, sounding very European. "You must go back to the car and wait for me. I will go through the records and return."

I shook my head, swallowing hard. "What exactly are we looking for?"

"Documented import activities. Anything that looks out of place. You were Mr. Barnes' friend. I thought perhaps you might know where to look."

"You want me to help you find proof my friend did something illegal?"

"You must trust me on this, Cauley. I am not out to destroy the memory of your friend."

"And this will prove Scott didn't kill himself?"

"It could."

His arm was still around me and I could feel the heat of his body through his open jacket, and my whole body warmed. He was treating me as an equal. Like a partner.

"I'm okay," I said. "I can do this."

I looked at the boarded window and felt my stomach slide. "Just promise me this will turn out all right."

Fiennes looked at me. "That is a promise I cannot make."

FIENNES SNAPPED ON LATEX gloves and handed a pair to me.

I blinked. "Federal agents wear rubber gloves?"

"Federal agents don't usually allow citizens to . . . how did you say it, *tag along?*"

"Yeah, I like that about you," I said and worked the rubber gloves onto my hands. I stood outside the back door as Fiennes flipped open his bag and pulled out what looked like one of those leather travel-manicure kits.

I felt like I wasn't contributing much to this endeavor. "When I busted into the shop last time there was no alarm," I said, trying to be helpful.

Fiennes looked up from the knob. "I know."

"Fine. I'll be quiet," I said.

He extracted two small, slim tools and slipped them into the lock. Within moments, he turned the knob and the back door swung open.

Swallowing hard, I followed Fiennes into the Blue Parrot.

The silence was the first thing that hit me. No scurrying of tiny paws, no fluttering of feathers. I went to flip on a light and Fiennes covered my hand.

"No lights," he said.

He removed a large, heavy-looking flashlight, just like Cantu always wears in his utility belt, and hit the button. But his beam illuminated a triangular patch of red on the floor and he searched the place like a television cop. He ran the beam along the high ceilings, careful to avoid the windows, and down, through the cages. All open, all empty. There was no Sam snapping his beak by the cash register, no slithering snakes in large aquariums.

"This isn't right," I said. "There's a guy, Burt Buggess—he helps look after the animals."

"I would ask for my money back."

"It's not like that. The Bug would be horrified. I'm going to call him," I said, pulling my cell from my back pocket.

"Later," Fiennes said. "Office?"

Shoving down the queasiness threatening to come up my throat, I pointed. Fiennes motioned for me to follow.

The office door was open, the computer quiet in the darkness. There was no blood, but I could feel Scooter's presence in his absence.

"Notice anything missing?"

I stared at the empty chair. "You mean besides Scooter?"

I made a wide path around Scooter's chair, trying to keep my mind in the present. The oak desk was still under the window. Telephone, green-shaded banker's lamp, and computer undisturbed on the desktop.

Fiennes moved past the desk, rifling through drawers, running his hands beneath them.

"What are you doing?"

"Checking for documents taped beneath the drawers and behind furniture."

"Oh," I said, making a mental note to remember that. He searched behind photos and in, above, and behind the bookshelf. His efficiency was astonishing.

"What are we looking for?"

He turned to the bank of file cabinets and began pulling open drawers. "Anything unusual." He stopped and looked at me. "Someone has been through these files."

I shrugged. "Crime scene techs go over everything."

"Not in this manner."

I peered into the long file drawer and ran my fingers along the gaps between files.

"Look," he said, shining the red beam on the folder tabs. "All of these bills of lading are domestic." He pulled several sheets from each file and shoved them into a manila envelope.

"I don't understand." I shook my head. "There should be foreign bills of lading. Scooter was importing animals from other countries. The Bug told me so. He said some of the animals got here in really bad shape."

Fiennes raised a brow. "Why would forensic techs take only foreign bills of lading?"

"Maybe the FBI took them."

Fiennes stiffened, but he didn't comment. I sighed. Boys and their agency pissing matches.

Fiennes moved toward the bookcase, where he began pulling books, flipping through pages. I stood next to him, watching as he pulled book after book, but one caught my eye. I slid a book titled *Living in Buenos Aires* off the shelf and frowned.

"Buenos Aires," I said, almost to myself. Fiennes pivoted and glared at me. He took the book from me, a little rougher than I thought necessary, and flipped through the pages.

"Nothing here," he said without looking up from the book. "Mr. Barnes was your friend. Perhaps you must search the desk." He shoved the book back on the shelf.

Wow. Touchy. I turned toward the desk and stopped. A wave of nausea rolled through me, but I moved the chair and searched the desktop, feeling Scooter's presence like a third person in the room. I hit the *play* button on the answering machine.

"You've reached the Blue Parrot." My breath caught at the sound of Scooter's voice.

On the recording, another voice sounded. "Leave-a-number. Leave-a-number," Sam's tinny voice trilled.

I laughed, and for a moment thought I was going to cry, too. Pulling out a pen and my notebook, I scribbled as the tape whirred. Three hang-ups, two calls about pet food deliveries, and a message from Scooter's parents.

"Scott, where are you? Please call us, hon. We're worried about you." My throat tightened. The message was from the day before Scott's death. I took a deep breath. *Keep it together, Cauley. You've got work to do . . .*

I scrolled through caller ID, writing down numbers, then turned the machine upside down and scribbled the code for remote message retrieval in case I wanted to listen again later.

Picking up the phone, I hit *redial* to see what the last number dialed was and got a disconnect signal.

Turning, I noticed Fiennes staring at me.

"You surprise me, Mrs. Peel."

I sighed. "My father was a detective, Mr. Bond."

I stood in front of the computer, not wanting to sit in Scooter's chair. Booting up the computer, I turned to the disk holder. "Hey," I said. "All the disks are gone."

I ran a few search functions on the computer, looking for document titles that might mean something, then ran a reverse search for documents created between Scooter's first incident and his death.

I felt a soft bump at the back of my legs.

"A chair from the lobby," John said, then stood behind me, his face illuminated in the blue light of the monitor. I nodded and sat.

"Come on, Scooter, talk to me," I whispered, clicking through documents in his *Favorites* folder.

Files buzzed across the screen as I did a hidden-folder search through the C drive. And there it was: a hidden file. It was marked *Hawaii*.

"Oh, Scooter," I said aloud, thinking of the same name on the file on my own desktop at work.

I jumped at the sound of metal clattering in the alley.

"*Jesus,*" Fiennes growled. He whirled and had his gun out, its muzzle glinting blue in the near darkness.

"Shit!" I said.

"We must get out of here."

More fumbling in the alley, then glass shattered at the back of the store, and a soft thud, as though someone had just landed on the linoleum.

My heartbeat kicked to three thousand b.p.m. and my hands shook as my fingers tapped the keyboard.

"This is it, I know it!" I whispered, reaching into the holder for a disk. And then I remembered that there were no disks. "Shit, shit!"

I heard the leather bag rumple, and Fiennes smacked a disk into my hand.

"Jesus, John, what are you, a Boy Scout?"

"Something like that. Hurry."

"I can't copy the file. It must be protected."

Fiennes slid in behind me, popping a fresh disk and a CD into the drives. The motor whirred and ground, and the monitor flashed like a strobe.

I stared at him. "Are you deleting the hard drive?"

He glanced toward the door. The sound of leather soles slapping linoleum sounded through the maze of cages.

They were heading toward the office.

"We must get out. Now!"

"What the hell are you doing, John?" I hissed, reaching for the keyboard. "That's evidence! What you're doing is against the law!"

"Ms. MacKinnon, you will find that I don't always play by the rules." He popped the disk out and left the CD in the drive. Then he shoved open the window, picked me up, and dumped me over the edge.

The breath slammed out of my lungs as I landed with a *whump* on all fours, the force of the impact shooting through my palms and knees. Fiennes landed lightly on his feet beside me, his hair perfect, bag in hand, the big envelope tucked in the crook of his arm. If I could've caught my breath, I'd have tripped him.

"Go!" He grabbed me by the arm and propelled me toward the Jeep.

"What about your car?"

"It's a rental. I'll send someone," he said, climbing into the Jeep. "Drive."

My hands were shaking when I jammed the key into the ignition. Nothing.

"Dammit!" I hissed, and turned the key again. The engine sputtered to life.

"Go!" Fiennes yelled, and I did.

The Jeep almost tipped as we took the corner and tore out of the parking lot. My mouth was dry, my heart pounded in my ears, and my knuckles were white on the steering wheel as we sped through the night.

"Who in the hell were they?"

"I told you, Cauley. There are dangerous men about."

Like that explained anything. "Shouldn't we at least call the police?"

"Do you want them to know you were with me on a federal investigation?"

We roared down the winding road, where tidy homes with manicured lawns zipped by in my peripheral vision. Inside, people were settling down for the night, watching the ten o'clock news. Probably none of them were worrying about earless bald guys slicing them into tiny pieces.

Suddenly, I was aware of a warm hand on my knee.

"You all right?" Fiennes said.

I stared through the windshield beyond the beam of the headlights into the overwhelming darkness and wondered what Tom Logan was doing tonight. Probably out doing what he did best. His job.

"Yeah," I said. "I'm as okay as I'm ever going to be."

I'D LEFT THE LIVING room light on and I could see Marlowe and Muse standing on the back of the sofa, staring out the wide front window.

"Your dog is inside," Fiennes said, tugging his leather bag from the cargo area of my Jeep. "Glad to see you are taking my advice."

"He's not my dog." I slipped the key in the lock and swung into the house, Fiennes right behind me.

Marlowe did his growling-snuffling routine while Muse streaked beneath the sofa. With attack animals like these, it was a good thing Fiennes wasn't some hardened criminal hell-bent on stealing whatever was left of my virtue.

I tossed my purse on the counter and the floor seemed to shift as the events of the evening caught up with me. I wasn't sure if I wanted to laugh or cry.

"You all right?"

"I don't know. We broke into Scooter's office," I said, trying to control the tremor in my voice.

"Come here," he said, and pulled me close. "You did good."

I nodded, but I wasn't so sure either one of us had done a good thing.

Tucking a loose strand of hair behind my ear, he said, "Well, Mrs. Peel. You must go change your clothes. You will feel much better. Can I get you something to drink?"

I nodded and walked woodenly down the hall, through the bedroom to the back bathroom, where I splashed cold water on my face. Leaning over the sink, I took a good, long look in the mirror.

"What in the hell are you doing?" I said to my reflection. "You just ransacked the office of your dead friend, probably committed at least three felonies, and now there's a hot customs agent sitting in your living room and your adrenaline is thumping like double-struck lightning. No good can come of this."

My reflection had no answer.

"Doesn't matter," I said. "We're going to finish this, and with the day I've had, I just don't care."

I dried my face, shook my hair out of the ponytail and stripped, changing into a comfortable old football jersey and a pair of shorts. Taking a deep breath, I psyched myself up to get down to business.

So what if John Fiennes was in my living room and every time I was around him it felt like the air was on fire? I could be calm. Casual. This was really no big deal.

I heard Marlowe growl. In the foyer, Fiennes was at the door where a young, blond guy with a body like a gymnast handed him a set of keys. I stared at the younger man.

Please, God, don't let Fiennes be gay.

"Friend of yours?" I said as the guy did a crisp military turn and disappeared.

"He brought me my car." Fiennes turned to look at me as I padded down the hall. "Nice shirt. From a boyfriend?"

I pulled at the fraying hem of the jersey. "Yeah, but it's old."

"Perhaps you should get a new boyfriend."

"Seems like a lot of trouble just to get a new shirt."

Fiennes chuckled, taking the Desert Eagle from his waistband to lay it on the end table. He retrieved a bottle of wine from his bag.

I stared at him. "Mr. Bond, is there anything you're not prepared for?"

"Don't ask the question if you don't want the answer. And please, call me John."

I took the bottle to the kitchen and poured two glasses of the rich red wine while he extracted the pirated disk from his pocket.

I held the glass out to him. He held the crystal by the stem, closed his eyes, and inhaled deeply. He looked very suave, unlike Diego DeLeon, who looked very stupid.

John set the glass on the end table next to his gun and pulled a black case the size of a trade paperback out of his bag.

"If that's one of those new laptops, I'm going to have to kill you."

"Do you have a gun?"

"No," I said. "If someone wants to kill me, they're going to have to bring their own gun."

"In that case, it's better than a laptop. It's a Tablet PC."

"With a satellite uplink?"

He grinned. "Maybe if you're a good girl Santa will bring you one for Christmas."

I was dead tired with all the adrenaline ebbing out of my body, but I couldn't help smiling back. "I've never been that good. Here. Hold this," I said, handing him my wineglass.

I headed to my little library to get the big white envelope and files I'd gathered that afternoon, then brought them back and dumped them on the living room floor. "I didn't have time to organize these."

"I see that."

"I reconstructed the file that was stolen when those bastards broke into my house as best I could." I stared down at the pile. "It includes some information I didn't have before."

John offered me my wineglass. "All right, then," he said, gently pulling my hand so that I sank down next to him. "Let's see what you've got."

TWENTY-ONE

THE WIND HAD PICKED up and lightning crackled on the horizon. Two and a half glasses of wine later, I was feeling much better, despite the fact that my cheeks were numb and I couldn't feel my ears.

"Here's what we have," I said. John and I were camped out on my living room floor where I organized copies, news clippings, Post-it Notes, and scraps of paper while he fiddled with his uber-computer.

"I've arranged it all by timeline, just for organizational purposes," I went on, ignoring the frown on his face and his increasing agitation with his computer.

I got up for a legal pad, then dropped down beside him, thinking aloud as I jotted notes of dates and descriptions in my own illegible brand of shorthand.

"High school football, his scholarship records. Transcripts from UT, his short-lived contract with the Cowboys, along with the papers they'd filed when they let him go. Documents on his marriage to Selena, medical records on his knee injury, financial information on the pet store, and the news clippings on the revamping of said pet store," I said, looking at Scooter's life, which was spread out on my living room floor. I wondered what my life would look like, spread out on little scraps of paper like that.

"Damn it," John swore, and I thought he was going to throw his little computer across the room. "The file is locked."

"We just copied that file," I said. "How could we copy a locked file?"

"We had a security disk when we copied it."

"Which we left in the computer to erase the hard drive. Y'all have software that'll copy locked files and erase an entire hard drive?"

"I could tell you, but then I'd have to kill you."

I looked at him to make sure he was kidding as he double-clicked the Hawaii icon. A password screen popped up on the monitor.

"If we'd had more time I could have copied the key codes," he said.

"Hey," I said, scooting closer to him. "Can I see that for a second?"

John handed me the computer, a little more roughly than necessary, I thought. I typed in *Selena* and got squat. I typed in *Obregon, Golly,* and *Coach.* I typed in *Dallas* and *Cowboys* and the number *24,* Scooter's jersey number, as well as all sorts of variations, all with the same results. Squat. I thought about the things that were important to Scooter, the things that were bothering him . . .

Closing my eyes, I replayed that day in my mind from the moment I'd crawled into the shed.

Did you know miners used to take birds with 'em down into the mine shafts?

"Sam," I said aloud. "No way. It can't be that easy." But then, as much as I liked him, Scooter was no MENSA candidate.

"What?" Fiennes said.

"We're still sharing information, right?"

"Of course," he said, and I moved a little closer.

"Sam," I said again, and typed in the name of the bird.

The computer made a cartoonish wilting noise and the screen went blank.

John stared at me. "You broke my computer?"

I gaped at the blank screen. *Oh, dear God. I broke a piece of government property in front of a government agent.*

I jumped when a high-pitched squeal emitted from the hard drive. The screen saver went into a psychedelic cyber-spin. An image of Sam appeared, his blue wings spread wide, and it morphed into a photo of Selena at the Miss Texas Pageant. A recorded version of Sam's shriek filled the room, and Marlowe leapt to his feet.

"What the hell?" John said.

"I think we found our password," I said.

"Clever girl," he said. "Cauley, I could kiss you."

I nearly fell over when he did.

It was a friendly little kiss, but it brushed my cheek near my ear and sent sparks skittering to some under-used parts of my body.

Marlowe let out a low growl.

"Oh, hush," I said.

The dog cast a disgusted look at both of us, then padded down the hall and into the bedroom, grumbling all the way.

"Cauley, you're a genius," he said, and I sat, synapses misfiring, as he turned back to his computer.

I cleared my throat. "Find anything interesting?"

"*Zorrita*," he said, and I moved closer. He double-clicked the file inside the file.

"It means *little fox*," I said.

"In this case I believe it means *vixen*," he said.

"Vixen?" I said, my brain stammering around the word. I looked at John. "Spanish is one of your five languages. But did you know that was Scooter's nickname for Selena?"

John's hands stilled over the keyboard and he looked at me. "That I did not know."

His fingers flew across the small keyboard and we watched as PDF files popped up onscreen in rapid succession.

"Foreign bills of lading," he said.

I squinted at the small print. "Are all those from Buenos Aires?"

"It would appear so. Notice the signature?"

"Selena," I said on a breath.

John nodded and dumped the domestic bills of lading he'd appropriated from Scooter's office onto the floor. Selena had signed none.

"Wait a minute," I said, rifling through the Business pile of my notes.

"I think I have something." Tearing though the notes, I got that sinking feeling you get when you can't find something you know you've got, when I remembered it was in the pocket of the jeans I'd worn earlier in the day.

Scrambling into my bedroom, I fished the photocopy out of my pocket and handed it to John, then grabbed another photocopy from the file I'd put together at the office.

He stared down at the paper, which was a page of the *Sentinel* reduced so it would fit on legal paper.

"What am I looking at?"

"This is the business article from the grand opening of Scooter's pet store, and this is the article from the grand reopening."

John looked more closely at the photographs that accompanied the articles.

"Selena wasn't at the first grand opening," I said, pointing at the aristocratic couple flanking Selena in the photo of the grand reopening. "Neither were her parents."

I pointed to her parents, and John looked at me.

"Selena is first-generation American—she's naturalized," I said. "Her folks are from Argentina, and when they reopened the pet shop, it specialized in exotic animals. See? Selena and her mother."

"They are very beautiful women," John said, looking closely at the photo.

"They're all right," I said, snatching the article out of his hands. The cutline under the photo read "Selenas Go Wild Over Exotic Animals."

I winced at the wordplay. "There's a special place in hell for people who write cutesy cutlines," I said.

"Selenas?" John said.

"Selena was named for her mother. Don't you think that's weird?"

John raised a brow. "Men are named for their fathers all the time," he said. "And didn't you tell me you were named for your mother?"

"Her last name, not her first," I grumbled. "It's not the same."

"I see," he said. Grinning, he dumped a pile of inter-company sales receipts on the floor. "According to these bills of lading, the pets were either bred in the United States or imported from—"

"South America," I finished for him. "And if the photo of the grand opening is any indication, Selena didn't get involved with the pet shop until they started importing exotic animals."

I stared at the pile of papers we'd pilfered from Scooter's office.

"Smuggling," I said. Something about the search of Scooter's office bumped the back of my brain. "Do you remember that book about moving to Buenos Aires on Scooter's bookshelf?" I said slowly. "Do you think Selena could be smuggling something from Argentina for El Patron, and that something is what everyone is looking for?"

I stared at the grand reopening photo, and my eyes wandered down the page.

"Wait," I said, a tiny bubble of excitement forming in my stomach. "Look at this."

John peered over my shoulder.

"In the Business Digest," I said, pointing to the column that ran the length of the business page. "'CenTex Distribution Sells to International Enterprises in Surprise Deal.'"

John stared at me as I snatched up a bill of lading from a nearby pile of papers and pointed to the logo at the top.

"CenTex. That's the shipping company the Blue Parrot used to transport most of their exotic animals from Argentina—where Selena's family is from!"

"So?"

"One of the reporters downtown told me he'd traced CenTex to El Patron, but he thought it was for money laundering," I said, the bubble expanding. "But CenTex wasn't purchased to clean money—it was to smuggle something in with the animals. Something from Argentina. And I think I know what it was."

I snatched up the article Ryder had given me on the Anschluss Eagle.

"The eagle," I said triumphantly.

John stared at me and I moved closer, the bubble of excitement growing in the pit of my stomach. "Don't you see? That's the missing piece of the puzzle. Scooter gave me a coin to give to Selena that day in the shed. He said it was for luck, but it looked just like this, only worn and kind of faded."

John went very still. "Where is the coin now?"

"At the bottom of Lake Austin."

His jaw muscles tightened. "Did he say he had more? Did he say where they were?"

"No, he was just really upset about Selena. But that's it, isn't it?" I was so proud of my conclusion, I picked up my glass for a congratulatory toast.

John's green eyes narrowed and he looked at me intently. "Clever girl," he said.

Still looking at me, he reached over and picked up the pieces of paper I'd laid in a connected line. "Very clever. You have quite an imagination. You should write crime novels. Don't you think we've already exhausted that possibility?"

My bubble popped so loud I could hear it in my head.

"Now," he said, tapping the papers into a neat stack and setting them aside. "Let's get back to the task at hand, Cauley, and not chase after some phantom connection with your El Patron people, or whatever you call them."

"Wait a minute—when you say *y'all have exhausted that possibility,* what do you mean? Exactly what did you exhaust?"

John's gaze went very cold, and for a moment I got a terrible chill, the kind that makes you stop and look behind you when you're walking alone down a deserted street at night.

I swallowed hard. "I just thought—"

"And I thought you were trying to discover whether or not your friend committed suicide, and if he did not commit suicide, the cause of his death."

I stared at the stack of papers he'd tossed near his gun on the end table and sighed. "You really think somebody killed Scooter?"

"There is a high probability."

"But we can't prove it."

John smiled and his face was kind again. "We haven't proved it *yet.*"

"You're going to help me?" I said, thinking of my promise to Scooter's parents.

"As much as I can," he said. He was looking at my lips.

He took the glass of wine from me and set it on the end table. He leaned closer, and he kissed me.

I was startled. My eyes went wide and my stomach fluttered and every cell in my body went on red alert. Wasn't this what I'd wanted from the moment I'd met him? I'd wondered what it would feel like, his lips on mine, his hands on my body. And now I knew.

His lips were soft and warm and went hard and hot in a flash of pure lust. He felt fierce and dangerous and very close, and I leaned into him, putting my arms around his neck, pressing hard against him so I could feel his whole body with mine.

"I want you," he said, and his voice was as low and sexy as anything I'd ever heard. "I want you, right here, right now."

"Oh," I said. *Brilliant.* Cauley MacKinnon, mistress of pillow talk.

John leaned in, and this time the kiss was hard; I could hear papers rustling beneath me as his body met mine. His breath came harder, and I could feel his heart hammering against mine.

"John," I said, wanting to tell him this was a big deal for me.

"Shhh," he whispered.

My breath caught when his hand slipped beneath my shirt. I don't think I've ever wanted anybody the way I wanted him at that moment.

Thunder rattled the front window. The lights dimmed, then brightened. John pulled back.

"Cauley," he said, looking down at me with those incredible green eyes. "I have to tell you something."

Now? Right this minute?

I pulled away, thinking of the blond gymnast with John's car keys. "You're gay."

He chuckled, running his fingers lightly over my cheek. "No, Cauley. I am not gay."

My whole body heated, but I waited. Nothing short of him telling me he was a fascist or a convicted felon was going to make me change my mind. And I might make an exception for the felon thing.

"I am leaving tonight. I will be back, but I have some things I need to take care of in Washington."

Our gazes locked, then he trailed warm kisses down my neck. I could feel his fingers, warm and strong, skimming beneath my shirt, just below my bra. He leaned me back and all I wanted was to tell him not to stop. I squeezed my eyes shut.

"John," I said, and sat up.

He blew out a long breath and sat up, too.

I shook my head. "I want to make love to you, but—"

Leaning back against the sofa, he ran a hand through his dark hair. "I know you do."

From anyone else that would have been arrogant. But the truth was I wanted him and we both knew it.

"Cauley," he said, looking into my eyes. "What am I going to do with you?"

I wanted to say, "Stay with me," but somehow found the good grace not to say it out loud.

In the silence, John got to his feet. He held out his hand and helped me up.

I wanted to say something—ask him not to leave, tell him I thought I might be falling in love with him—but the words didn't come. It was too soon, and truth be told, I wasn't sure I knew what real love was.

I stood, watching, as he packed up his computer and tucked his big gun back into his waistband. He turned to me and held out his hand, and I walked him to the door.

Outside, the night was dark, the air thick with the threat of rain, and his strong fingers wrapped around mine like a promise.

"I'll be back," he said, and he leaned in and pressed a kiss to my forehead.

Then he stepped out of the door. Lightning flashed green on the horizon, and he was gone.

Inside, the lamplight was dim, and I felt cold. Would it really have been so wrong to just rip his clothes off, right there on the living room floor?

He'd said he had to tell me something, and I was pretty sure that telling me he was leaving was only part of it.

Absently, I wandered through the empty house, wondering what I might be doing if John had stayed. Probably having the best orgasm of my short, deprived life.

So why did he tell me he was leaving?

Muse sat, perched on the desk next to the Magic 8 Ball, and I reached down to scratch her behind the ear.

"The thing is," I said to the cat, "I know he likes me. And there are customs opportunities all over Texas. It wouldn't be so hard to work out."

Muse twitched her whiskers, her gold eyes glaring skeptically. I scowled back.

"Oh, what do you know," I told her.

"What do you think, 8 Ball?" I said, picking it up and turning it over in my palms. "Will this *whatever-it-is* between me and John work out the way I want it to?"

Lightning crashed outside the library window and thunder shook the whole house.

Inside the 8 Ball, the little triangle tumbled in the blue liquid. *DON'T COUNT ON IT.*

I looked at Muse. "Electromagnetic interference," I said. "And besides, *DON'T COUNT ON IT* is not a definitive answer."

Closing my eyes, I shook the ball again.

The triangle flipped and the answer appeared.

MY REPLY IS NO.

I stood, staring down at the 8 Ball.

"It's broken!" I yelled and threw it at the bookcase.

Muse narrowed her eyes and hopped down from the desk. She gave me a withering look of pity, then padded down the hall to join Marlowe on the bed.

Alone again, I flipped on the DVD player. The television screen flickered to life. There was only one cure for this kind of malaise—chocolate and *Casablanca*. I fished a rock-hard, frozen Godiva bar from the freezer and the DVD spun; before long, Bogart was driving blissfully through Paris in springtime, teasing Ingrid Bergman about who she was and what she'd done before, completely unaware that both of their hearts were about to be broken into tiny little pieces because a bunch of Nazis didn't respect geographic boundaries.

Sighing, I scooped up the bits of research John and I'd been working on. I stood, gnawing a corner of the frozen chocolate and staring at the article with the picture of Selena and her mom at the grand reopening of the Blue Parrot, re-reading the cutline: "Selenas Go Wild Over Exotic Animals."

"Something about Selena . . ." I said aloud.

Lightning crashed so close to the house that the thunder was almost instantaneous. The lights dimmed as the thunder shook the house from foundation to rafters.

A chill skittered up my spine. As if I'd called him, Marlowe appeared in the hallway, fur bristling along his backbone.

"There is something about Selena," I said to the dog, and nearly screamed when a knock sounded at my door.

"Who is it?" I said, frantically searching for my phone.

"It's me, Cauley."

I swung open the door.

John Fiennes stood in the darkness, the storm lifting his dark hair. Lightning crashed behind him and he seemed very handsome and dark in the night.

I swallowed hard.

"I'm here until Sunday," he said.

Screw the stupid 8 Ball.

I opened the door wider and let him in.

TWENTY-TWO

"I thought you were leaving?"

"The gentle art of delegation."

"Are you going to owe somebody a big favor?"

His gaze raked the length of my body and he said, "I figure it's worth it."

The television cast a noir glow over the sharp planes of John's face.

"*Casablanca*," he said and smiled, catching the onscreen conversation. He took the remote from me, flicked off the television, and as his body closed in on mine, he said, "I was wondering . . ."

I would have smiled at his truly bad Bogart impression, but I could feel his gaze as though he'd touched me.

I backed up a little as he advanced, and he continued, "Why I'm so lucky . . . why I should find you waiting for me to come along."

"Oh," I said, and before I could say anything else, his lips were on mine, hard and hot, as he backed me into my living room, kicking the door shut behind him.

"Wait," I said against his mouth. "I don't have condoms."

"I brought my own."

"Of course you did."

"Besides," he said. "I'm a government agent. My physicals come with papers. Want to see?"

Did I.

He kissed me again, backing me all the way down the hall, into my bedroom, never breaking the kiss. I tore at his clothes as he worked on mine, and when I felt the edge of my bed at the back of my knees, a wave of apprehension washed over me. Could I really do this?

John broke the kiss, his hand hot against my bare breast.

"I want you," he said. "I want to take you in my mouth, kiss every inch of your body, and when I am finished I will do it again."

Well. When he put it that way . . .

We were on the bed then, a tangle of arms and legs, John's lips skimming from my mouth to my neck and down.

His hands were amazing, and he sent me over the edge almost immediately. To my horror, I felt tears, hot on my cheeks as everything crashed in on me at once.

"Hey," he said. "What is all this?"

I blew out a long, steadying breath. "It's just . . . everything."

This was going too fast and I knew it, but my eyes drifted shut as he leaned down and kissed my tears. I gasped when he plunged inside me. In that moment, I forgot everything. He moved against me as though some unseen force pressed him on and I moved with him, driving again and again until both our bodies shuddered. On a breath, we fell silent.

Nearly asleep, he wrapped both arms around me in a hold that was both comforting and possessive, and for that moment, I felt as though nothing and no one could ever hurt me again. I closed my eyes, wanting to remember the way he felt inside me, the way he'd shuddered against me, and the way he held me, pushing back the very bad feeling that, someday, time and distance would make me forget.

WE SPENT THE NEXT two days in bed, only getting up to eat and bathe, both of which we did together. I took the phone off the hook. Anybody who really needed to get hold of me had my cell phone number. Nothing else mattered.

Throughout the weekend, we didn't sleep, spending each moment as though it were our last, learning each other's bodies. Sunday came too fast.

Late that last morning, John drew a bath. I poured wine into two glasses and stepped over the wide tile edge into the bathtub. The water rose as I settled in front of him, his strong arms and legs wrapped around me.

I wished we could stay like that forever, and I made the mistake of saying so.

Behind me, John was silent, and I could feel his bare, slick body slide beneath me, but instead of making love again, he took my hand in his.

"I would like that, Cauley," he said quietly, his breath warm and sweet with wine. He examined my hand in his, folding his fingers around mine. "You are clever and beautiful and we would make handsome children."

Children? I swallowed hard.

"But my life is very complicated."

I swallowed. "I know."

He let go of my hand, reached for the shampoo, and gently worked a palmful into my hair. I sighed. He had great hands. My body melted as he massaged my scalp, and any doubts I had ebbed into a lingering sadness.

"Lean back," he said, and he poured warm water from the bath pitcher over my tilted head. "I'm coming back, you know."

I didn't say anything.

Stupid 8 Ball.

He set the pitcher down and reached around me, palming my breasts in his soap-slicked hands.

"And in the meantime, I'm going to make sure that you don't forget me." He nipped the damp flesh below my ear. Despite the warm water, I shivered.

He moved my wet hair and bit the back of my neck. His sharp teeth scraped my shoulder and his erection pressed hard beneath me.

"Cauley," he said. His warm, wet hands slid from my breasts down to my hips and he thrust, sliding hot and hard inside me.

I gasped. John was leaving. He said he'd be back, but he was leaving. "I can't," I said, but my voice sounded small.

"No?" he said, holding me tighter, rocking against me. Water splashed over the edge of the bathtub, onto the tile, and my whole body shook.

"I just . . ."

"Tell me no," he whispered.

The breath caught in my throat and I whispered, "Yes."

"We've got an hour to get to the airport," I said, stuffing his shirts into his bag. "And the drive takes at least that long."

We rushed to gather his clothes and I was glad, because the rush meant we didn't have to talk about the weekend, or his leaving, or the rest of our lives . . .

"I'll drive," I said. "I know the back way. And I'll check your BMW back into the rental company for you and have someone pick me up."

"No, I can—" but he stopped and turned to look at me and nodded. I could tell there was more to say. I figured he wasn't sure how to say it.

I tripped over Muse, who yowled, frankly, more loudly than necessary. "Sorry, cat," I said. "Shoot. I'm not even dressed yet."

A bubble of hysteria rose in my throat as the clock ticked, and I yanked clothes out of my drawer, throwing shirts and shorts onto the floor.

I wanted to wear something stunning. I wanted to be stunning. Something he would remember. Maybe come back for.

"Cauley," he said, and reached out and took my hand. I stopped throwing clothes and turned to look at him. He stared down at me and his eyes were so green they took my breath away.

Without a word, he slipped his dark polo shirt over his head and skimmed it over mine. It was still warm from his body, and the scent of him lingered in the soft fabric.

"Too much trouble to get a new shirt?" he said, and reached around me onto the dresser and tossed my old football jersey onto the rumpled bed.

"So maybe I should get a new boyfriend."

"Over my dead body," he said, and he leaned down, his lips warm on mine, and kissed me until I couldn't think straight.

WE WERE RUNNING LATE. Despite feeling weak-kneed from lack of sleep and an abundance of some truly mind-blowing sex, I hit Ranch Road 2222 and floored the little black BMW down the thousand-foot drop of Tumbleweed Hill. I felt the pressure of the decline in my ears. I felt the pressure of John's silence in my stomach.

Forty-five minutes later, we parked and hustled into the airport, where we stood in the luggage-check line.

"Do you have all your things?" I said, not knowing what else to say. My throat was tight, and I was having a hard time making the words come out.

"Give me your hand," he said, and with my hand in his, he squeezed hard. We didn't say anything else.

After his bag was checked, we moved toward the waiting area near the security checkpoint.

"I have to go," he said, and I nodded.

He leaned down and kissed me, long and warm and hard. Pulling back, he looked down at me intently, then stepped away.

Turning toward the bank of security monitors, he showed the guard his ID, went through the metal detector, and turned to look at me as a kaleidoscopic crowd of travelers coursed around him. Did any of them feel as awful as I did?

From behind the gate John looked at me, his eyes shining as though his throat was tight, too.

He touched his hand to his heart, to his lips, then toward me and mouthed, "I'll be back."

I swallowed hard.

"No," I whispered, as he turned and disappeared into the crowd. "You won't."

And I felt my heart begin to break.

I CHECKED JOHN'S BLACK BMW back into the rental company, and Mia picked me up in her Beetle and for once didn't ply me with questions. She chattered about Roger and their upcoming plans for a trip to Aruba before dropping me at my doorstep.

"You okay?" she said. I tried to smile, but it came off pretty weak.

Mia nodded, watching me carefully. "Call me tomorrow?"

I stumbled through the living room without turning on the lights. I crawled into bed, Muse and Marlowe snuggling in, happy to get back to their usual routine.

But I wasn't sure I'd ever be usual again. I lay there, listening to my body and thinking about my life.

I lived in a house that wasn't mine, with a dog and a cat that didn't belong to me. I may have been responsible for my friend's suicide, although I didn't think so. And his parents wanted me to prove it.

I turned, wrapping myself in the sheets, and pulled the pillow close, breathing deeply of John's scent, which lingered on the linen.

I wondered if he really would come back. Even if I never saw him again, I couldn't make myself sorry for the weekend.

I sighed aloud and then fell asleep, listening to the soft purr of the cat and the gentle breathing of the dog.

TWENTY-THREE

"The bastard stole my research!"

I'd woken up late, made a big pitcher of tea, and was ready to get back down to business when I discovered I had nothing to get down to business with. Outside, the sky was gunmetal gray and clouds banked on the horizon, perfectly matching my pissy mood.

I'd called Mia and Brynn, who'd broken land speed records to get to my house. They were standing in my home office, watching as I tore the place apart, looking for the research I knew I wouldn't find.

"A customs agent stole your research?" Mia said.

"It would appear so," I said.

I felt like my heart had been backed over by a certain black BMW.

My house was a wreck and my life was an even bigger wreck. And John was gone.

In addition to my life crashing into a million tiny pieces, my job was bumping the guardrail of the career track. I was on administrative leave for another two days.

I felt like screaming, so I did. "We broke into a crime scene, stole evidence, he screwed my brains out, and the sonovabitch stole my goddamn research!"

"But the sex was good?" Brynn said.

"This isn't about sex," I said.

"I think it is," Brynn said. "You haven't even had time to enjoy your post-coital languor."

Mia scowled at Brynn and turned to me. "*Cara,*" she said, taking my hand.

"Oh, stop it," Brynn said. "This puts your lifetime sexual achievements to what, a whopping three?"

"Three and a half," Mia said. "Todd Bryant. Prom night, senior year."

"Wow," Brynn said. "Soon you'll be organizing their names on index cards and cross-referencing them to keep track."

"It's just—out of the hundred things I could imagine coming from this, stealing my research would have been like, I don't know, number nine hundred thousand." I blew out a breath. "Am I really that bad at judging character?"

Mia and Brynn looked at each other, then Brynn said, "Want a list of all your bad characters?"

I sighed. "I guess I feel used. And a little . . . slutty. He as much as told me he was a dangerous guy."

"Oh, for fuck's sake. Why do you feel bad? Because you had marathon sex or because you think he's not coming back?" Brynn asked.

"He's not coming back," I said miserably. "I was just a three-night fling and a pile of stolen research to him."

"Well, according to your horoscope, you won't be alone for long," Mia said.

"Not being alone doesn't mean I'll be with John," I said.

"Hmm," Mia said. "True. The stars get fuzzy on the details. Have you seen Mark lately?"

Brynn snorted. "Mark is like an old flannel shirt. You keep it in the bottom drawer in case you need something comfortable."

I sighed. "I think that's why I tripped so hard for John. Because I'm trying to wean myself off of bourbon-soaked, midnight calls to Mark," I said, not believing a word of what I was saying.

Mia nodded thoughtfully. "What about your FBI agent?" she asked. "Maybe you should give him a call."

"Logan is not my FBI agent. And what am I going to do? Call him up and ask him to arrest John for taking files I helped steal from a crime scene? Besides, John's some kind of undercover customs agent, not a criminal."

"No, I meant call the FBI for you. You know. Like a date."

"Oh," I said and sighed. "Agent Logan has made it very clear his interest in me is strictly business."

"Maybe," Mia said dreamily, "he's just waiting for a starlit night to sweep you into his arms and declare his undying love, and then, *boom!* Fireworks."

"Mia," I said. "He's practically a reincarnation of John Wayne. I don't think he does starlit nights and fireworks. Plus, he thinks I'm a kook."

"You are kind of a kook," Brynn said, opening a bottle of wine. "But you're a cute kook."

"Thanks a lot," I said. We sat in a circle, Brynn and I on the sofa, Mia on the floor in front of us, and the concern in my friends' eyes was almost painful. I sighed. "I think mostly it's just that I'm alone. Again."

"Hey, you're not alone!" Mia said, raising the glass of wine that Brynn had just given her. "That's what friends are for."

Brynn lifted her glass and grinned.

"When you are sad, we will get you drunk and plot revenge against the rat bastard who made you sad, " Mia said.

Brynn clinked glasses. "And when you think it can't get any worse, we will tell you horrifying stories of just how bad it could be."

I smiled, but my heart wasn't in it. "I'm sorry. It's just . . . John. I was so sure there was something there."

"See? That is why you have got to start dating," Brynn said. "The only way to get over indiscriminate sex is to have more of it."

"Ah, *querida*, look at the bright side. At least you got two men following you around. Three if you count your friend the earless bald guy," Mia said, and wrapped her arms around me. "There's only one thing to do."

"Two things, actually," Brynn said. She got up and went to my answering machine and hit the *program* button. The machine said, *Press erase again to erase all messages.*

"No!" I yelled.

Mia and Brynn stared at me.

I had about six months of old messages from Mark on that machine. Comfort calls. I wasn't ready to erase them, but I didn't want my friends to know that.

"Don't have a cow," Brynn said. She punched the second *program* button and the machine barked, *Please record your message* in a mechanical male voice.

Wineglass in hand, Brynn leaned over the machine and in a breathy Marilyn Monroe voice, she said, "Hello . . . you've reached Cauley MacKinnon. I am available; however, I am not attainable. Leave your message and when I get over my snit, I'll call you back."

I couldn't help but laugh.

"I've got exactly what you need," Mia said, and she opened her big embroidered bag and pulled out a stack of *Chic* magazines, some DVDs, and a half gallon of ice cream.

"Mel Gibson," Mia said. "And Ben & Jerry's."

Storm clouds were amassing on the southeastern horizon and rolling into Hill Country at an alarming speed. I flipped on the Weather Channel to confirm what I already knew—Hurricane Jenny was bearing down on the Gulf Coast.

It was late when my friends left, barely beating the storm front. As I closed the door behind them, my heart felt a lot lighter, despite the fact that I'd been played like a cheap banjo by a hot customs agent.

I sighed. "Good friends are worth their weight in chocolate," I told Marlowe, who was working his way through what was left of a peanut butter sandwich.

I changed into my PJs, polished off the rest of the wine, and watched the rest of *Lethal Weapon 18*, letting Mel Gibson fog my brain of pesty thoughts of anything important.

Licking the last of the chocolate ice cream from a half-bent spoon, I rinsed bowls and glasses in the sink. Marlowe stalked into the kitchen, grumbling as he turned twice and settled at my feet on the throw rug.

Outside, the wind was picking up and I could hear it shift through the canyon behind the house.

As I rinsed the clinging bits of brownie from the bottom of a bowl, Marlowe growled low in his throat.

"Relax, tough guy, it's hurricane season. This is just a summer storm," I said, tucking the bent spoon into the silverware rack of the dishwasher. Marlowe was bristling and I found that I was bristling, too. The air was charged with electricity, the way it is when there's going to be a helluva storm.

Marlowe growled again and I went very still. The limbs of the magnolia tree at the front porch scraped the living room window like gnarled fingernails clawing a chalkboard. I was a little murky from the wine, but I wasn't inebriated . . . I didn't think.

Had I locked the front door after Mia and Brynn left?

"We're being ridiculous," I told Marlowe, who stalked alongside me as I went to check the front door, flipping on every light in the house along the way.

The wind outside began to gust and I yelped when lightning flashed outside the living room window.

I rattled the front door knob, making sure it was latched. It was locked, but I unlocked it and locked it again, just to be sure.

"See?" I told Marlowe. "All locked. We're fine." But the wind screamed through the canyon and the old house moaned with the force of it. My heart kicked, and suddenly I wasn't so sure we were fine at all.

"It's just the wind," I said, but the hair along Marlowe's back spiked. He didn't seem convinced.

"You're right," I said. "What we need is a distraction."

Glancing warily toward the front window, Marlowe padded beside me as I made my way to the sofa, where I settled in and proceeded to click though a hundred and fifty channels of crap before landing on a classic movie revival of the old Hitchcock showing of *Rebecca*.

I snuggled the quilt around me as the movie went on, getting creepier by the minute. Lightning crashed outside the front window at the same time the inferno flashed in the old black-and-white movie, and I nearly flew right out of my skin.

"I guess Hitchcock isn't the thing to watch when you're already feeling skittish," I said to Marlowe. I was about to change the channel when the creepy face of Mrs. Danvers flickered on the television screen, and I swear my hair stood on end.

I looked down at Marlowe. "Did I lock the windows?"

The dog grumbled, but he followed as I began systematically checking the locks, starting with the window in the kitchen. Thunder boomed so close that it shook the house, and the magnolia near the front porch crashed against the living room window. I rushed back to the living room, hoping the low branches hadn't broken the pane.

The window was intact, but with a bang that loud I was certain the tree was damaged.

I leaned over the sofa to peer out the window, but because every light in the house was on, the only thing I could see was my own reflection, distorted in the rivulets of rain.

I squinted against the windowpane, trying to make out the tree in the dark, and lightning struck again. My neck prickled and I watched my reflection dim, and in its place was the horrible, grinning face of Van Gogh.

I couldn't even scream.

The thunder was almost instantaneous, and it shook the house hard. The lights stuttered and went out.

I did scream then, and Marlowe threw himself against the window, snarling so hard that foam flew from his muzzle.

"Marlowe," I screamed. "Stop it!"

But he threw himself against the pane again and the glass shook, and I struggled, grabbing for his collar.

"Oh, Lord, please," I pleaded.

Marlowe snarled, scrabbling as I dragged him down the hall toward the bedroom, where I kept low, searching for the telephone in the dark.

I found the phone tangled in the bed sheets and quickly dialed 911. I didn't wait for a greeting.

"There's someone outside my house!" I hissed as I struggled to keep Marlowe under check as he squirmed and snarled, snapping his teeth.

"There's someone outside your house?" a female voice repeated.

"There-is-someone-outside-my-house," I repeated, panic rising in my throat.

"What is your address?" she said and I told her, but I was having a bit of trouble on account of my voice shaking.

"Has this person threatened you?" the woman said.

"Yes," I said, thinking about Van Gogh's promise to cut off my ears.

"Is he armed?" the woman asked, and I was about to answer when the front window crashed.

I screamed and dropped the phone. Marlowe lunged, choking, because I still had him by the collar. The dog dragged me halfway down the hall, my knees chafing against the hardwood floors.

"Marlowe," I hissed.

Lightning flashed again, illuminating the living room, and there I saw the big, wet lips and the sweaty, corpulent face that lurked in my worst nightmares.

Van Gogh's knife glinted green in the flash of lightning, but near him, there was a smaller, concentrated flash of fire, a small orange flame that didn't dim once the lightning subsided.

Grinning hideously, Van Gogh dropped a lighted match onto my Turkish rug.

Marlowe howled, the fur at his neck bristling. I kneeled there, wide-eyed, staring as the small flame hit the rug. It flashed and took off, zipping across the rug in long streaks, like someone had squirted lighter fluid there.

My heart stopped. Marlowe went wild, and in an instant, he broke my grip.

"No!" I screamed, watching as Van Gogh raised the knife to attack, but Marlowe was focused. The dog leapt and Van Gogh yelped as Marlowe's teeth sank into his knife hand.

My heart skipped. Warm, wet wind billowed and crashed through the shattered window, but Marlowe kept his grip on Van Gogh's big arm, snarling even as the man tried to shake him off, trying to shift the knife from one had to the other.

"*Weapon,*" a dark voice whispered, and I choked. My father's voice.

"I don't have a weapon."

"*You do, Cauley,*" the voice said and was gone.

I scrambled to my feet, tripping over the rug, and hoisted myself onto the kitchen counter, searching for a frying pan, wondering if the operator was still on the line, wondering if she believed me, wondering if police were on their way, cursing myself for not calling Cantu instead.

Lightning flashed again and the fire in the living room began crackling. The flames flickered, silhouetting the shape of Van Gogh fighting with the dog. The air filled with smoke and the sounds of growling and bitter struggle.

"Hold on, Marlowe!" I groped under the counter until I felt the rough edge of Aunt Kat's cast-iron frying pan, and I came up with it full force and headed straight for Van Gogh.

The fire was spreading, casting the living room in a weird orange glow. Dodging the mounting flames, I reared back and hit Van Gogh in the face so hard that the metal rang, and the reverberation traveled up my arm past my elbow to rattle my teeth.

Marlowe writhed and snarled but didn't let go. Momentarily stunned, Van Gogh made a muffled moan, probably because I'd loosened a couple of his teeth, and I reared back to hit him again.

"Drop it or I kill the dog," he lisped, shaking his left fist toward Marlowe's muzzle.

Swallowing a gasp, I dropped the frying pan, which made a gonging sound on the hardwood floor.

Van Gogh grinned at me, and he hit the dog anyway.

Marlowe yelped as he hit the floor, struggling to get his bearings.

My eyes went wide. "You lied!"

Van Gogh smiled through his own blood. "He's not dead."

I grabbed for the frying pan as the sound of sirens rounded the corner onto Arroyo Canyon.

Van Gogh lunged, the knife glistening with blood from his face, and I jerked away, barely missing the blow. He fell, but quickly scrambled to his feet. The sirens grew louder as a patrol car slid into my driveway, the headlights slicing the orange glow of fire in the living room.

"This isn't over," Van Gogh sneered in the weird light, and he turned, loping down the hall toward my back bedroom like he knew exactly where he was going.

He probably did, since it was probably him who'd broken into my house, stolen my computer, and left me the gift of a severed ear. I heard the back door bang open and the sound of the wind in the canyon grew stronger, and I knew Van Gogh was gone. For now.

My knees gave. Dropping to the floor, I picked up the phone and crawled toward Marlowe, choking on smoke.

"Miss? Miss? Are you okay?" the operator was saying. "The police are on their way. They should be at your door any minute."

"Better tell them to bring a fireman," I said. Marlowe seemed stunned but otherwise unharmed, and I hoisted myself up to find Aunt Kat's little red kitchen fire extinguisher.

A young cop busted through the front door, gun drawn but shaking. The kid looked just as scared as I felt.

"I should have called Cantu," I whispered to Marlowe, who was busy growling at the young cop.

"Where's the intruder?" the cop said, his voice cracking only a little.

Unhooking the nozzle on the fire extinguisher, I nodded toward the back door. He fumbled the radio from his utility belt.

"Fire department's on its way," he said, listening to his radio squawk. "You going to be okay?"

I nodded but said, "My cat's in there!"

"Out!" he yelled, taking my elbow and dragging me and Marlowe out the open front door.

"She's probably in the closet," I yelled.

With the dog and me deposited on the front porch, the cop moved slowly down the hall, creeping flat against the wall, coughing and talking quietly into the radio in his epaulet.

I told Marlowe to stay and ran back into the house, fire extinguisher at the ready. Muse was still in there, and stupid or not, I had to get her.

"Muse!" I screamed. "Muse?"

A big gust of wind rattled what was left of the front window as Marlowe leapt through the pane. The flames swelled, crackling, as they consumed the Queen Anne chair.

"Dammit, Marlowe! Get back!" I yelled, but he was barking madly.

Squeezing my eyes shut, I hit the lever on the fire extinguisher. The cylinder made a pitiful hissing sound and went dead.

"Shit, *shit!*" I yelled, shaking the bottle. "Muse!"

In a hot *whoosh*, the curtains were alive with flashfire.

No way could a fire spread this quickly.

There were more sirens, and in moments, two firemen with a big hose burst through the front door. Smoke swelled through the living room.

"Outside!" the big fireman yelled.

"My cat's in the bedroom closet!"

"We've got your cat. Get out!" he said, shepherding me and the dog onto the front porch again, and after a scuffle in the back bedroom loud enough to hear over the snapping flames, the younger, rangy fireman came out with a cyclone of a cat. He gladly handed her off to me.

On the porch, I turned in time to see the big fireman flood the living room with thirteen thousand gallons of pressurized water.

THE RAIN HAD STOPPED but the clouded night seemed darker than usual as I stood in the front yard bathed in flashing red lights and the halogen beams of emergency vehicle headlights.

Half a dozen cops and firefighters milled about in the yard. Outside the circle of lights, police radios squawked in the darkness like obnoxious night insects. Despite the heat of the evening, my teeth chattered.

Marlowe stood next to me, shifting from paw to paw, growling. In my arms, Muse writhed like she was possessed.

Beckett and Jenks had left that morning on a week-long gay rodeo thing, but the Bobs and everyone else on the street were wandering about in robes and pajamas, craning their necks and whispering behind their hands.

Cantu squealed around the corner in Arlene's station wagon. "Cauley," he said, bolting up the drive. He issued a sharp nod to a couple of the patrol cops. "What the hell is going on?"

"I'm all right," I said, hugging Muse close to me. "Did you draw this?"

"Went out for milk and heard it on the scanner," he said. "Your earless guy?"

My lower lip trembled, but I nodded. "I swear, I had all the doors and windows locked."

"Locks only keep out honest people," Cantu said, looking at the charred remains of the broken window. I told Cantu what happened, but my teeth were chattering and I shivered.

Cantu draped his jacket around my shoulders. "Your insurance company's taking a beating."

"I'm not going to report it. I just got one claim back and it's hard enough to get homeowner's."

Cantu shook his head and we turned in unison as the big fireman sloshed through the wet front yard, making his way toward us. He was holding something.

"Your house has been secured," he said. He handed me a charred, half-empty bottle of wine.

"Is the house all right?" I said.

"Damage is contained to the living room, but it's wet and you got some pretty good smoke saturation. You prob'ly oughta stay somewhere else tonight," the big fireman said. He had an enormous black mustache and dark eyes that glinted with disapproval. "Any reason your smoke detector didn't have batteries?"

"A friend of mine needed batteries for his Sims game."

Cantu snorted.

The fireman shook his head and pulled a notepad from his pocket. "You know how this fire started?"

"Yes," I said. "A big, bald, earless maniac broke in and lit a match."

The fireman looked up from his notepad. Cantu shrugged.

"No flammable liquids spilled?" the fireman said.

Frowning, I shook my head.

The fireman was scribbling away when Marlowe went on alert, ears pricked, tail stretched straight.

I slipped my fingers under the dog's collar and held tight. A battered gray Mercury screeched past the fire truck and squealed to a stop in front of Cantu's station wagon. I should have been surprised, but I wasn't.

Dressed in dark jeans and a black tee shirt with "FBI" printed in big white letters, Tom Logan badged the uniforms at the driveway and moved purposefully up the walk, his dark eyes locked on mine. It might have been concern, but he looked mad as hell.

Marlowe went wild, broke my hold, and loped down the stone path to greet him.

"You okay?" Logan said, his eyes still on mine. Absently, he patted Marlowe's head as the dog fell into step beside him.

"Hello, stranger," I said. "Fancy meeting you here. Have you got my house bugged?"

"I heard Armageddon broke out, and I only know one person who can incite that kind of panic," he said, stopping in front of the big fireman. Logan nodded at Cantu, and Cantu nodded back, somewhat grudgingly, I thought.

"Your earless buddy?" he said, and I nodded.

Logan's jaw muscle tightened. He turned to the fireman. "What've you got?"

"Brewster Dietz," the fireman said, his chest puffing imperiously. Looking past me, he talked to Logan, and his voice went about two octaves lower than when he'd spoken with us. Logan had that effect on people.

"You make this for an accident?" Logan said.

Dietz shook his head. "Spread fast. We'll get the arson dog in here. See if there's any accelerants."

Logan nodded, then headed toward the front door. Marlowe let out a strange, yodeling bark and took off after him.

"Hey!" I said, going after the dog, but Dietz put a hand on my shoulder.

"Guy knows what he's doing," Dietz said. "Let him do his job."

I stood in my front yard, Muse squirming in my arms as we waited. From somewhere in the living room, Marlowe barked three strange little barks. Within moments, Logan ducked out the doorway, Marlowe trotting along behind. Logan was flipping through his own notepad.

"Find anything?" Dietz said.

Logan squinted. "Too early to tell." He ripped a page from his small notebook and handed it to the fireman.

I rose to my tiptoes, craning to get a peek. The fireman nodded before folding it and stuffing it into his pocket.

"The way we figure," Dietz said, "the damage was contained to the living room. The girl's got mild smoke inhalation, borderline inebriation, and some very bad judgment. She busted back into the house and tried to put out the fire."

"Hey! I'm standing right here," I said. "And I was trying to get my cat."

Logan ignored me. "Too inebriated to drive?" he said to Dietz.

"I'll drive her," Cantu said.

"Thanks," Logan said. "But I'll take it from here."

Cantu and Logan stared at each other for a long moment.

"Hey," I said to Cantu. "Why don't you go on home. I bet Arlene's getting sick of you riding to the rescue. I've already told you most of what happened. Can I come down to the station and fill out paperwork tomorrow?"

After a bit more staring, Cantu nodded. "I'll wait for the techs to get here. Then we'll round up some uniforms and start a search pattern for your earless guy."

"Thank you," I whispered to him as Logan cupped my elbow.

Despite numerous protests, mainly from me, Logan herded me and both animals toward his old bureau car. I wanted to go back into my house and get a change of clothes, but Logan said I'd already come close to messing up a perfectly good crime scene.

"Hey," Dietz yelled after us. I turned to look at him. "Nice jammies."

Scowling, I climbed into the passenger seat, both animals jockeying for position.

"What was his problem?" I said.

Logan shook his head as he pulled out of the drive and I swear I saw the beginnings of a smile. "You were standing in the headlights," he said. "You can see right through your pajamas."

TWENTY-FOUR

In the end, home is the place where, when you have to go there, they have to take you in.

That may be true, but Robert Frost never met the MacKinnons. They'll take you in, but you'll pay for it for the rest of your life.

Despite copious amounts of red wine and a surplus of smoke inhalation, I filled Logan in on the events of the evening, beginning with my friends and Mel Gibson and ending with Van Gogh and the fire. I judiciously left out the part about John Fiennes screwing my brains out and absconding with my research. I was tired and sore and very embarrassed.

Logan handed me his cell and I called my mom just before we pulled past the front porch. He turned off the ignition and we sat in the driveway for a moment without saying anything.

"Your friends left before the fire started?" Logan said.

"Yes. I was cleaning up."

Logan had the good grace not to laugh out loud.

Marlowe leapt over me and landed on the driveway in front of Logan, looking up as though waiting for further instruction. I narrowed my eyes.

My mother met us at the back door, took one whiff of my smoke-saturated pajamas, and said, "Jesus, Cauley, what on earth have you gotten yourself into?"

Ordinarily, I would have been annoyed at her tone, but as she led us into the kitchen of the house where I grew up, it was comforting. Logan and I let the animals loose to explore.

"What the hell is going on?" the Colonel said, eyeing Logan.

I'd forgotten to introduce everyone, so Logan put his hand out to the Colonel. "Special Agent Tom Logan. FBI."

The Colonel nodded, looking Logan up and down, then reached out and shook his hand. "Thanks for bringing her home."

"Ah!" Mama said. "Cauley, baby. Are you hurt?" She turned to the Colonel. "Stephan. Get me the VapoRub."

I shook my head. "I just need some sleep."

Mama took me by the shoulders. "You look beat, honey. Let me draw you a bath."

In my peripheral vision, I saw Logan raise his brows.

"No bath," I said. The last time I took a bath, I got taken to the cleaners by a certain customs agent.

Logan grinned down at me. "You sure about the no-bath thing?"

If I hadn't been dirty and smoky and completely offensive, I might have thought he was flirting with me.

Logan looked closely at me, and I could feel his gaze like he'd touched me. Under his breath, he said, "You want to talk about what happened?"

"You mean the fire?" I said hopefully.

"Before that."

"I can't right now," I said. I couldn't tell him about John Fiennes. Even though there was nothing between Logan and me, sleeping with John seemed like a betrayal somehow. "Can I call you tomorrow?" I said.

Logan looked at me for a long time. "All right," he said. "Call me sooner if you need me."

I nodded. "Thanks, Logan. For everything."

He stood there for what seemed like a long time, and finally said, "What were you and your friends doing?"

"Having a pillow fight in our underwear."

Logan laughed out loud. He had a great laugh, warm and deep and true. "You know," he said. "Your new friend the fireman was right."

"About what?"

"Nice jammies."

The Colonel snorted and began walking Logan to the door.

"You're leaving?" Mama said. She'd been setting out the tea service and stopped, a china cup in her hand.

"Yes, ma'am. I've got some things to settle at the office, and it's going to be a long night."

Mama set the cup down and intercepted Logan.

"Mr. Logan," Mama said. "Would you like to join us for the Fourth of July soiree down by the lake?"

I closed my eyes, but I knew Logan was grinning.

"I'd love to, Mrs. Connor, but I don't know what my schedule's going to be like."

Mama smiled warmly as the Colonel walked Logan toward the door. I could hear Logan and the Colonel talking in hushed tones, and I couldn't shake the cloud of guilt over my weekend with John.

"What's wrong, baby?" Mama said, advancing on me. I shook my head.

There was so much to say that I couldn't say anything, and for the first time in my life, my mother let it go without comment.

I trudged up the polished stairs to my old bedroom, which was pretty much the way I'd left it. Canopy bed nestled opposite the narrow window seat; essay awards lined the chair rail. Drama ribbons and debate trophies scattered along the shelf on the south wall.

On an autopilot I'd thought long since extinguished, I made my way to the upstairs bathroom and brushed my teeth with one of the packaged toothbrushes my mother always keeps for guests. The perfect southern hostess. I wondered if I would ever be like her. I wondered if I wanted to be.

I filled the sink to splash my face. The water was warm and it felt like heaven, so I splashed again and considered a shower to get the smoke out of my hair, but I was so tired I thought my knees would give out. I slid under the sheets, kicking to loosen Mama's hospital corners. Staring at the ceiling of my childhood, I wondered how the hell I'd wound up back where I'd started.

It wasn't hard to figure out. I'd stood in the way of Scooter getting the help he needed, stolen evidence, spent two days debauching myself with a man I barely knew, got all my research stolen—again—and nearly got my Aunt Kat's house burned to the ground.

I rolled over in my old twin bed, wrapping the covers around me like a cocoon.

I wasn't sure what was supposed to happen next. In the larger scheme of things, it didn't really matter. I would tell Logan about breaking into the pet shop and about John taking off with the research. The debauching myself, I thought, probably didn't need to be told.

But I could tell Logan all that later. After all, in the words of Margaret Mitchell, tomorrow was another day.

THAT NIGHT, I DREAMED long, looping dreams about the fire. In the flames I saw the faces of Selena, Van Gogh, and John Fiennes, and then the dream skipped back to the day Scooter and I talked in the shed. I jolted awake several times, disoriented.

The night stretched on and on until the first rays of sunshine slipped through the twelve-light window and bathed my old bedroom in warm, golden light, the kind of brilliant, forgiving sunrise that comes only after a terrible thunderstorm.

The scent of bacon and homemade waffles drifted up the staircase, intruding on the slow waking that follows a really bad night. I inhaled the scent. The Colonel must be cooking breakfast.

For a moment, the past ten years slipped away. Then I realized I was having a hard time moving my head.

Marlowe and Muse had found their way into the bedroom and were attempting to suffocate me with a combined sixty-eight pounds of fur.

"Cauley?" Mama said from the bedroom door. "Come to breakfast, hon."

Bracing myself on my elbows, I sat up and looked at the alarm clock. Eight thirty.

"Church in an hour," she announced. "Daylight's burnin'."

"When we hear the ancient bells growling on a Sunday morning . . ." I grumbled, feeling terrible because I'd been skipping Sundays for more than a month.

"Don't quote Nietzsche on Sunday, Cauley, it's not nice," Mama said. She stood at the door wearing a cream-colored linen dress, pearls at her throat. She looked like a fading fifties movie queen, and I wondered if I would look like her some day.

"I'm having a really bad day and I'm not even out of bed yet," I said.

"That which does not kill us makes us stronger," Mama said.

"That which does not kill us makes us want to kill somebody else," I muttered.

Mama let out a long, beleaguered sigh. "All right. You going to at least make it to Sunday dinner? Your sister's bringing the children."

"I've got a lot to do today."

Mama stood silently. "Anything I can do to help?"

"Turn back time."

Sighing, she sashayed over, sat at the edge of the bed, and hugged me hard.

I sat up and let the hug seep all the way down to my bones. "Actually, there is something," I said. "Will you keep Marlowe and Muse for a couple of days?"

"Consider it done, baby." Mama pushed my hair out of my eyes and looked at me hard. Then, without comment, she rose and glided back to the door and turned.

"Cauley?"

"Hmm?"

"I like that Tom Logan. He's a nice man."

"Mama," I said. "He's just doing his job."

She smiled like she didn't believe me and pulled the door closed.

"Ah!" I said, and my mother's words hit me like one of those cartoon Acme anvils. My mother was right. Tom Logan was a nice man. I yanked the pillow over my head.

"I slept with the wrong man!" I yelled into the pillow.

Shoving the pillow away, I stared at the ceiling. "Ah, well," I said grimly. "Not the first time."

John Fiennes. Call me a sentimental idiot, because despite the fact that he'd screwed my brains out, then run off with every stitch of research I'd done, I believed John had feelings for me. I often have bad taste in men, but this time, I didn't think so. I was torn. Maybe he was trying to protect me by removing all traces of the stolen evidence?

I showered, wrapped one of my mom's big, fluffy towels around me, and rummaged through the dresser, where I found one of my old pairs of jeans and a tee shirt that said *Don't Mess With Texas*. The jeans were about two years too tight and so was the shirt. Since I'd left the house in my PJs, I didn't have a bra. I called a cab, hoping I wouldn't be involved in any accidents on the way home.

I took the stairs two at a time, trying to get out the door before anyone noticed my lack of proper undergarments—a definite no-no in any proper southern household.

In the kitchen, Mama was pouring coffee. The Colonel was at the table reading the *Sentinel*.

"Need me to carry you somewhere?" the Colonel said, looking up over the newspaper.

"Called a cab, but thanks," I said. I wanted to sit down and pour syrup over a stack of waffles and talk to the Colonel, see if he could help me untangle some of this mess, but if I did, I'd get roped into going to church, and I was running out of sick leave. I figured I'd call the Colonel when I got home.

"Aren't you going to eat?" Mama said, then she got a good look at me. "Good gawd, Cauley, where's your brassiere? What if you get in an accident?"

"I'll probably get better ambulance service," I said. "I gotta go."

I snitched a couple of pieces of bacon and a waffle, which would not make my jeans fit any better, and headed for the door.

"Your life is going down the toilet!" she called after me.

If she only knew.

TWENTY MINUTES LATER, I climbed out of the cab, paid the driver, and was standing in my front yard. The house looked like it was still standing only out of sheer stubborn will. The story of my life.

The man I thought I might be falling for slept with me, then stole my files. And I was perilously close to losing my job. I was going to have to start over. Again.

Sighing, I trudged up the porch steps and swung open the door.

"Oh!" I said, staring into my living room.

"Hey," Mia said. She was wearing cut-offs and a sports bra, and she was holding a mop. Brynn was kneeling next to her in head-to-toe Donna Karan, attractively accessorized with bright yellow rubber gloves and a pine-scented bucket of water. A Wet-Vac droned noisily in the corner. The house was hot and humid because all the windows were open to let the place dry out. Most of the water from the fire hose was gone, and my friends were mopping and scrubbing char marks off the end table.

"Did I hear Cauley?" Shiner came around the corner with a baking sheet of chocolate chip cookies, handing the first one to Mia. I grinned when she blushed.

I shook my head. "I love you guys."

"Yeah, yeah," Brynn said, handing me a sponge. "You and the 4th Infantry."

"When everything's dry, we'll come help you paint," Mia said. "*Chic* magazine had a whole spread last month on the best bachelorette pads."

Smacking his hands against his jeans, Shiner said, "I threw what was left of the rug and coffee table out back in my truck."

"Thanks," I said, wincing as I kicked aside a pile of wet towels before kneeling next to Brynn. "Jeez, this is a mess."

"Your mom called Mia, but we didn't get details. What happened?" Shiner asked, and their eyes went wide as I told them.

I shook my head. "Those flames spread way too fast. I'd bet my student loans that Van Gogh sprayed the place with accelerants. And speaking of flames, how mad is Tanner?" I said to Shiner.

"Mostly he's worried," he said. "He said you've got one more day of leave. After that, you can extend your leave, but it'll come out of vacation. You stay on this story, you gotta do it on your own time."

"I haven't been at the *Sentinel* long enough to get vacation time," I said. And I couldn't afford any more time off.

Shiner shrugged.

"Fine," I said. What I didn't say was that I had nearly twenty-four hours to get the Scooter thing figured out. I'd promised his parents I'd get to the bottom of it.

"We put some stuff we didn't know what to do with in your bedroom," Brynn said. "A couple of blankets. They aren't burned, but they smell like smoke."

"The whole place smells like smoke," Shiner said.

"I've got some aromatherapy stuff my herbal guy gave me," Mia said. "You want me to get a pot and start simmering?"

"No!" we all said in a chorus of alarm.

"Look at the bright side," Brynn said, pulling a damp DVD from under the sofa. "There's always Mel Gibson."

AFTER SUCKING MOST OF the water out of the sofa and floor with the Wet-Vac, we left all the windows open and set fans blowing on all the damp surfaces.

Mia, Brynn, and Shiner left, and once again, I was alone. Despite the efforts of the roaring industrial-sized fans stationed along open windows, the place reeked of smoke and damp fabric. It also felt empty without Muse and Marlowe, even though neither of them belonged to me.

Sighing, I called the Colonel, hoping he'd be home from church.

"Can I talk to you?" I said when he picked up the phone.

"You mean you want to tell me something and you don't want me to tell your mother?"

"I don't want her to worry, and I don't want her and Clairee meddling."

The Colonel sighed. "I won't say anything unless I have to."

Good enough for me.

I told him everything except the part about sleeping with John, which I judiciously left out, partly because I was embarrassed and partly because I was afraid the Colonel would get a big gun and go put a bullet in each of John's favorite appendages.

As I talked the story through, the frayed threads spooled out and the Colonel listened without comment.

I told him about my suspicions about the connection between the Nazi flight from Germany to Argentina, the Anschluss Eagle, and how at least some of the coins wound up in Central Texas. I told him about the bills of lading Selena had signed and how the shipping company used to transport the animals was purchased by a group that purportedly had ties to El Patron, who used the Necklace, the same burning-tire treatment as the Argentinean thugs, when they want somebody whacked.

"It's got to be these coins, because there's a customs agent involved and Logan says there could be smuggling, but it's not drugs or weapons. He said they've had dogs all over the place. But why would Scott and Selena smuggle? I mean, it's money. Why not just bring it in through the proper channels?"

"Well, if the coins really are Anschluss Eagles, they'd probably be confiscated, and somebody might even wind up on trial over the whole deal."

"What do you mean?"

"They're still deporting and trying war criminals. A couple of years ago, an international coalition traced large sums of money and gold to Argentina and Brazil, and there's some ongoing investigation into what kind of role neutral banks and countries played laundering money and moving around property that the Nazis confiscated from Jewish prisoners," the Colonel said.

"But how would they fence the coins if they could be confiscated?"

"Well," the Colonel said, considering. "It could work a couple of ways. Whoever's after those coins could be some nut-job Nazi memorabilia collector. Or they could have personal ties with the coins. Or it could be just some greedy bastard out for the gold."

"But you can't spend or trade them, they're too identifiable," I said.

"No, but you could melt them down—it's a lot of gold. What's the price for an ounce these days?"

My throat went dry. "You think I'm right? Somebody tossed Scooter's pet store and wrecked my house looking for these coins?" I shook my head. "That just sounds . . . incredible."

As incredible as it all sounded, it was a reasonable explanation for why everyone from the FBI to the Texas Syndicate had asked me what Scooter said in that shed and if he mentioned that he'd been hiding something.

"Everyone thinks Scooter told me where some kind of missing property is," I said slowly.

"The problem is you're dealing with thugs and you aren't thinking like a thug. Look, Cauley. You've got trained professionals chomping at the bit on this one. Have you told them all of this?"

"I told John—um, the customs agent—about the connections I'd found between the Nazi flight from Germany, Argentina, and Central Texas."

"What did he say?"

"He said I had a vivid imagination."

The Colonel was quiet. "You trust this customs guy? You said he stole your research."

I sighed, suspecting the Colonel knew there was more to that story.

"Why don't you sit down with your FBI agent friend and go over the whole thing with him?" he said.

"I knew you were going to say that. And he's not *my* FBI agent."

"And you're going to try to do it yourself." He blew out a long breath. "Okay. You're looking at the whole thing and it's overwhelming. It's like driving at night without headlights: you can only see a few feet in front of you, but you can make the whole trip that way."

"Been reading Doctorow again?" I said and smiled.

"Yeah, just like that," he said. "Cauley?"

"Yeah?"

"Don't be too proud to ask for help."

"Thanks, Colonel. I mean it," I said and disconnected.

I dragged a dry chair in from the library and sat down with my notebook. I didn't feel like going over everything again, but I had less than twenty-four hours to figure out if Scooter killed himself and if he didn't, who did, and if it was in fact the eagle coins everyone was wanting to know about, and if so, where they were, before I was back to writing obituaries.

"Come on, Scooter. Is that what you were trying to tell me? Where you stashed the coins?"

I tapped the pen to my lips. "Why did he call *me* that day he holed up in the shed and not the police?" I said aloud to no one.

"Maybe," I answered myself, "because he knew I'd been researching El Patron for a piece Ryder was working on."

I jotted that down in my notebook.

"And why did Van Gogh drive me into the lake?" I wondered. "He wanted to know what Scooter said in the shed. But all Scooter said was about Selena and how she was leaving him," I answered myself.

I got up and paced the short length of the hall.

"Tanner asked me to stay away from Scooter because of Selena. I'd nearly been dragged to a room by Diego DeLeon because of El Patron," I said aloud.

Selena was Scooter's wife. She'd engineered the big turnaround at the Blue Parrot by importing exotic animals. And she engineered the importing from Argentina. And then there was John Fiennes, a United States customs agent—why would he tell me there was nothing to my theory? Logan told me search dogs had been all through the place and found no evidence of drugs or weapons. But those dogs wouldn't have alerted on coins, I didn't think . . .

My head was spinning, so I went back to the chair and sat, staring at my notes. I thought about what the Colonel said about trained professionals and asking for help.

Sighing, I picked up the phone and speed-dialed Logan, mentally preparing the message I would leave on his voice mail.

"Tom Logan," he said, and I nearly fell over when I got his actual live voice, not a recorded message.

Recovering quickly, I said, "Hey, stranger. You got a minute?"

"Can you hold on a second?" he said, and I frowned, looking over my notes while I waited. The only thing that didn't fit tidily with anything else in the notes was Selena. I thought about her the way I'd known her best, small and blond and beautiful, playing Blanche DuBois off-stage as often as on.

Sure, she played on her looks and she could be manipulative, but I just couldn't imagine pale little Selena masterminding a plot to smuggle mysterious gold coins into the country.

I nearly jumped out of my skin when Tom Logan's voice came back on the line. "You there?" he said.

"Um, yes."

"You okay?" he said.

"Well, my house isn't on fire and I'm not getting chased into the lake by an earless German guy," I said, "but I think there is a German connection."

"What've you got?"

"I've been looking over my notes and talking to a few people, and I'm seeing some connections."

"Oh, yeah?"

"This might seem crazy, but will you hear me out?"

He made a loud snort, and being the eternal optimist I am, I took it to mean yes, so I told him about the animals imported to Central Texas from Argentina, the missing foreign bills of lading, and about the strange coin Scooter had given me in the shed.

There was a heavy silence on the line and he said, "Let me call you back on a land line."

The dial tone trilled, and I realized he'd hung up on me. Puzzled, I hit the *disconnect* button and jolted when the phone rang almost immediately.

"Cauley?" Logan said. "What the hell are you doing?"

"I think I'm on to something." I flipped through the notes I'd jotted.

Talking very fast, the way I do when I'm nervous, I said, "This whole mess started because Scooter called me, wanting to talk, but then all he talked about was Selena. But Logan, Scooter knew I'd been researching El Patron for Ryder."

"He mention El Patron?"

"Well, no, but here's the thing. El Patron has ties to the shipping company Scooter and Selena were using to import animals from Argentina. Everyone wants to know what Scooter said in the shed, including you and the customs agent, and I think Scooter was trying to tell me that they were mixed up with El Patron and that they were smuggling those coins. I think he was trying to come clean. Logan, he gave me a coin and I think it was one of those Anschluss Eagles like they found out near Bastrop two years ago."

"He gave you a gold coin?"

"To give to Selena."

"Where is it now?"

"At the bottom of Lake Austin."

There was a long, dead stillness on the line, and I said, "Logan? Are you still there?"

"Cauley," he said, sounding very tired. "I'm asking you to stay out of this."

I felt my eyes go wide, and the back of my neck prickled like mad. "I'm right?"

"Cauley. Do you know how crazy that sounds?"

"Well, yes, but—"

"No buts," he said. "You're about to mess up a perfectly good investigation. Just sit tight and all this will be over soon. I'll tell you what I can when we're done."

"Fine," I said, not feeling fine at all.

"Look," Logan said. "I'll call you tomorrow and we can go to lunch and talk all about it, but I need to get back to work now."

"Right," I said, and my voice sounded very small. "I guess I'll talk to you later."

He was quiet for a moment, then he said, "Hey, you're doing fine, kid. But you're in over your head."

I disconnected and the weight of the letdown settled over me. Looking over my notes, I shook my head.

"I know I'm right," I said stubbornly, keenly aware that no one was there to hear me. "Aren't I?"

Dropping the notebook on the counter, I looked around the empty house and wished Muse and Marlowe were home. I hadn't realized how much I would miss them. The house smelled like a big, wet dog, I thought, wrinkling my nose. Maybe I should do laundry. When all else fails, procrastinate.

I shoved the wet towels that Mia, Brynn, and I had used to soak up water into a laundry basket and wandered into my bedroom, thinking about Scooter and wracking my brain for something he might have said, something I might have missed . . .

Then I thought about John and felt a terrible sense of loss. I'd told John the same theory, a little less evolved, and he'd said I had an overactive imagination. And now Logan was insisting I stay out of it.

Frowning, I plucked a damp blanket from my bedroom floor and noticed a shirt and a pair of jeans under my bed.

It took me a few moments to remember that my friends had come over to help me get ready for a date with Diego the mobster-in-training several weeks ago and I'd shoved a pile of dirty clothes under my bed. Cauley's Code of Emergency Housecleaning.

Sighing, I took off the too-tight jeans and tee shirt I'd found at my mom's house and chucked them into the basket, too. Hefting the basket to the laundry room, I went to load the washing machine, checking pockets as I went. An ink pen and a receipt to the video store. Two crumpled dollars, Tom Logan's card with his cell phone number penciled in. An unlabeled microcassette.

I stood, staring at the cassette, trying to remember when I'd put it in my pocket.

Time slowed, and my heart skipped a beat.

That cassette was a record of my last conversation with Scooter.

My favorite mini recorder might be languishing at the bottom of Lake Austin, but I'd stuck the cassette and the coin into my pocket that morning when I'd been accosted by News Boy Salazar and his obnoxious television crew outside the shed.

I turned the cassette over in my palm. I'd undressed in the living room after my first meeting with Van Gogh, after I landed in the lake and came home hurt and tired and dripping wet.

I laid the cassette on the dryer, reached deeper into the jeans pocket, and came up with a dull, worn coin.

I stared at it. The eagle had two heads. The wings pointed skyward, and as I stared at it, the floor seemed to rock beneath me. The coin was dark gold and the craftsmanship was beautiful, the way some snakes are beautiful. I shivered. People had lost their lives for this coin, probably in the past as well as the present.

I nearly fell over when the phone rang.

"Cauley?" Jim Cantu's voice seemed very deep over the line.

My breath caught. "What's wrong?"

"Couple of things. I thought you might want to know your buddy Burt Buggess is in ICU."

The phone felt cold in my hand.

"Hey," Cantu's voice came over the receiver. "You okay?"

I shook my head, but said, "Yeah. I'm great. Where is he?"

"Brackenridge."

"Any problem seeing him?"

"Give me a few minutes and I'll go with you," Cantu said. I could hear a television and Cantu's kids fighting about something called *Blue's Clues* in the background. One of the kids sounded like he was coughing up a lung.

"You've got your hands full," I said. "I'm not snooping. I just want to see him."

"It's not him I'm worried about."

I sighed. "Would it make you feel any better if I called Logan?"

"He still in town?"

"He was with me until late last night," I said and braced for a wisecrack.

"You spending time with him?"

"Jim," I said. "He's just doing his job."

Cantu was quiet. "You could do worse, you know."

"I have done worse," I said.

"Call him," Cantu said. "If you don't get him, call me back."

"What's the second thing?"

"They took the accelerant dog through your house. He alerted at what was left of that little coffee table and your living room rug. Probably whoever broke into your house the first time was planning to do more than steal your files. Most likely you surprised your burglar when you came home early from your little date with the mobster."

"You mean Van Gogh was in my house when I came home?"

"Well, we got no forensic evidence it's your earless guy, but it's a pretty good bet," he said. "We're going to send a uniform to cruise your street for a while. Keep an eye on things."

"How come I didn't smell chemicals?"

"Some accelerants dry pretty quick and don't have an odor humans can smell."

I was quiet.

"Cauley?" Cantu said.

"Yeah?"

"Be careful," he said, and he paused. "And call Logan."

"Thanks, Jim. I really appreciate it," I said.

I disconnected and, true to my word, I called Logan on his cell and got his voice mail. Either he was on a stake-out and had turned it off or he was out of range. I left a hurried message that came out a little breathy, because I was rummaging for clean jeans and a fresh tee shirt.

As I dressed, I thought about calling John on the off-chance he might know something. If I did call, would I sound desperate and needy? I thought about the Bug lying in a hospital and dialed John, desperate and needy or not.

"You have reached the voice mail of John Fiennes," John's recorded voice announced. His voice still sounded like dark velvet and my heart did a sad little slide.

After two aborted tries at a message that didn't sound stupid, I was tempted to hang up and write a script. On the third try, I got it right. A calm mix between cool and confident. I hit the pound sign to hear what I'd said and the way I'd said it.

Listening to my own voice message, I only sounded somewhat desperate and needy, so I hit *send*.

I closed the windows, turned off the fans, got my purse, and double-locked the door behind me.

TWENTY-FIVE

I PARKED IN A spot marked *Police* and hustled through the sliding doors at Brackenridge Hospital's emergency entrance. A tiny little blue-haired woman who looked a lot like a garden gnome presided over the information desk.

"Mr. Buggess has been moved to Critical Care on the third floor," she said when I asked about Bug. "He's under police protection. I can't give you the room number, honey. Hospital rules, you know."

"Yes, I know. Thank you. You're a doll," I said, smiling with all my wit and charm. Who needed a room number when you could just go hunt down the gun guarding the door?

I took the elevator to Critical Care and looked for a beat cop. He wasn't hard to spot. He looked young—probably went straight from high school to the police academy. He was sporting a bad attitude and a closely cropped platinum crewcut that made him look like an ambulatory Q-tip.

Even in obits you get a press pass, just like the big boys, and I flashed it at the cop. He wasn't impressed. He eyed me with the suspicion cops always give media and crossed his arms in front of his chest. "Got anyone to vouch for you?"

"Detective Jim Cantu and half of Club West," I said. I stood in the white, antiseptic-scented hallway, waiting as he made the call.

"Right," he said into his radio. He swung the door open, still not looking impressed. I gotta work on my wit and charm.

Inside, the room smelled like rubbing alcohol and misery. Tubes and cables snaked in and out of the sheets, and a bank of machines beeped steadily in the corner. Burt Buggess looked like one of the illustrations of the Lilliputian capture in *Gulliver's Travels*.

"Mr. Buggess?" I said. A mountain of heavy gauze wound around his neck and there was blood seeping through.

His massive chest rose. "Thought you were calling me Bug," he said and opened one red-rimmed eye.

"Bug," I said, and I took his hand and smiled. "How you feeling?"

"Like hammered dog shit."

I nodded. "They say you've been out of it for a while. What happened?"

"Don't rightly know," he said. "I just picked up the last of the animals over at the Blue Parrot and I got 'em back to my place and was gettin' 'em settled in when this guy came out from behind the door and kicked the shit out of me."

I stared at his body, which was enormous, even when prone. "How'd they manage that?"

"Asked me where Scooter kept his shit. When I said I didn't know, he stuck me."

"Stuck you?"

"In the neck. Ain't that the shit? I never saw so much blood."

I shook my head. "Any idea who did it?"

The Bug opened both eyes and tried to sit up. "Same guy that stole my truck. Had a big bone-handled knife."

My stomach dropped. "Big earless guy?"

"He wasn't that big," the Bug said, and I smiled. I guess when you look like the Bug, big is relative.

"You know, Selena came by a bit ago."

I frowned. "How well do you know Selena?"

"She's a good girl, Cauley."

I thought about the gold coin in my pocket and tried to steady my voice. "Did she say anything about Scooter or the Blue Parrot? Did she say anything at all unusual? Like maybe something hidden . . . or stolen?"

"She was pale as a ghost, talkin' 'bout old times." The Bug frowned. "She said something about some kinda necklace, then asked me to take care of the animals from the shop."

I got a terrible feeling of déjà vu and hoped like hell Selena wasn't about to follow in her husband's footsteps.

"I'm worryin' about the girl." The Bug licked his dry lips. "A Detective Cando or something or other was by here earlier today. I asked him to call Selena's mama to check on her."

Drawing a deep breath, I stood, looking down at the Bug, formidable even tucked under hospital sheets.

"You going to be okay?" I said.

"The animals . . . they're at my house . . ."

"Take it easy." I reached over and patted his large, rough hand. "I'm headed to your house next."

Exiting the bug's room, I braved the afternoon heat but felt overwhelmed with a super-size case of dread.

First Scooter, then the mysterious Bastrop veterinarian, and now the Bug. I was up to my eyelashes in bodies and on my way to Paradise.

I called Mia on my cell phone and told her about Bug and the animals. She insisted on coming, as I knew she would. I pulled into her south Austin duplex, past a Virgin Mary statue that spilled water into a funky little wading pool. I hopped out but left the Jeep running because I was still having trouble getting the darn thing started.

"Is the Bug going to be okay?" Mia asked, skipping down the cement porch steps behind me to hop into my Jeep. She was doing hot pink today. Short skirt and clingy top, attractively accessorized with the big black Nikon slung around her neck.

"I don't know," I said. "He looked pretty bad."

Mia was quiet. "Do you know what's going on?"

"Not all of it," I said, thinking of the gold coin in my pocket and wondering where the rest of the blood money was stashed as we headed down the sloping hills of Loop 360. "I don't know where the coins are, and I don't know how El Patron fits into this whole scenario. I can't figure out how Scooter wound up in the middle of this mess."

"What if they just want the money?"

I shrugged. "There's got to be some clue in what Scooter said in the shed. The FBI, Van Gogh, and Texas Syndicate all wanted to know what he told me."

Mia frowned. "What did he say?"

"I could swear he didn't say anything important," I said, frowning. "But I have the tape."

Steering with my elbow, I wriggled the cassette out of my pocket, popped it into the mini recorder and plugged the adapter into the dash. I listened to the hissing tape, waiting for anything that sounded important as we turned down 2222, heading west to Paradise. The sun blistered the sky red as it sank behind the hills. To the left, Lake Austin snaked through its deep gorge.

I tipped my head as the tape whirred.

"Go away." Scooter's voice sounded hollow and staticky, and I shivered at the echo of the past.

"Oh!" Mia sucked in a breath.

On the tape, Sam squawked and then my voice.

"Hey, Scooter." The sound of grunting. *"Rough day?"*

Sam squawked again, I yelped, and then I said, *"Why'd you bring the parrot?"*

"Sam's a macaw," Scooter said. *"Sam's good company. Did you know miners used to take birds with 'em down into the mine shafts? They're sensitive to fumes."*

"The birds alerted when there was a gas leak?"

"No. They dropped dead. It was a sign things were about to go south."

Sam made a garbled noise, sounding like he was trying to talk.

"You know, if you want to off yourself with paint fumes, you're going to have to do better than a can of twenty-year-old latex."

"A lot you know. She left me."

I left-turned at Four Points and we were on 620, heading for Paradise as the tape rolled on, and for the life of me, I knew I was still missing something.

On the tape, I heard Sam shriek and the faint sound of his feathers ruffling.

"What about your pet store?" my voice said.

"I got a guy helps out, looks after the animals, cleans the kennels. Does some computer-type stuff at the shop."

I frowned at the tape recorder as it hissed. "Something's wrong."

Rolling back the tape, I listened more carefully. Sam squawked, and it sounded like a garbled imitation of a human voice. I looked at Mia in the rear-view mirror. "Am I crazy or did that bird just say *zorra?*"

Mia nodded. "I think he did. Why would an American bird say 'fox' *en Espanol?*"

"I don't know. Scooter used to call Selena *zorrita*," I said, thinking out loud.

We pulled into Paradise Cove and climbed out of the Jeep. Tails down, eyes wary, the horde of dogs met us in the Bug's front yard, but they didn't jump and yip the way they'd done before.

"I don't like this," I said and picked up the little rat-dog, heading to the back of the house. The key was in the pot plant out back, right where the Bug said it would be.

"Wow," Mia said when I let us in. The animals were quiet but fidgety. Some of the larger cages were empty. Muffin, the little white hound from hell, limped around the corner. Mia snapped a picture, then bent and picked up the fuzzy little land shark.

"Feed or clean?" I said, and Mia said, "Feed."

I set the rat-dog on the sofa.

Inside the Bug's wrecked living room, it was obvious there'd been a scuffle, but the crime scene techs had come and gone. I found it funny they'd left the pot plant, and I hoped the Bug wouldn't get in trouble for it later. If he lived long enough to get in trouble.

"You want me to call *mi compadres* to come help?" Mia asked.

I looked around at the mess and the restless creatures, glad the Bug couldn't see it. Maybe Mia's militant animal rights buddies were just what we needed.

"Yes," I said. "Some of these little guys probably need medical attention, and we're going to need help figuring out what to do with them if the Bug takes a turn for the worse."

Mia pulled out her cell, punched speed dial, and spoke rapid-fire Spanish while I went to the utility closet for provisions. I made my way back into the living room, trying to prioritize the cleaning.

A rustling sound came from the back room. My heart skipped a beat but slowed as a pair of large, familiar blue wings flapped into the living room.

I smiled. "Hello, Sam, you funny old bird."

Sam lighted on the lampshade next to an empty aquarium and cocked his head, looking at me intently with his onyx-black eyes.

"You hungry, big guy?"

He ruffled his feathers at me. Cautiously, I reached over to stroke his neck the way I'd seen Scooter stroke him a million times before.

"What's this?" I said, touching the bird's bright blue wing.

"What's what?" Mia said.

"Paint, I think. On his wing."

"Wow," she said. "Same ugly green as *Abuelita* Maria's kitchen."

"Avocado green," I said, and I heard my last conversation with Scooter as though he whispered in my ear.

"The birds alerted when there was a gas leak?"

"No. They dropped dead. It was a sign things were about to go south."

My heart thumped and I could see Scooter in that musty old shed, sitting next to the pyramid of old paint cans, and I shivered, thinking of the coin hidden in my pocket like a terrible secret.

"Sam, you're a hero," I whispered to the bird.

Excitement bubbled through my veins for the first time in a long time, and I turned to Mia. "I'm going to call Cantu. Will you be okay here?"

"*Mi compadres* are on the way. *Que pasa?*"

"I'm not sure," I said. "But I gotta go see a man about a bird."

TWENTY-SIX

THE SKY WAS DARK with the threat of rain when I right-turned onto 620 heading for Paradise Falls.

That green paint on Sam's feathers came from somewhere. Since I was fairly sure Sam the macaw had never been in Mia's grandmother's kitchen, I was guessing the paint came from Scooter's dad's shed. I looked down at the coin in my hand, and my heart went off like a pinball machine.

I jerked the wheel and nosed the Jeep up the hill toward the back of the Barnes place, where I would climb the fence, hopefully unseen.

This time, I would be more careful not to bump my head.

The falls in the near distance made a splashing water sound. The swollen moon shone dimly through the clouds, casting the hills in shades of deep blue and gray. I stopped near the end of the fence line and swallowed hard. Small shards of yellow light were spilling from the shed.

Someone had beat me there.

Heart pounding, I shoved the coin into my pocket and quietly crept around to the front of the shed to peek through one of the cracks in the weathered planks.

Selena.

She was sitting on the box-bench, right where her husband sat not so long ago.

She was small and thin, her arms folded tightly in front of her. The padlock was unhinged, so I pushed the front door open and carefully went in.

"Selena?"

She lifted her head and looked at me. I almost didn't recognize her. Her blond hair was wild about her shoulders, her face pale and blank. She was wearing white princess pajamas. Her small feet were bare.

In the dim light I could see the shed was a wreck, like someone had given it the once-over, the way they'd done at Scooter's pet store. The way they'd done at my house.

I nearly tripped over a rotten tire. Rusty tools were scattered along the dusty floor, but the warped cardboard boxes were gone.

"He's gone," Selena whispered, and the soft Spanish in her voice sounded like a sad song. "My husband is gone."

My gaze flicked around the shed. The front door was open behind me, the back door was closed. I wondered if it was locked.

Selena sat, staring straight ahead into nothing.

"Selena," I said carefully. "Is there someone I can call for you?"

I took a step closer.

"No," she snapped. I looked down and realized she was holding a gun. Jesus, not again. *I needed a negotiator.*

Selena yelped when I tripped over a rusty old shovel. *"Parada!"* she hissed. "No closer!"

"Selena, let me call someone for you. Do you want me to call your mother?"

"No!" She was on her feet, one hand over her stomach, the other wrapped around the gun.

I nodded. "You don't want your mother here?"

Selena shook her head and tears spilled prettily onto her cheeks. I looked down at the gun. It was a little Smith & Wesson, like the one Mark had given me. I was close enough that I could see one bullet in the cylinder. If she had a bullet lined with the barrel, that meant she had two.

Selena quivered. "I want you to leave me alone."

"I can't do that, Selena."

Her fair skin seemed tight over her delicate cheekbones.

"Selena," I said carefully. "I don't think Scott killed himself."

To my surprise, she laughed. It was a soft, ugly little laugh that seemed odd as it drifted from her lovely face.

"Selena," I said. "Let me call someone."

"There is no one," she said dully.

I looked down at the gun. It was shaking in her hand. I took a deep breath. "Selena," I said. "Do you know how Scott died?"

She nodded slowly. "I killed him."

"I don't think you did."

Her eyes were red-rimmed, and she looked like a small wild animal caught in headlights.

"Selena," I tried again. "Scott gave me something to give to you." Cautiously reaching into my pocket, I pulled out the coin and showed it to her. "He loved you, Selena."

A strangled noise came from her throat. Her hand shook but she took the coin, staring at it as though it was poisonous.

"The eagle," she whispered.

Nodding, I swallowed hard. "You know what I think?" I said. "I think by leaving Scott, you were trying to get him out of trouble."

Selena choked on a sob. "She hated him."

"I know," I said quietly.

"*Mi madre*," Selena said quietly. "She said he wasn't good enough."

"Your mother isn't here," I said, wondering if I should just reach over and take the gun from her the way Van Gogh had taken mine from me.

"Selena, Coach and Golly Barnes asked me to help you and I will help you, but I need your help to do that. Are there more coins like this one?" I asked, edging toward the box-bench.

"No further," she stammered, leveling the gun on me, and in that moment I could see Scooter clearly in my mind, sitting on the box-bench, surrounded by paint cans and a small arsenal of weaponry.

"Selena," I said. "Were you helping get these coins into the country?"

Her eyes went wide, her lips parted, but she didn't speak.

I looked over my shoulder, wishing like hell Logan was there. "Look," I said. "I saw Scooter's bird earlier this evening. He had paint on his wing. Do you know anything about that?"

Selena stared at me. "Sam?"

"I think the paint on his wing came from these cans. That's what Scott was doing the last time I saw him—messing with these paint cans. And I think that's why he called me that day. He knew I was doing some research that was related. About El Patron."

Selena flinched at that, and I took a deep breath and went on. "I think someone has been smuggling something with the animals imported for the Blue Parrot," I said, looking down at the coin in her hand. "And I think that something was Austrian gold."

Selena stared at me, her expression blank, which I thought was odd. It had been her signature on the bills of lading permitting the parrots and lizards from Argentina to enter the United States. But I was finding it more and more difficult to believe Selena could find her own car in a deserted parking lot, let alone mastermind a smuggling plot.

"I'm going to move now," I said. "I just want to open a paint can. You can watch me if you want."

I held up my hands and moved forward. Selena seemed to be in shock but she moved, mirroring me, still holding the gun.

I glanced around for something to pry a can open and found a rusty screwdriver on the floor. Selena's breath caught when I picked it up.

"Just a screwdriver. See?" I knelt so I could pry the lid from one of the cans.

Selena watched over my shoulder as I opened the can.

"Paint," she said.

"It's paint," I repeated dumbly as I stared into the can of avocado green latex. I was sure it would be empty of paint and full of Nazi gold.

"It's got to be here," I said. "Everything leads back to this shed."

Selena shook her head. She was still holding the gun, but at least she wasn't pointing it at my heart.

"Look, Selena, we need to find the rest of these eagle coins. People are willing to kill for them. Maybe even die for them," I said, and my gaze drifted toward the warped old box-bench.

"I'm going to move very slowly, but I need to look in that bench," I said, hoping like hell there wasn't a dead body in there, but honestly, who was left to kill?

"Why?" Selena said, still holding the gun, and she watched as I lifted the wooden lid. The hinges creaked like a coffin from an old Vincent Price movie.

I stood, staring into the big box.

"Clothes," Selena said, looking over my shoulder, appearing to come out of her daze a little.

Inside the box, piles of old clothes were wadded up and tossed about, as though someone had recently searched through them. "Yes, but somebody's been rooting around in here."

Frowning, I looked at the tangled crumple of clothing, thinking about how much scorpions love to hide in dark messes just like that.

I used the screwdriver to fish the clothes out of the box, one by one, dropping them on the floor of the shed until the screwdriver scraped the wooden bottom of the box-bench.

Selena crept closer and peered into the box. "There's nothing there," she said, and damned if she wasn't right.

"It's got to be here somewhere," I said, starting to feel like a fool. "Was your family wealthy in Argentina?"

Selena shrugged but seemed engaged in the conversation. "My great-grandfather and his friends were wealthy before they left Austria after what they called the Big War."

"Selena," I said, thinking of my conversation with the Colonel. "It was illegal to take assets out of the country in those days."

She looked like she was about to be sick. "Most grandmothers tell fairy stories with princesses and happy endings. My grandmother told stories of Anschluss—the spring of 1938 when troops marched into Vienna. Austria welcomed them with open arms. Within hours, the city's Jewish physicians and teachers were rounded up and made to wash the streets and sidewalks. And Karl Grynszpan, a Jewish jeweler, was forced to mint a special coin to commemorate the conversion of Vienna. The coins were made with gold gathered from the Jews."

I shook my head, feeling sick, too.

"It was my great-grandfather," she whispered, crying now. "He forced Grynszpan to create those coins, and then he escorted him to a train leaving Austria, and then Grynszpan was gone. Forever."

She shivered.

"Selena," I said, but she was on a roll now and I would have been hard-pressed to stop her.

Selena shook her head. "*Oma* said she and her family escaped Austria and came to Argentina. Argentina, *Oma* said, was going to be the beginning of a new generation." Selena smiled a strange smile. "That's what we called my grandmother. *Oma*. She refused to be *Abuelita*, like the other grandmothers. She had great contempt for Argentina and its people."

Selena sighed. "I am half Argentine, you know. No matter what I do, it is never good enough to win her love."

I winced, wondering what it would be like to grow up hating half of what you were. The Austrian grandmother who would never accept her granddaughter of mixed blood.

And I wondered if that was enough to make Selena sign those bills of lading. But it didn't make sense. I couldn't imagine fragile little Selena knowing what she was signing—knowing that those bills of lading would be used to smuggle coins that had caused so much pain. Knowing those bills of lading would eventually be the death warrant for her husband.

"Selena," I said, "did you sign forms to get the animals from Argentina to the United States?"

She looked confused. "I signed many things. Why?"

"I think some of what you signed brought those coins your grandmother spoke of to the United States," I said, looking at the coin. "Are you trying to tell me your grandmother was a Nazi?"

She flinched at the word, but shrugged. "My great-grandfather served in the Third Reich."

"That's terrible, but what difference does it make? I thought most of the escaped Nazis were caught and taken to Nuremberg to be brought up on charges for war crimes."

"Not all of them. They extradited the famous. My great-grandfather was famous. My grandmother, she was not so famous."

"Selena," I said, feeling like someone was sitting on my sternum. "I think maybe that wasn't a fairy tale."

Selena looked down at the coin as I looked around the shed. "They're here, I just know it," I said, and caught sight of the open paint can. Gripping the screwdriver, I knelt and stirred the clotted paint and found nothing but a terrible fashion faux pas best abandoned thirty years ago.

Leaning over the towering stack of cans, I began tapping the bases, listening for irregularities.

"Selena, can you give me a hand?" I said. She wandered over, watching as I moved the cans, prying lids and stirring as I went.

I wrenched the lid off the third can, jamming the screwdriver into the green paint, and hit something hard about an inch from the rim. It was filled with paint, but there, just below the surface, were the gold coins.

"Oh!" Selena said on a breath.

I fished one of the coins out and wiped it clean with one of the old rags from the box-bench, and there, in the dim yellow light, shone the golden image of a perfect two-headed eagle.

"Holy shit," I swore, pulling my cell phone out to dial Logan. "We've got to get out of here." My pulse kicked up 100 beats and I looked at Selena. Her eyes were wide, her face pale. "I can't promise everything's going to be okay, but Scooter's parents, they love you. They'll help you, they'll take care of you and your—"

The phone was ringing, but the sound of clapping hands stopped me cold.

"Very touching."

I could smell him before I saw him.

I turned, cringing to find what I already knew. Van Gogh's large body loomed in the doorway at the front of the shed.

"Drop the phone or I will be very pleased to blow a large hole in your pretty little head."

He smiled, and I noticed he was missing four front teeth. Assessing the situation, I dropped the phone, careful not to click the *off* button.

Selena scrambled toward the wall, the gun shaking in her hands. "Get back!" she said, pointing the gun at Van Gogh.

"There is no need for that, *querida*," a female voice said, and Selena's mother stepped into the light.

TWENTY-SEVEN

SELENA OBREGON STOOD JUST inside the door, dressed in crisply tailored Liz Claiborne. She looked a lot like her daughter, except she was holding a great big gun in a way that looked like she knew how to use it. I'd seen that kind of gun before. It was the same kind of rhino killer that John Fiennes carried.

The older woman lowered her cool gaze on me. "Where is it?"

She hadn't seen the coins, and I slipped the one I'd just wiped clean into my back pocket.

"Where is what?" I said, trying to look innocent.

Without warning, Van Gogh punched me hard on the cheekbone. Stars exploded behind my eyes and I tumbled backward, landing on my cell phone, which skidded across the dusty floor. Apparently innocent isn't my strong suit.

A gunshot rang in the rusty air and someone grunted.

"*Ach!*" Van Gogh roared. "She shot me!" He kicked me in the ribs and I rolled with the blow, and before I knew it, he had Selena by the throat. "She shot me!"

"Stop!" I screamed. "She's going to have a—"

"No," Selena choked beneath his grip. Shaking her head as much as she could under his fat fingers, I met her eyes and went quiet.

"Enough, Cronin!" Obregon said. "Let her go."

Her eyes were sharp and there was no affection in her voice. The smell of cordite hung heavily in the musty air.

"But *zorra*," he growled. "She fucking shot me!"

My head throbbed and my face felt wet. Blood, I thought. Too much blood, and then I realized I'd knocked over a paint can. I got to my knees and looked up at Selena's mother.

"*Zorra*," I said, and despite the pain in my head and ribs, I laughed out loud. "*Vixen*. You're what Diego DeLeon was twisting my arm about and what Scooter was trying to tell me."

And what Sam the bird had been trying to say when he'd warbled *Zorra*.

She smiled a beatific smile that didn't reach her eyes. "It makes no difference now."

I shook my head and couldn't stop the hysterical bubble of laughter. "It wasn't Selena," I whispered. "It was you. You signed those bills of lading to import the animals from Argentina, and you smuggled the coins with the animals. The animals were in bad shape, so they would smell horrible—the low-level guys in customs would be less likely to thoroughly search a cage full of urine and feces. And you probably engineered the deal with El Patron to get the animals here with a minimum of fuss. And you're ready to let your daughter take the fall for it."

"She shot me!" Van Gogh repeated like we hadn't heard him the first time. He was touching his fingers to the bloody bullet hole in his shoulder. "She fucking shot me."

"*Silencio!*" Obregon snapped, staring down at the overturned paint can. "Just shut up!"

She had seen what I had seen.

There, in the clotted green paint, was the distinct shape of dozens of large coins.

"My legacy," Obregon whispered in a reverent tone as she sank to her knees, dirtying her designer skirt. Her blue eyes gleamed over the grimy gold the way they'd never gleamed for Selena.

"Get them up and get this loaded," she said, motioning Van Gogh toward the van with her gun.

"You heard her," Van Gogh said. I nearly screamed when he grabbed me by the hair and yanked me to my feet.

Selena was still cowering in the corner. "Blanche DuBois after all," I muttered.

"Shut up," he yelled, and I set my jaw. I was dizzy. Blood and paint trickled down the side of my face, but I grabbed two of the heavy cans and went for the door, Selena's mother pointing her big gun at me as I moved.

Selena picked up two paint cans and followed. I blinked in surprise.

"Selena," her mother said. "Stop it. You are behaving like a peasant."

Selena gave her mother a withering look worthy of aristocracy and followed me out to the van, which was parked in a flat area along the back of the shed.

In the van, we stacked the paint cans in the cargo area. Selena's mother stood in the doorway of the shed, watching like a prison guard.

"I don't get it," Selena said. "Why *smuggle* the coins? Why not just bring them in?"

"And risk having them confiscated?" I said.

Selena nodded. "Or taxed."

As we made our way back to the shed to load more cans, Obregon and Cronin were busily wiping the green paint from the coins I'd dumped when I hit my head.

"Give that to me," Obregon said, and Cronin looked like she'd slapped him. "They belonged to my grandfather."

I swallowed hard as the realization hit me full on. "I've been touching Nazi gold. People died for that gold."

"Yes, well, certain collateral damage is to be expected."

An oily knot slid through my stomach. "And you killed Scooter for money."

"It's not money!" Obregon snapped, and beside me, Selena began to sob softly.

"Enough, Selena, this belongs to me. To our family," Obregon said. "*Vamanos.* Time is wasting. Get the rest of those cans into the van."

I looked around for a way out of this mess but didn't see an end in sight. With some effort, Selena lifted two more cans and followed me. Grunting, we moved toward the van, the wire handles of the paint cans digging into the soft flesh of our fingers.

As we shoved the cans into the cargo hold with the others, I noticed keys in the ignition. Well, well. Maybe Ms. Obregon wasn't as smart as she thought. Or maybe she thought we were really stupid.

"The only reason they are telling you this is because they are going to kill you," Selena whispered before we went back for the last of the cans.

"They're going to try," I said. "The keys are in the ignition. We may be able to get out of here, but we need to split up—make it harder for them to catch us. Can you run?"

She nodded.

"You know the way up to the house?"

She scowled at me. "Of course. Coach and Golly live there." Her face softened. "Scooter and I used to skinny-dip in the pool, just under the falls."

I couldn't help the wry smile. We had more in common than we'd thought. "I'm going to cause a distraction. When I do, you head for the house. Get up there and dial 911. They're doing periodic patrols out here so it won't be long. Tell them to call the FBI office and ask for Tom Logan. Tell him it's an emergency. I'll run for the van. Your mother will probably follow you, so you'll have to move quickly."

"You overestimate *mi mama*," Selena said. "This is the validation for her life and her whole life's work—the proof behind a family legend she's built her life around. She will hold on to her legend."

I shook my head in disbelief. "But she's your mother."

"Move!" Van Gogh yelled. "Get those cans into the van."

One final shove and Selena and I trudged back to the shed, breathing deeply. At least now we had a plan. It wasn't a very good one, but it was all we had.

"Inside," Obregon said, jerking her gun toward the door. My eyes darted around the dark, hilly landscape. If we ran right now, one of us would get shot. Probably me.

My mouth was dry and my head was pounding as we ducked through the door and into the shed.

Selena's mother held the last paint can, and her eyes gleamed in the dim, dust-moted light. "Selena," she said. "Get into the van."

Inside the darkness of the shed, Selena bowed her head. "No."

We all went quiet.

"What?" Her mother's composure cracked around the edges and her voice was shrill.

Selena didn't look up, but her voice grew stronger. "I said, I'm not going with you, Mama."

Holy hell. This was *not* the plan.

"Don't be *ridicula*, Selena. Get in the van."

Selena set her jaw.

"Oh, for Christ's sake," Van Gogh said, and he swung his fist hard, hitting Selena in the back of her head. There was an awful cracking sound and Selena fell forward over the shovel and crumpled on the floor.

"That was unnecessary," Obregon snapped.

"She will be easier to carry," Van Gogh said over his shoulder as he rolled the spare tire out of the van and into the middle of the shed.

My stomach twisted.

"Now," he said to me, grinning a wide, toothless grin. "What to do with you?"

I stared at the tire and broke into a cold sweat. This man was going to chop off my ear and torch me in a rotten Firestone. From the dusty floor, Selena made a small gurgling noise in the back of her throat.

"She's hurt," I said, dropping to my knees beside her. "Jesus," I said, looking up at Obregon. "What kind of a mother are you?"

I pressed my fingers to Selena's neck. Her breathing was feathery, her pulse fluttered.

In my peripheral vision, I could see Van Gogh advancing on me, his knife glinting in the dim light.

"This is not the time to be clever," he growled.

I leaned toward Selena's still features and whispered, "I'm sorry." Her head bounced as I jerked the shovel from beneath her.

Van Gogh lurched at me, the knife arcing wide, but I came up swinging. I swung the shovel hard and felt the impact all the way up both arms as the metal made contact with his head. Van Gogh howled and everything happened at once.

"You bitch!" he screamed. He'd aimed the knife at my heart, but my body rebounded after I hit him with the shovel. I went pivoting from the impact. Sharp, jagged pain ripped from my tailbone around to the front of my thigh, slicing deep as I spun.

He staggered backward into Obregon, who dropped the paint can and toppled off her designer heels.

I was operating on pure adrenaline, and despite the fiery pain in my leg, I windmilled the shovel over my head to hit him again.

Van Gogh caught the shovel in his free hand and jerked me toward him. He wrapped his big arm around my neck.

My hip hurt like hell and pain shot from my spine to my upper thigh, but I twisted under his grip, hoping to squirm out of his hold. I couldn't break free but in the scuffle, hoping to cause a distraction, I knocked over the last paint can and kicked it so that it rolled. He squeezed my neck harder, and I thought he was going to crush my throat.

Think, Cauley. *Where are his weak points?* I couldn't reach his bullet wound, so I bit his big fat forearm. You'd think some thugs would learn.

"Ach!" Van Gogh yelled, squeezing harder, and I heard a strange but familiar voice.

"I'll take that."

A shadow passed over us and Van Gogh turned toward the front door where John Fiennes stood, holding his large pistol steady. Selena's mother made a terrible hissing noise, but she steadied herself and smoothed her skirt.

"Get out of here, Fiennes," Van Gogh said. "This doesn't concern you."

"I think it does," John said. Without breaking his aim, he reached down and stopped the rolling paint can. Carefully, he pried the lid off and laughed, softly.

"So," he said. "It's true, then."

Nobody moved.

"John," Obregon said. "We paid you to help transport the cargo safely—we've upheld our end of the deal."

"The deal has changed," he said simply, tamping the lid back onto the paint can.

"What?" I said, choking under Van Gogh's grip.

"I'll kill her," Van Gogh said. I tried to gasp for breath and couldn't.

John shrugged. "Do what you must," he said, picking up the paint can. "She knows too much, anyway."

My eyes widened as John pointed his big gun at me.

He pulled the trigger. The noise was deafening and nearly shook the shed. I wanted to close my eyes, but couldn't, and I swear I felt the big bullet buzz by as it hit Van Gogh between the eyes.

Van Gogh's grip around my neck loosened slightly as he slumped to the floor, but his arm was heavy and he didn't let go. I fell with him, scrambling to get out from under his dead weight.

Selena's mother made a break for the back door. John caught her by the back of her neck and slammed her into the wall.

"Oh, no, you don't." He took her gun and shoved her hard into the corner. At the front door, he pulled the chain through the knothole and padlocked the door from the inside.

"A fine example of a mother," he said. "I do not wish to hit you, *Zorra*, but I will."

Pointing his gun at Obregon, he kneeled down and checked Selena's pulse.

"In case you are concerned, your daughter is alive," John said, and slipped Selena's little gun into his waistband. "Your friend Cronin, however, appears to be very dead."

"I knew it," I said, rubbing the choke-marks on my neck, feeling dizzy. "I knew she was lying. You're not with them."

John moved toward me, and I could feel his advance with my entire body. "Cauley," he said softly. "You are entirely too trusting."

"You're a Nazi?" I said, my voice ringing in disbelief.

"I'm a businessman," he said. "Do you know how much that gold is worth?"

"I know the value in human life you people put on it."

He gave me that killer smile that had once melted my bones. With his hands on my shoulders, he turned me around and examined the gash in my hip. "You will live," he said.

He pulled out his cell phone and called an ambulance, then ratcheted back the slide a bit on Obregon's gun, checking for ammunition.

"You've got one bullet. Use it wisely. And don't let anybody take this from you," he said, pressing the gun into my hand.

"But—" I said, but I stopped talking when he kissed me. It was a long, sorrowful kiss that made me feel strangely full and empty.

He broke the kiss and looked at me for a long moment. My vision went a little blurry.

"Help will be here soon," he said, then he turned, picked up the paint can, and disappeared through the back door. I heard the padlock on the back door click into place, then the roar of the van's engine. Then silence.

In the dusty quiet, Selena's mother began to laugh. It was an awful, sultry laugh.

A wave of bile swelled in my stomach.

"Look at you," Obregon said. "You let him get away."

She took a small step toward me.

"Stay back," I said, pointing the gun at her. She laughed again, and a cold sweat broke out on my forehead.

"Can't you see that you are hurt?" she said.

Well, when she put it that way. For the first time since I'd been stabbed, I realized I wasn't doing too well. The floor shifted and I had to fight not to sink down beside Selena.

"You're bleeding," she said, inching closer.

"Stop it!" I said, feeling weaker by the moment, like I was being drained. Tiny dark stars flashed in my peripheral vision, and I had a bad feeling I was about to pass out. "Stop it or I swear to God I'll shoot!"

Obregon moved closer, her cool, blue eyes fixed on me as she advanced. My skin felt cold, my arms and legs weak. Had I really lost that much blood?

"You won't," she said, closer now. "But I will."

My tongue felt like a wet bath mat, and I struggled to stay upright. "You killed Scooter."

She laughed. "No, *querida*, but I authorized it. He had simply outlived his usefulness. He was becoming a nuisance. He was not so smart, but he knew more than he should. He was going to report us to the authorities."

I could barely keep the gun steady, much less pull the trigger. My left leg was soaked with my own blood, and it felt like the blood was filling my shoe.

I could hear my heart slowing, pounding arrhythmically in my head. I leaned back against the wall to steady myself, so tired and cold I could barely stand. I got that nauseated feeling in the pit of my stomach that you get right before you pass out.

Obregon continued toward me and I couldn't keep my legs straight for one more minute. I slid down the wall until I landed with a thump on the floor next to Selena. My heart thumped slow and I tried to keep the gun steady on Obregon.

Help is on the way, I thought. *I just have to keep my eyes open. Breathe. Stay alive.*

"Just let go, Cauley," she said, still moving toward me, her words soft and soothing, her hand moving in front of me like a snake charmer. I had the insane urge to run, but I couldn't move.

"I'll take that," she said and reached for the gun.

The door behind her exploded.

The large form of Tom Logan filled what was left of the splintered doorway. He looked dark and dangerous and on my side. And he was pointing a large automatic at Obregon.

"FBI! Drop it! Now!" he shouted in that deep voice I'd come to recognize all the way to my bones. It may have been the best sound I'd ever heard.

I should have been surprised he'd come, but I wasn't. Tom Logan said if I ever needed him, I should call, and I had.

I watched, feeling oddly detached, like a spectator. Cantu maneuvered past him, a short-barreled shotgun braced against his shoulder, moving alertly as he scanned the shed.

Suddenly, I was aware there were more people in the room. A woman wearing a black raid jacket with big white letters that read "FBI" knelt beside Selena, feeling for a pulse. Two men in blue APD uniforms were handcuffing Obregon. Looking over, I saw another man in an FBI jacket rolling Van Gogh over and hand-cuffing him. I wanted to tell him it was too late, but I was too tired to form a complete sentence.

My pulse sounded like a slow bass drum thumping in the front of my head. My hands felt cold and wet, and I realized I was sitting in a very large pool of my own blood.

Logan dropped to a knee beside me.

"Hey," was all I could say.

His face looked grim. "Cauley," he said, and nothing else.

Logan pulled a small knife out of his pocket, hit a switch, and the blade snapped open. He rolled me to my right and sliced my jeans near the wound. I twisted at the waist, trying to see what he was doing.

Cantu dropped beside Logan. They looked at the long gash and my bleeding leg, then at each other.

Both looked more worried than I would have liked.

Everything moved in slow motion, as though I was floating just under the surface in a pool of water.

Cantu rose to his feet, jerking the radio from his utility belt. He called for two more buses and asked for an ETA, when the dispatcher told him an ambulance was already on the way. The thumping of my heart sounded slower.

Logan ripped off his white dress shirt, revealing a kevlar vest. I thought about the big slash in my rear and wondered if they had kevlar pants. I'd have to remember to ask.

"I'm sorry," Logan said. He got a pained look in his eyes as he stared down at me, the lines in his face deepening as he wadded up the shirt and pressed it hard against the gash in my thigh.

I screamed.

Pain shot straight up my spinal cord and the pressure he applied felt like he was pressing exposed nerve and bone. I heard the wail of sirens in the distance. Then the world spun twice and went dark.

TWENTY-EIGHT

WHEN I WOKE UP, I was lying on my side in the hospital and the entire left side of my body was throbbing with pain. I blinked and the room came into focus. My mother was standing over me with a green Jell-O mold. Suddenly, the events of the past few days crashed in on me. John Fiennes, the Anschluss Eagle. Selena and her awful mother.

"Where's Selena?"

"Well, look who's joined the living," Mama said, tucking the sheets tightly around my legs. Using my good leg, I kicked them free.

Tom Logan stepped into my field of vision. He looked tall and strong and very dependable, and my heart did a little jazz riff.

"They released her yesterday. She went home with her in-laws," he said.

"She's pregnant . . . " I said.

"The baby's fine," Logan said. "Doc says it's going to be a boy. We've, uh, helped them leave town until this thing blows over."

"Witness protection?"

"Not exactly," he said. "They'll be back for Obregon's trial. How are you doing?"

Mama bent down and whispered, "He's been here most of the night."

Great. My butt hurt like hell and the big gash was sending a pulsing pain from my knee to the middle of my spine. My whole body felt like I'd been hit by a truck and I was pretty sure getting a good look at myself in a mirror would make me feel even worse. I checked my pillow for drool.

"Well, I've got to go find Clairee," Mama said brightly. "She was having some young doctor examine her ankle, so I'll just leave you two kids to yourselves." She breezed toward the door humming something that sounded suspiciously like "The Wedding March."

"Subtle," Logan said, and I sighed.

"Your friends were here most of the night," he said. "Nurse Ratched marched in here and kicked them all out."

"Oh." I looked around at a forest of flowers. "How long have I been out?"

"Almost thirty hours," Logan said, handing me the little florist cards he must have gathered from the vases. He looked tired, but he sat on the side of the bed and watched me as I read the cards.

"My mom and the Colonel, Clairee, Aunt Kat, Tanner, Shiner, the girls."

I teared up. "Coach and Golly Barnes sent flowers with Selena."

I thought of Selena's awful mother and my throat went tight.

"Mama?" I called out.

She poked her platinum head around the doorway, just like she wasn't eavesdropping. "Yes, Cauley?"

"I love you."

"Of course you do, sweetheart," she said. "Eat your Jell-O." She disappeared around the corner.

Logan picked up the Tupperware of Jell-O and sniffed it while I laid the cards on the table near the bed.

I sighed. "He wasn't a customs agent, was he?"

"Let's just say he's a person of interest."

"He had a badge," I said miserably. "The business card I know can be forged, but a badge? What did he do, get it on the Internet?"

"Don't beat yourself up, kid. Some of those badges look pretty authentic if you don't know what you're looking at."

I shook my head. "He said he was a citizen."

"His dad was a lieutenant at Ramstein. His mother was a German national. According to our sources, his father met his mother when he was stationed at Ramstein. Fiennes went to live with an aunt in Argentina when he was five years old."

"He's El Patron, isn't he?"

Logan looked away.

I felt hollow inside. John Fiennes had stolen Nazi gold and very nearly stolen my heart.

I looked up at Logan. "Did he get away?"

"It's a small world. We'll find him."

"Knock, knock." Jim Cantu stuck his head around the corner, and despite the roller coaster of emotions rolling around inside me, I grinned.

"Am I interrupting?" he said.

"No," I said. "You're just in time to hear Logan ream me for overstepping my bounds."

"Good," Cantu said. "I'll take notes."

He produced a bouquet of daisies. "Arlene said to give you these. The kids drew you a card."

"Thanks," I said and smiled. "What about Selena's mother?"

Cantu slid a glance at Logan.

"We've got her," Logan said. "There was a lot of batting eyelashes and heaving bosoms." He shook his head. "She actually thought we were going to let her go. She lawyered up the minute we cuffed her."

I adjusted the blankets to make sure my bandaged backside wasn't showing through the hideous little green hospital gown. My head was pounding and the big gash in my gluteus maximus throbbed. "Am I going to be okay?"

"Okay as you ever were. What the hell were you doing in there by yourself?" Logan said.

"Hey," I said. "I tried to call you, and besides, I didn't know Selena was going to be there."

"Yeah, right," Cantu said. "You're goddammed lucky is what you are."

Logan nodded. "You're probably going to have an interesting scar."

I felt my face go pink, realizing that while unconscious I'd mooned at least half the men in the room.

"What?" I said, defensively. "Are y'all war buddies now, or are you just here to get a statement?"

"Don't know what the feds want, but you can come down to the station and give your statement when you spring this joint," Cantu said, and his cell went off. Cantu excused himself and went to the corner to take his call.

"We heard most of it," Logan said and handed me my cell phone. "You left your cell phone on. That's how we tracked you. But you're going to have to come down to the bureau for a debriefing."

I took my cell phone, and without looking up, I said, "Logan. Did you save my life?"

"Nah," Logan said. "We caught the bad guys, or most of 'em anyway. You saved yourself and probably Selena, too."

Cantu returned to the side of my bed. "I gotta get back to the station," he said, and he leaned over and kissed the top of my head. "Call me when you two get done playing Nick and Nora."

I waited until Cantu left, and I said to Logan, "I know why Selena's mother wanted the eagle coins, but what's the connection with John?"

"Greed," Logan said.

I felt sick. "So what happens next? With John, I mean."

Logan looked toward the window. "He can run but he can't hide."

I nodded, not sure how I felt about that.

A clatter of commotion rang outside the door, the sound of metal against metal, and I heard Miranda's silky voice say, "Just a quick word with Ms. MacKinnon . . ."

Then I heard my mother in full mama-mode roar, "Over my cold, dead, Liz Claiborne-clad body!"

Through the open door, I could see Miranda as she tried to wrench herself out of my mother's grip. She nearly made it into the room, a cameraman and sound guy trying to pry my mother off of her.

"Excuse me," Logan said to me, looking amused.

Miranda's face brightened to full-star status as Logan crossed the room.

"Special Agent Tom Logan, I presume?" she purred. "Miranda Phillips. I just have a few questions—"

"Talk to Public Information," he said politely.

"Yes, I know, but since you're already here, you could just answer a few questions—" She flashed her million-dollar smile just before Logan took her by the elbow and led her out the door, my mother still attached to her other arm. I heard them clattering and clanging down the hall, Miranda sputtering something about First Amendment rights.

Logan sauntered back into the room, smacking his hands together like he'd just finished a dirty job. He sat on the edge of my bed.

I grinned, trying not to look smug.

"Wow," I said. "You can be handy to have around."

"You have no idea," he said, and I could have sworn he was flirting with me.

My mother gleamed back into the room, the Colonel and a doctor in tow. She was carrying little cartons of chocolate pudding and handed one to Logan.

The Colonel leaned down and kissed the top of my head. "You okay?" he said. I nodded, but my chest felt tight.

"Good news," Mama announced. "They're going to release you from this wretched place this afternoon."

She looked at Logan. He rose from the bed and cleared his throat. Mama had the nerve to look disappointed. "You aren't leaving, are you, Agent Logan?"

Logan accepted the pudding and grinned. "I'll be back."

"Wonderful!" she said. "And you won't forget about the Fourth of July picnic Saturday?"

"Mama," I said. "He's just doing his job. He's got better things to do than sit around with us eating barbeque and watching fireworks."

Logan turned to my mother. "Thanks for the invitation, Mrs. Connor. Wouldn't miss it for the world."

"Brave man," the Colonel snorted.

I shook my head. "You don't know the half of it."

THE PHYSICIANS AT ST. David's released me right on time, probably because my mother was screaming for painkillers every two hours—for me or for her, I wasn't sure.

I don't think I've ever been so happy to get home. My friends had cleaned up the rest of my house under the watchful eye of my mother, the Queen of the Clean Freaks.

Muse and Marlowe met me at the door, and the whole place smelled like Fresh Scent Clorox. My butt still hurt but the pain was manageable.

I lounged in bed for the next forty-eight hours watching a Turner Classic Movies Dashiell Hammett marathon. I'd already used all my sick days, but it was the extended Fourth of July holiday, so I was taking full advantage. I'd made up my mind to skip the fireworks. I was watching *The Maltese Falcon* and in the middle of a pretty good wallowing jag when I heard a bang at my front door.

Marlowe lifted his head and growled.

Sighing, I grabbed a robe and swung open the door to find Mia and Brynn standing on the front porch with two big bags of supplies.

"Good gawd, Cauley, you look awful," Brynn said.

"Thank you," I said. "Hello to you, too."

"How's your behind?" Mia said, and before I could say anything else, they barged through the door.

"So you're going to the fireworks with Tom Logan?" Mia said, and my heart did a little lurch.

"I really don't feel up to going," I said.

Ignoring me, my friends tossed bags on the kitchen counter, ferreted out chips and queso, and headed straight for the bedroom, where they kicked off their shoes and sprawled on my bed with Muse, ready to offer helpful hints on proper picnic couture.

I shook my head and sighed. It was clear I was not getting out of the fireworks.

In deference to my stitches, I pulled a loose-fitting pair of denim shorts from a drawer, along with a white shirt and a red ponytail holder.

"I'm not going *with* Tom Logan," I said. "I hadn't even planned on going and I'm not even sure he's going, so clearly, we are *not* going together. End of story." I skimmed into the shorts, careful to avoid my stitches. "Does this make me look fat?"

"Fatter than what?" Brynn said, and Mia hit her with a pillow.

I grinned. Getting dressed by committee. Everything was back to normal—whatever that was.

I wondered if Logan would really be at the fireworks. He'd told my mother he would be there, and I had the distinct feeling that Logan was a man of his word. On the off chance that I'd see him, I rummaged through the plastic bag the orderly at the hospital had put my belongings into and pulled out the bloody, sliced jeans. Fishing in the pocket, I pulled out the coin I'd stuffed into my pocket when Obregon had burst into the shed. I looked at it for a long moment—the last of the Anschluss Eagles.

"What's that?" Mia said as I slipped it into the back pocket of my shorts.

"Nothing but trouble," I said.

MY FRIENDS AND I were a little late getting out the door, and my stomach was tied in knots at the thought of seeing Logan again.

We'd already missed the sunset when we loaded the folding chairs and a blanket into the cargo area of the Jeep. I whistled for Marlowe and we all motored down the street to the community park, where the tangy scents of barbeque and beer mingled with the smell of bug spray in the hot evening air.

"Cauley!" Mama said. "Sweetheart! Look who's here!"

I rolled my eyes as Mama hooked her arm around Logan, who'd been talking quietly with the Colonel. The sight of Logan made my breath catch. He was tall and dark and wearing jeans and a black polo shirt, his biceps stretching the short sleeves. For the first time in my life, I understood why Southern women get the vapors.

"Mia, Brynn!" Mama said, transferring her grip from Logan to my friends. "You have *got* to try the sangria. I made it myself!"

Near the bandstand, Clairee sat at a picnic table, munching on ribs and listening to the Bug, who was holding the little white hound from hell. Despite the nerves jangling in my stomach, I smiled.

Logan and I stood alone under the darkening sky.

"What did you call that the other day?" I said. "Subtle?"

Logan laughed.

The lake lapped the shoreline. People milled about with sparklers and turkey legs, and the snappy notes of a Sousa medley marched toward the darkening sky.

"Still got the dog," he said as Marlowe made a fool of himself, dancing and leaping for Logan's attention. I knew how the dog felt.

"Yeah," I said, watching Marlowe. "You know, he hates everyone but you. The way he acts, you'd think he was your dog in a previous life."

Logan grinned and I stared at him.

"You're kidding," I said. "Marlowe is your dog?"

"Sort of," he said, and we began walking toward his old bureau car, our bare arms brushing slightly as we moved.

"How can a dog be 'sort of' yours?" I said.

Logan ignored the question. "He's a great dog. Search and rescue, cross trained in drugs, bombs, and accelerants."

I waited.

"He belonged to my partner."

"Belonged?"

Logan's jaw muscles tightened. "She was killed in the line of duty."

She? I swallowed hard. "I'm sorry."

"Yeah, well, I figured a girl like you needed a guardian angel. I couldn't tail you all the time, so I sent the dog to keep an eye on you 'til this thing was over."

"What's that supposed to mean? *A girl like me?*"

"Stubborn, smart, nosy. Trouble-prone. That kind of girl."

"How did you know I'd keep the dog?"

"Because, kid, you are the Patron Saint of Lost Causes. Also, you're a sucker."

I grinned, but my smile faded as we stopped next to his car.

In the near distance, I saw Miranda setting up a live feed with her television crew. Probably doing a countdown to the fireworks.

I reached down to pet Marlowe. "Do you want him back?"

"Well, that's one of the things I wanted to talk to you about," Logan said. "I'm going away for a while. You feel like keeping him until I get back? You'll have to take him to his Thursday night search-and-rescue training."

I scratched Marlowe's chin, happy about the dog, but trying not to feel hurt that Logan was leaving. "He's some kind of husky, right?"

"Something like that," he said.

I frowned. "What's his name?"

"Dog," he said. "But he seems to like Marlowe better."

"You named him *Dog?*" I laughed. "Imaginative."

"I didn't name him, but it's from a John Wayne flick, if that makes you feel any better."

Behind us, a rocket burst red into the evening air. "What was the other thing?"

"Hmm?" Logan brushed my hair out of my eyes.

"You said keeping Marlowe was *one* of the things you wanted to talk to me about."

"Yeah," he said. "About that."

Logan stepped between me and the dog and kissed me, and my breath went away.

It was a gentle kiss, the way first kisses are supposed to be.

My heart thumped and my brain went blank.

He pulled back and looked down at me, his eyes as dark as a new moon.

"Hey," I breathed. "I thought you were just doing your job."

"Job's done," he said, and he leaned in, his arms around me as he kissed me again, harder this time, and I could feel it all the way down to my toes.

He stepped back, and for once, I was speechless. His hands moved up my lower back to my shoulders and he turned me toward the lake, his body large and warm and sure as he stood behind me.

"See?" he said, nodding toward the sky. "Fireworks."

We stood that way, wordlessly watching the fireworks, until Logan stepped back. He gave Marlowe a pat to the head, then opened his car door.

"You're not staying for the finale?"

"I already got my finale," he said, and I blushed when he grinned.

The finale really did begin then, and massive red, white, and blue fireworks exploded against the dark dome of the sky. The national anthem swelled around us.

I smiled, lost in the moment. "Oh," I said, my memory jogging. "I have something for you."

"All right, I give. What is it?" he said, watching as I searched my pocket.

"The stuff that dreams are made of," I said, and I pressed the coin into his palm.

He looked down at it for a moment, then at me.

He flipped the coin high into the air and it glinted dark gold in the moonlight. Catching it neatly, he tucked it into his pocket.

Logan eyed me for a long moment, then nodded. "You're going to be okay, kid," he said, and then he got into his car and disappeared into the night.

TWENTY-NINE

BACK AT HOME I was trying not to feel sorry for myself as I surfed through 400 channels of televised crap, looking for something to take my mind off a certain FBI agent who was missing in action.

Logan said he'd be back, and God help me, I believed him.

Muse was snoring on the back of the sofa and Marlowe was lying next to me with his furry chin on my knee. The dog was watching television, his little white eyebrows moving as I channel surfed. I landed on CNN and tossed the remote onto the end table. The anchorman was droning on about the latest congressional bickering, and I wondered if anyone knew just how precarious our little world was.

"So you're an FBI agent, too, huh?" I said to the dog. His ears twitched, and I could tell he was listening. "Well, that explains the way you snorted around the Turkish rug and the coffee table. You knew somebody doused them with accelerants, didn't you, big guy?"

Marlowe lifted his head and I rubbed his soft, velvety ears. "I guess sometimes you do get two guys, even if you aren't Ingrid Bergman."

The music swelled on the television and I jolted as the anchorman's voice changed the way it does when there's something important to report.

"Suspected fugitive John Fiennes was taken into custody this morning in Belfast, where he was caught transporting nearly fifty pounds of antique gold coins."

I sat up and Marlowe growled.

"Fiennes is the alleged leader of a Central Texas syndicate known as El Patron, which has ties to South American countries including Brazil and Argentina. Fiennes escaped from custody late this afternoon, but authorities say they have detained the coins, which are on their way to a lab for identification—"

I jumped to my feet and the dog stared at me.

"Marlowe," I said. "We've got some writing to do."

I rushed down the hall toward my computer in the den, then stopped short. Van Gogh was dead, but I wasn't sure where John was, and I wasn't about to get my hard drive stolen again.

I swung around and raced toward Aunt Kat's old Remington Scout in the library, moved the Magic 8 Ball, and jammed fresh paper under the cylinder.

I pounded the keys like I was possessed.

The old keys were harder to press than the computer keyboard and there was no delete key. Even so, the words had never come faster.

My Heroes Have Always Been Cowboys, I typed. *By Cauley MacKinnon.*

My fingers flew as the story bloomed on the page.

"Nearly three months ago, Scott 'Scooter' Barnes, a real hometown hero and former Dallas Cowboy running back, was branded a coward when he barricaded himself in a shed, allegedly threatening suicide. The coroner's department is currently reclassifying Barnes' death as a homicide and reopening the investigation. But Scott Barnes may have helped prevent an international tragedy with ties to Central Texas, Argentina, and beyond . . ."

Stopping a moment, I picked up the phone and dialed Tanner.

"Hey," I said into the receiver. "You got a minute?"

Tanner's tires spun gravel in my driveway forty minutes later as I ripped the last piece of paper out of the old typewriter. Marlowe growled low in his throat.

"Give it a rest, tough guy," I said to the dog and let Tanner in.

"It's ten o'clock at night! What in hell's going on?" Tanner said, his cigar puffing plumes of silver smoke.

"I thought you quit smoking."

"I did," he grumped. "You okay?"

"I'm fine," I said. "Put that cigar out. I've got something to show you."

He didn't extinguish his smelly cigar, but I handed him the stack of freshly typed paper and moved to the kitchen to get us each a Corona.

"You spelled *Pedernales* wrong," he said, turning the paper over in his hands, fingering the depressed text. "What the hell did you do? Write this on a fucking typewriter?"

"Just read it," I said and handed him a bottle of cold beer with a wedge of lime.

He paced as he read, and I watched his face brighten as he took in the story that would probably win both of us a Texas Press Association Award, typos or not.

"El Patron?" he grumbled, but his eyes jerked quickly from left to right as he read on. His expression changed, and I could tell he'd gotten to the part about John Fiennes and his escape from custody earlier this afternoon. I watched Tanner's face as he read about the stolen coins that were most likely going to be authenticated as Anschluss Eagles.

"Jesus," he said, sinking into the sofa.

"Yeah," I said.

I jumped when the telephone rang and the machine picked up.

"Cauley?" A dark velvet voice said. "Bond here. I wanted to tell you that I miss you and I am very sorry . . ."

I scrambled to the machine and hit the silence feature. There were some things Tanner didn't need to know.

"That him?"

I felt my cheeks redden but I nodded. Tanner shook his head. "Who else knows about this?"

"I don't know. Cantu knows some of it, but nobody outside Tom Logan and the bureau, except John Fiennes, knows all of it."

"And you got all the backup?"

"Authenticated all my sources," I said.

Tanner nodded. "This is good, Cauley. Really good. But you do realize I can't bump you to City Desk—"

I wanted to smack him. "I didn't do this to get off the Dead Beat," I said.

"You don't want a promotion?"

"Well, yeah," I said. "But I did this because I owe it to Scooter and his parents. He called me that day from the shed because he wanted to dime out his in-laws and those bastards in El Patron. He knew I'd done Ryder's background research on El Patron. You know what? Scooter was the one who started unraveling this thing. He's the real hero here."

Tanner was quiet for a long moment. "You gonna be in on Monday?"

"If I still have a job."

"Don't fucking tempt me," he said, heading for the door. "Be on time."

"You bet." I smiled and let him out.

I closed the door and walked back into the house, a riot of emotions rocketing around in my rib cage.

I jumped when the telephone rang again. The machine picked up and my heart jolted when I heard John's voice.

"Cauley? Are you there?"

Hesitating, I picked up the phone.

I waited a beat. "They're looking for you," I said.

"I wanted to explain."

"I don't need an explanation."

"I think you do," he said. "We came down on the wrong side of this. And I never expected to fall in love with you."

I felt dizzy, like I was car sick, but I listened as he went into a really bad Bogart impression. "But I've got a job to do," he said, "and where I'm going you can't go."

"If you say *We'll always have Paris,* I'm going to buy a gun and shoot you myself."

He chuckled at that, warm and low, then was quiet for a long time. I stood, holding the telephone as though it was my last connection with him, and I thought of Logan and his hasty departure earlier that evening. I blew out a breath.

"He's going to catch you," I said finally. "And I'm going to write about it."

"Perhaps," John said. "See you around, Cauley."

My breath caught and I closed my eyes.

"Goodbye, John," I said, and disconnected.

Muse hopped up on the kitchen counter next to the Magic 8 Ball and stared at me as I went back to the answering machine.

I hit *play* and the rest of John's message spooled.

I hit the *erase* button.

The mechanical voice of the machine said, *Press erase again to erase all messages.*

Muse glared at me and I hesitated. A year's worth of messages from men who'd left me.

I stood over the machine and pressed *erase* again.

All messages erased, the machine announced.

"I hope you're happy," I said to the cat. Muse gave me a self-satisfied smirk, hopped off the counter, and leapt to the top of the nearby Wurlitzer.

"Well, I guess I'm still the Obituary Babe," I said to Marlowe. "For now."

I picked up the 8 Ball and took it to the library and set it on a shelf above the old cigar box near the old Remington Scout.

"Rest well, Scooter," I said, running my fingers along the metallic surface of the typewriter. I opened the cigar box and took out my father's compass. It felt surprisingly warm in my palm.

Men may come and go, but the good ones never really leave.

"Thank you, Daddy," I whispered, and I felt his presence like a physical thing.

Beside me, Marlowe cocked his head and whined.

"It's okay, puppy," I said, but my throat felt tight. I set the compass next to the typewriter and moved into the hall, where Muse was still perched atop the Wurlitzer. I smiled.

"Logan was right," I said to the dog and cat. "We're going to be all right."

I hit the familiar series of worn plastic buttons on the old jukebox. Gears churned and the 45 dropped. The needle hissed as it hit the record.

The music started, and Aretha wailed, "When I'm down . . . and feelin' low, ah ooohh . . ."

Marlowe barked his strange, warbling bark.

"I know," I said to the dog. "It's Aretha."

Muse sat on top of the jukebox, her tail twitching to the beat. Marlowe yipped and pranced as the music swelled.

Then I threw back the rug, and the three of us danced until dawn.

THE END

395

Read on for a sneak peek at

Dead Copy

by

Kit Frazier

IN STORES MAY 2007

———————————

FBI SPECIAL AGENT TOM Logan is back in town, and he's got a proposition for obituary writer Cauley MacKinnon: he needs somebody dead. And who better to help fake the death of a weasely informant than Cauley, aka the Obituary Babe? But things go awry when the snitch is gunned down on the way to the courthouse, his sister is nabbed by a mysterious killer, and soon Cauley is up to her eyelashes in dead bodies and on the hunt for the missing sister with her search and rescue dog, Marlowe.

EXCERPT

ANSWERING THE PHONE IS always a crapshoot. It's usually the electric company checking to see if I'm dead because they haven't received a payment in two months or my mother calling to remind me that I'm on a swift approach to thirty and time's a-wasting.

It's never a good call, like my dream guy ringing from the driveway or Publishers Clearing House calling to tell me they're circling the block with a big fake check for a million dollars. Although if it was one of the guys from Publishers Clearing House, he would definitely be at the top of my Dream Guy list.

The phone trilled again. From the foot of the bed, Marlowe growled low in his husky-mutt throat. I cracked open one eye. Family or creditor, it was clear the phone was not going to stop ringing. My answering machine was broken so, short of faking my own kidnapping, I was going to have to answer it. Searching through the tangle of sheets, I nearly knocked Muse's grouchy little calico butt off the bed. *Jeez, what time was it anyway?*

"Sorry, cat," I muttered, ferreting the cordless out from underneath a pile of pillows.

"Cauley MacKinnon," I said into the receiver, my voice heavy with sleep and sounding a bit like Lauren Bacall.

I waited.

Nothing.

"Hel-loooo," I said into the silence and heard the unmistakable sound of heavy breathing. All the little hairs on the back of my neck lifted and I blinked myself awake.

"Look, you big jerk," I said with a mix of fear and false bravado. I was about to blast the bozo with a string of anatomically impossible suggestions when a deep voice drawled, "I need somebody dead."

Aha! This time it really was my dream guy.

Grinning like an idiot, I wrapped my quilt around me and snuggled deep into my big, empty bed. "Somebody *already* dead or somebody you want to *get* dead?" I asked. Just for clarification.

"The latter."

I nuzzled the phone to my ear and could practically see Special Agent Tom Logan leaning against his battered gray bureau car, looking like a tall, dark-haired, square-jawed Eagle Scout on high-octane testosterone. "Is this going to be one of those things where I have to help save the world and I get stabbed in the ass and then I don't get to write a Pulitzer Prize-winning article when it's all over?"

After a long pause, he said, "Probably you won't get stabbed again."

"Tom Logan, how you talk. FBI agents are so mercurial."

"How many FBI agents do you know?" he said.

"Enough that you shouldn't leave town again anytime soon."

I could practically hear him smile over the line and I wondered where things stood between us. The last time I'd seen Tom Logan, he'd thoroughly inspected my tonsils at the Fourth of July picnic and then disappeared into the night to go interrogate fugitives or use thumbscrews or whatever it was FBI agents did when they were called away in the line of duty.

"Yeah, sorry to leave in such a rush," he said, and he sounded like he really meant it. After a short pause, he said, "I need a favor."

"Right now?" I rolled my head to look at the little analog clock ticking away on the antique nightstand.

Four in the morning. It is my opinion that four o'clock should only come once a day, and it should come firmly entrenched in a happy hour.

In his deep Fort Worth drawl, Logan said, "I need an obituary."

I frowned. "An obituary?"

Anywhere else in the world, a request for an obituary in the middle of the night might seem crazy. But in Texas we have a special affinity for crazy. I hear up north they lock their crazy people in the attic. Down here, we prop them up on the sofa and invite the neighbors over for iced tea. In Texas, crazy is relative.

Rubbing my eyes, I said, "An obituary for who?"

"I can't get into it on the phone, I just need to know if you can do it. If you can't, I can get somebody else . . ."

"Well, of course I can do it," I said irritably. "Besides. How many obituary writers do you know?"

"One is all I need," he said, and I blinked in the darkness. Was Tom Logan flirting with me at four in the morning?

"It needs to look authentic," he went on, "with the right wording and on newsprint, printed on both sides so it looks like the real deal."

I sighed. Not flirting, apparently. But then, that was Logan. All business.

"Let me get this straight," I said. "You want a fake obituary on a tear sheet?" I said, wondering how I was going to pull that off. "And when would you need this real-looking fake obituary?"

"Now."

I bolted upright in bed. If Tom Logan said he needed something now, he wasn't kidding.

"Okay, just . . . give me a minute," I said. Stumbling out of my old four-poster, I stepped on the sharp corner of a DVD case for *The Searchers*. "Ow!"

"You okay?"

"It's four o'clock in the morning," I growled, snatching up the DVD.

Logan had given me the flick right after my house had been burgled and my movie collection trashed, probably hoping to win over another John Wayne convert. The movie wasn't noir, my favorite, but it was pretty good—if you like endings where the hero wandered off into the sunset alone. Which I don't.

But wandering off into the sunset alone is something I seemed to be doing a lot more of since I met Tom Logan . . .

"Is this going to be a problem?" he said.

"No . . . I'm ready, sort of . . ." With the phone wedged between my shoulder and ear, I tossed the disk onto the dresser and yanked open a drawer for a pair of jeans and a tee shirt, wishing I had time to find a killer summer sweater that fit so well it would make him think twice before leaving again.

I glanced in the mirror above the dresser and immediately wished I hadn't. Ordinarily, no self-respecting southern girl would be caught dead going out of the house with stage-three bed head. But I have found that self-respect is often highly overrated. I swiped a brush through my hair and gave up.

"Cauley? You still there?"

"I said I'm ready," I huffed, juggling the phone as I hopped on one leg, wriggling into a pair of jeans. "Where do you want me to meet you?"

"No need for that," he said. "I'm in your driveway."

Tom Logan was in my driveway?

Shit, shit, shit!

My heart sprinted as I ran a toothbrush over my teeth, fed the cat, leashed the dog, locked the front door of Aunt Kat's little Lake Austin bungalow, and skipped down the porch steps, where Logan's beat-up old bureau car was idling under the magnolia tree, headlights glowing against the warm, blue velvet sky. I couldn't help but smile.

The scents of fresh-cut grass and Mexican sage hung heavily in the predawn air, and I wished I'd had time to pop an antihistamine. We were well into the waning days of November, but summer and winter were at war over the brief bit of Texas autumn. We were stuck in that amorphous in-between time— a tedious, long stretch of hot and sticky that put everybody on edge.

Despite my post-summer restlessness, I was happier than I'd been in a month. I stood outside Logan's passenger door, the dog leaping at the window like a maniac.

Logan grinned, his face illuminated from the blue glow of the dash lights. Leaning across the console, he opened the passenger door from the inside. "Hello, kid. Long time no see."

My heart did a ridiculous little jazz riff and I felt my cheeks go red, despite the fact that it was four in the morning.

The dome light in the car was out, but the stars were bright in the autumn sky and I'd know that dark hair and those dark eyes anywhere. Even in the dead of night, Special Agent Tom Logan was hotter than a West Texas wind and twice as unpredictable.

My breath caught in my throat. He was wearing faded Levis and a worn, white tee shirt. Both garments bulged in all the right places.

I slid into the tattered and torn passenger seat after Marlowe, who was happily greeting Logan with a whole-body wag.

I knew how the dog felt.

Squinting at Logan, I said, "I am not a morning person."

"No kidding," he said, but he was smiling, scratching the dog's white, fuzzy muzzle as I buckled up. "You still putting him through his paces?"

Marlowe actually belongs to Logan, although I've been looking after the dog since Logan got called away on a big assignment. Or the dog's been looking after me. Sometimes it's hard to tell.

"Yeah, we do the training thing every Thursday night," I said. "He's great at the agility stuff, but so far, the only thing I've seen him search and rescue is a peanut butter sandwich."

Logan chuckled at that and handed me a trough-sized to-go cup of iced tea. "We doing this downtown?"

I shook my head and gratefully swallowed a big gulp of undiluted caffeine. "We don't do print or production at the *Sentinel* satellite, but we do have Cronkite."

"Cronkite?"

"It's a working model of an old-fashioned printing press. We use it to make mockups when kids come for Career Day and that sort of thing."

"Mockups?"

"We take a stock story and use it as a frame, plug kids' names in and they get to take home a personalized article. Only we try not to use obituaries."

"Right," Logan said. "You need to call anybody to make it happen?"

I shook my head. "It's early. The night-side crew rarely comes up front and we'll get there before day-side gets in. That way we don't have to explain anything."

Logan nodded and put the car in gear. "We've got to make a stop first," he said, and turned his attention to the big white dog who was straddling the console.

"Back," Logan ordered, and Marlowe leapt into the back seat.

Behind me, a nasally voice yelped, "What the hell? What's with the dog? I hate dogs!"

Startled, I jerked toward the back seat. As my eyes adjusted to the darkness, I saw a guy shielding himself from Marlowe with his forearm. He looked like one of those guys you see getting chased over a chainlink fence in a bad episode of *Cops*. His spiky black hair looked like it'd been hijacked off a hedgehog and moussed with so much product you could bounce a quarter off of it. The sleeves of his black tee shirt were rolled up to reveal biceps that didn't quite bulge. His features were straight and even, but there was something sort of vague about him that landed him on the ugly side of handsome. With his pointy nose and too-close eyes, he could very well have been a genetically altered weasel.

"Who's that?" I said to Logan, who was staring at the guy in his rear-view mirror.

"That," he said, "would be our obituary."

"WYLIE RAY PUCKETT," THE weasel said. "But everyone calls me Puck. My sister says it's somethin' to do with that Shakespeare dude."

Oh, good. A literary thug.

Puck lunged half-over the front seat to shake my hand. The smell of stale beer and cheap aftershave oozed from his pores, and when he took my hand, I had to stop myself from flinching. The guy's palm was sweaty as he leered at me in the dim light.

Marlowe growled.

Puck sneered at the dog, then looked me up and down through the gap in the seats. "You're the Obituary Babe? *You're* the girl who's gonna kill me? You don't look like an obituary writer. You look like one of those blond Gap babes on TV."

He seemed entirely too excited at the prospect of reading his own obituary, but I got the distinct impression that Wylie Ray Puckett was the kind of guy who inspired lots of people to want to read his obituary.

"What kinda name is Collie, anyway? You named for a dog?"

I narrowed my eyes. Despite his butchering my name, there was something familiar about him, something I couldn't quite put my finger—or my foot—on . . .

"Sit back and shut up," Logan growled.

"What? I'm just talkin' to the girl," the weasel said, but he sulked into the shadows in the back seat.

Logan watched him in the mirror. "He's testifying at the Obregon trial and some of his buddies in El Patron would rather he didn't."

"*He's* with El Patron?" I shuddered. The last time I'd had a run-in with Selena Obregon and her band of South American baddies, I'd been stabbed and run into the river and very nearly had my heart broken.

"Puck's their numbers guy," Logan said. "Word on the street is there's a hit out on him."

I bypassed the most surprising part of that statement—*That guy's an accountant?*—and went for the less obvious but more important question: "An accountant needs protection?"

"Hey," Puck said. "I know where the money is made and laid, babe."

"And some of that money came up missing," Logan said. "Seems our pal here has sticky fingers. He's agreed to dime out his buddies for a deal."

"It wasn't embezzling or anything," Puck grumbled. "It was an investment."

"How's that working out for you?" Logan said.

Puck folded his arms and sank further back into the seat.

I shook my head. "So we're going to stage this guy's death? Am I allowed to do this?"

"We've been outsourcing some projects—we're getting more leeway through Homeland Security. You write obituaries for a living, so it makes sense to source it out to you."

I couldn't argue with his logic, but I was the tiniest bit disappointed that Logan hadn't dropped by just to see me, even at four in the morning.

Especially at four in the morning . . .

Puck poked his head over the console. "Hey, I thought we were hittin' Mickey D's."

"The one out here's not open yet," Logan said. "And sit back."

Puck sat back in the seat. "Yeah, well, I'm hungry. I want a couple of those egg muffins. And some of those hash browns that come in the little paper things and a big ol' thing of Diet Coke. Hey, I can hear my stomach growling back here."

"That's the dog," Logan said. "Keep it down. He hasn't had breakfast yet."

I grinned, shaking my head. "How long have you been babysitting?"

"Too long," Logan said. "The sooner we get this guy dead, the sooner I can get back to my real caseload."

"Hey. I got an idea about that," Puck said, leaning between the seats again so that his head was bobbing above the console between Logan and me. "So we're goin' to court, right? So, we get to the courthouse, and see, I'm goin' up the steps to go make my statement, mindin' my own business, and then, *bam!*"

He was so excited he was frothing at the mouth. I leaned forward so as not to get any of his flinging bodily fluids in the near vicinity of my neck.

"These guys come out of nowhere," he went on, clearly caught up in his own criminal genius. "They come wheeling around the corner in a big, jacked-up 4 × 4 and they just *bam-ba-bam-bam-bam,* gun me down, but they're really FBI guys, see? They're shootin' blanks! Only nobody knows it but you, me, and the Obituary Babe here. Pretty cool, huh?"

"Sit back," Logan said. "We're not staging a shootout. Hits don't go down like that."

"Logan's right," I agreed. "Hits *never* go down like that. Nobody knows there's even been a hit until the cops find a dead body in a deserted ditch in the boondocks."

"Oh, what d'you know, blondie?" Puck said, and I stared at him in the rear-view mirror. He really did look like a weasel.

My great aunt Kat says there are three kinds of men: the ones you play with, the ones you stay with, and the ones that just need killing.

I hadn't known Puck long, but I suspected he fit rather nicely into that last category.

"My dad was on the job," I said quietly, but the weasel didn't know when to quit.

"No shit?" he said. "I always wanted to be a cop. I figure I'd be a good cop. You know that show *CSI?* I figure it out. Every time. Way before those dickheads on the show figure it out."

"You know," I said. "My dad used to say it's better to keep your mouth shut and let everyone think you're an idiot than to open your mouth and prove it."

"Hey," Puck said. "What's that s'posed ta mean?"

"Sit back," Logan said. His voice was quiet, but there was iron in it.

Puck sat back.

We dodged in and out of traffic and for a time I sat back too, watching the sliver of moon shine down on the rolling hillsides of Ranch Road 2222, the live oaks cast in shades of copper and blue in the early November morning. Big, beautiful houses cut jagged chunks out of the limestone cliffs, a reminder of Austin's relentless population boom. Even at that insane hour of the morning, we were boxed in by traffic. Lots of people visit Austin. No one ever leaves.

I turned from the window toward Logan. "So where are we heading?"

"To tie up some loose ends. What kind of shoes are you wearing?" he said, sliding a glance down my legs. Each of my nerve endings pinged *red alert!*

I cleared my throat. "Excuse me?"

"What kind of shoes?" he said, turning an abrupt right off Ranch Road 2222. "We're going off-road."

I gripped the dash as the car squealed onto Mount Bonnell Road. I glanced down at my Keds—glad for once that I'd forgone fabulous for functional.

"We're goin' up to Mount Bonnell?" Puck jammed his head over the console again, wiggling his shaggy, dark brows at me.

My upper lip curled into a grimace.

Mount Bonnell has one of the most spectacular views in Central Texas—miles and miles of rolling Hill Country to the west and the glittering Austin skyline to the east. It's also the hottest spot for the Mustang Mambo in the four-county region.

Puck was at the edge of his seat. "The three of us are going up to Mount Bonnell? Really?"

I stared at him.

Logan's jaw muscle tensed, and for a minute, I thought he was going to elbow the weasel right in his pointy nose.

"Three of us are going up," Logan said. "Two of us are coming back."

Puck's over-large Adam's apple bobbed as he swallowed hard and sat back in his seat, quiet for a change.

"We're doing it here? I thought most of these things went down east of Austin," I said.

"Most of them do. But we're on a tight schedule. Today's the only day he won't be accounted for. We stage the obit today and postdate it for next week. He needs to be seen in public a couple of times this week, then we put the word on the street he's been snuffed, flash the right people the obit, and he's out of it until his court date."

"And then you're finished babysitting?"

"Until some other disaster blows in."

"Hey! You callin' me a disaster?" Puck said.

Logan ignored him.

It was harder for me. I swallowed hard and stared out the window. I was going to help fake a death. It seemed surreal. But then, half the time I spent with Logan was beyond surreal.

I shivered. There were people—bad people—who were going to think Puck was dead. But if Puck could help put Selena Obregon and El Patron—her malicious band of murderers—behind bars, it was worth it. Even after four months, the mere thought of Obregon still had the power to make my stomach twist into a big, oily knot.

Logan turned into the narrow lot at the foot of the enormous limestone cliff, parked, and got out of the car.

I took a deep breath and climbed out after him.

Marlowe bounded out of the passenger door after me, probably using Puck's lap as a springboard, judging from the way the weasel yelped.

Logan pointed at Marlowe. "Back."

The dog leapt back into the car and waited. I shook my head. One of these days, I was going to have to figure out how he did that.

I stood beside Logan at the back of the battered car, which probably had been a piñata in a former life. The scents of cedar and blue sage wafted on the warm breeze and the sky was brilliant with stars—not a scene conducive to murder. In the movies, murders take place in cold, dark, gritty alleys—not on warm, beautiful, tree-covered banks overlooking a moonlit river. But this was Austin, where anything could happen and usually did.

Logan rummaged through the trunk, which was jammed with a large duffle bag, two radio consoles, a plastic tool kit marked *Crime Scene*, a box of twist-tie handcuffs, three large flashlights, and an assorted array of weaponry.

"Jeez," I said. "You use all this stuff?"

"Not all at once," he said, and I grinned. The edginess I'd been feeling started to ease.

Puck stumbled out of the car and gawked at the one hundred steps that lead straight up to the rocky point. Puck was probably in his late twenties, but his voice had a telltale smoker's rasp and his butt was shaped like it'd seen the top of too many barstools.

At the foot of the stairs, he balked. Probably afraid Logan wouldn't let him stop for a smoke break.

"That's a helluvalot of stairs." He turned back toward Logan and pointed at the park sign. "Says here this place locks up at ten, right? Maybe we should just do this here. You know. We don't want to mess this up 'cause some neighbor calls on criminal mischief or something. I could get made."

"Yeah," Logan said. "You're a real stickler for rules."

Logan shoved a clip into a huge .45.

Puck's eyes lit up. "Hey, is that the gun you're gonna shoot me with?

Logan stared at him.

"Can I see it?"

"No."

I shook my head. Texas men and their firearms—the final frontier.

Logan checked the clip and then handed me a Polaroid camera, hefted the duffle over his shoulder, placed his left hand at the small of my back, and guided me toward the stairs. A cold chill skittered up my spine.

"You ready?" Logan said, and I blinked.

Ready? I wasn't sure. Me on an honest-to-God FBI mission. My heart was pounding and I felt a little dizzy. But Logan was trusting me with this assignment and I liked the way it felt.

As we headed up the stairs, I could feel Logan's presence behind me, solid and strong. I'd forgotten how tall he was. His hand was large and warm and I could feel the heat of it through my tee shirt . . . *Good grief, Cauley, get a grip!*

To be fair, I hadn't seen him in months and I hadn't felt a hand on my back, not to mention any other part of my body, since Logan set off my fireworks and then left on the Fourth of July. I figured I was entitled to a little latent lust, even under the less-than-desirable circumstances.

The three of us trekked up the steps, with much wheezing and moaning from Puck, past the park rules sign at the top. *No one in after ten, no glass bottles, pick up your own trash, no throwing rocks off the cliff . . .*

Sounded reasonable. Mount Bonnell is the highest point in Austin. It's a small park but a spectacular one, with a narrow observation deck and a rustic pavilion at the top. Rock-throwing used to be a real problem at the park, which is one of the reasons they'd set a curfew. Some of the high-dollar homes perched beneath the peak had patched holes the size of small craters in their expensive Spanish tile roofs because some nitwit downed a couple of beers and thought it'd be a good idea to pitch golf-ball-sized rocks from the peak.

I gazed around in the tree-shrouded darkness. Puck had been right about one thing—the park definitely closed at ten. The place was deserted.

We were too high to hear the lake lapping the shoreline, but you could smell the fresh water, even at that distance. The only sounds were the rasp of rustling branches and a chirring chorus of cicadas.

"Stick close," Logan said, and I nodded.

Logan led us past the pavilion, where we picked our way along a crude deer path fifty feet straight down to an outcropping. Beyond that, the cliff dropped another seven hundred feet down to the lake.

"Stay away from the ledge," Logan said, setting the duffle on a waist-high boulder.

I looked down, way down, and my stomach lurched. "No problem," I said, edging back toward Logan.

Puck didn't seem impressed at the height.

"This is it? This don't look so bad. Hey! You see those houses down there? Jeez! Talk about *la mansiones*."

I followed Puck's pointing finger. He was right. Some of the homes perched below the summit were mansions—some I recognized from the ubiquitous two-page spreads that Meggie in the *Sentinel's* lifestyle section can't seem to stop covering.

Puck stood, peering over the edge like he was deep in thought and unfamiliar with the process. He turned abruptly and shouted, "Hey, y'all, watch this!"

The breath left my body and I thought, *No good can come from this . . .*

There are a number of universal truths in this world. One of the most time-honored is that when a redneck yells, "Hey, y'all, watch this!" you should get out of the way as quickly as humanly possible, as these are most likely the last words he'll ever say.

Puck picked up a rock the size of a softball and heaved back to throw it over the cliff. Judging from the look on Logan's face, it could have been Puck's last act.

But the skree beneath Puck's boots gave way, and as though he'd seen it coming, Logan grabbed him by the back of his neck and jerked hard. I swear I saw Puck's life flash before my eyes.

"Give me that," Logan growled, wrenching the rock from Puck's grip. "You keep that up and we're not going to have to fake your death."

Logan's voice was low and rough, and I had to give him an A-plus for not pitching Puck over the edge right then and there. Logan is a patient man, but I have found there are limits to his civility.

Puck's Adam's apple bobbed violently, and after a big swallow he said, "Jeez. Take a pill. I didn't mean nothin' by it."

"Yeah, you never do. Just stay there and don't move," Logan said.

Puck settled in by the rock as Logan unzipped his duffle, extracting a trash bag, a shirt, and a squeeze bottle of catsup.

Logan twisted a silencer onto the barrel of the gun. "Take off your shirt."

Puck grinned at me.

"I think he meant you," I said.

"Oh, yeah, right," he said. He hesitated, then yanked his shirt over his head, and he had the good grace to look embarrassed.

Puck had a red farmer's tan that ended abruptly at his neck and a tattoo on each arm—one of a Confederate flag and the other of an elaborate pot leaf wrapped around a skull and dagger.

Oh, good. An art enthusiast.

"How come you want my shirt?" Puck wanted to know.

Logan whipped the shirt over a low-slung oak branch, stepped back, leveled his weapon, and shot the shirt.

The gun made three weird *thwip, thwip, thwip* sounds, the shirt jerked three times over the branch, and the bullets pinged off a rock below.

Puck jumped. "Holy shit! What the hell are you doing?"

"Blanks," Logan said, tossing Puck the shirt.

Catching the shirt, Puck poked his fingers through three holes. "Blanks? So how come there's holes? This was a good shirt! Why didn't you shoot a hole in that other piece of shit shirt you just pulled out of the bag?"

"I told you to wear something old," Logan said.

"Well, yeah, but you didn't say you were going to shoot holes in it," Puck grumbled. He pulled the ruined shirt back over his head, careful not to muss his hair.

Ignoring him, Logan turned and leapt about eight feet down to the next rocky ledge. He shifted back and forth, checking for sturdiness.

He looked up at Puck. "Your turn."

Puck looked down, warily, watching Logan check the rock.

I waited.

Shrugging, Puck said, "See ya," and jumped off the ledge to join Logan.

"Not if I see you first," I muttered.

"Hey, where do you want me?" I called down to Logan.

"Right where you are," he said. "Just point the camera down the incline when I get him in position."

He turned to Puck. "Roll up your sleeves so we can see your tats, then get on your stomach, face to the side so we can get it on film."

Puck hesitated, but he did as he was told.

Even at that distance, I could see a shift in Puck's demeanor. As he knelt down on the rock, his back slumped a little and he wavered. I didn't know him very well, but I thought he was getting spooked.

"Hey," I called down. "This seems like a lot of trouble. Why can't you just give the money back?"

Puck sneered. "Aside from the fact that I don't have the cash, they don't let you do that, blondie." I didn't say anything, but he looked up at me, agitated. "I was buying out my sister's contract, okay? She don't need any of this shit rainin' on her."

"All right, get down," Logan said, his hand at Puck's shoulder. "We gotta get this done before daylight."

Logan shook the bottle of catsup and squeezed it in short, sharp bursts so that it spattered the rock, then poured three big globs on the holes in Puck's shirt.

"Ugh, that feels gross!" Puck yelped.

But I was still thinking about the sister. "Contract?" I stood, staring down at the bizarre scene unfolding. I knew the blood was fake and no one was hurt, but it was creepy. Puck lay in a crumpled heap halfway down the cliff, gaping red bullet holes in his shirt.

Unease prickled the back of my neck. Puck wasn't a likeable guy, but somebody out there wanted him dead. And he had a sister in trouble.

"Yeah," Puck called up, his voice muffled by his awkward position. "Her record contract. She's a singer and she's real good."

A musician. Anywhere else that might have been news, but Austin bills itself as the Music Capital of the World. Half the waiters and most of the cab drivers in Austin are musicians waiting for their big break. The other half are writers, but I don't like to go there.

"Move your arm out by your head and hold still," Logan said to Puck. "You ready with the camera, Cauley?"

"Yeah," I said, aiming the Polaroid straight down. I snapped three shots, careful not to get the toes of my shoes in the frame, and placed the developing photos on the boulder as the camera spit them out.

I peered down at the white-framed window of black film. The image began to surface from the void, and there was Puck, broken and blood-soaked on a boulder. I grimaced, fighting back a sudden wave of nausea. I knew Logan knew what he was doing, so I fought the urge to call down to Logan, *I've got a really bad feeling about this . . .*

"We done here?" Puck said. "I gotta take a leak."

LOGAN TOSSED PUCK THE clean shirt and led the way back up the steep rock-face as Puck wandered into a thicket of live oaks.

I grimaced. "He couldn't have waited?"

"Guess not," Logan said. He brushed off a nearby bench so we could sit down.

I shook my head. "You've got the patience of a saint."

Loganshrugged."He's a pain in the ass but he's a good informant."

I sat down beside him, suddenly very aware that we were alone. I smoothed out my hair, wishing I'd had time to do something that resembled an actual hairstyle before leaving the house. There ought to be a rule—a guy should give a girl notice before asking her to help fake a hit.

The predawn air was heavy with quiet. We sat there, looking at the lake below, and I felt the small space between us begin to buzz with electricity. Warmth began to pool in my stomach, spreading slowly to some underused parts of my body.

I snuck a glance at him from the corner of my eye. His dark hair was short, shorter than the last time I'd seen him. His chin was strong and his eyes were the color of warm chocolate. And we were on top of Mount Bonnell, the most romantic spot in Central Texas—if you weren't helping fake the murder of a guy who could be the poster child for celibacy.

Logan sat, staring out over the skyline. He was quiet the way my stepfather, the Colonel, is quiet when he's got something to say.

I waited.

"You know we're going to have to limit contact until the Obregon trial is over."

"Oh," I said, feeling like the breath got knocked out of me. I hadn't seen that one coming. I tried to swallow my disappointment. "Because we're both witnesses in the Obregon trial?"

He nodded and we sat there in silence.

"When you say limit contact, does that mean *reduce* contact or no contact at all?"

He grinned at that. "Let's try *reduce* and see how that works."

I felt a little better, but not much. Logan had finally waltzed back into my life, and now he was waltzing right back out.

We sat for what seemed like a very long time.

"Puck's sister's got a gig on Friday at The Pier. They're shooting some kind of music video there and it'll be Puck's last official public appearance. Maybe you could come and we can see how the *reduce* thing works out," he said, and I smiled with my whole body.

"Did you see that?" Logan said.

"Hm?" The only thing I'd been looking at was Logan.

"There," he said, nodding toward the still-dark sky.

"What? I don't see anything—" but then I did see it. A shooting star. And then another. My breath caught and I watched as bright stars streaked across the early morning sky. "Wow," I whispered. "Shooting stars."

He smiled.

"It's incredible. They must be late this year," I said, watching as tiny bits of comet blitzed the sky. "I've always had a thing for stars. Daddy used to say you were never really lost because you could navigate by the stars. One time I asked him what happened when the stars fell, and he just smiled, and I'll never forget this: he said that the important stars didn't fall, that they were always in the same place in the sky, even when the sun came up. He said, *The stars are always there, Cauley Kat. You may not always see them, but they're always there . . ."*

My voice trailed off, and I felt my cheeks warm with color.

"The Leonid meteor shower—we won't see another Leonid this active in our lifetime." He nodded toward the sky. "One of the most beautiful sights in the world and it only lasts a little while," he said, but at that last part, he was looking at me.

Our gazes caught and I swear I could hear my heart pounding in my ears.

"There must be hundreds of shooting stars," I whispered. "I don't think I have that many wishes."

"You only need one good one." Logan smiled, and his eyes did that crinkle thing at the corners that made my stomach flop onto my liver.

We were sitting close, so close I could smell the leather of his shoulder holster, his lips just a few inches from mine, and in that moment, I thought he was going to kiss me.

I jumped when his cell phone rang.

He cleared his throat and went for his phone. "Logan," he said, and listened. "About thirty minutes." He waited some more.

"Right," he said and disconnected.

He blew out a breath and clipped his phone back on his belt next to his badge. "Well, kid, we gotta go."

That was *so* not my wish.

I gazed up at the stars, still streaking across the sky, but I felt a lot less enthusiastic about it. *Somebody up there owes me a wish.*

He tucked the Polaroids in his pocket. "The obit needs to be dated for Tuesday. I've got a mug of our boy Puck on a CD. Can you do this yourself or do you need me for anything?"

Did I need him for anything? Clearly he didn't understand the whole wish thing.

"Um, no," I said, trying not to stare at his lips. "Just his vitals—name, age, where he was born. I know you want the pub date marked Tuesday, but I'll need the time and day of death . . . "

Logan nodded, his eyes still intent on mine.

The bushes behind us rustled. My heart dropped and the reality—and the unreality—of what we'd done came flooding back.

Logan was leaving. Again.

A loud rustling sound came from the bushes and Puck appeared, zipping his jeans as he came toward us. "Hey! Did y'all see all those stars?"

"Yeah, we saw 'em," Logan said. "We've got to go."

As he said the words, an enormous star blazed through the sky, so close to the earth that it looked like it might set the trees on fire and plummet into the lake.

"Will you look at that?" Puck said, staring as the star flamed into the horizon. "Ain't that the shit?"

"Yeah," Logan said. "It is."

But he was looking at me.

ABOUT THE AUTHOR

KIT FRAZIER (AUSTIN, TX) is a two-time first place winner in the Writer's League of Texas and Merritt awards. She is the managing editor of a regional magazine and, along with her dog, Tahoe, participates in search-and-rescue missions with the FBI and local police. Visit her website at www.kitfrazier.com.

www.MidnightInkBooks.com

From the gritty streets of New York City to sacred tombs in the Middle East, it's always midnight somewhere. Join us online at any hour for fresh new voices in mystery fiction, book club questions, author information, mystery resources, and more.

Midnight Ink promises a wild ride filled with cunning villains, conflicted heroes, hilarious hazards, mind-bending puzzles, and enough twists and turns to keep readers on the edge of their seats.

Midnight Ink Ordering Information

Order by Phone
- Call toll free within the U.S. and Canada at
  1-888-NITEINK (1-888-648-3465)
- We accept VISA, MasterCard, and American Express

Order by Mail
Send the full price of your order (MN residents add 7% sales tax) in U.S. funds, plus postage & handling, to:

> Midnight Ink
> 2143 Wooddale Drive, Dept. 0-7387-0915-8
> Woodbury, MN 55125-2989

Postage & Handling
Standard (U.S., Mexico, & Canada). If your order is:
> $49.99 and under, add $3.00
> $50.00 and over, FREE STANDARD SHIPPING
AK, HI, PR: $15.00 for one book plus $1.00 for each additional book.

> International Orders (airmail only):
> $16.00 for one book plus $3.00 for each additional book

Orders are processed within two business days. Please allow for normal shipping time.
Postage and handling rates subject to change.